GARLAND OF WAR

Linda Thackerley is seventeen and in love –
with Alan, her childhood sweetheart, now
on his way to war. In 1942 Linda escapes
from her wartime job to tour with a ballet
company, bringing the colour and spectacle
of dance to towns darkened by the blackout.
She discovers the excitement and the
harshness of a dancer's life – and realises the
intensity of her ambition. She wants to go as
far as her talent will take her, but can she
ever again be the shy, sweet girl Alan left
behind? How will the war have changed
him? If he returns...

GARLAND OF WAR

GARLAND OF WAR

by

Tessa Barclay

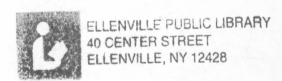
Magna Large Print Books
Long Preston, North Yorkshire,
BD23 4ND, England.

British Library Cataloguing in Publication Data.

Barclay, Tessa
  Garland of war.

    A catalogue record of this book is
    available from the British Library

    ISBN   0-7505-2009-4

First published in Great Britain in 1983 by W. H. Allen & Co.

Copyright © Tessa Barclay 1983

Cover illustration © Melvyn Warren-Smith by arrangement
with P.W.A. International

The moral right of the author has been asserted

Published in Large Print 2004 by arrangement with
Tessa Barclay, care of Darley Anderson

Magna Large Print is an imprint of Library Magna Books Ltd.

Printed and bound in Great Britain by
T.J. (International) Ltd., Cornwall, PL28 8RW

CHAPTER ONE

The stage was ready with its backcloth flawlessly stretched, showing the façade of a great rectangular temple and then palaces of beige stone fading into the distance. A cruel bronze sky had been painted above the buildings; this was to be a cruel ballet.

On a four-stepped dais upstage stood an ornate golden throne glittering with jewels. It was still fresh and garish, although it had been through twenty performances already in London before its transportation to New York for the first night of the Bordi Ballet.

The hum of sound from the auditorium could be heard from behind the front curtain of heavy gold-braided dark-blue velvet. Stage hands trotted back and forth, making sure the flats were bolted steady, inspecting the boards for flaws. Ballet dancers, they had learned, were snooty creatures who didn't like knots in the wood nor splinters that might tear their satin slippers.

The artistic director and choreographer of the company stood in the wings, outwardly calm. 'It sounds a restless audience,' she muttered.

'What d'you expect, Lin? They're not

ballet-fans, they're only here to show off their mink and diamonds.'

'Oh, David! We can't afford to be a flop!'

'We won't be,' said David Warburton with proud conviction. 'We'll knock 'em in the aisles.'

For answer Linda Olliver shivered and moved to the front of the stage, to peep through the shielded hole in the front curtain which gave a view of the auditorium. Row on row of glitter – satin, watered silk, men's stiff shirt fronts, the twinkle of diamond shirt-studs, the broader flash of bracelet and necklace. She even thought that over the backstage smell of resin and dust she could sense the perfumes – Shocking, Sikkim, Miss Balmain, Madame Rochas...

'I hope we were right to take on this tour,' she said, half aloud. 'I hope we're ready.'

'You'd never have forgiven yourself if you'd given up this chance,' David said in her ear.

She turned to him. They stood looking at each other, smiling, remembering. Once before he had said that to her. So long ago... Yet not so long ago, for that had been at the very beginning of her career – and her career spanned five and a half years.

Five and a half years, that had brought her tragedy and joy, triumph and failure, war and now – thank God – peace. But at the very beginning she had been with another man, the man she thought the most important in the world.

The delight of meeting again still cast a glow over them – almost as bright as the sun of the August afternoon. It beat down on Regent's Park on that Friday in 1942, so strong that the roses wilted in the blaze, the concrete defence block at the gate gleamed a dazzling white, and the barrage balloons overhead seemed like fat, lazy, silver fish.

In his khaki uniform, Alan was uncomfortable. But that wasn't important. His entire attention was taken up with the girl at his side. And he knew that Linda's attention was entirely taken up with him.

An entirely satisfactory state of affairs. He was on leave from training camp, he had a weekend of varied amusements before him. They were going to a performance at the Open Air Theatre – very romantic, very inexpensive. Then on Saturday Alan was going to a cricket match with some of the men from his training platoon, also on weekend leave. Linda would see him Saturday afternoon for a picnic in Richmond Park, at least in the part still available to the public now that most of it was taken over for agriculture.

It was a shame about Sunday. Sunday she had firewatch duty at her office and couldn't get out of it. Fire watching, one night a week, was now a compulsory duty for everyone, to make sure that fires caused by the German bombs were stopped as soon as they started. Alan, she gathered, would spend Sunday with 'the lads' in or around the Union Jack Club.

'I'll try to get something nice for the picnic sandwiches,' she suggested. He took it for one more proof of her anxious affection and hugged her arm against his khaki-clad side.

His confidence in her gave her a pang of guilt. If he only knew... Even now, while she was with him and ought to be thinking of no one and nothing else, her mind was ranging ahead to Tuesday. She was wondering if there would be time to get from the railway station to the theatre. Alan's train left about ten a.m. If she were lucky ... if she got a Tube train right away on the District Line... If she didn't have to hang about for a connecting train to Mile End... So many ifs, and none of them had anything to do with making Alan happy.

How could she be so self-centred? And so silly? Because if she for one moment let Alan think she didn't care about him, he might very well seek consolation among the ATS girls. Everyone said they were real go-getters where the men were concerned. 'Comforts for the troops,' unkind gossips called them. So smart in their knee-length skirts and trim jackets – who could tell how many of them had cast an approving glance at her handsome Alan?

Yet she knew she was scaring herself with a non-existent bogeyman. Alan loved her and she loved Alan. That was as constant as the Northern star, she quoted to herself, wondering if it was from *Romeo and Juliet*.

Alan broke in on this romantic thought with the prosaic suggestion that they might queue for an ice-lolly at the barrow of the vendor parked by the path. 'It's so *hot*,' he groaned. 'I wish they'd issue us with cotton for this hot weather—'

'Oh, Alan, don't say that!' She clutched at him in panic. Issue of tropical kit meant service overseas. The idea dismayed her.

Sensing her fears, he gave her a hug. 'Don't worry, I've still got a lot of training to do,' he said.

They queued patiently at the ice-cream barrow. By the time they'd found a shady bench to sit and eat the imitation-fruit-flavoured lollies, they had almost melted.

Somehow it struck them as exquisitely funny. They laughed and leaned against each other. When they had thrown away the lolly-sticks, Alan decided to steal a kiss and find out how strawberry-flavoured lips might taste. But they had been brought up not to make a display of themselves in public so by and by they got up, found a drinking fountain at which to rinse off the stickiness, and made their way hand in hand through

Queen Mary's Rose Garden towards the play.

Hardly anyone gave them a second glance: a tall yet compact soldier in the usual rough wool battle dress and a slender girl in a print frock clasped close to her narrow waist with a fashionable white belt. No one could have guessed that the girl at least was beset with a problem that bothered her conscience.

As soon as her Alan was safely on the train steaming towards his training camp, she was going to stop thinking about him and dash off to an audition for ballet dancers. The newspaper cutting about it was safely tucked in the handbag swinging from her free hand, an advert by the Gadina Ballet in yesterday's *Stage*.

'Fully trained ballet dancers for small *corps*. Girls Tuesday Orient Theatre, Mile End Road, 10.30 am. Boys Thursday s.t.s.p.'

It wasn't that Alan would mind... Well, perhaps he would. He'd always been tolerant with her obsession about the ballet, even when it had meant he couldn't meet her in the evenings in the old days at home. But now, when she only saw him on his infrequent leaves, it might be different. He might feel she ought to have nothing on her mind except the thrill of being together.

She ought to be ashamed of herself! She could almost hear her mother saying it. 'You're lucky to have a boy like Alan,' Mrs

Thackerley was wont to tell her. And it was true. He was marvellous – serious, considerate, and devoted to her. What more could she want? What more *should* she want?

Nothing, surely. Yet there was this nagging ache within her that might slumber yet never seemed to die. She knew, even while she sat through *A Midsummer Night's Dream* with her head on Alan's shoulder, that as soon as his train had left Victoria Station on Tuesday, she would be thinking of nothing but the audition.

She had some trouble finding the theatre which had been badly damaged during last year's air raid on the London Docks. A hand-printed placard announced: Orient Theatre Closed for Duration. Tacked to the edge of the placard was a second announcement: Stage Door Open. Audition 10.30 am.

Girls clutching zip holdalls or small attaché cases hurried up the side alley to the stage door. There they either greeted Tommy as an old friend or timidly gave names and addresses for the list he was preparing.

'Straight on down the passage, turn right, up the stone stairs, then follow the signs,' he instructed in a fatherly tone.

A stage-manager's prop room had been given over as a changing-room for the audition. In the big space behind the backcloth, girls who had already changed were warming up. Some were going through set exercises: '*Frappé*-one-and-two-and-three-and-four, and one-and-two-and-three-and-four...' Others were practising movements they thought would look impressive or showy – that whipping-round of the body on the full point known as the *fouetté*, repeated as often as possible to prove strength and agility.

For who could tell what the Gadina Ballet would be looking for? The announcement in *The Stage* had given few clues.

Linda Thackerley had less idea than most what the Gadina Ballet might want. This was her first audition. And what she was doing here, she scarcely knew. Even if – and this seemed so unlikely she couldn't really consider it seriously – they were to select her for a job, she couldn't take it. She already had a job, in a government office. And she couldn't leave it without permission, which certainly wouldn't be forthcoming.

'What are you doing here?' inquired a voice, exactly echoing her thought. Linda looked up from tying her shoes.

'Hello, Betty, I might have known you'd be here...'

'You bet! New ballet company? – I'd have to be in my coffin before I'd miss the audition, and even then the lid had better be screwed down tight to stop me.'

Linda laughed and tried her left foot on

14

the full point on the ground. The shoe was uncomfortable. But then all shoes were uncomfortable these days. The tiny output of the ballet shoe-makers went by government direction to the Vic-Wells company first and foremost, and then to such theatre companies or groups as had a genuine need. After that the dribs and drabs were available for sale to students and those not in work in the theatre. They were dipped in hateful shellac before the pink cotton-satin was stitched over, so that it took hours of bashing them against door-frames and fence-posts before they would bend to the human toe-joints.

Linda wriggled her toes about and tried again. 'You didn't bring your black shoes?' Betty Balcombe said. 'They're in better shape than those.'

The two girls knew everything about each other. They went to the same dancing class, the Business Girls' Ballet Group at the Mercury Theatre. There, under the watchful eye of the Rambert's junior ballet-mistress, they worked for two hours on two evenings a week. At weekends they took a class with Leryeva in her studio at Hammersmith – the Sunday class, it was called, a great omnium-gatherum of balletomanes and would-be dancers, enthusiastically urged on by the ex-ballerina.

Linda hadn't been at the last Sunday class,

15

because of firewatch duty at her office. So she and Betty had no chance to confer over this strange advertisement in *The Stage*, to discuss what to dance as a demonstration piece. 'Not many of us here,' she remarked as she began wrapping the ribbons of her right shoe around her ankle.

'Most of these will be from the provinces,' said Betty. She stared about her with undisguised curiosity.

They were a motley crew. Some were very young, underage by law and destined to be told to go away no matter what lies they told about being seventeen. Their mothers, aiders and abettors, would be lectured by the stage manager. But they would drag their daughters to the next audition, unquenched in their eagerness. Nothing was so indomitable as a ballet mother.

On that score Linda felt herself lucky. Her own mother was supremely uninterested in dancing, couldn't understand why Linda should be so devoted. 'Now you've got a nice steady job in the Civil Service, Lin, you'll give up all this ballet nonsense,' she'd said as she saw her off for London at Hedfield Station.

'Yes, Mummy,' Linda had agreed. She had even believed it at the time. Directed by the Ministry of Labour into a job described as 'necessary for the conduct of the war', it hadn't occurred to Linda that she'd be able to go on with classes. She'd pictured herself working from dawn to dusk on vital papers, deciphering important documents sent in code from battlefields overseas.

The Ministry of Supply was quite different. True, the hours were long and overtime was compulsory. But there was nothing exciting about it. The papers she dealt with were known as 'dockets': they were requisitions for dull items like kitchen equipment or carpentry tools. Within two weeks she was bored to death. The dance classes she took were her lifeline.

At seventeen-and-a-half, Linda's stage experience was limited to end-of-term concerts given by her ballet school.

For more than a year now Linda had longed for some standard against which to compare her ability. She felt she sometimes danced well – not as often as she'd like, but often enough to want to try out with the professionals, to experience the true tension of competing against old hands ... to try, in short, to be one of them even for half an hour.

There were sounds of activity on stage. Voices could be heard from beyond the backcloth, calling questions down to the auditorium. 'Where? Oh, I see – well, all right, but I'll need a light to read the music.'

The reply, scarcely audible, seemed to be in a foreign language. 'Please don't shoot

17

me, Madame,' said the pianist with a laugh, 'I'm doing my best.'

Betty Balcombe caught Linda's eye. 'He's got a sense of humour, at least,' she remarked. 'What are you giving him?'

'Schumann.'

'God, not *Butterflies?*'

'I thought so. Do you think I've made a mistake?'

'If he's like most rehearsal pianists he won't be able to read it! Four beats to the bar in the key of C, that's all they can do, mostly.'

'But Leryeva says it's a piece I dance well...'

'True enough, duckie, but who knows if the pianist will be able to play it?'

That thought had never occurred to Linda when she packed up her kit in the tiny bedsit that morning. The pianist might well be a hack supplied by the theatre management.

'What do you think I should do?' She was in a sudden panic.

'How about one of the classic solos? They're almost sure to have given him the music for the Tchaikovsky solos.'

'What are you going to do, Betty?'

'A bit of *Coppélia.*'

Betty was by now warming up by doing *grands battements,* high kicks with the foot immaculately pointed and returned to its starting point with the exactitude of a guardsman. Technically she was very strong, with an arched instep that seemed made of iron.

Linda began pinning up her long fair hair with nervous hands. She was sorry now she hadn't come in the black practice tunic and the 'good' shoes mentioned by Betty. Instead she'd packed a pale blue leotard that had once formed the basis of a costume for a charity performance back home, and her oldest point shoes, and her one good pair of pale pink tights. Tying her hair out of the way with a chiffon scarf, she decided she'd made a mistake. Betty, in her svelte black tunic and tights, looked much better.

But none of that should matter, Linda told herself. It's the dancing that counts.

As she looked around she noticed how the other girls had tried some little effect to draw attention. Striped shorts and a halter top, or a long soft satin ribbon round the waist so that the ends floated... A third girl was actually wearing a tutu.

Well, too late to worry about it now.

A tall, brown-haired woman in tweeds appeared among them. 'Well, girls?' She clapped her hands for attention. The group, perhaps forty in number, fell silent. The woman swept the area with a glance, pausing with something like amused irritation on the mothers clutching daughters by the hand.

'First of all, all those under fifteen should

19

leave right away,' she announced. She looked pointedly at two of the mothers, who looked down at the floor and set their lips mulishly. 'Look, I know the De Basil Company put a lot of brilliant babies on stage but that's not for Gadina. This is going to be a long, hard tour of the industrial areas and we can't manage programmes so that under-age dancers can be legally looked after. So ... out!'

After much muttering, several mamas and their offspring withdrew. 'Now,' said the director, 'I'm Alice Faulkner, assistant to Madame Gadina. Will you hold up your hands as I call out your names?'

The roll call was taken, the names of the departed five were crossed off. 'Those with experience in a ballet company please step forward.' One girl moved. 'Now you are ... um ... Dorothy Denby, right? Which company?'

'*Théâtre de Danse Française*, Miss Faulkner. We broke up when the Germans came into Paris.'

'I see. Danced since?'

'In the chorus of *Happy Feet*, Miss Faulkner. And summer show at Newquay until last week.'

Miss Faulkner scribbled on her list. 'Anyone with chorus-line experience? Musicals?'

One or two hands went up. Miss Faulkner moved among them, asking quiet questions, making notes. Betty's hand had gone up when she asked about musical comedy. Linda watched with something like envy as she was held in a moment's conversation with the assistant director.

'Right. Now, the rest of you, when you come on stage, Madame will probably ask where you trained and one or two other things. It's just for her own information.'

Linda suppressed a sigh. She knew the purpose of the questions. In ballet, your teacher counted for a lot. Anyone who could say she'd taken lessons from Spessiva or Genée would be at an advantage.

But what good would it be to Linda to say she'd trained at the Ida Simson School of Tap and Operatic Dancing? Even as she thought of it, she knew how absurd it sounded.

Yet when first she had achieved the glory of lessons at a proper dance school, she'd been so thrilled and happy she'd felt like a Catherine wheel awhirl with lights. Even now, when she remembered that day, something of that wild elation moved within her. And all thanks to Edith.

Dear Aunt Edith. The only member of the Thackerley family to have any money – and even that was relative, for in the midst of the Depression of the thirties to have a hundred pounds in the bank was riches.

Aunt Edith was considered by the rest of

the Thackerleys to be a bit 'different'. A schoolteacher until she married Uncle Freddie, she read a lot and could speak French. She had even travelled in France before her marriage. She liked to put records of opera and symphonies on the gramophone. When she and Uncle Freddie bought a wireless set, it was so that she could listen to a broadcast of *Faust*.

Stranger yet, Aunt Edith liked ballet. This was quite unconnected with Linda's interest – Linda had first been caught by the pretty movements of some girls in long tulle skirts who provided the background to the opening credits of a movie-magazine at the local cinema. Thereafter she'd liked the so-called 'ballet sequence' which formed a part of every pantomime, even those in the provincial theatres. Pantomime ballet usually consisted of an entr'acte called *My Lady's Boudoir* or *The Fairy Glade,* in which one rather good female dancer would perform the steps she was best at, backed by a chorus who tittuped about on their toes. Male dancers there were none.

But Aunt Edith had been to Monte Carlo and seen the Russians there. One wonderful day, she offered to take her ballet-loving niece with her on a trip to London during which they could attend a matinee of the De Basil Company, at the Alhambra Theatre.

The performance was a revelation to

Linda Thackerley. No little girls in fluffy pink tutus portraying My Lady's Powderpuff, no wavering line of unmatched girls in the background. Instead there was Riabouchinska in *Les Sylphides,* ethereally light, drifting, glowing. There was Toumanova in *Jeux d'Enfants* as the Top, whipping round as if powered by some magical electricity. There was the almost flamboyant muscularity of David Lichine, the first male dancer Linda had ever seen.

She came out of the Alhambra into the July sunshine in a dream. This was the real thing; a curtain of shoddy gauze had been swept aside.

'Did you enjoy it?' asked Aunt Edith.

Linda made no reply. She raised blank, sleep-walking eyes to her aunt. Edith was startled. Already she'd sensed that dancing meant more to Linda than a mere treat at the theatre, for the box of chocolates she'd provided had gone unnoticed after the first nibble before curtain-rise.

On the train back to Hedfield, half asleep already, the eight-year-old said wistfully, 'They were so beautiful...'

Afterwards, Edith Thackerley was to wonder if she had done a kindness to her niece. Linda talked of almost nothing else. She borrowed all the books in Hedfield Public Library that had anything to do with ballet and could be found sitting in a corner of the garden shed, poring over them. There was a lane behind the house, paved with smooth old flagstones and not much used except to put out the dustbins on Wednesdays. There Linda could be observed, waltzing about in plimsolls, attempting to reproduce the movements of Toumanova in her famous *fouettés*, trying to drift gossamer-like in imitation of Riabouchinska.

'That girl's proper silly,' her mother sighed to her sister-in-law. 'Pity you ever took her to that show in London.'

'You may be right. But it'll die out in time, Nancy.'

But Linda's infatuation with ballet didn't fade. For her next Christmas she demanded, and was given, a pair of dancing shoes. Her fury when she opened the parcel was almost tragic. The shoes were of patent leather, with full leather soles and criss-crossed elastic to keep them on. They were intended for young ladies going to a party. But poor Mrs Thackerley, knowing no better, had thought they were what Linda wanted. Nor, when she took them back the day after Boxing Day, was the salesgirl able to help. 'But those are dancing shoes, madam,' she insisted.

'No, like these,' said Mrs Thackerley, showing a photograph of Danilova cut from a copy of the *Daily Herald* by Linda.

'Oh, *toe-shoes!* Oh, I don't know where you'd get those. Nobody in Hedfield sells those. I imagine stage folk get them made specially for them.'

'I see.' Mrs Thackerley got a voucher to buy something else in place of the dancing shoes and went home. 'You have to get those toe-shoes specially made,' she told Linda, 'and I don't know where we'd get that done, and anyhow I expect it would cost a fortune, so that's an end of it, now, you hear me?'

Linda learned this wasn't exactly correct only a couple of months later. She was taken to a Red Cross Charity Concert at Hedfield Town Hall. And there, pirouetting around the platform, were four girls in 'toe-shoes' – girls about four years older than herself, but quite definitely not great dancers with the power to have shoes specially made.

Careful examination of the programme told her that these were the pupils of Miss Ida Simson. Miss Simson must have been the lady in the long green dress who came on at the end to take a bow.

What followed next was a campaign to be allowed to take lessons at Miss Simson's school. 'No, now, Linda, let's hear no more about that,' scolded her mother when she asked for about the eighteenth time. 'In the first place it's a waste of money, in the second place you should be working at your school subjects, in the third place your father doesn't approve of it.' And in the fourth place, they couldn't afford it. Income from the garage in which George Thackerley had a half-share was only enough for necessities or, if there was any to spare, it had to go on the education of their two sons. A girl would of course soon get married but a boy had to be educated for a career, so it was nonsensical to think of wasting anything on dancing lessons.

Linda had by now learned that it was impossible to get up on your toes and drift around like Riabouchinska just by trying. If you hung on to a chairback, you could raise yourself to the toes, but then you had to straighten your knees otherwise you looked like a curled whitebait. And if you straightened your knees and let go the chair, your ankles hurt, and you fell over. Moreover, try as she might, she couldn't see how to fit her feet neatly together when she was at rest. She understood it couldn't be done without proper lessons.

In the face of continual refusal, Linda stopped asking. Her mother was pleased. But if she thought her daughter had ceased thinking about ballet, she was wrong. Every time Linda got a Book Token as a present, it went on a book about ballet. Her pocket money went on tickets to see films that had dance scenes, though most of these proved disappointing, much though she learned to love Fred Astaire.

Only Aunt Edith understood how serious it was for Linda. Only Aunt Edith bothered to look into the books Linda bought. It made her catch her breath in astonishment to see that her ten-year-old niece was reading the life of Nijinsky by his wife Romola, or a serious history of the origins of ballet translated from the French.

Edith made Linda a present on her tenth birthday – twelve lessons paid for at the School of Tap and Operatic Dancing of Ida Simson.

Nancy Thackerley was furious. 'Good gracious, I spend a year or more knocking that foolishness out of her head, and then you go and do this, Edith! Well, you'll have to cancel the arrangement, that's all.'

'But she's always loved dancing,' sighed Edith. 'Long before I took her to see the Russian ballet, Nancy. It's just something she wants to do – and needs to do, perhaps.'

'Mmm,' said Nancy after a moment's thought. 'Maybe if she has a few lessons she'll get it out of her system.'

So Linda was allowed to go for her first lesson at Ida Simson's school.

It was, of course, an evening school. You went home from proper school, at half-past three, washed and had your tea, did your homework, and then at six o'clock you presented yourself at the dance studio in a short frock and ankle socks. Mrs Thackerley took her that first evening, carrying her gym shoes in a little linen sack with Linda's name embroidered thereon.

'Ah, here's our new little dancer,' Ida Simson greeted them. She was a tall muscular woman who seemed quite elderly to Linda, although later she realised her teacher then was only thirty-one. Two things were notable to Linda about Miss Simson. First, she wore a black dress with a tight-fitting bodice and short flared skirt, which exposed strong legs and feet ending in 'toe-shoes'. Second, her legs had bulging calf muscles, so developed as to be almost unsightly. Those had been hidden in the long green dress when she took a bow at the Town Hall.

Linda was aglow with excitement. She would take her place in the class, she would listen to the instructions of the teacher, and she would rise on her toes and twirl round the room like a rose petal in a breeze. The happy expectation was almost too much to bear.

Nothing of the sort occurred. Her first class was a disaster. First, she had no proper shoes. Gym shoes were forbidden, she must take class in her socks. A little humiliated, Linda took off the offending gym shoes and fell into place in the back row of assorted little girls.

The next disappointment was that they didn't begin to dance. 'First position,' called

28

Miss Simson. All the children adopted a stance with heels together but toes turned completely outwards, so that the line was straight across from one big toe to the other. Linda followed suit and promptly lost her balance.

'Hold the bar,' called Miss Simson, who from her great height could catch every mistake. When Linda had grabbed at the pole fastened along the wall of the room, Miss Simson went on at once: 'Second position!'

This one was easier. You simply took a little step so that your feet were apart although still in a straight line.

And so on, through the five positions which are the mainspring of classical ballet and which later became so familiar. That first evening she could only do two of them, the 'open' positions. When Miss Simson called 'Close up, close up!' she found it impossible to get her feet next to each other in the closed positions.

When the class had gone through the five positions a time or two, they began on the arms. These too had their specific 'positions'. Then they did arms-and-legs. So far not a note of music had been played and Linda hadn't enjoyed a single moment.

Through the exercises that followed she felt more and more alienated. True, the exercises were done to music, played on a piano in a corner of the room by a fat old lady. But the piano was so old and the lady played so badly that it was a pain to listen to.

'Now, centre of the room,' called Miss Simson.

The little girls left the *barre* and ran to form three rough lines on the parquet floor. Now came such dancing as the evening afforded to Linda. But she could make nothing of the steps called out by the teacher. Only by watching the others did she catch on, and by the time she'd mastered what it was they were supposed to be doing, that series of steps was over and they'd gone on to the next.

After half an hour there was a break. 'Point work!' called Miss Simson. Some of the older girls had occupied the short break changing shoes. Linda said timidly, 'I haven't any toe-shoes, Miss Simson.'

'Of course not, child! Good heavens, what an idea, at your first class! And don't call them toe-shoes. They're point-shoes, or blocks.'

'But ... Miss Simson ... what am I to do–?'

'You do the same exercises as the others, but on the *demie* – that means half-point. Right? Go along now, you stay at the back where you can watch the others.'

The rest of the evening went by in a muddled haze as Linda tried to catch what

Miss Simson was calling out and to watch how the other girls obeyed. Her perception quickened after half a dozen sequences: by watching the others she could soon get an approximation of the correct movements. But as to dancing, or drifting about like a rose petal, that was forgotten in the sweat and perplexity of trying to keep up with what was going on.

And when Miss Simson said, as she showed her out, 'Think you're going to like it?' her answer had been a fervent, 'Oh, *yes.*'

Hours of effort, of self-sacrifice and devotion, of actual pain and much dis-comfort, had gone into the dancer's education that had been the important part of Linda Thackerley's life. It was simply to put it to the test that she was here today, in this draughty bomb-damaged theatre, waiting to hear what Miss Faulkner of the Gadina Ballet would require of her.

Miss Faulkner had collected sheet music from those who had brought it for the accompanist. She set it in a neat pile on top of the old upright at the edge of the wings. She clapped her hands for attention.

'Right, on stage, please, dancers! Anyone below five foot four inches, front row. Those five foot four and over, back row. Madame will call out the sequences. Please pay attention and give us your best.'

A throaty, almost harsh voice spoke from

the front rows of the stalls. 'We will begin with a simple *enchaînement* – you should know this, it comes from *Paquita*, teachers use it much. Two bars introduction and then advance, *pas de bourrée, sissone, sissone,* arms in fifth *en avant...*'

The sequence of steps seemed to go on forever, difficult to catch because of the pidgin French used for ballet terms and the strong Russian accent of the speaker. She, Madame Gadina, remained invisible in the darkness of the auditorium, but the authority of her manner summoned her up for the girls straining their ears to hear her.

Unseen, to their left, the pianist walked on and took a seat. There was a preliminary ripple of finger-exercising and then, at the command from Gadina, the two bars of a strong two-four beat, the first indication they had of the rhythm in which they were to dance.

Linda counted in her head. '...And three and four and *pas de bourrée, pas de bourrée, sissone, sissone...*'

She was launched into the sequence, the great test. Could she dance well enough to measure up to the others at the audition? Had she anything of the true ballerina in her?

Or had all her years of self-sacrifice been a silly waste of time?

CHAPTER TWO

The first repetition of the steps was poor, with most of the girls feeling for the timing and the phrasing. 'Again!' called Gadina from the stalls. They repeated the sequence, a third time, a fourth time, running back line by line as they reached the footlights to begin again. They had done it twenty times and were beginning to take some pleasure in it when the voice below called a halt.

'*Assez, assez!* Thank you, children. Now we will all do some little *echappé* and *entrechat* work, to see the feet. Please to space yourselves out further. I need to see you. Ready? We shall have six beats to the bar – *ah, David, tu es prêt?*'

The pianist replied he was ready. To prove it, he immediately began a brisk little tune from Offenbach. 'You hear, children? No introduction – on my count – four, five, seex – *and–*'

The steps were fiendishly difficult, demanding the ability to jump lightly into the air and come down again on the same spot after changing the position of the feet twice while in the upward movement. By the end of the first eight bars, most of them had grasped it, but then the melody changed and caught out those who were relying on it to warn them of the jump.

The test went on for about twenty minutes. By this time most of them were running with sweat. Some were more breathless than they should have been.

'Very well, very well. Enough for showing the paces and warming up. Please clear the stage. Come forward when the name is called.'

They hurried to the wings, huddling together as if for protection. Opinion seemed to be divided as to whether it was good to be called first or last.

'Madeleine Strang... Come down to the front, *ma chère*... You have professional experience? Yes? – what company? Ah. And your teacher? Oh, *la grande Brunelleschi – da, da,* she is well-known to me... Very well, what are you to give us?'

'It is a solo arranged to Kreisler's *Caprice Viennoise*, Madame.'

'Very well, David, have you sorted him out?'

'Yes, Madame – ready.'

'*Harosho*. Begin, please.'

The pianist played the little six-note call that opened the piece. The dancer on stage, a square-shouldered girl with brown hair pinned up Edwardian style, settled herself with hands out to the side in a 'pretty' stance. 'Oh, God, Dresden china,' groaned Betty Balcombe in Linda's ear.

That was exactly the phrase for it. A specially arranged solo, showy, empty.

'Thank you,' called Gadina from the auditorium when Miss Strang was about eight bars into the waltz-like theme that follows the trilling introduction. 'Please go off stage-right and wait at the back. Next please. And you are...?'

One by one the girls walked on, answered Madame's questions, and performed the solos they had prepared. It was impossible at first to know how opinion was going among the group watching in the stalls, but it soon dawned on Linda that those who danced less well were stopped soonest. Nine girls had been auditioned when Betty's name was called.

'Good morning, you are–'

'Betty Balcombe, Madame.'

'Professional experience?'

'I just finished a summer season at New-quay, Madame, in the chorus of *Cornish Cream*. Before that I was in a tour of *Me and My Girl.*'

'The dancing in *Me and My Girl* is balletic?'

'No, Madame, not at all.'

'Your teacher?'

'I trained with Pauline Potter in Ealing, Madame, but lately at the Mercury.'

'Aha. Very well, what is your solo – have you given your music to the accompanist?'

'No, Madame, he says he knows it – the Spanish Dance, Act II, *Coppélia*.'

'Indeed. Let us see it, then. David?'

David Warburton, from his seat at the piano, caught the faint derision in Madame Gadina's tone. He was a little surprised himself. The dance Betty Balcombe had chosen was very difficult to perform – ballet feet but Spanish arms and head, all invested with a spirit of comedy that would be hard to capture at eleven-fifteen in a half-lit old theatre. Nevertheless, he'd do his best for the girl. She had courage, at any rate. He launched into the lilting bolero.

He knew the music well enough to be able to spare several glances at the soloist. A bit too heavy in her turns, and he wasn't sure she finished all her movements with precision but, oh, the gaiety and good humour she put into the performance!

Madame'll like her, he said to himself. He was proved right in that Betty was the first in the audition to be allowed to dance through to the end of her solo. As Betty finished, arm and leg flung up in a typically 'Spanish' stance, one or two of the girls in the wings produced a spatter of applause. David gave an inward groan. Madame didn't like to be prompted. Their approval might put her off.

'Thank you, Miss Balcombe, please go off stage-right and wait.'

There was no way of knowing what she was thinking. Sly old fox! David had known her almost all his life but was seldom able to tell what she was thinking. In general, she liked to take an opposite viewpoint from everyone else. If someone said English ballet was dull, she defended it with vehemence. If critics disapproved of ballets using the music of great symphonies, she explained that great music was likely to produce great dance. Yet the very next day she was quite capable of saying the exact opposite.

His family had never approved of his friendship with the strange old émigrée who rented from them the rambling old house in Cheltenham. A rum lot, Russians – smoking oddly-coloured cigarettes and putting raspberry jam in tea...

And ballet! Thank God at least David hadn't wanted to be a ballet dancer! Bad enough that he insisted on taking music so seriously, staying indoors to practise when other boys would have been out playing cricket or riding to hounds. But at least music was a social asset, a hobby that could be called upon for the entertainment of weekend guests. If his youngest son had decided to ask for ballet classes, Viscount Stroud would have been forced to put his foot down.

As it was, there had been much family uproar and distress when David asked to study music at university. The Warburtons had never had a musician in the family; the whole thing took them by surprise. Yet you couldn't exactly forbid it. After all, he pleased the vicar by always agreeing to play the organ when Miss Sykes was away, and a friend of the Warburtons had known Edward Elgar and said he was a perfectly respectable chap – although of course Catholic. So you could be a musician without going beyond the pale.

All the same, David certainly had some peculiar friends. Not least was Olga Gadina. Instead of being sensible and taking up church music, David spent most of his time mooning around with Madame Gadina or going to the ballet in London.

When war came, David Warburton knew his parents hoped he'd be drafted into some essential occupation. They knew, naturally, that the heart murmur left over from rheumatic fever in his childhood would prevent him from being taken into the armed forces. They had been quite appalled when David was assigned to ENSA, Entertainments National Service Association, at his own request.

Off he'd gone with a touring troupe, playing the piano for barrack theatre shows.

Well, it was national service, of a *sort*... But as to the suite of piano pieces he'd written in his spare time, entitled *Blackout Scenes*, well, the best you could say of them was that they had a sort of lilt to them, and they didn't last long.

In a word, David Warburton was a mystery to his family.

He was well aware of their feelings. But he'd long ago given up trying to explain to them. They knew nothing about music, less about ballet, and wanted things to stay that way. What was the use of explaining to them that British ballet was at the beginning of its evolution, with hardly any composers available to write for it? Some day soon, some young choreographer was going to look around for a musician who could work with him to produce a ballet that would make the world respect the English spirit. David meant to be within his line of vision.

The Gadina Company wasn't going to have a great effect on the future of British ballet. But it was a starting off point, a training ground. He already knew how dancers needed to know the music, to feel it in their feet. But there was a lot to learn about the staging of ballet, the blending of costume and movement and music, the understanding of personality and physique, the sheer economics of ballet.

So that was why he had pulled strings to

get a grant for the tour and obtained the post of musical director with Madame Gadina. He was prepared to do anything he was asked, to be a dogsbody, to play for auditions and rehearsals if called upon. That was why he was here today, to save Madame the expense of hiring an audition pianist. And great fun it was too, he told himself, watching an older girl go through the pyrotechnics of another *Coppélia* solo. Quite different from the Chapel at King's College on a cold winter evening, with the dons assembled to hear the music students show off their paces.

'Thank you, Miss Lamont, please go off stage-right and wait. Next?'

A slender girl in a pale blue body-maillot walked to centre stage. Her fair hair was tied up off her neck with a pale blue chiffon kerchief. There was very little colour in her face. The whole effect was wraithlike.

'You are—?'

'Linda Thackerley, Madame.'

'Professional experience?'

'None, Madame.'

'Where did you train?'

'In Hedfield, Madame. At the Simson School.'

The pause that ensued let it be known that Madame Gadina had heard of neither Hedfield nor Simson, and was unimpressed. 'And what are you going to show me?'

'The… One of the variations for Prince Florestan's sisters, Madame.'

'Indeed? You could not, Miss Thackerley, think of anything shorter?' The sarcasm knifed across the space between the auditorium and the stage.

'If … if you think it's too short to do one, Madame, I could do the other as well.' Linda was sorry now she had not handed in her Schumann music to be played by the pianist. Betty had been wrong – this accompanist would have been more than capable of playing Schumann's *Schmetterling* beautifully, with all its looping trills to show the flight of the butterfly in the sun. But it was too late now. She could guess the annoyance she would cause to this autocrat in the stalls if she begged a moment to fetch the sheet music from her bag somewhere at the back. No, she was committed to the variation from *Aurora's Wedding*, which she had chosen because she had studied it over some months and because the pianist was sure to have the music with him.

'*Là, là,*' said Madame Gadina in a strange tone, which might have been surprise or amusement. 'No, one variation will be sufficient, I feel sure. David?'

'Yes, Madame.' He let a tinkle of sound drift from under his fingers, to give this nervous girl some idea of his tempo. Nervous – but she had guts. To choose one

41

of the short, bright variations from a classic like *The Sleeping Beauty*, and what's more to offer to do the companion piece as well... He stole a glance at her from his place almost in the wings.

She had the ideal dancer's body – slim, leggy, yet not too tall for going on her points. How many dancers had he seen topping their male partners the moment they went on full point! This one had a willowy look, a born sylphide. She was blonde, which was a plus: so many ballerinas were either dark or hennaed their hair, striving for the dramatic, Russian look. She was pretty, or pretty enough – but that scarcely mattered, for make-up counted for so much in ballet that an insignificant face could be made magical with the use of Leichner.

All depended on what she did with Florestan's sister. He gave her a loud opening to ensure that she darted into movement with the right amount of verve, but then took his foot off the loud pedal. Let her take precedence: this was her moment, if she could bring it off.

Linda knew she had every movement and gesture right. She had studied and watched, she had practised again and again in the early hours of the morning to the strains of the music on a scratchy portable gramophone she'd bought in a junk shop. The basement of the big house where she had a bedsit was used as a bomb-shelter but, at about six in the morning, it was usually empty. There she would wind up the gramophone, unroll an old piece of linoleum as protection against the concrete floor, and work at the classical pieces she wanted to understand. No one ever interrupted; if they heard the music, they thought it was that mad girl who had the second floor room, wrapped in old sweaters and going up and down on her toes.

She knew she had it right. But was she dancing? Too tense, too nervous, too intent on staying with the fast tempo and the turn and twirl of the movement...

In a moment, it seemed, it was over. She wanted to cry, No, no, let me do it again – I can do it better. She stood still, panting a little, her hands coming to rest after the last upward flick of the climax.

'Thank you, Miss Thackerley. Please go off stage-right and wait.'

'Thank you, Madame,' Linda said, bobbing a curtsey, and ran off.

'Well, good for you,' Betty said as she hurried into the big space at the back. 'I had a peek through a crack – you looked like Pamela May.'

'Don't joke, Betty.'

'I'm not joking! You looked fine. A bit anxious, but we've all looked anxious.'

Linda draped her topcoat around her to stave off the backstage draughts. No one knew whether they were going to be asked to dance again but, in any case, cooling muscles must be protected even against the August air. There were forty-one girls now sitting or standing around in the back. Some had done their solos, some were still waiting to be called.

Half-an-hour later the audition solos were over. Miss Faulkner came back to speak to them. It was clear that she was to be what is called the *régisseur* of the new company, the principal who makes sure rehearsals are called and dancers are prepared for their roles.

'Will the following girls please stay,' she said in a quiet tone. 'The rest please leave – Madame has been glad of the opportunity to see your work but the company needs a particular type of dancer so it's no reflection on your ability if we don't take you. Thank you for coming.'

Linda began to gather up her belongings. Miss Faulkner began to read out names. 'Styles, Oakham, Balcombe, Radetzki, Macdonald, Chillerton, Thackerley, Harrison, Cobham – will those girls please come on stage?'

Linda stopped dead with her holdall and shoes in her hands. 'Me,' she gasped. 'Did she say me?'

'You're Thackerley?' said a tall older girl. 'She said your name.'

'But ... but ... I didn't expect...'

'Then bully for you,' said the tall girl. 'I'm Cobham, Alice Cobham. Let's go and see what they want now.'

Now there were only nine of them, the stage seemed vast. They went on nervously, to find the great lady herself sitting by the piano on the pianist's stool. She was clad in a moth-eaten fur coat.

'*Eh bien,*' she said. 'Now we have weeded out the *tshepukei* let us do something serious. What I want to know is to see if you are not only dancers, but artists. David will play three minutes of music for each of you. I have no idea what he is going to play–'

'Nor have I,' put in David.

Madame flashed him a glance from behind big horn-rimmed glasses. 'This is improvisation. I want to see what you can find in the music to put into dance. Clear?'

'Yes, Madame,' they murmured. They were all terrified. In no circumstances is it easier to look ridiculous than in improvising to music. Each had memories of their first dancing lessons as children: be a tree, Tessa. Think of what it's like to be a daffodil, Marion. Free expression, it had been called, and mostly used to get the children in motion, accustomed to using the floor space.

As you progressed through ballet class, 'improvisation' became rare. There was so much to learn in so limited a period that you couldn't waste precious minutes larking about pretending to be the Spirit of the Breeze or any other poetic fancy. Yet there were sessions when the teacher might be working on a new dance for an exhibition concert. At such times the dancer might be asked: See what you can make of that passage, dear... Just show me how you'd get from the *pirouette* to the *grand jeté*...

Sometimes it worked, sometimes it didn't. In any case, if you produced anything usable it was always appropriated by the teacher as her own. In a word, improvisation was a bore.

But if Gadina demanded it, they must do it. No one dreamed of protesting. They trotted into the wings beyond the pianist, who resumed his place as Madame went once more to the auditorium to watch.

The girls had automatically formed a line in the order Miss Faulkner had called their names. She called again from the auditorium. 'Styles!'

Audrey Styles walked on. The pianist crashed into what sounded like a summons by a band of trumpeters. Audrey leapt across the stage, drawing up abruptly as the sudden opening was succeeded by a quieter phrase. Later Linda learned that it was a theme from a Beethoven piano concerto, but at the time all she knew was that it looked damned difficult to dance to.

No one could have said that Audrey Styles did well, but she managed not to be at a loss until the pianist rounded off to a close.

'Hm,' Madame Gadina murmured to Alice Faulkner. 'Quick-witted at least. Good steady feet. She forgot to use her face, though.'

'Not bad, on the whole.' Miss Faulkner raised her voice. 'Oakham.'

The next girl was small and birdlike. She was the one wearing the tutu. David, left to make his own choices, decided to offer her the Fairy-of-the-Songbirds music from *The Sleeping Beauty*. Poor girl, she had either never heard the music or was in too much of a dither to recognise it.

'Dear God,' said Gadina under her breath. 'Thank you. Balcombe.'

Betty ran on. She had no idea what she was going to do but by God, she was going to smile while she did it if she died in the attempt.

David eyed her. He began to play a busy, lively tune by Eric Coates.

Gadina watched Betty's performance. '*Mon dieu*, what music-hall mannerisms,' she muttered.

'But she's very strong, Madame.'

'Like a pony... Well, let us ask her to stay.'

It was Linda's turn next. She was terrified. As she was called on stage, a momentary flutter of nerves seized her. She glanced around rather wildly. The young man at the piano caught her eye and gave her a wink of encouragement.

'I wonder if she can do anything with real music,' David said to himself. He looked down at the keyboard. Then, choosing itself, or so it seemed, a Chopin *Étude* began to trickle out from under his fingers.

Linda had been standing in a good 'starting position', hands held softly in front of her thighs, one foot slightly in front of the other but pointed and arched. As the music signalled itself to her, she drooped her head for a moment then, without pausing to think about it, rose gently on the point. The back leg came up in a momentary arabesque then she was moving, fluttering to the trill of the phrases.

She'd never heard the music before but for a moment she saw it in her mind's eye on the page, waves of semi-quavers unwinding like a stream. She felt her back bending to the shape, let herself trail like a wisp of cloud across the stage with hands aloft, then turned and turned all around its circumference.

'Who is this one?' inquired Gadina, sitting up to get a better angle.

'Linda Thackerley, Madame. Trained by

Ida Simson, whoever she may be.'

'Ida Simson did not give her that light-ness. She was born with that. Well, let's see what she does with the D major chords.'

They came almost as she spoke. Linda, startled, leapt into the air. As she came down, unheard though the boards had a creaking echo for others, the pianist smiled at her over the old upright. I'm doing this well, she thought, suddenly aware of the fact. And then she thought, I ought to do something difficult, not just twirl about ... the chords invited it. She leapt diagonally across the stage, *temps de flèche*, the arrow step, landing and taking off again buoyantly and defiantly, her feet fitting neatly each time they touched the ground.

The music was angry and discordant now. She let herself see storm clouds piling up on a horizon. She protected her head with crossed arms, ran and turned, ran and turned. This is silly, she said to herself, I ought to get in out of the rain! She darted under an imaginary tree and folded an imaginary cloak about herself, arms describing its folds as they fell to her sides. She was out of breath and longing for a pause – and it came. The music drew back, seemed to consider its own over-emotional sound, and became reflective. Linda drifted out from her oak tree's shade and, avoiding puddles left by the thunderstorm, darted in a series of intentionally pretty, neat steps to the front of the stage.

Mercifully the pianist played the necessary number of bars for the improvisation. He invented two gentle, thoughtful chords for her to come to rest and curtsey. Breathless, she did so.

'Thank you, my dear,' said Gadina. 'Next.'

Linda ran off. Madame had called her 'My dear!' Did that mean anything? Betty greeted her with a bear hug. 'I say! Get *you!* Was that your *Butterfly?*'

'What? Oh – no – it was improvised–'

'Fancy! It all looked sort of put-together.'

'Was it really any good?'

'Not bad at all, ducks. Well, here goes Harrison.' They all clustered round to look through cracks in the backcloth as Mary Harrison struggled with three minutes' worth of the main theme from Rachmaninoff's 4th Concerto. A flowing tune, she let it engulf her. 'Oh, you idiot, spread out,' Linda ordered under her breath. But Mary Harrison couldn't have done it even if she had heard her.

When the improvisations were ended Miss Faulkner came up backstage once more. 'Thank you. I'm going to read out three names and those girls are asked to leave with our good wishes. The fact that we can't use you doesn't reflect badly on your dancing – it's just that Madame has a particular

50

type of ballet group in mind and needs a certain choice of dancers.'

The girls stood huddled in dread and expectation. 'June Oakham, Mary Harrison, Helena Cobham – thank you very much, girls, better luck next time.'

'Thank you, Miss Faulkner.' They backed away, hiding their dejection. Betty grabbed Linda's upper arm in a grip of steel. 'We're in,' she hissed.

'What ... you mean ... us six? No more audition?'

'They're choosing six girls.'

'How do you know?'

'Oh, for God's sake, Lin, I asked around! They've got six other girls already, recommended dancers, you know how it goes between teachers–'

'Can I have your attention?' said Miss Faulkner, having crossed out names on her list. 'Have I got you down correctly?' She read out the remaining six, each of whom nodded or said yes. 'Very well. The tour commences in two weeks' time. You are asked to make your own way to Madame Gadina's studio in Cheltenham where we shall start practice and rehearsals on Friday. You are asked to bring as many pairs of ballet shoes as possible and supply your own fleshes, although we hope to get tights for other colours before we start the tour. Please think of a few stage names for yourselves –

with the exception of Marina Radetzki you sound a bit provincial for the Gadina Ballet Company.' She paused and looked around.

'What about digs, Miss Faulkner?' Betty asked.

'In Cheltenham you'll be put up in and around Madame's studio. I'm organising digs for the tour, no problem. Anything else?'

'What's the pay, Miss Faulkner?'

'You'll get £3 a week while we're getting ready and ten shillings more once we're on the move. You'll have to buy your own shoes, I'm afraid – you know how difficult it is to get shoes at the moment. Digs are paid for, and travelling expenses, unless you like to pay extra and go first class. No charge for hot drinks during theatre rehearsals – and that reminds me, be sure to bring your ration books. And your identity cards. You know, the usual things.'

Various other points were raised with the *régisseur* but Linda was too dazed to hear them. Exhaustion brought on by a very early start to the day, a long practice session before she left home, the exertions of the audition and the excitement of it were all taking their toll. She felt as if her head were full of cotton wool. She knew she ought to catch Alice Faulkner's attention and tell her she must withdraw from the company, but she couldn't rouse herself to do it.

'Very well, that's all for now,' Alice said. 'See you all by midday Friday at Cheltenham. Please clear the stage, we need it for some costume inspections we're having now.'

Chattering in pleasure and relief, the six girls went to the dressing area and changed. Even as they did so, elderly men with hampers of clothes were trudging on stage, totally uninterested in the spectacle of six rather pretty girls stripping down to their bras and panties.

'As soon as I've changed I must see Miss Faulkner,' Linda said to Betty, dragging her head through the neckline of her dress.

'Not now, lovey. They're in the midst of a collection by Nathan's.'

'Look, I've got to tell her. I can't take this job.'

'Why ever not, you idiot.'

'Because I'm in a reserved occupation, that's why! I can't just pack up and go.'

'Then why the devil did you come to the audition?'

'Just ... just to see if I could do it.'

Betty gaped at her. 'Are you telling me that you never intended to take a job if it was offered to you?'

'Well, I never thought I'd get the offer, Betty.'

'You're mad!' Betty said. 'You've just landed a place in a *corps* and you didn't even want it?'

'Oh, I want it. It's just that I can't take it.'

'Who says you can't?'

'Well ... the government.'

'Oh, the government! They're always making regulations but nobody really obeys them.'

'But you have to, Betty. I mean, you have to register for rations and put up blackout curtains and only travel when it's necessary–'

'Utter rubbish. There are people in this country who drive about wherever they want and live on steaks and caviar–'

'Oh, spivs and black marketeers, you mean. But–'

'Look, Lin, everybody wiggles round the rules in some way. You can't tell me it matters a hoot to the government if you leave your job in wherever it is–'

'Ministry of Supply.'

'What are you there, actually? I mean, you aren't a big wheel, are you?'

'Heavens, no. I'm a clerical officer.'

'There you are then. What the Dickens does it matter who clerics? It's far better for you to be off doing something more important, like dancing in a touring company–'

'How can you say it's important, Betty, compared with–'

'It's bringing culture to the masses, isn't it? Council for the Encouragement of Music and the Arts? Are you telling me Dame Myra Hess is less important than a filing clerk in a Holborn office?'

'No, of course not–'

'It's a matter of priorities. You go back to your boss and tell him you're off to join the Gadina Ballet Company and he'll give you his blessing.'

'No he won't. He'll tell me to fill out a form and it'll take six weeks to get permission.'

'Ho,' said Betty, stuffing her audition clothes into her holdall, 'then go first and tell him afterwards. Once you're on the road, they won't bother about you.'

They straggled out, into the late August sunshine. It was one o'clock. 'Off you go and do your packing,' Betty commanded. 'I'm going to hand in my notice at that rotten café. Cheltenham here I come.'

She darted off to swing aboard a passing bus. The other girls nodded and waved and hurried off. Linda stood hesitating. Should she go back into the theatre and confess to Alice Faulkner? The *régisseur* would be very cross. It would mean having to recall one of the girls she'd sent away, or finding a replacement some other way.

While she was standing irresolute at the mouth of the alley, she heard the stage door thud to a close and brisk footsteps. It was the audition pianist.

Now that she saw him standing up – as opposed to being half-hidden behind a piano – he proved to be a tallish young man about twenty-five, rather angular in physique to match his bony face. He had soft straight brown hair worn, according to present-day fashion, short and parted at one side. Despite the attempt at discipline, strands of hair stood up here and there so that they shone in the August sunshine like bronzed wire. He had a long stride which brought him to her in a moment.

'Hello,' he greeted her. 'On your own?'

'Yes, I … I was wondering what to do.'

'About what? Lunch? If you've nothing better to do, come on and have a bite with me. I reconnoitred a decent pub on the way here.'

The Harp was only a few yards away. It was fairly busy although over the bar the usual notice was displayed: 'Sorry, No Spirits, Only One Pint of Beer per Customer.'

'What'll you have – one pint in one mad swallow, or two halves?' David inquired.

'Oh … no thanks, can I have a soft drink, please?'

'Well, it'll probably be as intoxicating as this wartime beer. A half, landlord, and a lemonade.' He turned an amused glance on Linda. 'Do cheer up. It may not be good lemonade but it won't kill you. By the way, I'm David Warburton.'

'Thank you for the nice piece you gave me.'

'Liked it, did you? I thought you did, the way you seized it with both hands. Rather good, I thought.'

'Did you really think so?'

'Don't sound so surprised. You dance well. Where did you learn to get off the ground so easily?'

'You mean, steps of elevation? Well, it's easy to get off the ground when the music's right for it.'

'Is it? You surprise me. I've watched the class at Madame's studio and it always seems damned hard to me. You really are exceptionally light, you know.'

She couldn't very well reply, No, I didn't know. It would sound daft. But the truth was, she *didn't* know. She had a low opinion of her own abilities because until very recently she had had no one to tell her she was good. No one whom she respected, that's to say. Ida Simson she had soon learned to discount – in Ida Simson's view, if you could get up on points and do a series of pirouettes round the room, you were a star pupil.

'Are you part of the company or did you just come in to play for the audition?' she asked, remembering the rule of good polite conversation – always show an interest in your companion.

David jabbed himself in the chest with a forefinger. 'Musical Director, that's me.

Soon as I leave you I'm off to audition a few folk for the "orchestra" – we've enough funds to pay for a trio of piano, violin and flute. I've a hell of a lot of music to write parts for – you'll like it when you come to learn the ballets, we've got some nice pieces. But transcribing *Swan Lake* Act Two from full orchestra to three instruments is a headache, I can tell you.' He caught the barman's eye. 'What's on the menu, Fred?'

'Sandwiches – luncheon meat, tomato or cheese. And me name's Arnold.'

'I'll have two rounds of luncheon meat, then, Arnold, and ... what about you, Linda?'

'I'll have cheese, please – only one round.'

'He's only having one round too, dearie,' said Arnold, with a grin. 'There's a war on, you know.'

David began talking enthusiastically about his musical arrangements. 'Gadina's arranged a dance to pieces of Gluck – I've done a nice shape-up of the *Dance of the Blessed Spirits* – of course, it's nice having the flute for that...'

Linda tried hard to take it all in, waiting for a chance to ask him what he thought she should do about her dilemma. Perhaps she could send a message to Madame through David. 'Musical Director' – it must mean he was important, so Madame couldn't bite his head off when he announced that one of her chosen dancers had had to withdraw.

But she never got a word in. He gulped down the last of his sandwich, emptied his second half-pint, and took her hand. 'Well, goodbye for now, must dash. Are you on the phone? I'll ring you.'

'Yes – no – I'm in a sort of hostel.'

'Write it down on that.' He pushed a sheet of music at her which he took from a bulging jacket pocket. She obeyed, quite certain he would lose it before he had gone far. 'Right – I'll be in touch – sorry to rush but I've a violinist waiting to play for me – 'bye now.'

She made her way home on the Tube, mulling over her problem. She really couldn't go. Her mother would throw a fit. Besides, there was Alan. Alan would expect her to be in London when he got another weekend leave. How could he possibly reach her if she were off touring with a ballet company?

Alan Olliver was her steady boy-friend. They had been sweethearts since school-days, living in the same street in Hedfield, sharing the same childhood adventures. She'd been very proud to have Alan's friendship, for he was three years her senior. There had been prestige in having his regard, for between schoolchildren, three years is a vast gulf usually.

They were going to be married, of course.

'When the war's over,' that was the phrase. *'Après la guerre finie,'* as the French song had it. While he was off taking special training 'somewhere in Southern England' to be a commando, although that was supposed to be a secret, she was able to see him whenever he got leave. That was one of the reasons she was glad to be working nearby in London.

He thought her love of ballet was comical. He never actually said, 'You'll grow out of it,' but she could tell he thought so. It was just one of the oddities that made her lovable in his eyes. So long as it gave her pleasure to take lessons and give occasional charity shows, he didn't mind.

Yet she had a feeling that he would take it badly if she actually joined a professional group. She'd once dragged him to see the Vic-Wells Ballet in *Job,* and he'd been shocked – first at the profanity of putting a biblical theme into dance, and secondly and more importantly at the revelation of the human body in close body-stocking. 'I think it's disgusting,' he'd said with lips folded in disapproval. When she pointed out that there were great paintings showing the human body totally nude, he'd shaken his head. 'But they don't move about,' he said. 'Those dancers – I mean, one of them *writhed about.'*

She couldn't really understand his objection. To her, any movement made by the body in the course of telling a story through dance or mime was acceptable. The body was an instrument, that was all. But Alan couldn't see it. 'I don't mind the kind *you* do,' he said, unconsciously belittling, 'because that's graceful and pretty. But I'm glad you're never going to be up there in front of an audience looking as if you've nothing on!'

Linda had no idea what kind of ballets the Gadina Company might be presenting. But one thing was certain – they wouldn't all be numbers using dancers clad in romantic tutus. Even though she suspected Madame Gadina was one of the old school, who really preferred ballets about enchanted princesses and the like, she would want to pay lip service to the modern school. So there would probably be a few pieces in which there would be 'writhing about'.

Alan wouldn't like it, he really wouldn't. Apart from the fact that the tour would take her to the North of England, away from him, he would be … displeased. Tolerant though he'd always been about her classes, he wouldn't like it if she made a career of dancing. She had a feeling he thought it improper, somehow. Perhaps it had something to do with the male dancers. He kept saying he was glad she'd never danced with a partner. 'I wouldn't fancy that,' he'd always said.

Shaking her head at her thoughts, she went on to the Mercury Theatre for the Business Girls' class. For the rest of the evening she forgot her problems in the glories of practising double pirouettes round the dance studio along with twelve other devotees.

But the problems were still there next morning. She went down to the bomb-shelter with her old portable gramophone, her body retaining its night-time warmth under two sweaters and a pair of leg-warmers knitted from precious scraps of multi-coloured wool. She wound up the gramophone and set the needle in the worn recording of *The Teddy Bear's Picnic* – first-class for the *barre* exercises with which every class must begin. As she did the precise bending and stretching that would flex her muscles for the 'neatness' steps, her mind was occupied with the thought of what she ought to do.

At the Ministry, soon after the afternoon tea-break, she was called to the telephone on which private calls were permitted. 'Lin? What train are you taking on Friday?'

'I'm not going, Betty.'

'What!' There was a pause. 'You're joking?'

'No, I've thought it over, Betty. I've no experience, and–'

'Oh, do shut up! How many of those girls had any experience? Damn it, Lin, that's what touring is for – to let you learn what you need to know about the life, so that you can adapt to everything.'

'No, but I mean – Betty – I didn't have a real teacher–'

'D'you think I did? Oh, you're talking nonsense. Look here, what time do you finish this evening? I'll meet you for a drink and we'll talk it over–'

'I don't think it's worth wasting your time–'

'What time, Linda?'

'I must go, Betty. We're not supposed to stand chatting on the phone. Goodbye, good luck on the tour.'

She put back the receiver feeling she had made a very sensible decision. That being so, it was odd that she should feel so dejected as she went back to her desk.

The evening meal at the hostel was over by seven. She sat down to do some mending while listening to the radio in the big communal sitting-room. The first item on the news bulletin caused a complete hush among the girls chatting there.

'Buckingham Palace announce with deepest regret that His Royal Highness the Duke of Kent was aboard a civilian Sunderland flying boat shot down by enemy action over the Bay of Biscay–'

The rest was lost in exclamations of horror. The women in the big room, in common with all the others, had taken the

Duke to their hearts after his romantic courtship of the Princess Marina.

'Fancy firing on a civilian plane!'

'Damned Jerries – a bunch of savages!'

'You can bet they knew he was on it!'

'Sh, shush, let's hear the rest.'

The heartfelt expressions of sympathy from the BBC to the King and Queen in their bereavement were being read out when the gnarled old maid came to the door. 'Miss Thackerley? Is Miss Thackerley about?'

'I'm here.'

'A gent to see you in the hall, miss.'

It must be Alan, with an unexpected twenty-four hours pass! She flew into the hall.

It was David Warburton.

'Good evening,' he said. 'Thought I'd turn up instead of ringing. Betty told me she didn't have much success on the phone.'

'Betty?'

'She came to see me, told me you'd decided not to join the company.'

'She saw you? I didn't know she knew you?'

'She didn't. Come on, come out and have another lemonade.'

'No, I've got things to do–'

'Don't be silly,' he said, gently but firmly. 'This is important.' He took her by the arm and led her out, letting the big heavy oak door swing shut behind them.

The late August evening was warm and heavy with the scent of stock and roses in the neighbouring garden. He drew her arm through his and set off at a leisurely pace. 'Betty rang Miss Faulkner and asked for my address. It appears she saw us at lunchtime yesterday going into the pub – her bus was at the traffic lights. So she thought I might have some influence on you over this business.'

'It's no use arguing about it, David,' Linda said in an anguished voice. 'I've thought it all through and I realise I should never have let Miss Faulkner keep my name on that list. I can't go. I'm in a reserved occupation, and I can't leave it.'

'Oh, you are an idiot,' he replied calmly. 'Hundreds of girls can push pieces of paper around on a desk. Only a few can dance. You ought to be doing what you're good at.'

'But I'm not good – I mean, not good enough. You don't understand. I showed up well at the audition, but that was a fluke.'

He stopped to stare at her. 'Well,' he said, 'that makes you unique. You're the first dancer I ever met who didn't think she was Pavlova and Markova rolled into one.'

'Oh, that's nonsense! Every dancer knows there are things she needs to improve – that's why we keep on taking class and trying to learn.'

'Yes, but every other dancer I've met thinks

that her particular combination of talents and flaws makes her irresistible on stage. Look, Linda, I know about dancing – I've been friends with Gadina since I was a schoolboy. I've watched dozens of dancers, through Gadina's school and on to the stage. I know what I'm talking about. You can dance.'

'But not well enough for–'

'Yes, well enough for the troupe. Believe me, you're a joy to watch.' It was true. He had found her a delight on stage. But more than that – he wanted her to come on the tour so as to get to know her. There was something about her quiet, fair-skinned face that had stayed with him after he hurried away from the pub yesterday. Besides, she was a better dancer than any of the girls they'd have to call on for a replacement, at least for the present.

Blushing with pleasure at his praise, Linda walked on. His opinion carried great weight with her. He was one of the *cognoscenti*, clearly more at home in the world of ballet than she herself. If he liked her dancing, it must be true – she did have talent. But enough to take a place in a company?

He took her to a pub in Chelsea from whose saloon bar windows they had a distant view of the Thames. Because of Double Summer Time, brought in to lengthen the working day still further, the black-out curtains weren't drawn yet. They sat in silence, staring out. She said, remembering: 'Did you hear the news?'

'What news?'

'About the Duke of Kent.'

'No, what?'

She told him about the loss of the Sunderland. He frowned, sighed, and shook his head. 'Damned shame. Why would they bother to go after him?'

'Propaganda? "We know who's on every plane"?'

'Makes you feel–'

'Unimportant,' she supplied.

'Linda, you're not unimportant. You have something that matters. You'll always regret it if you don't take this chance,' David urged. 'If you wait until the end of the war, when the regulations are relaxed and you're free to leave, who knows – there might be a lot of other dancers to compete against.'

'But you don't understand – I never meant to make ballet my career.'

'No? Then why on earth did you take classes?'

'Because ... I don't know. I wanted to, that's all.'

'And you want to dance. In a theatre, I mean – not in a dance studio.'

'Well ... it would be nice to have space to...' She let the words die away. She was remembering the improvisation of yesterday, the feeling of freedom as she threw herself through the space on stage. How wonderful it would be to do that to the sweeping sound of a full orchestra! And to have colour and movement around her, the glow of lights, the impulse of a story to convey to hundreds of people intent on every movement!

She pulled herself together. 'When you get called up,' she said in a serious tone, 'you'll have to go. You just can't ignore wartime regulations.'

'Well, in fact, they took one look at me and decided I was substandard,' David replied. 'But that's different. If you were doing something vital, like training an anti-aircraft gun or nursing in a field hospital, there'd be no argument. What I'm saying is that a replacement could be ordering whatever it is you supply by next Monday morning. Isn't that true?'

'I suppose so. But if we all began making excuses like that, there'd be nobody to do the dull jobs, would there? I know it sounds … soppy … but there is such a thing as duty.'

'Oh yes. A big word. Are you sure you're not just hiding behind it?'

'I don't know what you mean.'

'Are you scared to go with the tour, perhaps? Scared because it's new and demanding, whereas a desk job is easy and–'

'Oh, you know nothing about it,' she burst out with some resentment. She felt she was justified in her anger against him. It was easy to see he came from a family who could afford to give him whatever training he asked for. He was clearly doing what he wanted to do – his enthusiasm and his talent were all turned towards the work of providing ballet music. What did he know about 'easy' options, he who'd never had anything else?

'I'm sorry, I didn't mean to offend you,' he said at once, with a smile of real apology. 'But it does seem a possibility. You are scared, aren't you? Because it's your first job as a dancer?'

'Not in the least,' she lied with a little jut of her chin. 'And if you don't mind, I think we ought to finish our drinks and get home, for there's almost sure to be an alert again tonight – they're sure to attack somewhere on a fine night like this.'

The late dusk was falling. What she said was true, an air raid was quite likely, although there was no knowing where it would occur. But he knew, and she knew he knew, that she was using it as an excuse. His arguments made her uncomfortable – she wanted to get away from him.

He saw her to the gates of the hostel. 'Think it over,' he said, 'and when you do you'll see I'm right. You owe it to yourself to come. So I'll see you on the Cheltenham train on Friday morning – eight-forty from Paddington. Betty will be on it too, so don't miss it.'

'I don't think so,' she said, shaking her head.

'If you're not coming, you'd better ring Alice Faulkner and tell her. And rather you than me – she'll bite your head off for this trick you've played.'

'Goodnight. Thanks for the drinks.'

'Oh, two lemonades and some straight talk – think nothing of it.'

He waited till she went indoors, then stood for a moment looking at the blacked-out windows of the house, noting its shabby paintwork and worn, sagging fence. Not much of a setting – surely she would rather leave it and go out to take her place in the theatre? Even though wartime theatre was shabby too, it had compensations beyond anything to be gained from nights spent in this dreary house and days at a routine office job.

He turned away, sighing, and as he did so, the sirens began their rising and falling notes. Oh, damn – she'd been right about the alert. Let's hope she isn't right in her view of the so-called duty, he said to himself. Because if she is, it's a rotten waste of a good dancer.

Linda slept fitfully and woke rather later

than usual. That being so, she was unable to have her full work-out in the basement. It was always chancy after an alert, anyhow – sometimes people went down to spend the night if there had been an early warning. Nothing had actually happened. The raid – if there had been one – had gone elsewhere. So she found the shelter empty and had half-an-hour's limbering up before hurrying upstairs at seven-thirty to get a bath before the breakfast gong went.

The day at the Ministry branch office was long and tedious. And then it was her turn on fire-watch rota. Fire-watchers got a free meal in the canteen at seven, without having to give up any coupons for it. Linda gulped it down, glad of the fodder to help provide energy for her next dance class. But she gave up the chance of seconds of the jam roly-poly to get to the coinbox phone. She was trying to contact Alice Faulkner and tell her she wouldn't be at Cheltenham tomorrow.

But the trunk operator told her there was no chance of getting a call through to Gloucestershire for the foreseeable future. All lines were busy. Linda ruefully reflected that there were masses of army camps out to the west and their calls would take precedence of private traffic.

As she stepped out of the callbox in the hall of the office block, Frank joined her. He was a wages clerk, he kept trying to sit next to her in the canteen. 'Phoning your boyfriend, Linda?' he inquired.

She shook her head, her thoughts on the wire she was now going to write. As short as possible because she couldn't expect a long message to be accepted at the moment– 'There's a war on'. Yet she must convey apology and regret. 'Sorry unable to join company, war work detains.' No, that sounded weird. 'Prior commitment prevents...' No, that sounded as if she had had another ballet offer.

'You dashed off from supper pretty fast,' Frank was saying. 'Missed coffee – want some now? There's some in the flask in the watch room.'

'Not at the moment, thanks,' she said, and retired to the women's quarters to compose her telegram.

The women's quarters consisted of a former storeroom furnished with four beds, very hard and twanging, clad with army blankets. Linda could never understand why army blankets had to be grey.

She sat on her bed and wrestled with her message. 'Regret service duties prevent...' That was better. She didn't need to confess that the 'service' was the Civil Service and that she was a lowly clerical officer.

She was due on duty on the roof at ten o'clock. Before that she must have got the wording right and telephoned it to the Post

Office. She was still deleting and inserting words when she heard someone come in.

She didn't turn her head. It was probably Lucy Mason, the other girl on duty with her at ten.

'All on your lonesome?' said a voice. And it certainly wasn't Lucy Mason.

'Frank! What are you doing in here?' Linda was appalled. The men were not allowed to enter the women's quarters – although she heard fanciful rumours of 'goings-on' among some of the other fire-watching teams.

'I've come to see you, that's what,' Frank said, sitting down beside her on the blanket-spread bed. 'Come on now, Linda, you know I've been after you for weeks now.'

'I don't know anything of the kind and if you don't get out of here I'll report you.'

'Who to?' Frank inquired, putting an arm round her. 'If you really want to know, they've other things on their minds in the watch room.'

'We'll soon see,' she said, springing up to leave.

Frank grabbed her at the shoulder as she tried to rise, and with a strength that surprised her pulled her back. 'Come on, don't be so toffee-nosed,' he said in her ear in a breathy whisper. 'Why not grab some fun like the rest of them?'

'Let go,' she said, wriggling out from

under his hold with a suppleness that, in its turn, surprised him. 'You're drunk!'

'Not a bit, sober as a judge, and all afire with love for you, dear,' he replied. He lunged across the bed and caught at the skirt of her summer dress. His jerk at it caused her to lose her balance. She fell back on the blankets. He threw himself across her. She scrabbled with her feet and got enough purchase to bend her knees. With all her dancer's strength she straightened her legs, almost springing through his embrace and hitting his chin with the crown of her head as she did so. He gave a howl of pain and lashed out. His arm swept her to one side and he seemed to be falling on top of her.

Suddenly he was yanked back. Lucy Mason's face appeared behind him. She had a handful of his shirt in her grasp. 'Come on, Romeo,' she said in her matey, jokey way. 'You made a mistake, eh. Thought this was the men's quarters?'

'Oh,' Frank was gasping. 'Oh, she's split my lip! Oh, I'm bleeding!'

'Buzz off, mate, will you? There's some styptic in the first aid box for your lip. Go on, off with you, or I'll have to report you.'

'It's her fault,' groaned Frank. 'She asked me to come–'

'I didn't!' cried Linda.

'No, of course you didn't. Scarper,

Frankie – otherwise I'll do you a more severe damage than Linda did.'

Frank went out with both hands to his jaw. Lucy Mason looked at Linda and shrugged. 'Now you know why so many girls wear siren suits for fire-watching,' she said. 'Good as a chastity belt, they are.' She indicated her own severe dungaree-style outfit in dark blue serge. 'Worth the clothing coupons just for the protection.'

'I didn't invite him–'

'No, I know you didn't. He's a well-known louse. You all right?'

'Yes, just shaken, that's all.'

'Funny, the ideas men get – a girl gets orders to spend the night time hours on duty here and they take it for granted it's all for their comfort and relief. Bloody arrogant fools.'

'I've never had it happen to me before, Lucy–'

'You've been lucky, child. Sarah Lavington in Surplus Stores has had to take compassionate leave – she's preggie by some bloke who got a bit carried away during the spring, and what's more, he's married with two kids.'

'Oh, lord,' said Linda. She looked about the dingy room with distaste. 'Fancy … *here*…'

'Yes, not romantic, is it? Come on, kiddie, let's get a cup of coffee and sort ourselves out for "upstairs".' She looked at the notebook and pencil on the bed. 'Letter-writing?' she asked, picking up one of the discarded sheets.

'No, it doesn't matter,' Linda replied. She took the square of paper and crumpled it up. 'I've changed my mind.'

At eight-forty next morning she was at Paddington Station, having raced home at six to throw her dancing gear and a few clothes into a suitcase, obtain her ration book from the manageress of the hostel, make sure she had her identity card and her Post Office savings book.

Frank had made up her mind for her in a way no one else could have done.

CHAPTER THREE

The shakedown period of two weeks was insufficient for the company. But then, any shakedown period is too little – two weeks, two months, six months, there's always more that needs to be done before the work is perfect. Designers see some way to improve the costume, the choreographer wants to neaten the *coupés* and *relevés* or change the sequence in the last variation, the dancer can envisage a new phrasing that will help save breath for the last great leap...

The girls had been found sleeping quarters in the big old house in which Gadina lived and had her school. The boys (few in number) had camp beds in an old summerhouse. Luckily the weather continued fine and warm into September.

Costumes had been bought ready-made for some of the ballets; *Homeland,* for instance, to music by Smetana, required only the usual 'peasant' outfit with a different colour skirt for the soloists. For two of the ballets, dresses were even now being evolved by a pair of devoted seamstresses who did all the costumes for Gadina's school displays.

The musicians rehearsed in a church hall by themselves when they weren't needed for work with the dancers. Their *ensemble* improved noticeably over the two weeks. So did the work of the dancers.

There were twelve girls forming the *corps de ballet*, four of whom were already selected for small solo parts. Others might be given solos as Gadina thought fit. There were three boys only, because almost every male dancer was already called up or with the Vic-Wells or Rambert companies. Of Gadina's three, one was a citizen of the Republic of Eire and not subject to call-up, one was waiting for his papers, and the third was only sixteen although, tall and muscular, he looked older.

The 'stars' were Maria Petrowsky, nee Mary Petersfield, and Carl de Breuve. Mary's father had put money into the company, which in part explained her stardom, although she was a good dancer, strong and effective despite her thinness, which seemed to be caused by a neurosis about food. Carl was a great bonus – well-trained, strong, sunny-natured. All the girls adored him as they would a kindhearted big brother. His homosexuality, which Linda didn't divine until well into the tour, was discreet – as it had to be if he wanted to avoid trouble with the police. He had come to the company at Gadina's invitation after taking lessons with her for more than a year while hoping for an opening with one of the established companies. It was a mystery that they hadn't snapped him up – but so much the better for Gadina.

The daily routine was hard but necessary. They were all up soon after six, competing for the washing facilities. Then they would gather in the studio at the front of the house for exercise and warming-up. Then class, taken by Gadina herself.

She was a tyrant, armed with a long wooden pointer with which she thumped the floor to emphasise the rhythm. Occasionally, in moments of great frustration, she would aim thwacking blows at an offender, but she never intended them to hit their mark – for what ballet-mistress in her right mind would want to bruise a dancer's legs?

Class lasted two hours, from seven to nine. Then breakfast – tea, piles of fresh toast with plenty of margarine (for Gadina had her friends among the tradesmen), a protein item such as fish or an egg or a precious sliver of bacon. Then 'freedom' until ten, although almost every girl had been press-ganged into sewing costumes – stitching on trimmings, binding the stems of artificial flowers so they wouldn't prick when tacked to the dresses, and when all else failed, darning the points of ballet slippers to improve their 'hold'.

At ten rehearsals began. The *corps* worked in Gadina's studio under Alice Faulkner, the soloists sometimes worked there with them and sometimes in the church hall. From time to time all would be united – *corps*, stars and the trio of musicians. During the first week these encounters ended with Olga Gadina throwing her pointer at someone or pushing back her chair so hard that it fell over. But towards the end of the second week it began to seem possible that they would be able to give a performance.

They were to travel on the Wednesday, to make their debut in a half-week engagement as part of a variety bill at the Grand, Manchester. They would dance Thursday, Friday, Saturday matinée and evening. The ballets were *Polonaise* to music by Chopin and a direct steal from *Les Sylphides*, *Sugar Plum* from the *Nutcracker Suite* danced by Mary and Carl, and the *Dance of the Reedpipes* from the same ballet fiddled-about-with to lead into a coda and finale.

'Is this ballet?' Linda asked David as they ended a fairly disastrous dress-rehearsal on Tuesday in a theatre hired for the day by Gadina.

'It's what the public wants, Lin.'

'But it isn't *saying* anything.'

'It's saying that this is a group of dancers who want to entertain the public–'

'Oh, entertain–!'

'Listen, Lin, if it was good enough for Markova and Dolin it's good enough for us.'

'But they only did music-hall when there wasn't an audience for ballet – they wouldn't do it now!'

'There isn't an audience for us yet, that's all. We've got to have a running-in period, Lin, you must see that. Today was the very first time we'd all been on a stage together.'

'Yes, and it was dreadful, wasn't it?'

'Don't worry, you know it's a tradition that a bad dress rehearsal means a good performance.'

'Ha,' said Linda, and went into the house to pack.

She had many anxieties besides the prospect of a first night in a big provincial theatre before an audience who didn't know anything about ballet. She had to explain to her mother that she was off on tour with a ballet company. They had a routine of writing to each other once a week so thus far she had claimed to be spending 'some free time' in Cheltenham taking lessons with Madame Gadina. But soon letters would have to follow her on the touring route, which meant that her secret had to come out. She dreaded what her mother would say. She even feared she might come after her to the first address she would give her, the theatre in Bolton where they were to play the week after their Manchester debut.

Then there were the fears about her own abilities. She had enjoyed the hard work at

Madame's studio but touring would be different. Already she found she liked some of the company, didn't care for others – yet it was important to be able to work in harmony with them all. Madame still frightened her, Alice Faulkner was cold and stand-offish, Mary Petersfield's intensity was often hard to take, and two of the girls in the *corps* were boring and self-centred to the point of caricature.

The men – 'the boys' – scared her, but for purely technical reasons. So far in her training she had never done double work, dancing with a partner. During the two weeks' rehearsals she had learned how to be held in the course of the dance, but more was to come – she was going to have to learn how to be lifted, and the prospect was terrifying.

In the old classical ballets, the *corps* was used to decorate the stage behind the ballerina. Little more was asked of them except to be proficient and look pretty. Now, as ballet made greater demands, every girl had to learn how to float through the air at the end of a man's arms, how to dive into space with the full confidence that he would be there to catch her.

If there had been plenty of time and plenty of boys, the lessons would have been easier. But the girls without experience had to catch up as fast as they could, with only four boys to partner all of them. Carl was strong and dependable, the Irish boy Terrence had done some double work before. But the others were learning as the girls were – and were as frightened as the girls. What's more, they got very tired. The outlook was depressing, yet they had to master the techniques or one-third of their repertoire would be unusable.

Added to all this was the problem of shoes and tights. A dancer needed new shoes after about eight performances. It was highly unlikely that, in wartime, they would get enough to supply their needs. The difficulty was as great for the boys as the girls, for men's shoes are thinner than girls' and come into contact with the stage over a greater area. It was just conceivable that one could patch a blocked shoe over the toe, but a man's shoe would need patches at the toe, at the ball of the foot, and perhaps even at the heel – which really meant making a new shoe.

As to tights: 'Thank God for crochet hooks,' they would say to each other as tiny runs were picked up so as to be unnotice-able. Small holes they could deal with themselves; bigger disasters would have to be taken to the invisible menders with pleas for immediate attention. If only rayon were not so apt to give way... They had heard that a marvellous new material called nylon was being used for stockings and tights in

America, but if there were any available in Britain no one in the Gadina Company had as yet seen them.

On the Wednesday morning they gathered at Cheltenham Station – seventeen dancers, three musicians, the wardrobe mistress known as Cissie and her assistant Pat who doubled as dresser, Mary Petersfield's maid Beryl, Brian Hampson in charge of scenery, props and if possible lighting, Alice as *régisseur* and business manager, and the Artistic Director, Madame Olga Gadina. There were press photographers and reporters, to Linda's surprise.

'Are you looking forward to launching a new artistic force in the provinces?' one serious-looking young woman asked Linda.

'Oh ... yes ... certainly.'

'You regard yourselves as crusaders? Pioneers?'

'We regard ourselves as dancers,' Betty Balcombe said in a cross tone, coming to join them from the station buffet where she had been buying wrapped sandwiches for the journey.

'Oh, so you take a practical view of the enterprise?' suggested the reporter.

'Well, I certainly don't think of it as converting the heathen. There have been other ballet tours, you know.'

'But of the Black Country? Dancing in factory canteens?'

84

There was a pause. Betty looked at Linda. 'Canteens?' she mouthed at her, silently.

'We just want to dance well for anyone who wants to see us,' Linda said.

The sound of the approaching train put an end to the interview. 'Thank you. You are...?'

'Linda–'

'She's Lina Takarova,' Betty cut in, 'and I'm Bettine Balzac.'

'Balzac? Any relation to the novelist?' called the reporter as she was pushed aside in the rush for seats.

'Oh, of course. He was my great-great-grandfather.'

'Betty, how could you?' Linda said as they tumbled in after four other girls and shut the carriage door.

'People like that ask for it,' Betty said in an angry tone. 'It's not enough that we're a new ballet company – there's got to be something more, to make a story.'

The train was greatly delayed, often shunted into sidings while more important traffic took precedence. They reached Manchester after dark and in the rain. 'It's always raining in Manchester,' muttered a voice from among the dancers as they emerged from Piccadilly Station.

As they dispersed in search of their various lodgings, most of them passed the variety theatre in which they were to make their

85

debut the next evening. It was a Victorian building, painted ochre once but now peeling and sad. Because of blackout regulations, no lights showed on its canopy, but as the taxi went by there was just light enough to read the bill of tonight's show: 'Canova and his Performing Cats – 2 Lions 2! Daisy and Dennis, Fun with a Song or Two!' After that the print became too small to see from the roadway.

'Oh, lovely,' sighed Betty. 'We're coming in after Canova and his lion-taming act. We've *got* to be better than that!'

The digs were across town from the station, towards the Ship Canal. The landlady had the door open before the taxi had stopped. 'Oh, my dears, how lovely to see you at last! I was beginning to think your train was bombed! Come in, come in! Dancers – oh, I do love having dancers as my guests!'

Betty, Audrey Styles, and Linda were each given a hug and a wet kiss on the cheek. Their luggage was taken in by a shuffling, shadowy figure – 'my hubby,' said Mrs Goodge dismissively.

It was cheering to be welcomed so warmly but less so to discover they had missed the evening meal. 'I kept it as long as I could, darlings, but it dried up in the oven so I had to put it in the pigbin.'

They were dismayed. Betty, a seasoned

tourer, insisted they must have something. 'We've been travelling all day with only four LMS sandwiches amongst us, Mrs Goodge. And we have class and rehearsal first thing tomorrow.'

'Exactly, I know, darlings, it's awful, but I haven't anything to offer. There's a war on, you know.'

There's a war on ... the unending excuse, now three years old. For every shortage, every lack, every failure of service, every inconvenience – there's a war on. Sometimes the words were said to those who had best cause to know it – those who had lost men in the Dunkirk retreat, the capture of Hong Kong or Singapore.

There was no need to tell it to the girls. Their awareness of it was reinforced by every newspaper headline, every radio bulletin. Almost always the news was bad. This morning, for instance, the BBC had been preparing the way for some depressing announcement about the Russian city of Leningrad. 'They are meaning St Petersburg, of course,' Olga Gadina had said, half in irritation, half in anxiety. St Petersburg, the home of the Maryinsky, where she had trained, made her debut, and fallen in love with a young nobleman shot by the Bolsheviks.

There's a war on. From the possible capture of a great Russian city to the lack of a decent meal at the end of a long, wearying day – it served as catchphrase for disasters great and small.

But Betty wasn't prepared to submit to this small defeat.

After much protest from Betty and support, though muted, from Linda and Audrey, they were offered fish and chips from a nearby chippie – so long as they would pay half the cost.

'It's a con,' Betty muttered. 'She ought to pay the whole thing. I bet what you like she didn't have a meal ready in the first place...' But there was no alternative if they were to stay the pangs of hunger enough to sleep and be ready for next day. What made Betty even more furious was that she was certain Mr and Mrs Goodge each got a fish supper out of the deal.

Yet next morning, after a night in a fairly comfortable room with one double bed and one single (for which they tossed best of three) they found a substantial breakfast awaiting. 'I understand, darlings. You need to stoke up. I was a dancer myself, you know. Julia Jenner, High Kicks and High Jinks – that was me.'

'She'll show us her cuttings book at tea,' groaned Betty as they set out for the theatre. 'It's inevitable.'

The Grand had better equipment than its exterior suggested. Faded and grubby it might be, but it had been built by an owner who wanted to show respect for 'artistes'. The dressing rooms, though spartan, had an adequate supply of warm water (not hot, that was asking too much with a war on) and the lighting was good for make-up. There was a rehearsal room at the back where Madame at once began morning class.

It was a pattern that was to become familiar to Linda from that day forward: as much breakfast as possible in lodgings, to provide energy for the morning's work. Then a brisk walk to the theatre, a quick look at the noticeboard by the stage door to see if Alice had changed the programme or had any remarks to pass on from Madame. Then limbering and class – and no matter what might have happened the previous night, a good performance or a bad, class was always severe and thorough. Then special tuition for those beginning to understudy the principals. Then lunch, usually in a British Restaurant where it was possible to get a substantial and nourishing meal for one shilling and sixpence.

The afternoon was free if there was no matinée. But 'freedom' to a dancer means time to learn and improve. If there was a well-known teacher in the town, almost everyone turned up in her class at least once during the company's stay, to see if they could find out anything helpful to their technique. Of course there was always laundry to do, hair to shampoo, mending, foot care. Some of the girls had dreadful feet, Linda was shocked to see.

The evening performance followed the rule set in Manchester. The audience applauded wildly. At first it was heartening and exhilarating, but it began to dawn on them by the time they reached Blackburn that these enthusiasts had no discrimination. They were just pleased to see something pretty or clever. They clapped loudest at the showiest bits. The show-business reporter would praise them in the local paper, but it meant nothing. When that realisation came to them, they were disheartened for a time.

'Well, it's better than being booed,' Betty said philosophically. 'And at least we're giving them what they need – an escape from dreariness.'

After the first shock of pleasure and then disappointment, Linda made up her mind to disregard applause. She knew within herself whether she danced well or badly. And she was aware that she was improving all the time.

Madame's classes were wonderful. There were times when Linda wanted to wring the old lady's neck, and moments when she was actually, physically afraid at the anger she had evoked by some mistake. Gadina would swear in Russian, give orders in English, but when she wanted to praise she spoke French. It was extraordinary; she had lived in Cheltenham seventeen years but had never learned the language so well as the French she had been taught at the Maryinsky. When, rarely, she was pleased, she would tell a dancer: *'Tu as bien fait. Très bien, mon enfant.'* Rarer still was: *'Magnifique! Exquise!'* These infrequent happenings were referred to by her dancers as 'Madame's French Flashes'. So far, Linda had never earned one.

To her astonishment she was asked to understudy two of the solos, danced by Patricia Eland, one of the four named dancers on the billing under Maria Petrowsky. It must mean Madame – or perhaps Alice – thought well of her dancing. 'On the other hand, they have to give it to *someone*,' she said with a sigh to David, who was playing for her during an hour's private rehearsal.

'That's not the way to look at it,' he scolded. 'She could have given it to Betty or Marina. She chose you.'

'She couldn't give it to Betty. Betty's too muscular. But Marina or Lallie could do it.'

'There you are then. She chose you instead.'

'Only because they've already got understudy to do.'

'All right, if you're determined to think you're not good enough, why don't you go and tell Madame she's making a mistake?'

'Are you out of your mind?' cried Linda in horror. 'Come on, let's have another try. From bar thirty...'

They were in a basement room in the Premier, Blackburn. Class had been held in it that morning. Now it was half-past two in the afternoon and Linda was struggling with a small variation from *Polonaise*. In practice clothes, she looked nothing like the fairy-like wraith who was supposed to drift across the stage summoning her sisters to dance in the moonlight.

Over the top of the battered piano, from which he was attempting to coax liquid Chopin phrases, David watched her: slender and blonde, with lovely fluid lines and feet that scarcely seemed to touch the boards. But still with no personality to project, and perhaps not very strong...

One day, perhaps, she would graduate to a proper ballet company. David, his hands occupied with the keys and his eyes with the dance, let his mind wander. One day he hoped to be part of a great company himself. He wanted to write full-scale orchestral music for ballet. For this very reason, though Gadina didn't know it, he had hinted and coaxed and bullied until friends in high places accepted the idea of a small touring ballet directed by the former colleague of Anna Pavlova, Olga Gadina. If ever David should gain promotion to a big company, his work with Gadina would stand him in good stead.

Already he had to his credit the transcription of the works of Chopin, Gluck, Smetana and Tchaikovsky for his trio. He was now working on re-orchestrating melodies from Bellini's *Sonnambula* for a twenty minute ballet of the same name. He had two or three ideas of his own which, in due time, he hoped to present to Gadina. In one of them there was a role Linda ought to get...

Lina Takarova's debut as soloist in the Gadina Company took place at the Saturday matinée in Bury, Lancashire. It called forth no cries of *'Exquise! Charmant!'* from Madame. Instead, as the company came offstage and made for the dressing rooms to change, Madame put herself in Linda's way.

'Even if most of the leg is hidden by the long romantic tutu, it is important to have straight knees, no?'

'Yes, Madame.'

'Did you think I would not see the knees were not straight?'

'No, Madame.' Linda waited, holding her breath, for Madame to say she was so disappointed in her that she had decided not to let her continue the understudy. But

Madame stood back and raised the skirt of the long black dress she always wore (so as to appear 'regal' as company director at curtain call).

'Even though no one can see, my knees are being straight,' she remarked.

It was only too true. The slender legs, apparently untouched by age, were as straight as the proverbial willow wands. Madame went up on the half-point. 'Straight,' she said.

'Yes, Madame.'

With a nod the company director dismissed her. Alice, appearing at her shoulder, said, 'I thought she did rather well. Wouldn't a word of encouragement have been in order?'

'Encouragement my dancers are hevving from the public. From me what they are needing is a little cruelty.' And Madame walked off to inspect the make-up of the village prankster in *Homeland*.

But her 'cruelty' had encouraged Linda. She knew her performance had been literally weak-kneed, and she was disappointed in herself. Yet there were two things about it that satisfied her, almost. One was that she had maintained the air of dreaming enchantment that the part demanded, despite her nervousness. The other was that the magical ability to leave the ground almost without effort seemed to be increasing. It had something to do with her breathing; whenever she tried to analyse it and time it, it didn't work. But when she let her dancing self take over – that other Linda who knew without teaching how steps should be phrased, actions should be merged – the result was a lightness, a winged-ness, without effort.

The only cloud in the sky was her worried mother. 'An Investigating Officer came from the Ministry of Labour on Wednesday,' she wrote. 'He asked if I knew where you were, but I only said I thought you had taken a job in dancing. Linda dear, I really think you should go back to your real job before you land in serious trouble.'

Her real job. How could she leave the company and go back to an office job, now, when she was just beginning to learn something about real dancing? Too inexperienced for solo work after only three weeks out with the company, nevertheless she had been given this golden chance. She would stay, and she would learn, and the devil take the consequences.

Alan had been understanding, in the end. She'd got through to him on the phone from Cheltenham, after hours of trying. At first he'd been shocked by the news that she'd joined Gadina's company.

'How can you leave your job?' he said. 'You're in a reserved occupation.'

'I know that, Alan. It's just … I want to see if I can do it.'

Suddenly Alan relented. She'd always had this funny notion about the ballet, a fixation, they called it. She might as well get it out of her system now, because once they were married… 'You're daft,' he said, warmth in his voice. 'Utterly crazy. But I like you just the same.'

'Do you, Alan? Do you still?' she asked anxiously.

He laughed. 'Yes, but when I'm going to see you, Lord knows.'

Betty Balcombe too had her problems. She was engaged to a sergeant in the Royal Engineers. 'I mean, when we got engaged he wasn't in the army – I never thought of myself as being engaged to a sergeant,' she explained to Linda over thick cheese sandwiches at lunch break. 'But he rang me yesterday to say he thought he would be going overseas soon–'

'Oh, Betty, should you be talking about things like that on the phone–?'

'We have our special code. We agreed that if he was being posted he'd tell me he'd been to the flicks, and if he was going overseas he'd been to see a double feature.'

'And that's what he said?'

Betty nodded, her dark eyes sombre. 'It's terrible. I mean, when you read how Rommel is swooping back and forth over our boys in the desert ... Harry might be sent there. All of a sudden, he's important. I ... never really thought about it when we got engaged – he wanted to because he thought it would make me behave when I was on tour. The ring, you know, scaring off the wolves...' She held out her left hand with its small diamond, which spent most of its time in her handbag while she was dancing or taking class.

The following Monday they were to open in the Carlton Theatre, Rochdale. There was no rehearsal room big enough in the shabby little theatre, so they took class on stage. The barre was provided by a row of chair backs, which didn't make life easier. Moreover, in an excess of zeal at having high-class performers like ballet-dancers in his theatre, the manager had had the floor washed. Even putting extra rosin on the shoes didn't seem to help much. When they came to do centre practice, they slipped all over the place.

'*Bratschknyei! Skoteenyei!* You have the grace of elephants! Boys at the back – when I say *entrechat-quatre,* I expect to see your heads far above girls! Should be easy, for girls are flat-footed, all flat-footed! Once more – David, more slow so these flat-ironings can make preparation and *perhaps* get off ground – ready, and *one*-and-two-and-three-and-four...'

The class became aware that the doorkeeper's messenger was hovering in the wings. One of the girls in the front row dared to bring it to Madame's attention.

'What do I care if he is waiting. *I* am waiting, I am waiting to see some correct technique. David, at the correct tempo, eight bars of two-four. *And*-one...'

'Miss Gadina,' ventured the messenger, a sickly-looking ex-millboy, 'it's important.'

'Important?' said Madame, rounding on him. '*I* will say what is important!' To David, who had ceased playing: 'Why are you stopping? When I wish to stop, I will say. Play two-four time, please, pianist!'

David went back to the beginning of the passage, the class faced forward, and once again they attempted to rise into the air and perform that twinkling of the feet in mid-stride which is known as the *entrechat*. Audrey skidded and fell. The girl next lost concentration and stopped. Madame's pointer went flying through the air like a missile. Audrey dodged.

The result was a tirade in Russian which luckily none of them understood. In the midst of it the stage-door messenger appeared with a piece of paper folded in his hand. Madame broke off her remarks to turn on him with glacial politeness.

'Well, my friend?'

'I've a note here.'

Madame held out her hand.

'It's for Miss Balcombe.'

Silence fell. Madame held out her hand. The messenger, cowed by a glance that had brought princes to her feet, gave up the note.

In front of the startled gaze of the entire company, Madame opened it, read the few lines it contained, and folded it. She put it in the pocket of her old cardigan. 'That will be all,' she said.

'Er… There should be an answer, miss.'

'No answer.'

The boy hesitated. Madame took a step towards him. He turned and retreated with haste.

'Now we are beginning again with our work,' said Gadina. *Entrechat-quatre*, boys only, strict tempo–'

'But Madame–'

The old prima ballerina looked at Betty. 'You spoke?'

'Madame, my note–'

'There are no notes during class. There is no speaking during class. When class is over, is time for the note. Begin, pianist – strict tempo. *And*-one–'

'Madame, I must insist–'

'You insist? I insist that we work. Step back into your place. Everything this morning is bad. No concentration, no technique, no grace – all like carthorse. Until we can do simple *enchaînements* we cannot end class.

99

Until we end class, we cannot rehearse on this accursed stage. So you hold up everyone with your talk, Betty. Are we all ready? Two-four time...'

They worked on, and to their amazement satisfied Madame enough to move on to the next step. Then as if they had eyes in the backs of their heads the whole company became aware as they were turning *en attitude* that the messenger had re-appeared.

'Madame Gadina,' he said in a loud, firm voice, 'Miss Balcombe's wanted at the stage door.'

'Tut kuraj!' said Madame, giving him a glacial smile. 'You are a brave man, my friend. Have I not made it clear I do not wish to be interrupted?'

'It's not you, it's Miss Balcombe as is wanted,' persisted the boy, who had clearly been tipped well to make him brave. 'It's her fiancé waiting for her.'

'Harry!' gasped Betty.

'Ah, it is the fiancé! If it is the King of England, he does not call a dancer from my class until it is finish. Go tell this Harry – he can wait.'

'But he says he only has a few hours, miss. He's got a train to catch.'

'And I have a class to conduct.'

'Madame,' cried Betty, running forward, 'I think he's on embarkation leave–'

'I am not caring what excuse he has. You

100

know I do not wish my dancers to have love affairs – this interferes with the dancing. It is my strict rule – no romantic nonsense.'

'But you must have known I was engaged when I joined the company,' Betty insisted. 'You must have seen my ring?'

'Ring, ring, who cares about little piece of glass on the finger of a vain girl? Go back to your place. Already is ten o'clock, we have not finished elementary exercises, when shall we ever reach partnering, and when the rehearsal? You wish us all to suffer because you have young man waiting?'

'N-no, Madame,' stammered Betty, 'but if I could be excused–'

'I have *told* you,' cried Gadina, 'we have work to do. Do you disobey me?'

'No, Madame, but–'

'Go back to your place. We will work. David, three-four time, *allegro*–'

To Linda's consternation, Betty backed away, fell into her place in line, and took up the position of arms and feet for the attitude-turn. The class went on, the messenger did not return. When it ended more than an hour later everyone was wringing with sweat and a spirit of dejection had settled over them all.

'Now,' said Madame Gadina, pointing at Betty, 'you may go to speak to your Harry. But be back here in fifteen minutes for rehearsal of *Polonaise*. We must see if we can arrange any groupings on this slippery floor.'

Betty dashed away, still wiping her face with a damp towel. 'She's just being a bitch,' Audrey Styles muttered to Linda. 'We could mark Betty's place while we rehearse–'

'Betty won't show up,' Linda said with conviction. 'I wouldn't, if I were her.'

But Betty did show up. She came back, looking flushed and tearful, went through the rehearsal like a zombie, and rushed off as soon as the late lunchbreak was called. As she ran, Madame called after her: 'Prompt at the theatre at six o'clock, Betty.'

Later Linda heard the story. Harry Whitworth had forty-eight hours' embarkation leave, most of which he had spent in travelling to Rochdale from a camp in the south of England. He would have to leave again while Betty was performing in the theatre. If Madame had let her go from class, they could have had almost eight hours together. Instead they had three.

'But why did you come back?' Linda demanded. 'I never expected you to.'

'What, and face Madame afterwards? She'd have skinned me alive.'

'But he's your fiancé, Betty!'

'I know.' Betty's tears slipped down her cheeks. 'I just didn't know what to do. It was awful for Harry – all I did was cry and hang on to him.' She gulped and shook her head.

'I think he thought I was upset because he was leaving – but the terrible thing is, I was upset because of how Madame treated me...'

The performance that night was poor, but the audience seemed quite unaware of that. When Madame Gadina appeared at the end in her long black dress to take a bow as Artistic Director, they didn't notice that the company allowed a space of about two feet to separate her from the dancers.

Afterwards they all gathered in an all-night café the boys had found near the station. What the habitués – train staff, lorry drivers, drifters – thought of this sudden influx of exotic strangers was shown in the stares of amazement.

Terrence, the Irish boy, had elected himself spokesman. 'What we have to do,' he announced, 'is hand in a protest.'

'A protest!' This was greeted with awe. 'To Gadina?'

'Who else? We've got to make a stand, for Pete's sake! We're only four weeks into the tour and already she's trying to take over our private lives. Well, I for one am not going to stand for it.'

They sat over their stewed tea and processed-cheese sandwiches nodding their heads and looking indignant – all except Betty, who seemed too sunk in misery to care, and Mary Petersfield, who kept saying they were wasting their time.

From somewhere Terrence produced a sheet of paper and began to write with a leaky fountain pen. 'We the undersigned–'

'You want us to sign it?' Carl interrupted, shaken.

'We're standing up to her. An anonymous protest wouldn't show much courage, would it?'

'No, Terrence is right,' David agreed. 'We've got to sign it and it's got to be unanimous.'

'I'm not going to sign it,' Mary said. She got up, shivering and rubbing her arms as if she were cold. 'I think it's a waste of time. She's the director of the company. We have to abide by her rules.' She looked at Betty, who was stirring her teaspoon round and round her murky cup. 'I'm sorry about your boyfriend, Bets, I really am. But it's your affair, not mine, and after a working day that's lasted thirteen hours so far, I'm in no state to stand up to anybody. I'm for bed.'

She went out. For a moment the protesters were dashed. But Terrence's Irish blood was up. 'Come on,' he said, 'it's only what you'd expect of Mary. It's so important to her, being a prima – she'd rather die than offend Gadina. But the rest of us have more principles, haven't we?'

They all agreed they had principles. When the protest had been worded to Terrence's satisfaction, they all signed it – all the remaining dancers, David and his two musicians, and the assistant wardrobe mistress who promised to get Cissie's signature before going to bed.

That done, the meeting broke up. They felt as if they were starting the French Revolution. *'Liberté, Egalité, Fraternité!'* they cried, suddenly laughing and pleased with themselves. They were going to present the protest to Madame before class next morning.

When they assembled on stage at nine next morning, Mary was noticeable by her absence. 'Staying away until we've presented the protest,' Audrey remarked scathingly. 'Typical!'

They spent the usual pre-class period with their private limbering exercises. The beginning of class seemed to be delayed. Ten minutes past, a quarter past, and still no Mary – and what was stranger, no Gadina.

She arrived at twenty past, unusually flustered. Her thin face looked pinched, her hair was untidy. 'Before we begin class I appeal for excellent work all through so we can finish on time. We have to rehearse a new cast. Mary is having influenza.'

'What?' Cries of consternation and concern. Some recalled that she'd seemed shivery and listless last night.

Madame thumped on the boards with her pointer. 'Come, come, dancers – we must no time wasting. Take place at the barre, please. David, you are ready? We begin with our *pliés*. Right hand on barre, left hand in first position, please remember, soft elbow, soft hand – *and*-one-and-two-...'

Linda found the protest, much creased and soiled, on the floor of the passage to the dressing rooms when they had packed to leave on Saturday night. She picked it up. Later she showed it to David.

'We forgot all about it,' she said in shame. 'It was important, but we just brushed it aside the minute we had something else to think about.'

'Something more important?' he suggested.

Linda thought about it and half-shook her head. 'There must be something wrong with our priorities. How could it have been more important to switch roles around and learn steps at top speed, just to get the dances on stage? Betty was treated really badly–'

'But that was Betty's problem,' David put in. 'We were all sorry for her and wanted to show support but in the end it was up to her. She herself did nothing. And to tell the truth ... neither did the famous Harry.'

'What could he have done?'

'Dunno. He's an engineer, isn't he? Perhaps he could have set a bomb under the theatre.'

106

They laughed, but Linda refused to be diverted. 'What it comes to is, Betty was a coward.'

'I'm afraid so.'

Linda threw the last pair of slippers into her case and snapped it shut. 'I just felt so ... ashamed for her,' she murmured. 'I mean, if he really meant anything to her...?'

'Perhaps that's what she learned,' David picked up her case for her. 'Perhaps she realised what came first.'

Their next engagement was Rawtenstall, a half-week stay where they would be dancing in factory canteens, smelling strongly of Woolton pie, a wartime non-meat dish, or chops. Mostly chops. This was the fulfilment of the threat that had been hanging over them ever since they left Cheltenham. It was a short journey by local train so they arrived soon after midnight on Saturday. Alice took up a post in the ticket office to read out the names of their digs, most of which were in turnings off the main street.

Linda and Marina Radetzki were set down by the bus conductor at the turning. They walked up, trying to make out house numbers in the darkness of the black-out. Finally, at number thirty, they saw a small pocket torch set on the hearth-stoned step to light up the number. 'This is it, Linda,' Marina said with relief in her voice. As they walked up the path the door flew open, to reveal against the subdued light of a carefully shaded bulb a stout, apron-clad figure.

'Is that you, dears?' asked a loud whisper.

'Yes, from the Gadina–'

'Come in, come in – it's a right chilly night. Let me take your cases. I've got hot cocoa ready for you and pikelets – do you like pikelets?'

'Oh yes!' Already they had learned to welcome any form of food, no matter what title it might bear. Their landlady, Miss Allnutt, shooed them into a bright kitchen where a dark red fire glowed behind polished steel bars.

'There, take off your coats, tired, are you? I've a hottie in each of your beds, don't empty the water away in t'morning, dearies, use it for washing, eh, isn't it awful the things we have to do – but there's a war on.'

In a moment they were sitting at a table covered by a chenille cloth and drinking cocoa made with powdered milk and sweetened with saccharine. Miss Allnutt dumped the dish of crumpets, kept warm on top of the range, in front of them.

'Now,' she said, stepping back to survey them with her hands wrapped in her apron, 'which of you is Linda Thackerley?'

'That's me,' Linda said, pausing with her hand outstretched to the dish.

'Well, love, I don't know what you've been up to, but Mrs Goodge in Manchester sent me a p.c. to say there'd been a policeman asking for you there.'

Marina gasped. Linda sat up and stared at Miss Allnutt. 'A policeman? What did he want?'

'Mrs Goodge didn't say. She just said one of the boys in blue had been by, with a sticker for Miss Thackerley.'

'A sticker? What's that?' Linda asked, bewildered.

'A warrant, dear,' said the landlady, 'a warrant.'

CHAPTER FOUR

The word caused an intake of breath from both girls. Marina was round-eyed with disbelief.

'What've you been up to?' asked Miss Allnutt. 'Shoplifting?'

'Of course not!' Linda was shocked at the mere idea. 'It's just ... a thing about ... wartime regulations...'

'Oh, buying on the black market,' Miss Allnutt rejoined, sitting down suddenly at the table. 'My, what a relief! I'm glad it isn't anything really bad. I wouldn't ever shop you, of course, but I'm never happy covering up for a wrong 'un.'

'Oh, it's nothing criminal, honestly it isn't,' Linda insisted. 'But ... I never thought it would ... I mean ... the *police*...'

'Oh, you don't want to worry about them, dearie,' their landlady said comfortably. 'Good old Mr Plod – he's about three stops behind you, isn't he? Nobody's telling anything so he has to trudge along behind, and I don't think he'll ever catch up, if you want my opinion. And another thing, lass – it'd be a good idea to use your stage name all the time, eh, 'cos he's looking for Linda

Thackerley and not for a Russian dancer called Push-'er-ova.'

'Takarova,' Linda corrected automatically. Most members of the public got their names wrong to some degree.

'There, you see? They don't know which one is you and they have to go round all the digs trying to sort you out. And they take ages at it, and you're always off two towns further on in the tour. I shouldn't worry about it, if I were you.' She pushed the dish of pikelets at them. 'Eat up, you ought to be in bed, it's well past my bedtime I can tell you, even though I used to be a real night owl when I was in the profession, oh yes, I was a right one, I can tell you.'

Marina looked at Linda, they suppressed a sigh and prepared to listen to the reminiscences of the landlady. So far every lodging had been in the ownership of a former stage performer who wanted to relive past glories with them. Moreover most of them had husbands or sons in the Forces. The 8th Army was now sweeping back across the North African Desert to retake the towns from which they'd been driven – Sidi Barani, El Alamein... Landladies produced over-exposed snapshots of grinning, suntanned men in baggy shorts – 'My Stan. Been gone eighteen months now. Soon be home now they've got the Afrika Korps on the run.' Or, sadly, 'My Walter. No news of him since Hong Kong fell.'

But by and by, seeing their eyelids slip shut, Miss Allnutt relented enough to pack them off to bed. They undressed in the dark and fell between the sheets, faces still greasy from the melted marg on the pikelets. Just before they drifted into sleep Marina whispered: 'What was it you bought on the black market, then, Lin?'

Linda yawned. 'Ballet shoes, what else?' she muttered, and fell asleep.

On Sunday she sought out David at the factory canteen where he was trying out the acoustics for the trio. When he heard her tale, he laughed aloud. 'Oh, so you're wanted, are you?'

'It isn't funny, David! At the moment they're trying to catch up with me at my digs but they'll come to the theatre in the end.'

'Perhaps. But the police must have other and more important things to think about. As they say, there's a war on. I should think your arrest takes a very low priority, duckie.'

So it proved. No one appeared asking for her in Rawtenstall. Moreover, the problems of giving three performances in three different factories in totally different conditions each time kept her busy enough to forget the police. The town remained in their minds afterwards as the place where Carl got the sneezes. Something in the manufacture of carpets was apparently irritating to his mucous membranes so that all during the afternoon rehearsal he had sneezing fits and streaming eyes.

The local chemist supplied something that dried him up enough to perform. Nevertheless, during the *pas de deux* from Act Two of *Swan Lake* he had to abandon Mary and rush to the back of the platform where he gave two convulsive sneezes before dashing back in time to grab her as she came down from an unsupported arabesque. The audience noticed nothing amiss.

They had danced in Burnley and were in Preston when the dreaded blue uniform showed up at the theatre. It was a Thursday afternoon, the company were dispersing to relax for a few hours before the evening performance. Alice was in the office dealing with financial matters, Madame Gadina was in conference with David over the planning of the new ballet, *The Sleepwalker*. Linda, coming out of the front entrance, saw the constable walking round the side towards the stage door.

Her heart missed a beat. She drew her headscarf closer about her face, bent her head to the bitter November wind, and hurried away in the opposite direction. She had shopping to do and tights to collect from the invisible mender. Then she hoped to be in time to get the permitted four inches of hot water in the bath before one of the other two girls in the digs used it all. She went through this programme, resisting the temptation to swing aboard a country-bound bus and hide out in the moors until the danger was past.

She wasn't surprised to see David Warburton coming up the path to the house at about five that afternoon. She let him in and, contrary to the landlady's rules, took him up to the room she shared with the two other girls. They were both absent, one at the hairdresser and the other taking a piano lesson at a neighbouring house.

'The police were at the theatre–'

'I know, I saw the constable. I dashed away–'

'That was lucky! The stage doorkeeper brought him in to see Gadina, who left him to me – I suppose she thought I'd understand his Lancashire accent better.'

'So what happened?'

'Oh, I acted dim. When he said he was looking for a Linda Thackerley, I showed him tonight's programme with all the names – no Linda Thackerley. After a good deal of head-scratching he retired, satisfied that you're not with the Gadina Company.'

'Oh, David!' She threw her arms around him and hugged him hard. 'Oh, you're marvellous! It's such a relief!'

'I told you it was nothing to worry about–'

'Yes, and of course I should have believed you, but when Miss Allnutt said a warrant–'

'Incidentally, it's not a warrant, it's a summons – that's a lot less fearsome. Anyhow, it's all over. You don't have to worry any more.' David was enjoying the moment, feeling like a Sir Galahad who had rescued a maiden from a dragon. It was very pleasant to be standing in this over-furnished room, with Linda's arms about him and her body still scented from her bath close and confiding against his.

He dropped a kiss on Linda's parted lips. They both decided it was a brotherly kiss, and simultaneously ensured that no more followed it by moving apart.

'I must get ready for the theatre,' she said in a flustered tone, flushed and disconcerted from the warmth of their embrace and David's closeness.

'Yes, and I've got to get a meal of some kind. Shall I wait for you – and we could eat together?'

She was tempted. Why not? They were colleagues, friends. All the same... She shook her head. 'No, I've got things to wash out before I go.'

'Righto. See you later then.'

When he had gone she found her handbag and took out the snapshot of Alan. The familiar features sprang out at her. And yet he seemed somehow very distant. His letters

115

took a long time to find her, and he had never been a good correspondent. The last time she'd actually seen him was over three months ago, before the audition.

Everything had changed so much since then. She was a different person, almost – not an office clerk, but a dancer. And not just a dancer in the background but a soloist.

She checked herself there. Now, now, you know very well you wouldn't have got a solo in any other company. It's only because this is such a small group, and we have to cover every role somehow in case of illness or mishap.

Yet she was different. Eight weeks on tour had changed her. She had more confidence in everyday life, and despite the way her heart had failed her this afternoon at sight of the policeman, she had more courage than when Alan used to champion her against the other kids in her street.

Moreover, her horizons had widened. Her own experiences, and chat from other members of the company, had shown her that the view of life approved by her parents was not the only one. Carl and his boyfriends were taken utterly for granted by the members of the corps. A one-night romance by one of the girls was noted and dismissed. The admiration lavished on the dancers by the rich intelligentsia – such as it was – in each town opened new doors. Parties in settings of surprising luxury, gifts of items supposedly unobtainable – those new-fangled nylons, chocolates – propositions ranging from marriage to love-by-correspondence: all of these had flitted through Linda's life since she left London.

Oddly enough, she said little about them in her letters to Alan. To him she stressed the hard work – and that was the greatest part of her existence, indeed. She told him about her friends, about Gadina's autocratic rule and her sudden bouts of kindness.

But she had scarcely mentioned David.

A sudden pang of conscience assailed her. She abandoned any notion of washing stockings, and set herself to write a long letter to Alan.

The tour was now due to turn eastwards, towards Halifax. The month was November, and David was hard at work on the music of *The Sleepwalker* so that Gadina could do the choreography. It was urgently necessary to enlarge the company's repertoire so that costumes could be 'rested' and cleaned. Moreover, Gadina wanted a new ballet for Christmas presentation.

David was pleased with *The Sleepwalker*. It owed most of its plot to the opera – innocent girl suspected of immoral behaviour because she walks while sleeping into the room of a man. But for the purposes of ballet it had been much truncated. David had hoped Gadina would give the role of the heroine to Linda, but such a notion didn't even occur to the director. Naturally Mary Petersfield would take the principal role and her understudy would be Esme Resselle, one of the accepted soloists.

There was a chance for three girls, in a little trio for the heroine's friends. To David's delight, Linda was chosen. Yet she was oddly unenthusiastic.

'What's the matter?' he inquired in bewilderment. 'I'd have thought you'd be delighted at the chance of a special number.'

'Oh, I am, don't get me wrong. It's just...'

'Well, what?'

'What would you say the tone of the ballet is?'

'The tone?'

'Would you say it was bright? Boisterous? Happy?'

'It ends happily,' he pointed out.

'Oh yes, but after twenty minutes of drifting about in the moonlight and a few "rustic" dances.'

'What are you getting at, Lin?'

'It's not a bad ballet. It's just that it's awfully like everything else we do. It's samey.'

'Oh, thanks very much–'

'No, no, I'm not getting at you, David. The music is nice and the story is – well, quite dramatic. I've never seen the opera–?'

'It's never performed these days. That's why I chose it – the music will be new to the audience. And the story's unusual–'

'But not the dances. We'll even be using some of the costumes from *Homeland,* and probably the same backcloth. What I was thinking was... Well ... it's not great fun for Christmas, is it?'

'It's all we've got, sweetheart,' David said, somewhat annoyed at her criticism. Yet later that afternoon, when the session in the hired drill hall was over and Gadina had gone away to dream up a variation for Carl, he came back to Linda.

'What in your opinion would be great fun for Christmas?' he demanded.

Linda, deep in the problems of getting her practice gear into a collapsing paper carrier bag, turned to look up at him. 'Well, people in these parts like pantomime–'

'You're not suggesting we should put on a pantomime!'

'No, of course not. But there are things traditionally associated with Christmas...'

'Fairy godmothers? Cinderella?'

'We couldn't afford it. Even in a potted version there'd have to be a carriage and glass slipper...'

'Christmas trees ... *Babes in the Wood...*'

'Too gloomy. *Wind in the Willows–*'

'That means animal masks–'

'God forbid. *Peter Pan?*'

'Who on earth would dance Peter?' They looked at each other and began to laugh.

'No, let's be sensible,' Linda said. 'Think about what they put on Christmas cards. Holly, robins, stage-coaches–'

'That limits the ballet to Christmas only. We can't afford that, Lin. We need something that could be used throughout the tour – and we'll still be out touring at Easter.'

'Dickens?' Linda suggested. 'Everybody always associates Dickens with Christmas, but we "did" Pickwick at school and there's an election in that–'

'Dickens? *Sketches by Boz?*'

They thought about it, Linda trying to re-pack her carrier bag while she did so. 'Mr Micawber,' said David.

'That schoolmaster–'

'You mean Wackford Squeers in *Nicholas Nickleby.*'

'Do I? Then there's Tiny Tim–'

'Scrooge–'

'Too many men,' she protested. 'What about some women?'

'That one who was a lone lorn female ... Mrs Gummidge.'

'Little Nell.'

'Oh, God – we don't want a deathbed scene if this is supposed to be a happy ballet, and all Little Nell's famous for is her death. No, wait – Miss Havisham – the mad old lady in ... *Great Expectations?*'

'We don't want any mad old ladies, we want fun and romance. What about a pair of young lovers?'

'Well, then, Estella and Pip from *Great Expectations–*'

They made a list on the back of an envelope. David groaned at the thought of having to read half a dozen novels to find descriptions of the action. But a worse problem presented itself after the first rush of enthusiasm. 'What about music? There wouldn't be time to get anything written.'

'Oh, don't be silly, David! What about all that stuff the Victorians used to play and sing in their parlours, before they had the gramophone and radio? Why, my own mother – she used to play a piece called the *Pixies' Polka,* and my Uncle Edward used to sing songs like "Asleep in the Deep".'

'By God, you're right!' David stopped and gave her a searching glance. 'How long have you been thinking about this?'

'Well, about Dickens – ten minutes. But about a ballet with some bounce and good-humour – three weeks. I was thinking along the lines of a birthday party, but the Dickens idea is better – it gives a definite setting and ought to please the critics.'

'But will it please Madame?'

At first it did not. Gadina had never read a book by Dickens and had no intention of starting now. Moreover, her attention was taken up with *The Sleepwalker*. She didn't want to be distracted by another ballet.

'But this would only be a suite of dances, Madame,' David urged. 'Each dance would have the name of a Dickens character and would summon up that character – Mr Micawber is funny and has pathos, Sarah Gamp is a roistering old bundle of tricks, Estella and Pip can be very romantic–'

'Estella. That is a pretty name. It would be suitable for Mary?'

'Oh yes, very suitable.' No one more suited to the part than their tense, neurotic prima ballerina. 'Then there's Tiny Tim, who'd have to be danced by one of the girls dressed up as a boy–'

'Audrey?' suggested Madame, caught up in the idea.

'Yes and you see,' David said, knowing the streak of sentimentality that ran through Gadina's iron framework, 'he's a little lame boy who gets cured, so we could have this lovely dance where he gets up and walks and then–'

'And then he hears a lively tune and he dances! Oh yes, that could be very touching.'

They decided on eight dances. David was relieved of the responsibility of reading the books by learning that his woodwind player, Arlen Jones, was a Dickens devotee who could tell him all he wanted to know. He told him an unwelcome piece of news – that *Sketches of Boz* didn't refer to any of the novels. Undaunted, David stuck to the title for the ballet.

To his delight, Gadina decided, quite unprompted, that the idea of Little Dorrit flitting lightly through the Marshalsea Prison summoned up the figure of Lina Takarova. To David's way of thinking it was only fair that a ballet, so quickly devised and so easily put together, should contain some kind of reward for its inventor.

If any of the major companies had mounted such a work in peace-time, the highminded and serious critics would have torn it to shreds. But in wartime, its tinkling music and familiar characters gave delight the moment it was put on. Even Gadina's choreography, which was very run-of-the-mill, seemed to suit the easy familiarity of the whole thing. The critic in Doncaster, where it was given its first performance in Christmas week, voted it the 'best Christmas piece in town'!

Linda's debut as Little Dorrit was the most thrilling experience of her life to date. She felt she had helped to shape the role while it was being created by Gadina. By little things, by the way she reacted to unsuitable steps and phrased those that seemed right, she made the solo into a gentle, tender little cameo. She would have liked something with more gaiety, but Arlen assured her Little Dorrit was sweet and loving, not bright and cheerful. So with every turn of her head and flutter of her hands she tried to convey a quiet, devoted daughter of the kind Charles Dickens liked to imagine.

The best actual choreography was in the two parts for the 'stars', Carl's solo and Mary's duet with Rodric, whose young and rather hesitant manner was exactly suited to the part of Pip. Yet the critics actually mentioned the 'charming dance by Miss Takarova as Little Dorrit' – a paragraph which Linda promptly cut out and folded into the back of her diary. Her first review as a professional dancer!

The following week they were in Hull. The weather for the first week in the New Year was atrocious – bitterly cold and with snow flurries blowing in on the exposed North Sea coast. The town seemed wrapped in barbed wire. Air raid warnings were more frequent here than in any other town they had so far visited and, what was more, it more often meant actual aircraft overhead. German bombers, on their way home from Midland raids, often unloaded the left-overs on Hull and other east coast ports.

Linda was sharing with Lucy Daniels, a girl with whom she had little in common. Yet one night the cold was so intense that

Lucy actually crept into the same bed with Linda, for mere animal warmth by which to get to sleep.

The company longed for the week to be over so they could move on. They were due next in Goole, a small shipping port which Betty Balcombe knew. 'It'll be as cold there as Hull,' she predicted. At which everyone gave a moan of disbelief.

The town's population had been much swollen by an influx of naval trainees and engineering personnel. Audiences were good; despite the cold and the blackout, the Town Hall was full for every performance. It was as she came off-stage at the halfway interval that Linda received a call to the doorkeeper's telephone.

'For me?' she queried, at once alarmed that it meant something had gone wrong at home in Hedfield.

'Yes, miss, they rang before, I said you'd be free in half an hour if they rang back.'

A voice she didn't at first recognise greeted her on the phone. 'That you, lass?' it said. 'This is Mrs Hopgood of Cleaver Road in Hull. Listen, dear, I had a copper here asking for you this morning.'

Linda went cold.

'You there, dear? They'd sent him from t'theatre. He said he had a summons for you.'

'He ... asked for me by name?'

'Oh yes, Linda Thackerley alias Lina Takarova. I told him, I said, "What d'you mean, alias, it's her stage name, is that." But all he said was, where had you gone.'

'Did you tell him?'

'Nay, lass, but he'd find out from t'theatre, wouldn't he? They'll be sending on mail and suchlike. Listen, dear, I don't know what it's about, but he did say as they'd been on your track for months. So happen you'd better get out of there while you've the chance.'

'Thank you, Mrs Hopgood. It's very kind of you to take the trouble–'

'No trouble, dear. I know what it is to have problems. Best of luck.'

What ought she to do now? Pack up and run, as Mrs Hopgood suggested? But there was no sense in that. Where would she run to? And the company – she couldn't just walk out on them.

The second half of the programme was *The Sleepwalker*. Linda danced with a fierce concentration on what she was doing, urged on by the feeling that this might be the very last time. For subconsciously she was already coming to a decision about what to do.

After the final curtain she followed Gadina into the wings. The old prima ballerina was lighting one of the brown cigarettes she allowed herself in moments of relaxation. 'May I speak to you a moment,

Madame?' Linda asked.

'Now? If it is about new shoes, I cannot help. No more are being available. Next month, perhaps, we get a supply.'

'No, Madame, it's not about shoes. I have to tell you that I'm in trouble with the police.'

'The police?' echoed Madame, in a voice that turned into a squeak of alarm.

'The landlady at our last digs in Hull has just rung to let me know – they've been there asking for me.'

'But for what? What have you done?' Gadina took Linda by the wrist. 'It is a man? You have a lover, you have had a quarrel?'

'No, Madame, nothing like that. Can we go somewhere, so I can explain.'

Frowning, Gadina drew her Spanish shawl around her shoulders and led the way to the green room. As they went, David caught sight of them. One glance at Linda's face was enough to warn him there was trouble. He followed them, closing the door behind them. Gadina looked at him in surprise. 'You are concerned in this trouble?' she demanded. Her eyes in the wrinkled face looked from one to the other. So it was a crime of passion, as she had suspected. But between the cool David and the quiet Linda?

'I left London and my job there without permission,' Linda began. 'I joined the company under false pretences.'

'False pretences? I am not understanding this. What have you pretended?'

'That I was free to come. I broke government regulations. I worked in a government department.'

'Oh, God,' gasped Gadina, crossing herself, 'it is political!'

'No, Madame, it's nothing serious, really,' David put in. 'Linda should have had permission before she left her office.' He tried to explain in simple words, but he could see Gadina had retreated behind a fog of dread and old remembered horrors. She came of a generation in Russia that had suffered from the Cheka, the secret police. To her, anything to do with police was alarming, as witness the speed with which she had absented herself when a uniformed constable presented himself at the theatre in Bury. Now all she could gather was that Linda had held some government position – she was unable to imagine anything as lowly as a ledger clerk.

'All we have to do,' David was urging, 'is say she isn't here if they ask. They pass on reports to one another, from one town to the next – they can't really be bothered to keep track, I'm sure of that. So if she stays out of sight–'

'You are telling that we should lie to the police?'

'Not lie, exactly – just not tell them the truth.'

'This is terrible,' moaned Madame. 'Who are you, child, to put us in this terrible position, that we are hiding you from the political service?'

'Madame Gadina, it's not like that,' David said. 'It's a routine inquiry – her office have reported that she left without permission and–'

'We will not speak of it any more! Tell me nothing! All my life I have stayed out of politics–'

'But this isn't politics, Madame–'

'Silence, child! Why did you do this to me? I who have taught you everything and given you solo roles to dance!'

'I'm sorry,' Linda said, shaken at the terror in the old lady's voice. 'I never saw it in quite that way–'

'Go away! Go home and stay indoors! I shall think of this and tomorrow I will tell you how I have decided to deal with it. But now, go away – I don't wish to be speaking to you any more.'

Linda went to the dressing room to take off her make-up and change. The other girls had almost finished. They were all fairly quiet, tired after a hard day and not elated at the prospect of turning out into the dark, cold night of the Humberside. David was waiting for her by the stage door.

'The old girl's got the wind up good and proper,' he remarked as they made their way, heads down against the wind, towards the residential side of the town.

'It surprised me. I always thought she could stand up to anything.'

'Not this, it appears. She's scared of the cops.'

'It's understandable, I suppose.'

'Well, let's hope she gets a bit of dutch courage by tomorrow.'

Linda slept deeply from exhaustion. The cold seemed to use up any surplus energy left over from the already exhausting routine of class, rehearsal and performance. Next morning she was scarcely prepared to deal with the problem left over from last night. She regretted now that she had confessed to Madame: it would have been better to rely on the grapevine between theatrical land-ladies, and the discretion of stage door keepers. No one is so impenetrable as a stage door man when he wants to be.

Yet a sense of justice had forced her to speak. By and by, it seemed, there would be a confrontation. Better to have Madame prepared for it.

When she reached the theatre Gadina was already there. Class was assembling. Gadina didn't deign to notice her. She changed into practice clothes, took her place at the barre. The rest of the class assembled. David arrived and took his seat at the piano.

'We will begin with our *pliés*. Right hands on the barre, left hands in first position. *Pliés* in first and second, hands come out, *à la seconde*. *Relevé*, feet to fifth, *plié*, hands follow. Repeat with the same hands and feet, sixteen counts. *And–*'

The stage doorkeeper appeared in the wings. 'Madame Gadina!'

Madame turned. Instead of telling him to be off, she looked at him with frightened expectation.

'There's a policeman here, asking to speak to you.'

There was a startled pause. The members of the company looked at one another in surprise. They waited for Madame to blaze in anger at the man.

Instead she said, 'Please to tell him I am very busy. This is morning class, will take an hour-and-a-half. Tell him, if he will be kind enough, to come back at lunchtime.'

'Yes, Madame.'

'And now we do our exercise. Please, David?'

David sighed and hunched his shoulders in a shrug. Then he began to play the slow, definite beat for the class. When the first exercise was over, Madame beckoned to Linda. 'The rest of you, carry on. You should be doing *battements tendus en croix* and then *dégagés* – four-four time.'

The old lady took Linda into the wings. 'So here is the policeman who was supposed not to be on the track, eh? They are not so stupid, policemen! He has come for you, of course.'

'I expect so, Madame.'

'What do you intend to do?'

'I ... I thought perhaps you'd see him and tell him—'

'Tell him what? That you are not here? This would be nonsense! He has only to ask any other member of the company and they will be pointing out.'

'I suppose so, Madame.'

Gadina clasped and unclasped her slender, muscular hands. 'Linda, please to go back to your office! I see now, you are important in the government and if you continue to trying escape, they will come for us all in a Black Mary!'

'Oh, no, Madame,' Linda objected, startled almost into laughter.

'But yes! You speak so careless – but I know, I! I have seen the police when they set out to track down a political suspect! You will have us all in jail, and in wartime who will come to the aid of a foreigner like me, who already am questioned if I am pro-British when the war is starting. Go back, Linda – and they may leave the rest of us in peace!'

In the face of the blind panic she could see

dammed up behind the old ballerina's frightened eyes, Linda had no choice. 'Very well, Madame,' she said. 'I'll go home now and pack.'

'And go straight to the train, do not wait for the police to fetch you. I tell you, child, it is better to go of your own free will than to be dragged back a prisoner.'

'Yes, Madame.' The habit of obedience, now so deeply ingrained after months with the company, brought the words of submission to her lips. Besides, what else could she do? Gadina no longer wanted her, regarded her as a Jonah, a danger.

She collected her clothes from the dressing room, pulled her coat over her practice tunic and changed shoes. Then she hurried out of the theatre. A wet sleet was falling. She was lucky enough to catch a bus for the short journey to her digs.

The landlady had a timetable. There was a through train at noon, otherwise she would have to change at Doncaster. She threw her belongings into the suitcase, watched from the door by Mrs Summerson. 'Had a row, have you, dearie? I can see by your face you've had a row. She's a right old hag, I hear. Will you be coming back? I'll keep your bed for you...'

'No, I don't think so, thanks, Mrs Summerson.'

She dragged the suitcase downstairs. At the

door she gave the obligatory hug and kiss to the landlady. 'Half a mo', dear, you're forgetting your ration book.' It was produced from a capacious handbag on the hallstand. 'Oh, I am sorry you're going! A nice quiet girl – you're the kind of lodger I like. Well, bye-bye, dear, God bless.'

She was early for the train, but that was just as well because she would probably have to fight her way on board. She bought a cup of railway tea to while away the time and warm herself, for the cold on the platform seemed to enter her very bones.

Noon came, no train. An announcement was made over the Tannoy– 'The twelve-oh-eight to King's Cross has been delayed. Passengers should expect a wait of at least half an hour.' No explanations, of course, but it could be anything from a bomb on the line to a wait for a VIP. Linda finished her tea and went out to see how many other passengers were waiting.

The first person she saw, with a sudden rush of gladness, was David Warburton. 'Oh, thank heavens, I thought you'd have gone by now–' he said.

'No, the train's late. What are you doing here, David?' she demanded.

'I've come to see you off, what else?'

'No, I meant, how did you get away? Who's playing for rehearsal?'

'Freda's doing that. They're taking *Sketches*

by Boz, it's all easy stuff. Listen, Lin, what's happening?'

'Madame asked me to leave. She's scared about the police.'

'Oh, lord! What are you going to do?'

'I don't really know. Go to London, report to the Ministry of Supply, wait and see what happens.'

'Who's your boss there? Is he a decent chap?'

'I've no idea, David. I've never seen him.' She searched her memory. 'I think his name's Sandford – Leonard Sandford.'

'And where are you going to stay?'

'Dunno. I'll try that hostel first – they may have room. If not, it'll be a YWCA.'

'God, it sounds terrible. Well, look – don't lose touch, Lin. Send me your address.'

'Yes, all right,' she agreed, in a dispirited tone. She was going to miss David.

The train could be heard approaching. The crowd on the platform surged forward. David took her case. 'I'll get you a seat,' he said.

Weeks of travelling with the Gadina Company had given him a certain amount of experience of the in-fighting needed to get on board first and find a place. His face appeared at the grimy window, beckoning. She struggled aboard. He had put her suitcase on a seat between a stout lady with a bright piece of knitting and a mother with two toddlers. 'Here we are.' He picked up the suitcase, pushed her into her place, and wedged the case on top of the other luggage in the sagging net rack. He bent to kiss her briefly on the cheek. 'Don't look so down,' he murmured. 'They can't eat you.' He stroked her cheek.

'Want to bet?' Unexpectedly, she felt herself on the verge of tears.

'This Sandford bloke might be kind-hearted–'

'It's my problem, David,' she said, swallowing hard. 'You're needed at the theatre.'

'I suppose so.' He sighed and edged his way out of the compartment to the crowded corridor. 'Bye for now, Lin. Don't forget – let me know where you are.'

'Goodbye, David. Thanks for ... coming, and everything.'

Already he was being heaved out of sight by the struggle of would-be passengers making their way up the train in search of a seat. When the train began to steam out of the station she had a glimpse of him on the platform, then he was gone.

The journey took four hours. At King's Cross she found a phone box and dialled the Holborn office where she used to work. She asked for Establishment Branch.

'This is Linda Thackerley speaking.'

'Who?'

'Linda Thackerley. I'm reporting back –

I've been gone three months.'

'Oh, *that* girl. One moment please.' After a slight pause an authoritative voice took over. 'Miss Thackerley? You've cost us a lot of time and wasted energy. Where are you speaking from?'

'King's Cross – my train just got in. What do you want me to do?'

'You must report here for consideration of your case, but it's too late today. Hold on one moment.' Mr Pitt set down the receiver, dialled a number on the internal phone, and was put through to the office of the department's Controller. The call was taken by the Controller's personal assistant.

'Miss Johnson? I wonder if Mr Sandford has a free space in his diary tomorrow?'

'Tomorrow?' Miss Johnson turned the page of her official book. 'The morning is relatively clear. Is it something important?'

'Our runaway, Miss Thackerley, has come back. I'll send the papers up to you for tomorrow.'

'Shall we say half-past ten? We can spare fifteen minutes at that time.'

'Half-past ten. Thank you, Miss Johnson.' He picked up the outside phone. Linda had heard his side of the exchange. 'Report at the outer door at ten-twenty tomorrow, Miss Thackerley.'

'I don't have my pass any more, I'm afraid.'

'Don't worry,' Mr Pitt said ominously, 'the doorman will be expecting you.'

'Er ... excuse me, before you go ... what's likely to happen?'

'There'll be a court case. The fine ranges from twenty pounds for a brief absence to a hundred pounds for flagrant violation.'

'A hundred pounds?' Linda gasped. 'I haven't got a hundred pounds!'

'Should have thought of that before you went, shouldn't you?' said Mr Pitt, and hung up on her.

Next she rang the hostel in Fulham. The manageress told her her room had been taken by another Civil Servant. 'My dear, the hoo-ha after you went! I had investigation officers –'

'Listen, Miss Lingholm, do you know where I could get a room for the night?'

'You'd better try the YWCA down the road at Euston, my dear.'

She was thankful to be greeted with acceptance at the hostel. The place was gloomy the lighting was low, for economy, the blackout in the downstairs rooms permanent. Her cubicle was tiny but she was used to hard living by now. At least there was a good supply of hot water so that she could have a long, relaxing bath. The cafeteria provided a substantial meal, mostly root vegetables and gravy but filling enough to make her feel sleepy. But before she sought an early bed she had to ring her mother and tell her what had happened.

'Oh, I'm so glad, Linda!' cried Mrs Thackerley at her news. 'Don't worry about the fine, we'll find the money somehow. But it's such a relief to have you back where you belong instead of racketing round the country with a lot of theatricals.'

Next day, Linda dressed carefully in a navy skirt and jumper and her best coat and her fully-fashioned Lisle stockings. The weather in London was grey and very cold but dry. She decided against tying her hair up in the ubiquitous headscarf but instead wound it up at the back in a severe, classical knot. She ate a good meal in the cafeteria: The condemned man ate a hearty breakfast, she quoted to herself as she tucked into four slices of toast.

She felt tense and restless. She had done no class yesterday nor today: her body felt unstretched, unused. She was scared, too. To try to relax herself she decided to walk to the grim old Victorian building in Holborn, formerly a publisher's office before it was taken over by the Ministry.

The doorman directed her to a first floor office. There she found a young woman of about thirty, who told her to sit down on a leather-seated chair against the wall. Presently a buzzer summoned the young woman. She went in with a notebook, then came out in about ten minutes to say that the Controller would now see Miss Thackerley.

Leonard Sandford had had a phone call about Miss Thackerley the previous evening as he sat with his wife in his dining room in Hampstead savouring a precious glass of his vintage port. It was from a chap at his club, asking as a favour for an old friend, name of Warburton, to treat with leniency the young runaway from his department. An affair of the heart, he assumed.

The Controller was exasperated. He had been interrupted in the savouring of that first magical mouthful of the 1927 Cockburn. 'I believe the papers came to my office this afternoon,' he said. 'I'll take a look in the morning.'

The papers now lay before him on his blotter. He had opened the folder and taken a glance. This chit had been gone three months, evading every attempt to find her. He looked up as Miss Johnson showed her in.

He saw a slight girl of about average height, in a plain tweed coat worn open over a dark skirt and jumper. She was fair and pale and rather thin. She didn't look as if she'd been off on an enjoyable escapade with her lover. In fact she looked quite unwell. Oh, thought the Controller, so that's why she's come back. She's having a baby.

'Well now, young lady,' he said, his

140

annoyance with her evaporating, 'you've led us a fine chase, haven't you?'

'I'm sorry, sir.'

His eye was travelling over the sheet of notes in front of him. Bury? Blackburn? Rochdale? They hardly sounded ideal background for a romantic interlude. 'You realise that we are considering your case with a view to prosecution.'

'Yes, sir, but I'd like to point out that I came back of my own free will.'

'So I gather, and what interests me is – why?' Now we'll get it, he thought. He's left her and she's pregnant and there'll be floods of tears.

'Well,' began Linda, 'Madame was so panicky about the policeman–'

'Madame?' Good lord, had she spent three months in a brothel?

'Madame Gadina. She's Russian, you see, and had to make a run for it just after the Revolution, and had the Cheka – or was it the Ogpu – after her–'

'The Ogpu?' said Mr Sandford.

'It gave her a basic fear of police and of course she couldn't see that ours are quite different – but in any case, they were getting closer–'

'Who? The Ogpu?'

'No,' Linda said, looking at him in surprise. 'The local bobbies. They kept sending a man to the theatre–'

'What theatre?'

'Whichever one I was dancing in.'

'You've been dancing in a theatre?'

'Well, yes, sir ... I thought you knew that. With the Gadina Ballet Company.'

The Controller picked up the sheets of paper in the folder and began to read rapidly but with concentration. He looked up. 'Let me get this right. You left the Civil Service without permission to go with a ballet company?'

'Yes, Mr Sandford.'

'And it's genuine? I mean ... you really can dance?'

Linda coloured slightly. 'Of course.' She hesitated then opened her handbag. From the back of her diary she took the cutting about her debut in *Sketches by Boz*. 'Look.'

He took it, baffled, and read it. 'In the part of Little Dorrit, Miss Tarakova gave a delightful performance with steps set to a charming arrangement of the melody, "The Last Rose of Summer". This solo, danced between pools of light on an empty stage, was most notable for the lightness and delicacy of movement. Miss Tarakova will go far.'

'Tarakova?' said Mr Sandford. 'That's you?'

'Takarova,' she corrected automatically. 'They got my name wrong.' She looked down at her shoes on the Civil Service imitation-turkey carpet.

Then she heard a strange sound and raised her head.

Mr Sandford, the Controller of Ministry of Supply Branch 2f (Factory and Catering Supplies), was laughing.

CHAPTER FIVE

Mrs Sandford was dying to hear the story of the romantic runaways when the Controller got home that evening. She had been told about last night's phone call.

'Oh, it's not like that at all,' he reported as she handed him his gin-and-tonic when he came in. With a good deal of amusement he reported the interview.

'So what are you going to do to her?' Peggy Sandford inquired. 'You surely aren't going to take her to court?'

'Well, I ought to. But honestly I think she's been punished enough. Three months out in the Black Country working from dawn till midnight on short rations – what she needs is a couple of good steaks inside her, not a prosecution. You should have seen her, Peggy – two pennorth of skin and bone.'

'Poor little mite,' said Mrs Sandford sentimentally. 'Why don't we invite her here for a meal?'

'What!'

'Invite her. We can't offer her steak, but we could get some good fish – turbot, perhaps. And–'

'Peggy!'

'Leonard,' said Mrs Sandford, fixing him with a disapproving eye, 'I hope you're not turning into a stuffy old Civil Servant?'

'I hope not, my dear. I'll see what I can do for her.'

Linda was due to return to his office late the next afternoon when, after consultation with his advisers, he would give her his decision. In fact he consulted no one. The whole thing tickled his fancy enormously. He asked her to sit down when she was shown in, told her that after much cogitation he'd decided her three months on a CEMA tour could be regarded as war work, and that therefore he would not pursue the case in court.

She sat looking at him, accepting everything he said. She was really a very appealing little thing. 'Look here,' he said, 'my wife says you should be given a good meal. How about coming out for something to eat – it would give you a chance to tell me all about your tour.'

Her eyes widened. 'What, now?'

'Why not? It's six o'clock, the toil of the long day is o'er... Where would you like to go?'

Linda was taken aback. By his well-barbered and well-tailored appearance he wasn't the kind of man who would know the whereabouts of the nearest Lyons Corner House. 'It's very kind of you,' she faltered. 'I leave the choice to you.'

'Righto. I'll just make a couple of phone calls. You go down and wait for me in the hall.'

'Yes, sir.'

The first call was to his wife, to say that he was taking her advice and giving the dancing child a good meal. 'Don't keep anything for me, I'll have eaten.'

'Oh, Leonard, take care,' teased Peggy. 'This isn't the proper behaviour from a Controller to a clerical officer.'

He knew of a quiet little place in the Strand, to which he took her by taxi. He could see she was nervous and a little over-awed, yet her innate grace saved her from seeming awkward. From the limited menu imposed by the five shilling limit she chose cream of chicken soup with croutons, braised steak with as many vegetables as she was allowed, and a large helping of steamed pudding. When she saw him watching her with amusement, she coloured a little and apologised.

'It's because there never seemed to be enough to eat while I was on tour,' she explained. 'Dancing burns up an awful lot of energy yet we never seemed to get food that would replace it – sugar's on ration and glucose is unobtainable except on pre-scription. You should have seen us scouring the shops for honey...'

'It's all right, I'm glad to see you enjoying it.' He himself had eaten sparingly, although he had drunk most of the bottle of expensive Burgundy. 'Now that we've sorted out your court case, what else do you need besides a good meal?'

She considered. 'I need to take a good ballet class,' she said. 'I had a lesson this morning with Leryeva in Hammersmith but my mind wasn't on it, of course. I was too worried about maybe hearing a magistrate say I was fined a hundred pounds.'

'You mean you're still going on with your dancing?'

'Oh, yes, Mr Sandford. I couldn't give it up now. Not now I know I can...' She let the words die away. How could she explain to him, a non-dancer, the delight and exhilaration of taking an audience with her through the phases of a long sequence, showing them the meaning of the movements and the beauty of the classical style? How could she describe the sense of wonder as her own body obeyed the inner commands – turning, soaring, drifting, bending, seemingly without effort to the beholder but with so much discipline from her own will?

'But my dear girl,' objected Sandford, putting his fingers over hers as they rested on the table by her wine glass, 'you do realise you're still restricted by Regulation 58(a) of the Defence Act? You can't leave

147

your job—'

'But I can apply to be released, can't I? I know it might take a while, but if the authorities take into consideration the fact that I—'

'Skipped from your job? Eluded the police for over three months?' He heard her sigh and tightened the handclasp. 'I might be able to put in a good word for you, of course.'

She turned her head and looked at him. He got the full gaze of the clear grey eyes – innocent, anxious eyes. She wriggled her hand free from under his.

'It's very good of you, sir,' she said in formal tones, 'but you've done enough for me already. I'm ever so grateful. And please tell your wife it was a lovely idea to give me this lovely dinner – it's been a real treat for me.'

Well, he thought, she's not so innocent as her gaze seems to say. Nor as much of a working girl as she's pretending, with her 'ever-so-gratefuls' and so forth. But he had deserved the rebuke, he knew that. Must be the wine, he told himself.

'Glad you've enjoyed it,' he said.

His wife Peggy inquired how the evening had gone and required full details of all Linda had told him about the Gadina Company. She was a thwarted romantic, secretly in love with the Robert Taylor of

Camille. To her husband's astonishment, she sent Linda an invitation to a belated New Year party for the last Saturday in January.

'My dear, she won't come,' he assured her. 'She knows it's unsuitable.'

But Linda thought it over and accepted. Intuition told her that Mrs Sandford was interested in her: perhaps Mrs Sandford would influence her husband to recommend Linda's release from the Ministry.

She had telephoned her mother with the good news that there would be no prosecution. 'Thank goodness for that! Your father and I would have come to court and spoken for you, of course, but it would have been such a disgrace, Lin – none of our family have ever been in any trouble of that kind before.'

'I'm sorry, Mummy, I know you were upset about it.' She couldn't bring herself to say, 'I shouldn't have done it.' She knew now that she would have done the same again if the chance presented itself but, for the moment, she would wait to see if she could get official permission. This, too, she kept to herself. Instead she said, 'Mr Sandford has been very kind and considerate. I'm going to a party at his house on Saturday.'

'Linda!'

'Oh, it's all right, Mummy, the invitation came with a note from his wife. She wants to meet me–'

'I really can't see why! You've been extremely wicked and thoughtless – she ought not to be encouraging you!'

'Yes, Mummy.' One day, she thought to herself, I won't have to keep saying yes to people in positions of supposed superiority. I'll be a person in my own right. I am a person already, when I'm dancing. One day … one day…

'Well, I've some marvellous news for you,' her mother went on, 'although you really don't deserve it. What do you think? Alan's been desperately trying to get in touch with you the last few days, nearly climbing the walls because he couldn't find you. He rang me in the end and if you give me your phone number at the hostel, dear, I'll give it to him. He's being transferred from his training camp to "somewhere in the south" and from what he was saying, it's not far from London. He'll be able to see you perhaps two or three times a week, Linda!'

'But that's wonderful, Mum!' Then she broke off, wondering what it meant. Alan had volunteered for commando training; each time he was moved to some new camp she feared it was the final training before he went off to do some frightening deed. During the first few weeks of her tour with the Gadina Company, news began to be released to the newspapers of the commando raid on Dieppe and even in the midst of her own exhausting regime she'd thought of Alan, learning the special skills to suit him for just that kind of attack.

'He'll be in touch, dear, so I'll feel more at ease about you. With Alan keeping an eye on you, you can't go far wrong.'

'No, Mummy.' She listened demurely to a short lecture on getting plenty of sleep and taking shelter the moment the sirens sounded, exchanged messages with the rest of her family, and rang off. To tell the truth, they all seemed distant from her now, even her mother, who had seemed so important in her life. She had outgrown them somehow.

Alan rang that same evening just as she was about to win a place in the bath rota. He was delighted to be in touch at last but went on to administer a scolding for her 'disappearance'. 'When they told me at the theatre you'd left the company, I took it for granted you'd gone home. But your mother had no idea where you–'

'It was all quite sudden. I rang her as soon as I got fixed up with a place to stay.'

'But meanwhile I'd no idea where you were–'

'I did write, Alan. The letter just hasn't reached you yet.'

'Well,' he said in a tolerant tone, 'you always were a bit impulsive. Now I've got you pinned down again, I'll take some of the time off that's due to me and we'll do a show or something. How about the day after tomorrow? We can go to a matinée.'

'I can't, Alan. I'm back at the office in a bit of disgrace. I have to keep my nose to the grindstone, and I certainly won't get an afternoon off.'

He was only momentarily dashed. 'Oh, well, that's understandable, I s'pose. You have rather asked for it, Lin, swanning off like that. Well, Saturday afternoon, then.'

'I can't, Alan. I've accepted an invitation to a party.'

'What?' She could tell this didn't fit in with his idea of having to suffer for her misdeeds. 'Whose party, if I may ask?'

'My boss – and his wife,' she added quickly.

'Your boss?' He couldn't argue with that. 'We-ell, I s'pose you'll have to go, if you've said you would. Sunday, then.'

She found she didn't dare say she wanted to go to class on Sunday. She knew he would disapprove. He sided with her mother: she ought to concentrate on her Civil Service career and stop messing about with ballet.

They arranged at last that he would call for her at the hostel about noon, they would have 'a nice lunch' somewhere and then go to the Albert Hall for the *Messiah*. Alan, a former choirboy, liked a good oratorio. She agreed to it all, mentally vowing to be up and out to a class with Leryeva by nine in

152

the morning. The old ballerina was fond of urging her students to come to her early, for Sunday mornings she had few in her first class.

Linda got out her best dress before going to bed that evening so as to get it to the cleaner first thing on her way to work. It was an all-purpose best dress, maroon marocain, very creasable but attractive in its simplicity and complimentary to her fair hair and skin. It wasn't very fashionable, but then, who was these days? Only the very rich could afford to have clothes made or altered to fit changes in outline but in any case, fashion was rather static for the present. Perhaps she ought to shorten the skirt? But no, she wouldn't have time. It must serve as it was.

Madame Gadina had given her dancers regulations for party-going, for the three or four occasions when rich manufacturers had offered hospitality to them. 'It is fitting to accept compliments but you are forbidden to take up private invitations. No one is to drink spirits – they redden the skin, and though helpful in moments of crisis they do not improve the physique in general. You may drink two glasses of wine – three if it is white, but prefer to take red wine, which has more iron in it and is beneficial to the blood. Eat all you are offered, for energy.'

Linda wasn't offered any wine at Leonard Sandford's party. The main drink was a fruit punch concocted by the hostess from the snippets in the bottom of various bottles plus some cooking sherry and a couple of flagons of real cider from a friend in Evesham. Half a glass of this was enough to convince Linda that she didn't like it. But with the remaining half a glass she looked as if she was enjoying it with the food, which, being mainly unrationed fish in some form, was plentiful and good.

Mrs Sandford had decided to take a special interest in Linda. She shepherded her around among the guests. When newcomers came, she sought her out and introduced her. Thus Linda found herself being introduced to Mr Bordi, a man of perhaps forty and with enough flash of dark eyes and black hair to announce his Italian origins.

'Linda is a dancer, Niccolo,' said Peggy Sandford.

Mr Bordi bowed and murmured something about being delighted. But truth to tell, his expression said he had met thousands of dancers.

'Mr Bordi is in the theatre too, Linda. I'm sure you two will have a lot in common so I'll leave you in his care.'

Bordi, trapped with a glass of the sticky fruit cup in one hand and sliver of toast with salmon mayonnaise in the other, stifled a sigh. 'You are in work at present, Linda?' he inquired politely.

'Yes, I'm in Mr Sandford's department in Holborn.'

Ah, so she was not only a dancer but an out-of-work dancer. His interest in her was even less. Still, he could see no way of pretending he was needed elsewhere for the moment, so he went on: 'You are "resting". Anything in prospect?'

'Oh, well, it depends on getting my official release. When I came back from Goole and gave myself up, the first thing I did after getting back to the office was to apply for release so I could rejoin the company.'

This incomprehensible statement had the merit of at least not being a request for a job. He raised thick dark brows. 'Company? What company? I thought you said you were in an office–'

'Yes, but only because of the wartime regulations. I went on tour with the Gadina Company without permission.' She sketched in the facts for him, aware that now he was paying attention whereas at first he had thought her a bore.

'*Santo cielo!* I too was caught by the wartime regulations for a while, but I was unable to run away! You've shown remarkable initiative, Signorina Linda!'

'I was silly, really. I see now I should have made a plan a long time before I was directed into the Civil Service. In your case...' she was feeling her way ... 'I suppose it was something to do with being interned?'

'I was lucky. I had already offered my services to the government and my long-standing opposition to Benito Mussolini was well-known.' He smiled down at her. 'You have never heard of me.'

She went faintly pink. 'I'm afraid not.'

'Well, since you have spent your life struggling with the difficulties of learning ballet, why should you? I am in the theatre, as Peggy told you. But I am one who puts on shows you would think very frivolous – musical comedy.'

'Several of the girls with Gadina had danced in musical comedy,' she offered, without adding that in general it was considered a handicap by Madame.

'Are you interested in dancing with such a company?' he asked. 'That no doubt is why Peggy put us together – so that I could offer you a job.'

'And would you?'

'Why not?'

'But you haven't seen me dance.'

'If you can dance well enough for Gadina, I imagine you dance well enough for *Gypsy Princess*. Or, quite soon, I put on *Die Fledermaus* – there is dancing in that but less than *Gypsy*. Send in your name to my manager.'

'I've still to get my release from my job–'

'Oh, there will be little problem in that, I

am certain. If Peggy Sandford is working for you behind the scenes, her husband will be prompted to see that the pieces of paper go quickly from one office to the other – *non è vero?*'

Linda too had gained the impression that Peggy knew how to handle her husband. She smiled. 'Well, I hope so,' she said, yet avoided saying she would apply to his manager. If she got her freedom, she wanted to rejoin Gadina.

Next morning, at Leryeva's studio, she asked to be allowed the use of the phone. She rang the theatre in Ripon, which town the company would have reached last night if they kept to schedule.

It was ten-thirty. Class should be over. Her guess was correct for Gadina came to the phone almost at once. 'Yes, who is here?' she asked in the loud voice she always used when speaking into a receiver.

'Madame, this is Linda Thackerley–'

'Ah, yes, where are you speaking from? You are ringing from a prison – I thought that would not be allowed?'

'I'm not in prison, Madame, and not going to be. Everything is all right about the police – the case has been dropped. Madame, it seems my boss is going to help me get permission to leave the Ministry so I could rejoin the company–'

'Ah, no,' Gadina interrupted at once. 'No,

157

the risk is too great–'

'Risk? But there'll be no risk, Madame–'

'My dear child, do you take me for an idiot? Once you have a police record, there is always risk–'

'I assure you, Madame Gadina, I've no police record and the authorities have no interest–'

'Besides,' Gadina interrupted, louder than ever in her alarm, 'do you think there is a hole in my ballet line, waiting for you? Naturally I am having to replace you, and there is no vacancy for you, Linda, so this is all a waste of my time, speaking to you when I should be starting rehearsals–'

'Madame, please! I think in about three weeks I could–'

'No, you have caused me enough trouble, girl. Now goodbye, I am busy.' The phone was hung up at the other end.

Linda replaced the receiver and turned to find Leryeva watching her with sympathy. 'You are in Olga's bad books, eh?'

'I'm afraid so.'

'She is always difficult, Olga. I remember when we are learning solos in *Bayadère*, she is complaining that her steps are easier than mine so she does not seem to dance so good, and Kchessinskaya, who is teaching us, said to Olga, "Difficult, difficult, with difficult dancer we give easy steps, with easy dancer we give hard steps." But in the end, she comes to senses. First she is difficult, then she relents.'

'I don't think she will this time,' sighed Linda. 'I gave her a fright – she finds it hard to forgive.'

'*Eh bien*, wait a day or two, then try again. And now, *seladkya*, I'm afraid I must ask you for the two shillings for the phone call.'

Linda went home to the hostel to shower and change into something pretty for Alan. She tried to cheer herself up for him, because it seemed unfair to be depressed when he was going to spend his time and money on her, yet she couldn't help knowing she would rather have had the rest of the day to herself, to get over the disappointment of Gadina's words.

Alan greeted her with a whistle of appreciation when she came down to the hall to greet him. She was wearing her best coat and a little fur hat, a Christmas present from her parents. Her legs were clad in a precious pair of real silk stockings, worn last night and washed just after midnight so as to be ready for today.

Alan looked different. He seemed taller and broader. His uniform, with its special shoulder-flash for the Commandos, seemed to fit better than when last she saw him. The months of training had changed him, just as her time with the ballet had changed her. They rushed into each other's arms but when they kissed, it was awkwardly. They had to get used to each other again. Their meetings now were so infrequent – so different from Hedfield, where they had seen each other every day so that every feature, every characteristic, was dearly familiar.

Somehow he seemed to have more authority. He had always been inclined to order her about, even from schooldays, and always she'd loved that. Her schoolfriends used to say, in admiration: 'He's so masterful!' and she'd thought it only fitting, that the man should have the right of command. But now Alan had an appearance of innate power, something to do with supreme physical fitness. He had been trained to hair-trigger effectiveness in action. It gave him something new – a magnetism for which she had no name.

Though she was too innocent to know it, its name was sexual attraction.

He for his part thought her as wonderful as ever – fragile, slender – too slender, perhaps, worked too hard by this fiendish ballet mistress. All his protective love rose up in him. He put his arm round her shoulders as they set out to walk to the Tube station, and felt her shiver with pleasure at the embrace. For a moment he was startled: usually she took his actions as almost comradely – but he felt a stirring of something new in her. Her love for him was subtly changing. To himself he phrased it very simply: 'She's growing up.'

He stole a little secret glance at her, and found that she was gazing up at him, eyes blazing. His arm tightened around her in reaction. She smiled and came closer, moving against him.

In the station he had to let her go to buy tickets, and was sorry. But as they came on to the platform for the train, she saw the bunk beds for those who took shelter at night for fear of air raids. There was something gaunt and dreary about them in daytime, without their determinedly cheery occupants. She shivered, and drew close to Alan, taking his arm for protection.

'It looks so ... sort of sub-human,' she murmured.

'It's all right, sweetheart,' he reassured, leaning his cheek down to hers. 'It's just that there's a war on.'

Other passengers, seeing them so close, frowned in disapproval. Really, the war...! People never used to make a show of themselves like that in the good old days of peace. Linda and Alan drew apart at their disapproval – but nothing could change the current of tenderness that ran between them, communicated without the need to touch.

They lunched in a Kensington restaurant. 'Joe Fielder recommended this place,' Alan told her. 'He gets around, Joe does.' The restaurant in Kensington High Street, was nothing special. It suddenly struck Linda that Alan was really quite unsophisticated, to be so impressed by the white tablecloths and printed menu. But that was somehow lovable – open and artless. Artless ... was that a word she should think of in conjunction with Alan? She didn't mean it in any critical sense. She loved him for wanting to please her with this special meal in what he took to be a special place.

Over the meal he gave her news from home. He had been back to Hedfield on leave while she was touring so he had little stories about their former schoolfellows, their neighbours, their respective relatives. She listened, enjoying it, but gradually realising that he was closer to them than she. Their affairs still interested him deeply. With remorse she saw that she found them shadowy, unimpressive. Gadina was real. The other dancers in the company were real. David was real. But these people Alan was talking about might almost have been in another world.

'I'll be at this camp for at least another two weeks,' he told her, 'and there's no problem getting a pass for most evenings – of course, we have to take turns and Joe likes to grab all he can – he's got about six girl friends, oh, he *is* a lad!' This led to a long account of the escapades of Joe Fielder, who was a subject of mixed admiration and alarm to Alan. 'As a matter of fact, there's a patrimony suit against him–' He broke off.

'A what?'

'Never mind,' Alan said, embarrassed. 'You don't want to hear about that.' Strictly brought up, he was furious with himself for even beginning to talk about such a thing to Linda. You didn't talk about such things to nice girls.

They walked from the High Street to the Albert Hall. The day was bright but very cold; they could see their breath on the air. They embarked on a foolish competition to see who could make the longest puff of steam, and it caused some amazement when Linda won.

'But ballet training teaches you breath control, Alan. I'm surprised that you're surprised.'

'I suppose that's true. You'll be getting out of condition now, with your ballet days behind you.'

'Behind me? Whatever makes you say that? I'm going to go on taking lessons, Alan. I always have.'

'But it's pretty pointless now, isn't it? I mean, now you've had to admit defeat and come back.'

Her chin jutted over the collar of her tweed coat. 'I didn't admit defeat. Madame

Gadina got scared and ordered me to go. Otherwise I'd still be up north, dancing.'

'Come on, now, Lin... You proved your point. Now it's time to settle down to your proper job–'

'Dancing is my proper job,' she burst out in indignation. 'It's what I do well! Sitting at a desk answering requisitions for fish fryers isn't my real work.'

Her vehemence made him pause to look at her. 'You're not still thinking about making a living in ballet?'

'Why not? Mrs Sandford told me last night that her husband will pilot my request for release through the proper channels. I sent it in the very first day I was back in the Ministry.'

'Lin!' he said in exasperation. 'What's the point of all this?'

It was too big a question to deal with as they walked to the Albert Hall, and in any case the concert-goers were beginning to jostle them as they stood on the pavement staring at each other. Their conversation was lost while Alan produced tickets and they went on the usual trek to find their seats. Settled at last, Linda found she didn't want to start an argument. After all, this was a day's leave for Alan. It was wrong to be at odds with him about anything.

The famous old oratorio could not fail to hold them. They came out discussing the merits of the singers, personal problems were forgotten. They found an ABC tea-room for a snack – tea and toast and jam. The place was quiet, dark-painted, rather steamy.

'Lin,' Alan said in a very serious tone, 'I hope you're not letting this dancing thing become an obsession.'

She made herself keep her attention on the tea she was pouring from the metal pot into thick cups. 'You've always known I was keen on ballet, Alan.'

'But not to the extent that you wanted to go on the stage and do it, darling. Look here, be reasonable – I'd no objections to your having a hobby like that, but I certainly don't want my girl getting involved any further with ... well, oddities.'

'Dancers aren't odd, Alan. They're just like you and me – except that they have a special talent in using their bodies.'

'I don't want to go into a discussion about what they can do or can't do. All I'm saying is, it seems pretty pointless to me to get your release from the Ministry and go back on the stage. I mean, it'd only be for a few months. Everyone says the war will end this year.'

'Really?' she said, offering him the sugar. 'But we haven't even got a second front going yet.'

'That'll come. I see the preparations being

made, Lin. You can take my word for it – the war will be over before the end of the year.'

He was a few years her senior and had spent a year in the army. She felt she couldn't argue against his superior knowledge – so she turned to another angle. 'Even if it is only a few months ... I'd rather spend them dancing than sitting at a desk.'

'But what good does it do? We'll be married as soon as I'm demobbed, and that'll be an end of your career anyhow – it'd make much more sense to stick to the Civil Service, where at least you'd get a marriage gratuity. What'll you get at the end of six months in a measly little company like the Gadina? You told me yourself they hardly had two pennies to rub together–'

'Madame Gadina doesn't want me back,' she blurted out. 'I rang her this morning and she said...'

'Oh, sweetheart.' He could see it had hurt her, and took her hand. She found that his had a hard palm and strong fingers now – different from the lad who had started a short career in the Hedfield Building Society when he left school.

She blinked hard to get rid of the smarting that might be tears, picked up her cup with a free hand, and took a big swallow. The tea was boiling hot. She coughed and spluttered. Concerned at first but then laughing, Alan thumped her on the back. When she'd recovered he sat with his arm about her. She leaned against his strength.

'You always were a funny little thing,' he told her kindly. 'I suppose I'll just have to put up with your funny ideas.'

It didn't occur to her to say, 'Don't patronise me.' In the world where she was brought up, women were expected to be in the background. In her view, Alan was being kind and forbearing to her. She was being wayward and selfish, and it was very wrong of her. Her mother had said to her on the telephone, 'Now don't you go upsetting Alan with your nonsense – he's got a war to fight.' She agreed with this precept: she must not upset Alan, she must stop being silly and instead be thankful to have a wonderful boy wanting to marry her.

After they had said a long and tender goodnight at the porch of the hostel, she went upstairs to sit in thought in her cubicle. What Alan said was true. When they were married, she would have to give up all thought of dancing as a career. The mere notion of trying to run the kind of household he would expect while rushing back and forth to a theatre was absurd: she would have laughed at the thought if it hadn't been somehow so sad.

When she married Alan after the war they would settle down in Hedfield, of course. Because he had a job waiting for him, they would have no problem about income. Because he was with the Building Society, they would get help in buying a little house. Soon they would have a family – they had never discussed children but she knew Alan expected a son.

An idyllic future – once the war was over. Why then did she feel tears trickling down her cheeks in the darkness?

She was summoned out of this self-pitying misery by a call along the corridor. 'Linda Thackerley! Linda Thackerley! Phone call!'

She jumped up and ran out. There was an extension on each landing, so she hurried to the nearest and picked it up. 'You're through,' said the hostel receptionist on the main phone.

'Linda?' said David Warburton. 'Linda, I've been trying to get hold of you all afternoon and evening!'

'I went to hear the *Messiah*.'

'Oh.' A pause. 'Was it good?'

'Yes, lovely. What did you want to talk to me about?'

'About Gadina. Listen, sweetie, don't be too depressed by the way she went on at you. You know what she's like – speaks first, thinks afterwards.'

'But what she said was true,' Linda said, with a crack in her voice. 'She's replaced me, there's no vacancy for me in the company.'

'Oh, that's just a way of talking. No

replacement really equals the replaced dancer. Lorraine Powers is good, nice *retirée*, has quite a sense of character, but she hasn't replaced you. For instance, she's not dancing Little Dorrit. We've shuffled everybody around to fill the various roles. And besides, Ariel Johnson is talking about leaving.'

'Leaving? What on earth for?' Linda cried in genuine astonishment.

'For more money, as a matter of fact. She's been offered something in a summer show in Bournemouth and she wants to leave fairly soon to go and take tap lessons for that.'

'Tap lessons!'

'Gadina, of course, is furious. It'll end by Ariel having to leave before she's nagged to death. If your release from a reserved occupation is really coming through, you could be coming straight back to us.'

'Oh, David! Do you think Madame would really take me back?'

'I'm working on it,' he said with a laugh.

'Why are you so good to me?' she cried in a voice full of gratitude.

'It's because when I write the music for my great ballet, I want you in the starring role.'

'Oh, you are an idiot! But thank you for speaking to Madame. If you can persuade her to let me come back I'll be so – so *happy!*'

'Isn't it funny! She's a tyrant and a heartless sergeant-major, yet you want to come back.'

'The truth is,' Linda said in surprise, 'I've missed her.'

CHAPTER SIX

By the end of February, Linda was back with the Gadina Company. Madame greeted her grudgingly: 'So, I welcome you back, but if you had been honest with me you need never have been sent away.'

Linda said nothing. Privately she thought that if she had been honest with Madame, she would never have been accepted in the first place.

The welcome from the rest of the company was strangely warm and touching. It was like being enfolded by her family. They told her she looked well, which was true, for the month she had spent in London had been easy compared with the harsh regime of touring. She found her friends weary and yet determined. Betty had been promoted to understudy the lead of *The Sleepwalker, Polonaise* had a completely new set of soloists so that Mary could get two or three evenings a week on which she didn't dance every item.

'She's getting more and more tense and tired, and who can blame her,' Betty confided. 'Madame is trying to arrange programmes so Mary can get a week off and go home for some rest, but Mary herself doesn't want that – she feels if she goes she'll be replaced as the star.'

'Madame should put her foot down. I'm surprised she takes so much notice of her.'

'Lovey, if you were trying to mount your first three-act ballet and needed money, you wouldn't antagonise Mary Petersfield.'

'Oh, I see.' Mary's father, reputedly a millionaire, was financing the company in part. But the interesting thing was the new ballet. 'What's it about?'

'Well, we've only just started on it. It's based on an old Russian fairy tale–'

'Oh, help,' groaned Linda.

'But it's not a bad plot, actually. This old king displeases a magician, who is going to kill him, but the king's daughter volunteers to take his place, so the magician takes her and keeps her prisoner. She has to amuse him and dance for him.'

'You surprise me,' said Linda.

'Yeah... Well, one day she manages to dance her way through a maze that's supposed to keep her prisoner and meets a young man–'

'Fancy!'

'You're not taking this seriously! They dance, and the magician finds them together and magics the pair of them so they have to be his servants. But they're saved when a pure flake of snow touches the hero, and he fights Enyesto and carries the princess to safety–'

'Whereupon her father orders a ball and they all dance. My hat! I thought you said it wasn't a bad plot?'

'It comes across better when you dance it. And Carl is really marvellous in the fight scene. A lot of it hasn't been worked up yet – the pure-snow-flake hasn't got any steps and every time we come to it Madame says, "We'll mark it" and goes on to something else. As far as I can gather, snow-flake comes in with a party of dancers and bobs about – there's quite a lot of music for that, and then there seems to be a solo, and then a *pas de deux* with Carl before he's rescued from the enchantment.'

'Who's dancing that?'

'No idea. Mary's the princess, of course, and there are dances for the courtiers among which I've got a solo, and so has Marina, and there's rather a nice trio for Terrence and two girls – all in all, it's not bad, although of course very like any Pepita ballet you've ever seen.'

Linda took part in the first working session with the new ballet while they were in Bradford. Then there was a busy week split between two manufacturing towns, where they danced in factory canteens and town halls without scenery. For this week Mary allowed herself to be persuaded to take a break which meant that everyone moved up in rank: Linda found herself dancing the lead in *The Sleepwalker*, to her own astonishment.

A week of blessed relaxation followed in Ilkley. The small moor town was pleasant, the weather had relented a little as March began. There were actually real hotels where they could stay. Performances in the little theatre were packed out. Mary having returned, looking a little more rested, work began on *The Willing Prisoner* again.

'And now, Linda, you will see why I was so angry with you when you had to leave us,' Gadina remarked to her as they assembled after a coffee break following morning class. 'I always saw you in the part of snow-flake.'

'Me?' Linda gasped.

'*Da, maladoya,* who else? Snow-flake must be very light, yes? Whirl about, not touch the ground – because if she does, she melts – no, she must float about until she lands on the hand of the young man and releases him from the magician's spell. And you are the girl with the lightness, so you are the snow-flake.'

'Oh, God,' said Linda in a sudden panic.

'You do not say thank-you? Gadina gives you a big part, a solo and a *pas de deux,* and you have nothing to say that you are pleased?'

'I am pleased, Madame. I really am. I'm

just … overwhelmed.'

'What is this overwhelmed? Is something wrong with the legs, the feet? No? Then we work. David, please, we begin today on the long passage in Act Two. We will have the lead-in, where first we hear the music of the snow flurry and Carl looks up. Carl, please – centre stage, you walk with dragging feet, shoulders sag, very depressed… Chime-chime of bells, snow flurry overhead – look up – oh, *idyoht,* not jerking the neck, snow is not sudden. You glimpse it, you look up… Better, now, please look opposite-prompt… Snow-flakes … who, now … Audrey and Susanne, please flutter on and then off – the first few flakes, yes? Oh, no!' The pointer hit the floor with a terrible thump. 'Flutter! *Pas de bourrée,* very fast to the beat–'

'But what are the arms doing, Madame?'

'*They are fluttering!* No, no, not up and down – you look like *Swan Lake!* No, in front and then back *en avant, en arrière* – ah, dear God! Not both arms back at the same time, how can you be so stupid?'

So it went on, Madame attempting to convey what she had in her mind in a mixture of ballet-French, English, and angry Russian. Finally the *corps de ballet* were on and 'fluttering' to her satisfaction. 'Now, then, Linda… You dart on – very fast, very light. *Glissade devant* – you are going into *saut de basque* – now wait, what did I

175

want next – ah yes, please mark this with me – forward, arms up to couronne. Arms stay up, turn, go on, go on, how many bars, David? – two bars – *Balloné, ballon*é… Yes, arms still up…'

So it went on, each work-session winnowing out the chaff of unexciting movement until at the end of ten days Gadina had the passage forming the entry of the snow-flakes and Carl's first contact with them. The solo for the leading snow-flake went much faster. By a process of hesitation, suggestion, consideration, Linda managed to modify Gadina's original intention of a sparkling sugar-plum-fairy variation.

'Snow-flakes are fragile things,' she murmured at one point. 'They do sparkle, it's true, but if they touch the ground they get muddied, and if the temperature goes up a degree or so they turn to sloppy sleet…'

'Sleet, yes, this we have had a great amount in this winter,' Gadina agreed. 'Certainly, I see what you mean, poor little snow-flake – and also, she is going to die when she touches Carl – the warmth of his hand will melt her, no? So, perhaps it is correct… Not too much brilliance… So what you must do is glow, Linda. Please, again – David, the last four bars, and less brightly, so that Linda can be more wistful…'

The music was a collection of melodies from the work of the Russian composer

Glinka. To tell the truth, the music was rather shallow and the steps were often quite predictable. Yet to Linda's astonishment her solo began to enthral her. She worked on it in every spare moment, with David obligingly playing the accompaniment.

The new ballet was for Newcastle. 'A great city,' Gadina explained. 'The Athens of the North.'

'No, that's Edinburgh,' David objected.

'Edinburgh? Ah, well, we are not being booked for Edinburgh. Newcastle is important, no?'

'Oh, important enough. They get air raids from the Germans to prove it. I should think the government will be pleased that we're honouring Newcastle with the premiere of our new ballet.'

'Oh, as to *goh*vernment,' said Gadina, rolling it off her tongue scornfully, 'if they are pleased, perhaps they are showing by giving us more money.'

David greatly doubted that. He had had to pull every string he knew of to get the original vote of funds to launch the Gadina Company. All the same he felt that the new ballet deserved its due – imperfect though it was in its naivety and lack of originality, it had some good things in it.

Notably the entry of the snow-flake, her solo, and the strange duet with Carl.

He rang a friend in London, an elderly

musicologist who had taught him orchestration and occasionally wrote pieces for the heavy Sundays.

'What, travel to Newcastle? To see a ballet *set to Glinka?* Are you out of your mind, dear boy?' Potterton cried. 'And in any case, I know nothing about ballet.'

'Then get someone else to come. Perhaps a theatre critic.'

'My dear lad, no one is going to grind all the way up to Newcastle in a slow train just to look at some footling work by a second-rate company.'

'Oh, it's not so second-rate, Stuart. Some of the dancing is very good and though the works we do are a bit derivative, they're good theatre.'

'No, it's out of the question. *The Times* wouldn't commission it.'

'Come on, Stuart – I'll pay your fare and your hotel bill. Surely they'll take a piece if you tell them you're doing it for the fee alone. Sell them on it for the patriotism – small hardworking group touring the factory towns, cheering the populace, fine exponent of the ballet-education of our great Russian allies in charge, chances for young British dancers, hardships only make us keener – and now a new ballet for the people of Newcastle, sorely tried by air attacks–'

'Absolutely no, my boy,' said Potterton.

However, the idea had its attractions. When he put it to the Arts Editor of *The Times,* he was greeted with a moderate interest. 'Sounds like a week-end piece,' his editor said. 'We're always accused of being obsessed with London events... All right, if you like to do it on spec, I'll give it a favourable eye.'

David arranged for tickets for the first night of *The Willing Prisoner.* It was a Friday, the idea being that they would launch it with two successive performances, travel on the Sunday and remedy any defects in rehearsal Sunday afternoon and Monday. They would perform it Monday and Tuesday evening in Sunderland, rest it two days, and put it on again Friday and Saturday. The following week they were doing factory halls and canteens again, circumstances in which it was impossible to put on a long ballet. When they moved south again towards Stockton and Middlesbrough, the new ballet would get further airings.

The theatre reporter for the *Journal and Mail* was astounded when he heard a *Times* man was coming. All at once, from being a boring chore, his visit to the Gadina Ballet became important. As a way of earning a little extra, he alerted the *Yorkshire Post.* So the company found they had quite a row of pressmen for the first night.

'You see? Three-act ballet with lots of variations,' said Madame. 'This is what people are liking. *Sleepwalker* is nice, *Sketches by Boz* makes audience clap, but *real* ballet is three-act with many solos.'

David refrained from telling her that none of the reporters had any idea there were three acts and 'many solos' in *The Willing Prisoner*. His main worry was that they'd yawn their heads off all through Act One, and might slip off after the first interval to file their reviews. He very much wanted them to see Linda's section as the liberating snow-flake. To that end, he arranged for the house manager to ply the reporters with refreshments in the first interval so that they would want to stay on for the second interval. People these days would do almost anything for a glass of watered down scotch and a free snack. Food was becoming an obsession as rations grew ever more strict. Rationing of even bread was being forecast.

To say the company was nervous would have been like saying Romeo was fond of Juliet. All of them, except Carl, were scared stiff. There were too many costume changes, too many different parts to dance under various guises, almost no one had a chance to draw breath. From being a gentlewoman of the court in Act One, Linda had to rush off and change for the snow-flake role. That done, she had to be part of a *pas de quatre* in the ballroom scene at the end, nip off and change, come on as a wedding gift (The Ruby Rose) and generally look festive until curtain.

It was the same for everyone. They all kept saying, 'It's too big a ballet for such a small company,' yet not one of them dreamed of refusing to perform. They threw themselves into it heart and soul, and were rewarded by the applause of the audience for every showy display of technique which Gadina had arranged.

When the moment came for Linda to enter as the snow-flake, she was suddenly quite calm. For a strange moment, as she waited in the wings, a cool glow seemed to enter into her. Everything receded – even the tinkling music from the trio in the pit, which would herald her entrance. She suddenly knew she was going to float through the air, light as gossamer. Her breathing was slow and regular, her body felt weightless.

She saw the twirling skirts of the other girls. She heard her summons. She leapt on stage, felt her foot touch the boards only momentarily before she was up again, up, darting, floating, turning, speed and light personified.

Some sixth sense told her of a stir in the audience, but she paid no heed. It wasn't important that almost everyone in the King's Theatre had sat forward, amazed, at her entrance. She was slowing now, as the music slowed to show the breeze had died. She evaded Carl's grasp, leapt so that she seemed to go through his very fingers. Drifting now, more gentle but if anything even more light, she eluded her partner with ease.

It was a good piece of choreography. Watching it from the wings, Gadina was pleased with it. She had no idea – nor had Linda – how much of it was due to the suggestions and gentle guidance of the dancer. All she knew was that she was seeing good theatre, good ballet: if nothing else of her life survived – and her career had been wrecked by the Revolution – she would be remembered for this passage of perfect dance.

The applause at the end of the Second Act was for Linda – there was no doubt of that. Startled, but happy, Linda was ordered in front of the curtain with Carl for a special bow, then another, then another. Carl was careful to take Mary forward: she deserved approval for a very good performance of a long, showy passage earlier in the act. But the entire company could hear that the applause rose in volume when Linda went out.

When it was all over, when the usual first-night hugs and kisses had been exchanged and the usual first-night party was held over two bottles of sparkling wine, David announced that the *Times* reporter had telephoned his review to London in time for the Saturday editions. 'I think he liked it,' he said. 'But of course, he knows nothing about ballet – music is his thing.'

A few eager spirits rose early next morning to buy copies of the papers straight off the mail train. David rushed into Linda's digs at seven o'clock, waving a copy of *The Times*. 'Linda, Linda! Look at this!' He thrust the folded copy under her nose, dislodging the toast from her breakfast plate.

'An out-of-London ballet premiere is a rare event but *The Willing Prisoner*, presented by the Gadina Ballet Company last night at the King's Theatre, Newcastle-upon-Tyne, was intended as a tribute to the courage and war-work of that great city. Worthy of its task for certain great moments, the ballet owes much to such famous works as *Lac des Cygnes* and *La Belle au Bois Dormant*,' she read. 'The music is appealing through its familiarity for anyone who knows *A Life for the Czar* or *Russian and Ludmilla*, and on the whole well-arranged by David Warburton who leads the hardworking trio of musicians. Special mention must be made of the excellent flute-playing of Arlen Jones in a passage derived from a theme in Karaminskaya. Of the dancing, much could be said: long roles are well sustained by Maria Petrowsky as the

Princess and Carl de Breuve as Anton, her rescuer. But the best dancing came from an unknown, Lina Takarova, as the snow-flake who frees Anton from his enchantment. It was a most touching, charming *pas de deux*. On the whole, the work is sparkling and will no doubt please audiences at Christmas for years to come.'

Linda sat back in her chair. 'There's more,' said David, and withdrawing *The Times* he gave her the *Newcastle Journal*.

The report was longer, because the event was of greater local importance. 'Go down to the foot of the column,' muttered David over Linda's shoulder.

She obeyed, and found there her own name. 'Lina Takarova is a revelation of grace and lightness as the snow-flake. But more than that, she endows the part with pathos. A very moving performance, and yet in the following act this same dancer was notable for the brilliant solo as the ruby rose. Clearly this is a name to watch for.'

She handed the paper back to David. 'It's amazing...'

'It's great. Now you're a somebody, Lin. Aren't you glad you didn't settle for a desk job in the Ministry of Supply?'

She laughed, but there was a tremor in it. How strange it was... If she had been guided by good sense, none of this could have happened. But then good sense asserted itself and she said, 'Well, of course, it's lovely, but we're still only a penny-ha'penny company with bookings into places no other company would touch. It's nice to be praised, David – but it makes no difference to the fact that next week we'll be struggling with an unsuitable stage in Sunderland.'

'Aren't you pleased to be representing British ballet among these dark Satanic mills?' he teased.

'I am, you know I am. But don't let's get carried away.' She was thinking of Alan, and how he would receive the news that she'd been singled out for her performance. She could just imagine how he would sigh and hope it didn't mean she was thinking she could make a real career out of it.

Nevertheless, the whole company was lighted up with enthusiasm by the praise they'd received. If Mary Petersfield was a little miffed at sharing the glory with Linda, she didn't say so. Only Carl murmured mischievously to Linda, 'It's pretty hard on her after she twisted her father's arm for money to mount the thing – and then you run off with all the applause!'

In Sunderland everything went wrong. The old variety theatre had a stage intended for stand-up comics to work at the front, the lighting equipment was poor, and Carl injured a foot on a nail sticking up from the stairs. Though they danced poorly, the applause was just as great. It depressed them, made Gadina furious. Then when they moved on the following week to their factory commitments, the costumes for *Homeland* went astray. They had to dance the same programme of three short ballets wherever they went. 'We can only be thankful that workers don't work in more than one factory at a time,' remarked Alice Faulkner, 'otherwise they'd complain at seeing the same things.'

Many of the dancers had ailments. Injury to muscles was commoner than it used to be. They were all suffering from fatigue, from the lack of comfort and proper rest, from poor food. The men were especially tired: lifting a one-hundred-pound ballerina is no easy task. Most dancers have no superfluous flesh but all there is consists of muscle which must be handled carefully, and then the whole thing must look easy, almost casual. The male dancers of the Gadina Company needed extra rations, just as a manual labourer did – but they were not forthcoming under touring conditions.

The company made its weary way southwards. The tour was to end at Easter which that year was very late, April 25th. The wintry weather was unwilling to relax its grip but as they travelled the temperature did begin to climb up a little from zero.

They were in Peterborough when Alan

turned up at Linda's digs. He knew better than go near the theatre, for Linda had told him the tale of Betty Balcombe and her sergeant. She found him installed in the landlady's private snuggery, sipping sherry and looking very much at home. 'There you are, dearie... Your young man arrived while you were having your bit of practice, so I says to him, I says, just sit you down and have a drop of something while you wait.' In Linda's ear she added, 'Ain't he handsome! You're the lucky one!'

Lucky, it turned out, wasn't exactly the word. Alan had come to say he had his posting for what he called 'action-stations'. He had no idea where he would be going or what he would be doing but implied that it would be dangerous. 'I was thinking, Lin ... I know it's a change of plan... But could we get married before I go?'

'Married?' They had always talked about waiting until the war was over. 'What makes you ... I mean...' But she knew. She had sent him cuttings of her debut in *The Willing Prisoner* and though he'd written back in congratulation, she could sense it worried him. 'Now don't go getting ideas from this,' his letter had ended. 'It's nice to have made a success and you deserve it, but it's only a passing thing, after all. Marriage is for ever, darling.'

On the one hand... On the other hand...

This was what he had been telling her. Marriage was more important. Marriage was what women aimed for. Marriage, and a home of their own, and children... To be a dancer was exciting, but they had always planned on being married when he was twenty-one, if the war had not spoiled everything.

Now he was twenty-two, about to be sent on some dangerous mission, and scared he would never know whether Linda really loved him. This was to be his proof: she would become his wife and thus belong to him, belong to *him* and not to the world of ballet.

She couldn't say, 'I don't want to.' Before she joined the Gadina Company, one of their chief laments was that they had to wait, 'there's a war on.' Now he was wiping out that obstacle. He had a special licence, everything was arranged, he had rung her parents to say he was on his way to claim her.

'You rang home?'

'Yes, and they were delighted. It's what they've always wanted, after all, Lin. And us too – we've always planned and talked...'

'Yes, but I never expected...'

'I know, it's sudden, and not like me, is it?' He grinned, white teeth gleaming in a face made brown by long outdoors training. 'I've changed, you see. Knowing you might be wiped out in a week or two makes you realise you shouldn't put off the good things in life.'

'Oh, *Alan!*'

'Don't get upset, darling. I'm not going to get myself killed if I can help it. But there's a risk, after all. I'm not in a unit that's going to sit safely on a shelf at HQ.'

He was playing on her emotions but it was not intentional. His impulse to claim her and bind her with a gold ring sprang from a simple and genuine need. He had loved her all his life and was afraid he was losing her at the moment when he needed every reassurance he could grasp. Linda must prove she loved him. And the proof was to get married.

She understood. None of it was put into words but she sensed his needs. And she loved him. No matter how she might have changed since she began to dance, she was still the Linda Thackerley who had played tag with him in the recreation ground, fielded for him at cricket, embroidered his initials on handkerchiefs as a birthday present, walked hand in hand with him home from church. She was his Linda: she never questioned that. And he was hers. If he needed her, she must go.

He had four days' leave. He wanted her to marry him next day so they could have three days' honeymoon. He had heard of a hotel

189

in Cambridge, recommended by the famous Joe Fielder, and had booked a room. Everything was arranged. She had only to say yes.

'I'll have to talk to Madame Gadina–'

'Surely you don't need her permission?' he burst out. 'Or is it going to be like your pal Betty Balcombe – she locks you in the theatre?'

'No, no, it's nothing like that. But I have to explain, Alan. She'll need to re-plan all the programmes. They won't be able to do *Prisoner*–' She broke off. She'd been going to say that so far no one had been designated to cover that role and before she went to the church she must go to the theatre, to teach snow-flake to someone for tomorrow night.

'I'll sort it out. I must rush now to catch Madame before afternoon rehearsals. Mrs Tyler will be able to give you some lunch, I expect–'

'But what about you? I wanted to take you out, somewhere posh–'

'I can't, Alan.' She gave him a quick hug-and-kiss. 'I have to get back to the theatre. I'll be as quick as I can.'

'Hi!' She turned back at the door. He held out a page of clothing coupons. 'This is for you to buy the dress.'

'But–'

'Go on, it's all right, I bought them off someone for you.'

She accepted them reluctantly. The fact of

her reluctance showed her how little she was ready for this sudden change in her life. But she must get to the theatre.

Gadina was in the manager's office complaining about a lack of advertising for her new ballet. She swung round on Linda with an expression already full of annoyance. 'Ah, so you have come to say the sweetheart is here and you want the evening off to having dinner with him. Well, let me tell you, it will not be so! I am not rearranging my programme.'

How could she possibly know Alan had arrived? Yet the grapevine was so swift between theatre landladies that no doubt word had been passed on. Linda said, 'It's more than that. Alan has asked me—'

'I am not interesting in what Alan asks. I have a ballet company to direct, and Alice has toothache so I am having office work to do, and I cannot be bothered with—'

'Madame, I must have three days' leave.'

'What? What is this? Must? The only "must" for Gadina is the dance. You cannot have day's leave. It is impossible.'

'I must have three days off. I'm getting—'

'You are getting tired? This I am knowing. So are we all – tired and worn out. But all the more we are going to work, and rehearse, and make our dance perfect, so that when we return to Cheltenham for farewell performances, we are being asked to stay together, tour again after summer–'

'Madame, I'm not asking to leave the company in the lurch. I'll teach someone snow-flake if you'll choose an understudy–'

'You are telling me how to run company? Nonsense! *Devoshka moi,* I need no suggestions from you.' There followed a passage in Russian which by its force and rapidity demonstrated a very angry spirit. 'And as to taking days off, who are you to demand this? If there are any days off to be taking, Carl should have, or another of the boys, who are exhausted – but no, they do not ask, they are not selfish! So it is No, do you hear me? *Niet, niet, niet!*'

It was intimidating. The old lady was breathing fire, her hand was raised as if to strike Linda. It was enough to make any dancer quail. Yet Linda heard the echo of Alan's question: is it going to be like your pal Betty Balcombe?

The manager had taken the opportunity to escape from his own office when Linda came in, leaving the door open. The tirade coming from within had attracted two of the girls from the company. They hovered outside, listening with awe to the row. When David Warburton walked up, arms full of music scores, they beckoned to him to stop and listen. Shamelessly he did so: in many ways a ballet company was like school.

In a small silence that had fallen after

Gadina's total refusal, Linda drew a breath. She wasn't going to be like Betty Balcombe. She wasn't afraid to stand up for her rights.

'Either I have three days off or I leave the company,' she said.

'Eh?' said Madame inelegantly. 'You leave?'

'I don't want to. I'm asking for three days, and it doesn't seem much. I'm getting married and I want it for my honeymoon.'

The old prima ballerina sat down slowly in the manager's chair. 'Married?'

Outside the door there was an echoing murmur. 'Married…?'

'Yes, Madame. My fiancé is going overseas and has three days' leave. We want to be married before he goes.'

'But this is madness!' Gadina cried. 'You are not wanting to be married? You are a dancer!'

'It's possible to do both, you know,' Linda said in a practical tone that upheld her own lack of conviction. 'But that's not the issue. I'm taking three days off. I'll teach snowflake to whoever you choose, but you'd better hurry up because after this evening's performance I'm going.'

'This is unheard-of! You defy?'

'Yes, Madame, I defy,' she agreed flatly.

The other girls burst in. 'I say, Linda, congratulations! I'd no idea you were thinking of–'

'Yes, lots of luck, darling!'

'Me too,' said David, putting conviction into his voice, 'I wish you all the best, Linda.'

'Thank you.' She met his eyes for a moment and thought he looked unhappy, but her mind was on Gadina.

'Very well,' said Madame Gadina. 'Three days. Teach Marina snow-flake. I am thinking this is mistake but you are determined, yes?'

'Yes.'

'It is settled, then. Find Marina and tell her. As for me, I take aspirin, for you have give me big headache.'

Linda impulsively took the old lady's hand. 'It'll be all right. I'll be back on Friday.'

'So. But you will not have mind on the ballet once you are married. I have seen, many times. It is mistake, Linda. *Tu as beaucoup de talent mais il faut le servir. Servir, tu comprends? Ah, nichevo!*' she burst out, with one of her sudden changes. '*U menya bolit golova, no nichevo! Slushete, maladoya* – you will be sad over this! *Zhenatya* – married – what dancer wants to be married. *Tu feras grand erreur, tu verras!*' With that she pushed her way between the others and went out.

'We-ell,' remarked Daisy Overton. 'That's what you might call a pep-talk for intending brides. Pay no heed, lovey – I'll bet you'll be

194

very happy. Who is it – the young man in the commando outfit?'

Linda spent a few minutes telling them her plans and listening to their congratulations. She didn't notice that David had soon followed Gadina out. As soon as she could she went in search of Marina Radetzki to tell her the news but, as she expected, Marina had already heard. 'Get *you*,' she greeted her. 'Standing up to Gadina! That's what marriage does for a girl, is it? Perhaps I'll try it.'

'Marina, can we find time this afternoon to go through snow-flake? About four o'clock. Then you can watch tonight and let me have any queries before we leave the theatre.'

They agreed on the arrangements then Linda went hurrying out again. In Peterborough's main street she noticed a shop window with pale coloured dresses, tempting the buyer to think of Easter. She stared at them for a long time, blankly, trying to summon the energy to choose between apricot and rose. She was reminded of the clothing coupons in her hand bag. After a long hesitation she went into the shop to exchange them for a wedding dress.

It seemed she really was going to marry Alan.

CHAPTER SEVEN

Cambridge was full of American service-men, mostly flyers from the airfields of East Anglia. They either trudged about with guide books and cameras to record their visit for the folks back home, or hung around the hotels waiting for the strange British opening hours to let them have a drink.

The hotel recommended by Joe Fielder was not far from Parker's Piece. It was small and rather shabby, as almost everywhere was, what with the lack of available paint and no one to use a paint brush. But it was clean and quiet and looked out on a green square bordered with fine chestnuts. When they were shown to their room, Alan walked to the window to look out. 'All right, eh?' he said when Linda joined him.

'It's lovely, Alan.' The snow was going, there were even snowdrops to be seen pushing their helmets up under the trees.

'We'll have a lovely time, darling. It's only a short honeymoon but it's going to be marvellous.'

She knew he was nervous, and so was she. She was what was called 'a good girl' in the circles in which she was brought up – no experience of sex, not even much knowledge of it. Her mother, embarrassed, had given her a short lecture when she reached the right age but it had conveyed little except that from now on she must be particularly careful to keep herself 'nice' and never to wash her hair at certain times of the month.

Among the ballet company there were those who could tell her more. Marina had had a six-months affair with a naval officer, from which she would recount entertaining moments – but the lieutenant sounded like a man-about-town with a keen sense of the ridiculous. It hardly seemed to fit with the solemn moment that came later that day, when they had had lunch and taken a brisk walk through the steely-cold city.

'Let's go to bed,' Alan said suddenly.

'But it's too early, darling. I'm not sleepy.'

'Not to *sleep*, Lin.' He looked at her, flushing at having to explain to her. But his mouth was determined and as she moved towards him she saw something in his eyes that she recognised for the first time. Recognised and welcomed.

It was physical desire.

She undressed more quickly than he. She was accustomed to getting out of her clothes with celerity. She turned back the bed-covers and sat on the edge, fluttering with nerves,

197

hot and cold by turns.

Alan turned from the last wrestle with army underwear. He gave a little gasp. 'Good God, there's nothing of you, Lin!'

'Oh ... I'm sorry ... I know I'm a bit skinny...' She looked down at her familiar body. 'It's the dancing, you see.'

'Darling, you're beautiful.' He swung himself over the bed to sit beside her and take her in his arms. 'Just like a lovely little greyhound.'

'But did you want to marry a greyhound?' she said, laughing a little. She looked at him over her shoulder. 'There's more of you, that's for sure!'

'Oh, yes ... muscle, that's what commando training gives you.' He pulled her close and began to kiss her at her neck and ear, little soft kisses that made her shiver with sudden arousal. 'And at the moment, my angel, all that muscle is just aching for you.'

Their love-making was a revelation to her. Not only about Alan, but about herself. She had always been too busy to think about herself as a physical creature except where it concerned her dancing. Now she found there were nerves that responded with a force that left her breathless, powers that swept her away so that she came to her senses to find she was clutching her lover with hands that had turned into claws. Later, when they were at momentary peace and examined each other, she found she had made weals in Alan's back with her nails.

'It's all right,' he soothed when she began to blurt an apology. 'I like it. In fact ... I think you're marvellous.'

'Am I, Alan? I'd no idea what ... what to expect.' She held him closer. 'Had you?'

'Oh, the other fellows go on all the time about... Well, you don't want to hear that. But I knew that with you it would be different ... wonderful ... and it is.'

Early next morning she woke to find a grey light filtering into the room. They had left the black-out undrawn last night so they could see the stars. She pulled herself up on an elbow and studied her sleeping partner.

My husband, she said to herself. My *husband*. Not just Alan, my boy-friend. He belongs to me, I belong to him. We're man and wife. And it's so tremendous... Why did no one ever tell me?

They spent the three days in a daze of happiness and desire. They were sure no one else had ever felt as they did. They turned to each other to share a moment's amusement over ducks on a pond, touched hands when they met again after a passer-by had separated them. They looked at the beauties of Cambridge and scarcely saw them because they were too beglamoured by each other.

Time had ceased to exist and yet they knew that Thursday evening was coming closer. At seven o'clock they went to the station. Alan had to see the Rail Transport Officer about his travel warrant. She stood with his kitbag and her own small holdall at her feet, shivering but not from the cold wind that swept through the small station.

They travelled together to Peterborough. She got out. He came out on the platform with her, to carry her bag. He stood looking at her with something like despair. She threw her arms round him. 'Oh, darling, darling, be careful! Come back to me safe and sound!'

He made no reply, but kissed her almost savagely. The whistle blew, the guard was showing his green lamp. They clung together while the train began to move. He dragged himself from her arms and leapt into the carriage entrance, then leaned back, dangerously, to try to see her in the blacked-out station.

'Don't forget me, Lin!' he called back to her. 'Think of me when you're dancing!'

Then he was gone, his voice drowned by the shug-shug of the steam train and the rattle of the wheels. He was going North, but more than that he couldn't let her know. He would write, he said, as soon as he had a Forces Postal Address to send her. It might be days before he reached his destination.

She had promised to write every day and send the letter as a packet when she knew how to address it. She stood on the platform trying to remember everything he had said, so she might find a clue to his future whereabouts. She needed to know, to picture him in some surroundings – hills, moors, the coast...

When she got to her digs the landlady took one look at her and set her in a chair by the fire in her snuggery. Without more words she made sweet coffee from a precious bottle of coffee essence, laced it with rum, and made Linda drink it. Then she said, 'Hot bath and bed – up you go.'

There was no thought of disobeying. It seemed only right that someone should tell her what to do, for her head was empty, her heart was breaking, and her body was like ice.

When she woke next morning, very early, at first she couldn't think what was wrong with her. She lay staring up at the ceiling. Then she became aware of the narrow bed, the single pillow. Remembrance flooded through her. She turned over on her face and began to cry, stifling the sound with the pillow so as not to disturb the other boarders.

She was at the theatre for class at nine. The other dancers were still gathering. They crowded round her, giving her good wishes, hugging and kissing.

'We've got to have a party!' someone cried. 'A wedding celebration.'

'Oh, no,' gasped Linda, but the protest was drowned in the hubbub of approval and suggestion.

'Tomorrow night after curtain... Anyone got any booze...? Mrs Hodges would let us use her sitting room... Train's at twelve-thirty – is that enough time? Let's have it on the train, folks! That's the solution!'

Madame Gadina appeared. Everyone fell silent. They were on edge to see how she would treat Linda, who had after all defied her. The old ballerina walked to her usual position at the front of the stage by the footlights.

'Good morning, dancers,' she said.

'Good morning, Madame,' they chorused.

'Please form three lines as usual,' she said, 'girls in front, boys at the back. We will begin as always with our *pliés*... Ready, David? *And*-one-and-two...'

That was all that ever passed between Madame and Linda about her marriage.

Though she had not taken class for three days, she danced well that night. She knew it, and the rest of the company knew it, even if the audience was unable to tell that something wonderful had been laid before them. When she came off at the end of *Prisoner,* Madame was standing in the wings.

'*Tu as bien fait,*' she said, in a trembling voice. '*Tu m'as donné beaucoup de plaisir ce soir et je te remercie, ma belle.*'

Linda was staggered. To be told she had given pleasure to the old lady was the greatest compliment she had ever been paid. 'Thank you, Madame,' she said uncertainly.

'Well, go on, do not be standing there like statue, go back, take another call!'

Later Linda told herself she had danced for Alan, as he had begged as the train carried him away. But as the days went by and the performances enthralled her attention, she knew she danced well because she needed to dance well – for herself, because that was why she was born. It shamed her, but she couldn't alter the fact. Perhaps she was selfish?

The tour ended in Cheltenham, with three triumphant performances of *The Willing Prisoner* to an augmented orchestra, and on the other evenings the usual three short ballets. On the Saturday on which they were to break up, the theatre was packed to the doors with a full complement of standing tickets.

There was to be – of course – a party. On stage after curtain. Linda accepted the glass of white wine which Gadina approved, and was sipping it with her feet up on another chair (strictly forbidden during class or rehearsal) when a faintly familiar voice spoke her name.

'Linda T'ackerley? Is this you?' She looked over her shoulder. A tall man with black hair and a sallow complexion was examining her. 'So it is you! Lina Takarova is Linda T'ackerley!'

'It's ... Mr Bordi, isn't it?'

'*Si, si,* I am flattered that so great a dancer remembers me. When I think how I patronised you at Leonard's party. "Contact my manager", I think I said. You forgive me?'

'Don't be silly. You'd no idea who I was – and in any case, everything's still the same. I'm an out-of-work ballerina.'

'Out-of-work? Absurd! After what I saw tonight, there must be a queue of ballet companies wanting you–'

She shook her head, disturbing the diadem of dark red sequins she wore in her Ruby Rose costume. 'There aren't all that many ballet companies if you come to think of it,' she pointed out. 'Vic-Wells, International, Rambert – and they've all got enough ballerinas without offering a place to someone with my limited experience.'

'I find that hard to believe.' He sat down on the stage at the side of her chair, waving a negative at her when she offered to give up the one on which she had her aching feet. 'You say you have limited experience? Yet what I saw–'

'I know about six other roles besides what you saw tonight. I've never danced modern ballet, I've never done comedy or real character–'

'But you are delightful, Linda. I know what I say – I handle dancers and singers every day of my life. You have that special quality.'

She shook her head. 'I don't think so.' She was measuring herself against Riabouchinska, Markova. She knew she fell far short.

Yet the fact of his approval warmed her. He had a shrewd, dark glance that implied a penetrating intelligence, and it was wonderful to receive praise from an intelligent man after so much foolish adulation on the tour. But more than that: he was an impresario, a man of the theatre whose experience encompassed work in his native Italy, and in America before he made his home in Britain.

While they discussed her performance of this evening, he praising, she disclaiming, she became aware of his personal magnetism. She scolded herself inwardly: it was such a cliché, wasn't it, to be attracted to the dark, handsome foreigner. Yet it was more than his looks, more even than his prestige as a theatre manager. It was the fact that he was taking special interest in her – and she was more flattered than she expected. Generally she took enthusiasm for her dancing with a pinch of salt. *She* knew her faults, if others did not.

But when Bordi spoke well of her, it was suddenly important to believe it.

'*Eh bene!* I tell you you have great appeal, and if you say you lack experience, appeal is better! I will think about–'

'Hello,' David Warburton said, coming up with a plate of the little snacks called *zakuski* which Gadina loved to eat at parties. 'Hungry? Have some herring-and-sour-cream.'

'Thank you, no,' Bordi said with a shudder. 'How can the Russians have won back Stalingrad when they feed on such things?'

'Perhaps it's because they feed on such things, Nicco. Makes 'em tough.'

'You two know each other?' Linda said in surprise.

'A little. Signor Bordi wanted me to write some incidental music for a propaganda film last year but I couldn't fit it in.'

'Films? I didn't know you made films, Mr Bordi.'

'No, it is relatively new. I put myself at the disposal of the British government when the war broke out and they asked for suggestions, so I said I thought an outsider's view of their world might make good propaganda. Thus, they offered me the chance to make films, little films, you understand – fifteen minutes of *Brave London* or *The Shepherd on the Downs.* You have seen none of these?'

'We don't have much chance to go to the pictures,' Linda apologised, reaching for another snippet of herring on toast. 'We're in the theatre most of the time. I'm sure your films are very good.'

'Ah, listen to her. The polite English miss! I tell you, my films are quite good, but I believe I now have an idea that may make a fine film. A very fine, unusual film. Tell me, Linda, you have had any film experience?'

'Me? Goodness, no.'

'I wonder... You are now out of work?'

'Alas, yes.'

'Can you be in London by Wednesday of next week? I will fix up for a test–'

'No, no,' Linda cried in alarm. 'I'm not an actress!'

'*Capito!* You are a dancer. It is possible to film dancers as well as actresses, you know.'

'But dancing has nothing to do with war–'

'You are wrong,' Bordi contradicted. 'War has its flowers as well as its thorns. In Flanders, in the First World War, there was the poppy – that is right, *il papavero,* no?'

'Quite right, Nicco, but I don't quite see–'

'Ballet is the flower of this war in Britain – no, it is a whole garland of flowers. I see it suddenly. And I see that it would make a good film.'

'"The garland of the war",' murmured

David. 'That's in *Antony and Cleopatra*, I think. It never struck me before, but you may be right, Nicco.'

'That is why I am useful,' Bordi said with an upward flick of the head that sent a black lock flying back from his brow. 'I look at the British from outside, and I can tell you to be proud of what I see. And I believe a film about this would be worth doing.' He turned his dark glance on Linda. 'I should have to show you to one or two people who must approve. So can you audition on Wednesday?'

'No, really, I can't. I have to go home to Hedfield–'

'Linda!' David burst out. 'Where would you take class in Hedfield? And how would you hear of any jobs?'

'I know, I know, but I *must* go home. I haven't seen Mummy and Daddy in over six months, and I must pay a visit to my in-laws.'

Bordi frowned. 'In-laws?'

'You don't know, of course. I'm married now. My name's Olliver, not Thackerley.'

'*Mio Dio*,' gasped Bordi. 'When did this happen?'

'About six weeks ago.'

'And the husband – he is in ballet too?'

'He's in the army,' Linda said with a smothered grin at what Alan might say at the idea of being a ballet dancer. More seriously she added, 'He's on active service.'

'Oh, I see.' She thought he looked put out, but couldn't understand why. It was nothing to do with him one way or the other.

'So Wednesday is not good. Can you come Thursday?'

Linda burst out laughing. 'I've just told you! I have to go and see my family. I can't arrive on Monday, stay two days, and then tell them I'm off to an audition on Thursday.'

'Why not?' Bordi asked, reasonably enough from his point of view.

'Because...' Well, because they would probably imagine that with the ending of the Gadina tour, 'all that kind of thing' was over. It was what she had more or less imagined herself. She could foresee the arguments she would have with her parents if she said she intended to persist, that she was wanted for an audition less than a week after leaving Gadina.

'I'm sorry, I don't think it's possible,' she said, making it sound very firm and formal. She didn't know that there was disappointment in her voice. 'Besides, I don't really want to be in films. I want to dance.'

'*Certo*, I have already said – in the film you will dance. You must come, Linda. I will arrange it – Thursday afternoon, at the Gaiety Theatre – you know the Gaiety, at the foot of Aldwych? *Fledermaus* is playing

209

there at present, the stage is good, clear for dancing because we have big choruses and also three short ballet inserts... Yes?'

'No, I'm sorry. It's just not on.'

He scrambled up from the floor, dusted himself off from the rosin always present on a ballet stage, and went away without another word.

'You're being silly, Lin,' David said, offering her the tray of *zakuski*. 'This is a chance most girls would give their eye-teeth for.'

'Oh, you don't understand!' She sprang up so suddenly she almost knocked the food out of his hands. 'My parents are dead against the whole thing so it would mean a long, silly argument–'

'But they haven't even come to see you dance, Linda. What right have they to give opinions?'

'Well, I ... I always told them I only wanted to do the Gadina tour just to prove I could do it. It was understood I'd give up after that.'

'You don't want a career in ballet?' He was staring at her in disbelief.

'Of course I do!' It was forced out of her against her will. 'But, you see ... Alan...'

'What about Alan?'

'He... We always planned to get married and settle down. It's been understood all our lives. Now we *are* married, and as soon as the war ends – and Alan says that'll be this year–'

'Oh!' It was a snort of denial. 'That's pie in the sky!'

'Yes, perhaps, but... Don't you see, one way or the other, I'm going to settle down in Hedfield.'

'Not if I can help it! I won't let a talent like yours go to waste!'

'It's none of your business–'

'Of course it's my business! It's the business of anyone who– Besides, I'm writing the music for a ballet that needs you, Lin. Don't walk away from the world you belong in! Don't waste yourself on being Alan's wife–'

'It's not waste! He deserves–'

'What do you deserve? To be doomed to domesticity? Never appear on the stage again, never drift through the air and feel as if you had transcended everything on earth–'

'How did you know that?' she gasped. 'How can you know how I feel–?'

'Oh, I understand all that, Lin. I'm not a dancer and never could have been, but I see it sometimes in a dancer's face. On the stage, sometimes, but in class, too – everything meshes and merges, the body works without having to be urged, and the real aim of the dancer ... is won.'

They stood in silence, apart from the rest of the party, an incongruous pair, she in her dark red sequined tutu and diadem, he in his rather worn evening suit. They were not looking at each other but at some scene they both could see and understand.

'I can't come,' she said. 'I can't audition. Alan wouldn't like it.'

'But Alan's off somewhere, where you can't explain it so he'd understand. And it's not as if you were being asked to go swanning off to Hollywood, is it? Bordi's asking you to audition for some sort of propaganda film – it's all to help the war effort.'

'Ye-es, but...'

'You ought at least to turn up. What harm can it do to dance for him and his pals, and hear what they're suggesting?'

'I don't really think I...'

'You'd spend a day in Town – stay overnight one night, perhaps. Then you could be back with your family until Nicco gets things rolling.'

'I don't even know what's involved in filmmaking.'

'Oh, they don't hang about – they haven't the film to waste or the money to spare. I suppose it might be three weeks' work – maybe four. How could Alan object to that?'

'If it was only something short like that...'

'You'll turn up?'

'Well, I suppose ... I'd have time to get tights mended and give my practice tutu a good wash–'

'Oh, listen, Linda! Look here – you're not going to audition for ballet-teachers. These'll be film financiers, perhaps even men from the Ministry of Information. Wear something *they'd* think of as ballet.'

'You mean Sugar Plum, *Swan Lake?* I haven't *got* anything like that, David. Only amateurish things I used to wear for charity shows and stuff.'

David took a pace or two about, thinking. 'You could wear that,' he said, with a gesture at the Ruby Rose costume.

'But it belongs to Gadina.'

'Ask her to lend it.'

'What?' The mere idea filled her with alarm.

'Dammit, Lin, you're going to be auditioned for a part in a film. Nicco has asked you personally. He's not a nobody and you're not a nobody! You're a star of the Gadina Company–'

'Oh, don't talk rubbish, David. I'm not a star–'

'You're a soloist with the Gadina Company. That gives you *some* status. Anyhow, what harm can it do to ask? She can't eat you!'

'Want to bet!' she responded.

She sought out the company's director as the party was breaking up. Gadina was sitting on a hard wooden chair, feet together, back straight, head up, receiving the

213

farewells of her dancers. To each she gave her hand. Each bowed over it. The men kissed the back of the hand, the girls bent so their foreheads almost touched it. 'Goodbye, thank you for working so hard for me,' she said to them one by one. She was smiling a little, there were tears at the rims of her eyes. She looked quite different – old, proud, vulnerable.

'Madame,' Linda began after she had bowed and been thanked, 'may I ask a great favour?'

'What?' Madame looked guarded: most favours were about giving recommendations.

'May I borrow the Ruby Rose tutu to use at an audition next week?'

'Audition? Who auditions?' the old lady demanded, black eyes snapping. 'De Valois? If so, she is very quick to snatch – and if you are loyal, I may have another tour–'

'No, Madame, it's not for the Vic-Wells. Nothing like that.'

'Like what, then?'

'It's for a film test, Madame,' David put in. 'And it would be a great boon if she could have the Rose tutu – and the one for snowflake too.'

'Film?' The wrinkled mouth turned down in disapproval. 'I am not liking ballet in film. American girl, twirl-twirl-twirl, bad music and, worse, not straight knees!'

'It's not for a spot in a revue film, Madame,' David explained. 'Niccolo Bordi has some idea for a propaganda film–'

'Ballet is not for propaganda. Ballet is for itself.'

'Yes, Madame Gadina, but there is a war on–'

'Oh, you are thinking this I don't know? War, war ... I have been in one war, and though this one is less terrifying for me, I do not approve that everything is turned to be used for killing.'

'Nothing Linda does is going to help kill anybody,' David soothed. 'Bordi wants to show ballet in Britain in wartime, I suppose.'

'Vic-Wells also?'

'Er ... no, I don't think so.'

'Linda is not ballet in wartime. I am ballet in wartime, also de Valois, and International...'

'I don't know what Bordi has in mind. All I know is he saw Linda and got some sort of idea. Now he wants to show her to some other chaps – government men, I suppose.'

'Oh, if it is *government,* you will be as old as Gadina by the time they grant the money to make the film, *ma chère!'* With a hoot of laughter the old lady patted Linda heavily on the shoulder. 'Very well, borrow Ruby Rose and snow-flake. Please to return them personally to Cheltenham, cleaned and any tears mended.'

'Yes, Madame,' Linda said.

'Government,' chuckled Gadina. 'Ha! How long did we having talks over Gadina Company, David? A year? Film is much more money – oh, you will be eighty years old when film is made!'

When Linda reached Hedfield next day, her mother was on the station platform to greet her. She clasped her daughter in her arms so that Linda had some trouble releasing herself to leap back into the old-fashioned compartment to rescue the muslin bags holding the two precious costumes.

'What on earth are those?' Mrs Thackerley said in astonishment.

'Costumes I borrowed from Gadina. They're for an audition on Thursday.'

'Audition! Oh, *Linda*...!'

'I'll tell you all about it on the way home. Have we got a taxi?'

Mrs Thackerley stared at her daughter in disbelief. 'A taxi! I took it for granted we'd go on the bus.'

'With these?' Linda laughed. She gave one of the muslin bags to her mother, picked up the other and laid it over her arm, then hoisted her suitcase. At the rank the usual two decrepit taxis were waiting. Linda pushed her mother into the first one, clambered in, and gave her home address.

'Now,' Nancy Thackerley began at once, 'let's have this out! I'm amazed you should think of joining another company, Linda, I really am! You know Alan hates the idea–'

'It's not a company, Mummy. I'm auditioning for a film.'

'A film!'

Linda explained. Her mother was silent. Surprised, Linda waited for the outburst – but it didn't come. 'A film,' mused her mother. 'We-ell, fancy ... a *film*. You mean, like Leslie Howard and people like that? We-ell ... I never thought a child of mine... Fancy!'

Films, it seemed, were impressive, important. Neighbours and friends went to see films. Whereas ballet was odd and 'arty', marking one out as eccentric, films were acceptable, even exciting.

The battle was already won by the time Linda's father came in from the garage to greet his daughter. Mrs Thackerley burst out with the news. 'What do you think, Harry? Our Linda's going to be in a picture, the government's going to make it, she's got to go up to London about it on Thursday – isn't it wonderful?'

Nobody remembered to ask whether Alan would approve.

There was no one in Hedfield with whom to take class. Linda did her own practice and centre-work to the strains of the old portable gramophone brought home by her mother from her former digs in London. She hired the church hall at ten shillings a morning, Tuesday and Wednesday.

On Thursday Linda presented herself at the stage door of the Gaiety. The doorkeeper took her to the old green room where, to her surprise, she found David Warburton. 'I didn't realise you'd be here,' she said.

'Well, who else could play the music? I rearranged it, don't forget. Anyhow, Nicco is thinking about hiring me to do incidental music for this flick, if all goes well.'

While he was explaining Bordi himself came in with two men and a woman. One of the men was in uniform with a flash saying 'MOI', Ministry of Information. The civilian was a wan-looking specimen, introduced as 'Verdon, the writer.' The woman seemed to be a secretary or note-keeper.

'What's he going to write?' Linda whispered to David as they were ushered through passages to the stage. 'Ballet?'

'No idea.'

There was only a working light on stage. In the stalls, a group of about a dozen people was seated. Bordi went to the front and began a speech of explanation.

'I had Joe working on a script all week. It's pretty rough still, as you comprehend, because I only gave him the project on Sunday, In essence, it goes like this. The

218

film's message is that in the midst of war, Britain still cares for and nourishes the arts. Britain wants its people to have what is good in life. So the government has sent out this little touring ballet company.'

'Which little touring ballet company?' queried a voice from the auditorium.

'It's fictional. We haven't thought of a name yet. I had discussions with various people and it's quite hard to get the lend – the loan – of a *corps de ballet* so we've decided to do as little as possible showing anything like a full performance but instead have only the solos or duets. If we need to show a line of dancers, I can supply girls from the *corps* of *Fledermaus*.'

'Righto, Nick. So it's an imaginary ballet company, with an imaginary *corps de ballet*. Do we have imaginary soloists?'

'No, we do not. Linda?' He half-turned. Linda walked to his side, and he ushered her forward, one-handed, in some slight imitation of the *danseur noble* presenting his ballerina.

'Here is our ballerina,' he said. 'Lina Takarova, otherwise Linda Olliver of the Gadina Company. The film will concentrate on her. We'll show her dancing, making up, exercising, travelling–'

'Now look here, old man, we're not going to throw money away on cars and petrol–'

'You don't understand. We'll show how

219

the ballerina has to share the trials of every-day life. She'll travel by train, like everybody else – and don't worry, we won't be shunting camera crews up and down the rail network, we can do most of the railway scenes on the outskirts of London, some-where like St Albans.'

'So far not bad,' said another voice. 'Let's hear the rest.'

'Well, that's all, really. We show her in all her everyday routine – practising, rehears-ing, and then performing. We'll show the man too, but less extensively because–'

'Because the general public will think he's a pansy–'

'No, Letherwood, because in fact Alex-ander Prebble has his calling-up papers and has to join his unit in thirty days' time. So we'll just have to do what we can while we have him.'

Linda had seized Bordi's hands convul-sively at the name. Prebble? The star of the Vic-Wells? The man who had trained with the De Basil?

Bordi paid no heed to her excitement. He was in an argument with someone in the stalls. 'We can do it in the time available so long as you don't waste any of it,' he insisted. 'Give me yes or no today – the details we can settle later. But if you say yes, we can start this very afternoon to film Prebble at class – he's in the studio of Anna

Leryeva in Hammersmith and she's agreed to let us film there. Of course it'll be rough – the lighting will be poor – but this is after all a documentary film.'

'My word, you have been beavering away, old chap. I admire you. But look here – if the film really hangs on the ballerina, we really have to get some idea of what she can do.'

'Of course. Linda, would you go and change? Miss Nelson will show you where.' A plump lady appeared from nowhere and led Linda away, the theatre dresser.

Meanwhile David was introduced to the group in the auditorium and played a few excerpts on the piano of the music he'd noted down for the opening titles of the film. Murmurs of approval greeted him. He waited by the piano, hands on the keys, until he saw Linda come to the wings in the Ruby Rose tutu. Then he played a loud chord to summon attention, rippled an accompaniment as she walked to the point at backstage left where she would begin, and gave her a few bars of reminder. She glanced over her shoulder at him. Though she was wearing costume, she had only sketched in the make-up. Her face was pale, her grey eyes enormous with fright.

He played her introduction. She took up the opening pose – right foot *dégagé* behind, arms *demi seconde*. As the first bars of the variation trilled out she was off across towards the footlights – *brisé-volé, brisé-volé* in the series so well-known from the Bluebird Variation (and borrowed direct by Gadina), then directly into a step forward that brought up the back leg in a swift arabesque.

Both she and David knew that she didn't dance as well as usual. She was nervous, she was under-practised, the piano gave less beat to the music than the trio she'd been accustomed to. But the effect to the non-expert was dazzling – a slight blonde girl in a dark red short skirt of tulle and a crown of trembling ruby drops, fluttering up and down from the bare boards like some exotic hummingbird.

The ending of the solo was more stately, intended to give some validity to the title – a rose made of gemstones. There were grand open movements of the arms, slow turns that melted into curtseys. The finale was a series of *fouettés* and an arabesque pose. It was greeted with a ripple of applause from below.

'Very nice, dear. Thank you. Would you like to rest for a bit while we have a talk?'

Linda bowed and went off. In the dressing room she got out of the tutu and the head-dress. 'You wanting the white, dear?' the dresser asked.

'Yes, I imagine so.' She splashed water on her face, on her upper body, dried, sprinkled talc, tied her hair in a chiffon scarf and did a little work on her eye make-up. She was just stepping into the white tutu of snow-flake when there was a tap on the door. The dresser opened it to reveal the secretary.

'Mr Bordi says will you get dressed and come to the manager's office when you're ready, please? To discuss a contract.'

'But ... don't they want to see this second piece?'

'Oh, no, Miss Olliver, the Ministry of Information people were quite delighted with what you've already shown them. Shall I tell Mr Bordi you're coming?'

Speechless, Linda nodded.

It seemed she was going to be a film star.

CHAPTER EIGHT

Linda knew so little about film-making that she was at first quite unaware of the miracle Bordi had performed by getting *Count Every Step* into production so swiftly.

As she learned later, it was done like this. First Bordi convinced a ballet-loving Cabinet Minister that Alexander Prebble should be given a four-week deferment to help in the making of an important propaganda film. This arranged, he went to the Ministry of Information with the idea that since Prebble was being given a month's deferment to have the chance to record his brilliance before it was wrecked by military service, the chance should be taken to make a film. The project was put under consideration, Bordi sold the true scenario to a journalist conscripted into the service of the MOI, the go-ahead was given, and technicians, cameramen and film stock were made available.

No money was accessible at the moment. Bordi was paying everyone out of his own pocket and would be reimbursed when the paperwork caught up with him – probably in about three months' time. He had conjured up a screen-writer, a costume designer, and a composer.

Bordi was everywhere at once – coaxing, inspiring, arguing, driving – but always, always, encouraging, building up her confidence.

'I know I'm going to freeze up in front of the cameras, Nicco.'

'And I know you are not.'

'I wish you hadn't put your own money into this!'

'I shall be repaid. Besides, that is what I do – invest money in production.' He smiled. Certainty was in every line and plane of his dark-featured face. 'You must believe me, Linda. You will do well.'

And because it was Nicco who said so, she believed it. He had become so important as a guide and friend that she ought to have been wary. She wasn't free to give anything of herself to a man so much older and who led such a different life. She was a dancer, dedicated to the dance. She was also a married woman. What was there left that Niccolo Bordi could claim?

But she trusted him. She felt an inner certainty that he would never ask for any reward for the chance he was giving her.

Linda's delight at meeting Alexander Prebble was wrecked by the fact that she was in a panic, having been shown the scenario outline. It called for her to perform the *pas de deux* from *Swan Lake* Act II with Prebble.

'But I've never danced Odette!' she cried in dismay to Joe Verdon.

'No? I thought that little tinpot company of yours included *Swan Lake* in its repertoire?'

'Yes, but the highest I ever got was one of the zombies.' At his look of surprised inquiry she explained, 'One of the leading swans.'

'Oh, I see... Yes, it comes back to me now, Nick did say you were an *aspiring* ballerina. Well, love, you do know the steps, I take it?'

Of course she knew the steps. It would be a dull and stupid dancer who did not know the steps of one of the greatest pieces of ballet ever staged. 'But I've never actually–'

'Look, darling, we're here to show you rehearsing and working with Preb and getting ready for the performance and then dancing the damn thing, aren't we? Here's your chance to practise it until you get it right and then go on stage and do it.'

'In four weeks?'

She related all this to Alexander Prebble, known to all as Preb. He smiled down at her from his six-foot height and looked thoughtful. 'We're not going to have to do the whole of Act II, right? It's just the *pas de deux?*'

'"Just"!'

'We'll make it. I hear you're a quick

learner and we're going to be together day in and day out, as far as I can gather. What we need is a ballet-master for coaching. I wonder if they've thought of that in this daft script of theirs?'

No, she had seen no mention of a ballet-teacher. 'Right,' said Preb, 'we'll insist they import Leryeva. She'd love it, getting the chance to go on film showing everybody how to do everything.'

The film studio was a former wholesaler's warehouse on the northern outskirts of London, commandeered by the Ministry of Information. At Preb's behest, a permanent set was built, a dance studio with mirrors and barre. Leryeva was installed, to reign in splendour wrapped in several shawls and a car-rug round her knees, drinking continual glasses of Russian tea sweetened with raspberry jam provided by a minion with a primus stove.

There Linda and Preb worked day by day. Learning to do double work was a revelation to Linda. She had had some experience with the Gadina Company but not enough. She found Preb was quite different from Carl de Breuve: he was less jovial and good-tempered, but not temperamental – in fact, he was almost businesslike. He would work tirelessly at the ballet-mistress's command. When she was momentarily satisfied and called a break, he simply went off the set, wrapped himself in an old blanket, and went straight to sleep on the floor.

The cameras recorded their efforts. Nothing was missed out – Linda's nervousness, her little war-dance of triumph at achieving in class a perfect version of the famous fish-dive from *Aurora's Wedding,* the moment when a shout from some technician startled them so that they fell in a heap together.

Linda wrote about it all to Alan. She wrote less frequently than formerly because the pressure of learning and working was so great but she tried to let him know how important it all was.

She would then feel guilty about thinking only of herself, and write a few paragraphs about the war news to assure him she was thinking of the part he was playing. Wasn't it wonderful that the North African campaign had ended so well? Thanksgiving services had been held in the churches, she'd gone to the one in St Martin-in-the-Fields. But how awful about the bombing of the Eder dams – no matter how much it might shorten the war to flood the industrial areas, think of all those drowned German families...

Then she bethought herself that the censor would probably black out that last bit, as being likely to spread 'gloom and despondency', so she scrapped that sheet and started again, inquiring teasingly if he could get his favourite radio programme, *The Brains Trust,* in whatever savage spot he now dwelt.

All she knew about Alan at present was that he was somewhere in Scotland – this from a reference to 'enjoying the whisky', which she knew he didn't drink. He was somewhere rather wild but he couldn't say where. He had been in an action but he couldn't say what. All had gone well but he couldn't say how. She sensed he was as busy as she was, had no time to miss her. He wrote that if the film was for the Ministry of Information it must be all right though he couldn't see why people needed to be informed about ballet. He wished her well.

The day came when the filming was to move into the disused theatre that was to be the set for the ballet performance. Cameras were placed in the stalls, on a platform in front of the grand circle, and one in the wings. Other shots would be taken later from difficult angles, in the gods or at floor level.

When Linda put on the Swan Princess headdress for the first time, she was trembling so much with emotion that she could not fasten it. The designer had chosen a band of white feathers across the top, ending in two wings against the ears, with a secondary band of silver behind it to highlight her fair hair. The dresser settled it firmly and tied the tapes under the chignon in which her hair was dressed.

The tutu itself was very simple – a plain white satin bodice with a band of feathers from right shoulder to left waist, the merest whisper of ostrich fronds at the shoulder straps.

The girls from Bordi's *Fledermaus* company had been drilled in the swan dances by Leryeva. 'You will never be asked to join De Basil,' she told them with a sigh, 'but only keep quiet behind the soloists while the cameras work, and it will do.' In fact their main use was to dress the stage.

Linda met Preb by the rosin box. He was serious and concentrated yet relaxed. 'Oh, Preb,' she whispered, grasping his arm, 'I hope I'm not going to let you down...'

He smiled. 'Listen, Lin, this is my swan song. I had another six or seven good years in me as a dancer, but the army's going to put paid to all that.'

'Oh, Preb–'

'It's all right, I've come to terms with it. Ballet isn't an essential occupation, like doctoring or driving a train. So I'm going, and my feet are going to get ruined by army boots and my muscles are going to be pulled the wrong way by basic training... Oh well, there's a war on. But if you think I'm going to let us look bad on what may be the last thing I do in the theatre, you're nuts.'

Thus encouraged, they went through the obligatory little exercises that fill in the last moments before performance. In the pit David Warburton was chatting to the orchestra. The lighting cameraman was clambering about in the grand circle. All at once the director called out, the clapper boy walked flat-footedly on stage and called out the shot with a click of his board, the orchestra began the famous music, the swans tripped about the stage to form clusters of tulle and it was time for the prince to walk on, looking for the swan princess.

Afterwards, when they were accepting the congratulations and applause of the technicians, Linda wished they would all be silent. If she was to hear anything she wanted it to be the applause of a theatre audience, telling her they had done well, conjuring up the pure magic of the ballet. She knew they had danced well. But she wanted lovers of the ballet to tell her so, not a camera crew and a continuity girl.

And then it was all to be done again. The lighting technician wasn't quite pleased with the shadows among the *corps de ballet*. And then again, to record the foot movement. And then, next day, again, to have close-ups when they were doing what the director called 'the difficult bits'.

And then another day in the same

costumes, miming curtsey and bow to the applause, accepting bouquets provided by the props department. And then, one more day, Preb's last day, when he would record the solo for the prince, from Act III, short and vivid and full of the high, disciplined turns in the air for which he was famous.

He too was greeted with applause by the studio crew. But it was to Linda that he looked, and to Leryeva. 'Was it all right?' he asked, almost uncertain. 'Was it worth putting on film?'

'You danced well, my dear boy,' Leryeva said, tears streaming down her face. 'But then you always do.'

'Positively the last appearance of Alexander Prebble,' he sighed. He put an arm round each of the two women. 'Well, it's not a bad last performance – at least people will be able to look it up if they want to. More than other dancers have had.'

There was a party to send him off. Everyone was more bright than they actually felt. Niccolo Bordi arrived with two bottles of champagne, toasts were drunk and prophecies were made about the war ending before ever Preb got into any fighting. The dancer nodded, perhaps thinking he'd have some fights in training camp the moment the other recruits heard he was a dancer.

In the end he slipped off quietly with a

quick kiss on the cheek to Leryeva and Linda. Linda went to the cubicle in the warehouse which had been given to her as a dressing room, there to put her head down on her dressing table and cry her heart out.

She didn't hear the door open. She didn't even know Bordi was there until he took her by the shoulder and tried to raise her.

'What are the tears for?' he asked in amazement. 'Why are you unhappy?'

'Why, for … for Preb,' sobbed Linda.

'There, there.' He took her in his arms, let her cry herself out, then offered her his handkerchief. But she found cotton wool on the dressing table to tidy herself up. Bordi watched her through the mirror. He had an odd expression on his face. 'This man means something to you?' he said. 'After so short a time? I thought the British were supposed to be so cool and reticent.'

'Of course he means something to me! He's the greatest dancer I ever danced with!'

'Yes but… To cry over him?'

'Well, he's going to throw away everything he's worked for. Even if he isn't killed or injured, his career's ended – a year in the army will undo all his training.'

Bordi frowned. 'And it is for this you're crying?'

Linda brushed her hair back from her flushed cheeks. 'For the waste,' she said on

233

a stifled sob. 'I know it can't be helped but … it's such a waste.'

'And the man himself? You don't cry for that?'

'What?' She was puzzled for a moment, then shook her head. 'I don't even know him, in that sense.'

'Ah,' said Bordi. She was surprised at the relief in his voice.

David came in, carrying three glasses of wine on a tray. 'Feeling low?' he inquired. 'I thought you might. I brought you a little sustenance.'

'David, it's awful.'

'I know, love, but at least he's one better than Nijinsky – we've got some of his dancing on film. I know he was pleased about that.'

'We should have got all his great performances! We just don't *care* enough.'

'That's what this film is about, in a way, isn't it? Trying to show people that ballet can belong to everybody… Well, drink up and I'll see you home. You look a wreck.'

Once she was at home in the flat she was sharing with Betty Balcombe, the memory of that little scene with Nicco came back to her. 'Ah,' he'd said in relief.

Nicco had been jealous. Jealous!

At first the thought amazed her so much that her hair brush, jerked into immobility, tangled in her long fair hair. Then she was aware of a little thrill of pleasure. But then she thought: oh, Italian men – they get possessive very quickly. It means nothing.

She wasn't sure whether she was glad or sorry over that conclusion. Glad – of course, she was glad. She didn't want to get involved with Nicco. And yet there was something enticing in the thought that the great Niccolo Bordi might be attracted to her.

Next day the shooting schedule resumed, without Preb. Now the cameras concentrated almost entirely on Linda, either on stage or in preparation for performance. With the *corps de ballet* she danced the mazurka from *Les Sylphides* and, with Gadina's permission, the snow-flake section from *The Willing Prisoner,* which Linda taught as ballet-mistress to the other girls.

As they neared the end of the schedule in the theatre, the script-writer approached Linda. 'Listen, I don't want you to think I don't approve of everything you've been doing, but I can't help thinking it's kind of...'

'Moonlit?' she suggested, remembering her own criticism of the Gadina Company's repertoire.

'Right! I was wondering, couldn't we film you doing something a bit more ... well ... common? A bit more human?'

'Such as what?'

'Dunno. I was thinking – there's a can-can

in the opening music David has arranged.'

'I'm perfectly willing. What does Peter say?' Peter was the director.

'Oh, he's perfectly happy to film whatever we show him. It's just that this film has got to please a wide audience and everything we've put in the can so far is a bit sad.' He nursed his long chin a moment. 'We need something a bit saucy, lots of leg and frilly pants?'

'Why not? It sounds fun.'

'Right, I'll see if I can get back that old Russian bag to work something up–'

'Good gracious,' Linda said, 'you don't need a choreographer to arrange a few steps for a can-can. Let me talk to David and see what he suggests for music, and I'll try to put something bright together for you.'

'You could do that?'

'Don't see why not,' Linda said with a sudden complete confidence.

When she sought David out and told him Joe Verdon's idea, he gave a faint groan. 'Oh, God, not a can-can! It's so corny … I mean I can do it – I can beef up the Offenbach or arrange some Suppé – but what's the point?'

'Joe wants something with a bit more of the common touch–'

'Yes, but why does it have to be a can-can, which was supposed to be danced by laundry girls in the Moulin Rouge in eighteen-fifty? Why can't we have something

236

a bit more to do with Britain?'

'Because – I don't know – what, for instance? We don't have much in the way of native dance. "Knees Up Mother Brown" and "The Lambeth Walk"... Other than that, the "Jolly Miller" and Morris dance.'

'There's music hall,' David suggested. 'We have some marvellous old tunes. The "Old Bull and Bush"...'

'"Daddy Wouldn't Buy me a Bow-Wow"...'

'"My Old Dutch"... No, that's rather sad. What else is bright and funny?' David asked.

'That one about following the van... "My Old Man Said, Follow the Van"...'

'That's it! Suppose we imagine a fictional ballet – we're not going to have it all, just a bit for you to dance. Based on the music hall–'

'We'll call it that – *Music Hall*–'

'Then on you come...'

'Calf-length frilly skirt, button boots, wide-brimmed hat... Carrying a birdcage–'

'Good, that's it... And the orchestra's been playing something like a military march ... which dies off into...'

'My old man said, Follow the van,' Linda sang, and began to develop the steps. *Sissone*, very slow, lots of flounce... Set down the birdcage... '*Dilli*ed, and *dall*ied...' High kick over the birdcage – oh yes, frilly knickers to show off...

The minute Joe Verdon heard about it, he was sold on it. David sat straight down to work on the music. Linda went into the studio's dance-practice area and began to work. In half an hour she had the steps for the first chorus of the song. She ran to David. 'What do we do after we've danced out the main theme? It gets a bit dull if we just do it again.'

'Listen to this.' He played the last four bars of 'Follow the Van' and ran it straight into a trilling version of 'Only a Bird in a Gilded Cage'. 'That's her canary singing to her, the one in the cage. Can you use that?'

'Oh yes, gorgeous! She can do a sentimental waltz to it – just let me try it.' She ran up the steps to the stage from the orchestra pit and began to dance. She imagined a birdcage in her arms, like a partner, and looped about the stage as if in raptures, her feet taking her into the air in little twinkling movements of elation.

It look longer to get costumes and write band parts than to devise the dance. Meanwhile Linda worked on it, simplifying and improving it. Everything had gone so easily that she was sure it would be a flop in performance, but the only problem turned out to be the camera crew bursting into song when the well-known tunes surged forth in the street-band arrangement provided by David.

'That thing's got personality,' David told her. He was more impressed than his tone implied. When he thought back over her career with Gadina, he realised that *Sketches by Boz* had been Linda's idea, that most of the dances had been from her suggestions because Gadina knew nothing about Dickens, that the snow-flake in *Prisoner* had owed much to Linda's opinions and guidance. Perhaps, somewhere inside that quiet girl, there was a choreographer waiting to get out.

The director declared himself satisfied with the dance sequences and turned his attention to reaction shots of audiences, continuity sequences showing the company supposedly travelling. Now Linda had to do some acting, even speak some written dialogue. She dreaded it, yet it came easily in the end.

Peter Hawker, the director, was pleased with her. 'She's no trouble,' he confided to David. 'I thought ballerinas were supposed to be temperamental?'

'Not this one. Linda's one of those who is never going to stop learning. It's what makes her interesting.'

Bordi appeared for an end-of-film party. They drank beer, ate sandwiches filled with unidentifiable paté, and exchanged little presents. Linda was taken aback by the present-giving – warned on the morning of the day, she didn't have enough money with her, nor would have had even if she had known. But everyone was glad to accept signed photographs. It made her feel odd: she'd never thought of herself as a 'celebrity'. And there was a sense of something ending as she shook hands with the crew she'd come to know so well. Even David wouldn't be around: he was going to closet himself with the edited film and write incidental music.

Bordi took her to lunch at the Ritz next day. It was faintly comic to think that the meal they ate could not cost more than five shillings, by law – yet that the wine he chose cost more than her week's salary as a film actress.

'What are your plans now?' he asked as they sat looking out over the June greenery of Green Park.

'Oh, work, as usual. I've been lucky enough to get a place in Guancini's class – he says I need to concentrate on increasing strength–' She broke off. 'You don't want to hear all that.'

'So ... you are going back to class, I understand that. But what of your career, Linda?'

'I've kept in touch with Madame Gadina. She says she hopes to take a company on tour again in September. Mary's father is putting up more money so they don't have to bother too much about getting a grant.'

'You would go back to that?'

She met his surprised gaze. 'I don't know why you say that. It's the only company I know, after all.'

'But you're somebody now, my dear–'

'So you say. So they implied yesterday when we broke up the film crew. But all I've done is dance in a half-hour film for MOI, and that hasn't even come out yet.'

He beckoned the waiter to remove the hors d'oeuvres. When he had left them Bordi said, 'Colbert is interested in you.'

It was Linda's turn to be surprised. 'But he doesn't even know me!'

'I showed him the rushes of your dance sequences. He was very impressed.'

Colbert? Impressed? Pierre Colbert was one of the legends of the dance world. Trained at the Academie de la Danse in Paris he had started off as a fine classical soloist. But soon he'd become an *enfant terrible,* persuading the management of the Opera to let him put on modern ballet that scared the audiences. He took Greek legends and stood them on their heads, made ballets about modern politics, dressed his dancers in next to nothing and used gestures and mime that shocked the conservative.

When the Nazis invaded his country, Colbert had kept out of their way by travelling south until at last he was able to slip through the Spanish border. In Spain he had put together a ballet company but the government of General Franco were unhappy with him. He was asked to leave. By a long and difficult route he at last arrived in Britain where, because of war shortages, he had been unable to get a new company together.

'He did the dances for my *Fledermaus*,' Bordi explained to Linda. 'He thought it was *kitsch* but he needed the money. Now he's talked me into financing a company which will go international when the war is over – I'm collecting the backing now.'

Linda waited, unspeaking.

'So what do you say?' Bordi demanded.

'Are you telling me I could join a company directed by Pierre Colbert?'

'What did you think I was telling you?'

She was silent again.

'What's the matter? I thought you would be pleased, *piccina*.'

'I am … I really am… It's just too much to take in. Colbert really wants me in his company?'

'He wants to see you, to talk about it. You understand he has his own ideas about the ballet–'

'Oh, of course! And I'm not against them, only…'

'What?'

She'd been thinking how shocked Alan would be at some of the ideas portrayed in Colbert ballets. 'He's a bit ... outrageous at times.'

'We have made an agreement, he and I. He will not do anything to offend public decency in this country because I have explained to him about the Lord Chamberlain's office and the danger of being closed down. If it is that, Linda *mia,* don't worry. He will be basing the repertoire on some of the classics – *Swan Lake, Sleeping Beauty, Giselle–*'

'*Giselle?*'

'Ah, that pleases you? Yes, some time next year, when he has a *corps* that he is familiar with and soloists he likes, we plan to put on *Giselle* – new costumes, new scenery, bringing back some lost variations. But first he must collect dancers he can work with. He asked me to invite you for an audition some time next week.'

'I'd love that. Where and when?'

'Here is his telephone number. Ring him later, make the arrangement. You are pleased, my dear?'

'I'm dazed, that's the truth, Nicco. I never expected anyone like Colbert to be interested in me. It's a chance to learn, to extend myself... Thank you, Nicco. I don't know how to tell you what this means to me...'

'Good, good,' he said gently, taking her

243

hand. When she was happy, she became beautiful as she did when dancing. She was different from any other girl he had ever met – shy, fair, young, quiet – totally unlike the women of his homeland. But his homeland was far away, losing reality after ten years in London. His life was here now – and he had begun to want Linda to play a part in it.

Pierre Colbert sounded short-tempered when she rang him. 'Who? Olliver? Oh, yes, the little film dancer. Yes, it would be interesting to see you in person.'

'Mr Bordi said you wanted to audition?'

'Ho! I know you can dance. I have seen your filming. What I want to know is, have you any intelligence?'

What I want to know is, have you any manners, thought Linda. 'Would you like me to come to see you?'

'We meet at Guancini's – he tells me you are taking lessons with him.'

'Yes, Mr Colbert. Every morning at ten.'

'I see you there tomorrow.'

'Yes, Mr Colbert.'

When she had put back the receiver, she blew out her breath in a gust of annoyance. Why did she spend so much of her time saying 'Yes, sir' and 'No, sir'? Perhaps she should develop the kind of temperament the film director had expected to find in a ballerina. But all that kind of thing was such a waste of time.

One thing was certain. She wasn't going to let this semi-Marxist Frenchman push her about. With the great old teachers it was different: they had years of hard experience behind them and had earned the respect of their students. But fiery political maestros were quite a different proposition: Colbert was still young, in his mid-thirties, and what he was famous for, mostly, was causing uproar in the theatre.

By the time she went to Guancini's class next morning she had talked herself into a mood of pugnacity towards Colbert. So it was a considerable surprise to find herself melting the moment he shook hands and smiled.

'Ah, Mademoiselle Olliver! I believe I was not polite to you yesterday when you telephoned. Forgive me, I had just burned my hand trying to heat that dreadful powdered milk which scorches the bottom of the saucepan.'

'It's quite all right,' Linda said, throwing away her resolve to be cool with him. 'You do your own cooking, then?'

'Oh, life in the bedsit! It is full of *catastrophes* for anyone like me. I fuse the lamp, I run out of *monnaie* for the meter, I pull the blind cord and the blind fall down!'

Linda laughed. She recognised it all.

'Now you will permit that I watch your

lesson? Then perhaps you will let me take you to have coffee – not that the abomination they drink here is coffee. But let us dare.'

Guancini's other students had arrived: a principal from the Vic-Wells, the star of a West End musical comedy, and two young girls whose parents could pay for expert advanced guidance. The class began.

Throughout the next hour Linda was too busy to think about Colbert. So when she eventually joined him and he took her holdall from her, she was pleased afresh at his manner. He was a not very tall man, with the dark sharp looks of his Provençal forebears. But he had charm by the cart-load.

They went to a Lyons in Marylebone Road. Colbert screwed up his face at the first taste of the coffee but munched his currant bun with enthusiasm. 'In France we don't have these,' he explained. 'I like them very much.'

'They were much better before the war – lots of currants.'

'Ah, always people say, "Things were much better before the war." But I don't agree, you see, mademoiselle. I looked around and I saw much that was bad. If the world had been so good, it would not have fallen into the hands of fascism.'

'I don't know anything about politics.'

Linda changed the subject quickly. 'Bordi told me you were going to do the classics – particularly *Giselle*.'

'Ah. And you want to be with a company that does *Giselle*. No doubt you see yourself as the great new *Giselle*.'

Her utter astonishment at the words made him raise his eyebrows. 'You do not see yourself as *Giselle?*'

'Not for the next year or so, if at all,' she said, pausing to think. She had never until this moment imagined dancing the greatest role in ballet and now that she did, she knew she wasn't ready for it. If she ever would be, there was much to learn first, and much to experience – because *Giselle* called for depth of character as well as dancing.

'If I made a ballet about politics – about what men do to each other in the name of patriotism – would you refuse a part?' he inquired.

'If I thought it was a bad ballet, yes.'

'I don't make bad ballets.'

She laughed. They both knew he had some momentous failures in his past. 'So long as you stick to *Swan Lake, Sleeping Beauty* and *Giselle*, I'll have no quarrel with you,' she said. 'As to the rest, let's just see how it goes, shall we?'

'Who is interviewing whom?' he remarked. 'It is I who should make the conditions.'

'Very well. What are the conditions?'

'We start work next week – afternoon rehearsals. Later, when we are in our theatre, we shall have class in the mornings. You will be engaged as a soloist – I see you as Odette, alternating with Lascelles, and I think I would give you Bluebird to dance, perhaps also one of the leading roles in my *Paragon.* Then I am doing a new ballet – about how the gods send a message to earth with the god Mercury and he gives it to the wrong people – this is what you call an allegory, no? I thought when I saw your filmed dancing – she would be good as Mercury.'

It was about six times as much as she had expected. She'd thought he saw her as a leading member of the corps with occasional solo opportunities. It dawned on her that she was being offered almost top-billing with the new company.

Her silence perplexed him. 'Isn't it enough?' he said in irritation. 'I'm not going to offer you Princess Aurora or Sugar Plum – you are not really suited to those although one day you may dance Aurora.'

'I don't know the whole of *Swan Lake,*' she blurted out. 'You do understand that? I only learnt the *pas de deux* from Leryeva, for the film.'

'Ah, I see.' He covered her hand with his. 'You are scared? Don't be. You will see – you will do well.'

Thus comforted, she nodded agreement. He paid the bill and led her out. 'Come and talk to Nicco. There is all this nonsense of contracts and so on. Nicco will be pleased. I almost think he would have withdrawn his backing if I had not engaged you.'

For a moment the words chilled her. Favouritism... But then common sense prevailed. No one as shrewd as Niccolo Bordi would risk money just to get a job for a girl he liked.

Soon she was in the midst of the familiar scenes – ballet class under Colbert himself every morning, long and difficult rehearsals every afternoon. The company was quite different from Gadina's, however: apart from strict discipline in the dance, there was no effort to rule the private lives of the dancers. Romantic involvements were common, intrigue tended to blossom, and there was strain, certainly, between the pro-Communist Colbert and the Russian members of the company – who were mostly the offspring of White Russian émigrés.

Sometimes Linda thought Colbert regretted that he hadn't joined the Free French fighting units. He was more fiercely joyous over the Allied landing in Sicily than even Niccolo Bordi. Bordi said sombrely, 'There will be great bloodsheds. We Italians take revenge – and there are many old scores to settle.' Colbert said, 'Let them be settled, then! To clear the way for a better world!'

Linda took no part in the arguments. She was too busy learning eight new ballets.

The premiere of *Count Every Step* was given in September, in a programme at the Leicester Square Cinema with a feature film staring Stewart Granger and Wilfred Lawson – 'Which can't be bad,' as Bordi shrewdly remarked. The members of the production team reassembled to attend the film and have a celebration. To their surprise, the little supporting film was greeted with actual applause by the audience in the cinema.

'Darleeng,' Leryeva said, embracing Linda, 'you showed up very well. I liked particularly the *petits battements* against the left leg in the *pas de deux*–'

'*Petits battements!*' Betty Balcombe cried, waving her arms in the air in excitement. 'My God, our little Linda can actually be a Swan Queen!'

'Well, Linda dear,' her mother remarked, flustered and pleased to be invited to the premiere with her husband, 'I thought the bits where you danced in those nice costumes were lovely, but I don't think you should have let them take pictures of you in those terrible long thick socks and grubby cardigans.'

David couldn't be at the premiere. He was off with Gadina again, opening with *The Sleepwalker* in Carlisle. He sent a telegram next day when he had read the reviews: 'Incidental music ignored, dancing praised, seems you have made hit, don't forget poor starving musician.'

Linda cut out the reviews and, after some hesitation, sent them with her next letter to Alan, just in case he didn't see the daily papers off in his wild remote camp. She received no reply but there was nothing unusual in that: his letters had become quite infrequent, due to events he could never explain to her when at last he wrote.

Air raids on London were becoming more common again. It was tit-for-tat now – huge raids mounted by the Allied air forces on German targets, reprisals taken by Germany. Every night when the weather was suitable, air armadas of United States and British bombers set off from the airfields of East Anglia, Northumberland, and Kent. Reports next day of a thousand planes in action were not uncommon. The Ruhr, Dortmund, Bremen, even as far east as Dresden – the Allied bombers would reach out in horrific numbers to batter the enemy into submission. Some said that the air marshals wanted air power to win the war, rather than the infantry on the ground. It was a matter of prestige, some muttered.

The Luftwaffe, desperate to obey Goering's orders to wreak vengeance, sent over as many planes as they could muster. There seemed to be no more pretence of respecting civilian populations or ancient cities. Great buildings toppled, museums, cathedrals – on both sides they were demolished by fire and explosion. The people in or near them were destroyed. Total war, it was called.

The first night of the Colbert Ballet was almost ruined by an air raid warning at the beginning of the third section of the programme but though the theatre manager invited anyone who wished it to take shelter, hardly anyone moved. The last ballet, *Aurora's Wedding*, began to the surge of the fine orchestra Bordi had provided. Outside thumps and crumps could be heard. Still the audience didn't budge. Linda was halfway through the solo variation of the Bluebird when an enormous explosion shook the building.

For a moment the lights dimmed and faltered. Then they came on again. A great sigh of relief went up from the auditorium. Linda, just coming down from an *attitude*, held the pose longer than required. The orchestra, momentarily startled out of concentration, looked at the conductor, whose baton swept on. Linda's foot came down, her hands and arms flicked in the ending of her position, she was off and away on little winged feet. The audience sat back, watching her.

Whistles and fire-bells were ringing outside in the street. A film of dust drifted into the theatre, settling visibly through the beams of the limelights. Linda ended her variation and poised for congratulation. The audience applauded. She curtseyed, gave a little cough as the dust got into her throat, waved the dust away from in front of her face with an impatient hand, and was greeted with a cheer of appreciation.

From that moment she was the darling of the ballet-goers who followed the Colbert Company.

'*Eh bien,*' said Colbert, 'you have endeared yourself. This is good. Because when I do my ballet of Mercury and the Gods, I want them to laugh at you but to sympathise too. This Mercury, you see, is eager to do his duty but everything he does is wrong.'

They began to work on the choreography. The music was a score by Darius Milhaud, very spare and witty. The steps were complex, sometimes acrobatic and sometimes pure classical Russian. Linda often had her doubts about how they would work.

'This isn't danceable,' she protested one afternoon as they toiled with a scene in which Mercury had been driven out by an angry King.

'*Comment?* You have the rheumatism? Or the brain is too tiny to understand them?' Colbert flared.

She drew back, but smiled. 'Mercury's costume is going to have little boots with wings on the heels, yes?'

'Of course. And a winged helmet.'

'Well, let me tell you, Pierre, you can't do *entrechat-six* with wings on your heels.'

He had been facing her in annoyance. Now he turned away and began to pace the rehearsal room. Then he stopped, threw back his head, and began to laugh. '*C'est vrai!*' he guffawed. '*Tu as raison!* How could I have made such a foolish mistake?'

'It's because you work it out intellectually, Pierre,' she suggested. 'You don't feel it in your muscles as a dancer would, your brain is working but not your body.' Nor your heart, she might almost have added, but refrained. She didn't like the works of Colbert that she had so far learned. She thought them clever but sterile, not destined to live in the repertoire.

Colbert cancelled all the work on the scene so far. They resumed, but he seemed preoccupied. That night, after curtain call in the theatre, he surprised her by coming to her dressing room with some sheets of paper.

'*Chérie,*' he said, 'these are my notes for *Messager des Dieux*. Look at them for me, *hein?* What you said this morning... That

254

struck me with force. Perhaps I think too much and feel too little. Look at my notes and see if you think my plan is too much of the head, not enough of the body.'

She was reluctant to accept the task, but he insisted. 'Who else can I turn to? Bordi is clever, but he is not a man of the dance, he is a man of the theatre, of the spectacle. If I give it to Susanne Lascelles, she will pout and say the part of the nymph is too short for her. I must give her more to do. But you, I believe, I can trust.'

She took the sheaf of notes. They were untidy, written in French interspersed with little sketches. 'Of course I'll read them. But I don't know if...'

'Read, only read! You will have opinions, I know, and will be honest.'

She read them that night on the way home on the Tube. They were difficult to follow, and she was tired. Next morning she re-read them over breakfast, while Betty scrambled eggs and made toast. 'What you got there?' Betty asked. 'Love letters?'

'No, Pierre's working notes for the Mercury ballet.'

'What? Wonder Boy's trusted you with his precious baby? I *say*, Lin! He must think a lot of you!'

'He ... well, I think he tries to see everybody as an equal. He's a Communist, you know.'

'An equal, oh yeah? Who tells everybody else what to do? Who gets cross when other people don't behave? From all I hear, he's as much a tyrant as Gadina, only in a different way.' She took her place opposite Linda, munched toast for a moment, then said with some seriousness: 'You be careful, Lin. He may be asking you for your opinion or help, but you can bet he doesn't want criticism.'

'Oh, but he said—'

'Never mind what he said. You be careful what you tell him. He's not a man to have for an enemy, I should think.'

There was no opportunity for discussion that day. That evening she was putting on her Swan Queen costume when the stage doorkeeper put his head in the door.

'Miss Olliver, a phone call for you.'

She knew it must be important. Calls were not accepted for any of the cast while the performance was going on – unless urgent.

She ran to the doorkeeper's office. It was her mother on the line, in Hedfield.

'Linda… Oh, Linda, darling, there's a telegram here for you!'

Alan had named Linda as next of kin, but had always taken it for granted that she would come to her senses about ballet, settle down at home, and behave like a normal human being. So her address, as far as his records were concerned, was with her parents in Hedfield.

She felt a deathly chill seize her. 'Open it, Mummy.'

'Oh, darling … I don't want to… Wait a minute.' There came the faint rustle of paper. '"Regret to inform you–" Oh, Linda! Oh, my dear – it's Alan – oh, Linda, my poor baby…'

'Mummy, what does it say?'

'He's dead, dear. Oh, Lin, how awful! Lin? Linda?'

Linda had put down the old-fashioned earpiece of the doorkeeper's phone. He, wise old man, brought a chair to her and made her sit. Into the phone he said, 'Hang on a sec. Miss Olliver's not feeling too good.'

'Linda?' quacked the phone. 'Linny, dear?'

'Here, miss, drink this,' said the door-keeper, offering a glass of water.

She pushed it away so violently the water splashed all over her bare arm. She snatched up the receiver. 'Mummy, it's a mistake!'

She heard her mother sob. 'No, dear. It's an official telegram.'

'I don't believe it. He can't be dead.'

'Oh, darling, it's true, it's true. Oh, Lin dear, why aren't you here with me so I can comfort you?'

Linda stared at the phone. Then she hung up the receiver. She got up out of the cane chair in which the doorkeeper had set her.

'I must get back…'

'Just sit down again, miss. I'll get Mr Colbert.'

'No, I...' She walked blindly past him, brushing past other dancers making their way to the wings. In her dressing room she closed the door and stood leaning against it. Her dresser had the Swan Queen headdress in her hands, and advanced anxiously. 'Miss Olliver, five minutes to curtain–'

Linda shook her head. She walked to her dressing table and sat down. Puzzled, the dresser hovered near her, holding the feathered headband over her head. Linda bent her head suddenly and hid her face among the clutter on the dressing table.

'Oh, dear,' whispered the dresser. 'Bad news?'

No reply. Panic-stricken, Mrs Burton ran out. She met Colbert hurrying towards her already, summoned by the doorman. He was in his costume as Rotbart, the villain of *Swan Lake*.

'What's the matter?'

'She's in a state of collapse. She had a phone call.'

'Oh, *diable!* There is a husband in the army, no?'

'Yes, and I think...'

He pushed past her, went in. *'Ma chérie,'* he said gently, leaning over Linda.

She didn't look up.

'Linda, what has happened?'

Still no response.

'Come, Linda, you must tell me. Is it the war? Your husband?'

'He's dead,' she said, her voice muffled against the surface of the table.

'Ah, *ma pauvre petite ami...*' He knelt at her side, but turned to say over his shoulder to Mrs Burton, 'Tell them to hold the curtain.'

'Hold it?' Linda said, looking up.

'We will delay ten minutes. Madame Burton, fetch some brandy–'

Linda pushed herself to her feet. She put one hand behind her back. 'Burton, unzip me,' she said in a flat voice.

'*Comment?*' cried Colbert. 'You are not taking off the costume–'

'Of course I am. Mrs Burton, help me–'

'But, *chére amie,* you must dance! The audience is waiting! You cannot let them down.'

She stared at him, as if he were speaking some foreign tongue.

'Come now, put on the headdress, go on the stage, dance! This is best – to fight back against grief–'

Linda shook her head. 'I'm not going to dance.'

'But you must! There is no understudy here–'

'Do you think I care?' she said, in a sudden flare of anger. But it died. She moved away towards her dresser who obediently began to unfasten the back of the white satin bodice.

'Linda, you cannot do this! You danced through an air raid – you can dance through this–'

'No.' She shook her head. 'My husband's dead. Why are strangers more important to me than my husband?'

'But it is the tradition, Linda–'

'Then it's inhuman. Go away, Pierre, let me get dressed and go home.'

'Linda!' He took her by the shoulders and shook her. 'You can't let me down like this! You must get a hold of yourself!'

She let him shake her about like a rag doll. When, in dawning shame, he stopped, she gave him a bitter smile.

'Is this the way to treat a war widow?' she said.

He went red. Then, shaking his head and looking stricken, he hurried out. He put a message over the Tannoy to the dancers that they would be making an alteration to the programme and sent the house manager in front of the curtain to say that, because of a sudden indisposition, Miss Olliver could not appear. As there was no replacement at such short notice, they would repeat *Les Cerfs*. He begged the audience's indulgence and was rewarded by seeing at least half of them remain in their seats. But those who had come specifically to see Linda Olliver got up in disgruntlement and went home.

Mrs Burton took Linda home in a taxi, and stayed until Betty got back from her theatre. 'Miss Balcombe, dear, her husband's been reported dead and she's gone to pieces. Can you get her to bed? I'd call a doctor but I think she'll get over it if she can get some sleep.'

'Oh, my God,' Betty breathed. She threw herself out of her coat and winter boots, ran into the bedroom. Linda was sitting on the side of her bed with the make-up for the Swan Princess still on her face.

'Darling, how awful.' Betty put her strong arms round her, pulled her face against her shoulder regardless of the greasy make-up against her precious woollen dress. 'Linda, I know what this means to you. I'm so, so sorry.'

Linda made no reply. Betty couldn't tell whether she had even heard.

By degrees she got the make-up cleaned off the white face, put her into a nightdress, got her into bed. She made her drink brandy and hot milk. The phone began to ring. She told first Colbert then Bordi that Linda seemed numb but steady, was in bed and asleep.

But Linda was not asleep. Nor did she close her eyes all night.

Next morning she was up before Betty, as

usual. She was drinking weak tea at the kitchen table when Betty came to join her. 'How are you, love? All right?'

'Yes, thank you, I'm all right.'

'What are you going to do?'

'Go to the theatre, of course.'

'Oh, darling, do you think you should?'

'Oh yes, why not?'

Baffled, Betty watched her put on her coat and hat and fetch her holdall with her practice clothes. But once Linda had gone out, she didn't hurry to the Tube as usual to make her way to the Regent Theatre. Instead she walked with her head bent towards Holland Park. She found herself there at nine o'clock, sitting on a frosty bench when she should have been in practice tunic.

She took a taxi but was late getting into the theatre. Colbert was on stage. The class was standing about looking anxious. As she walked into the wings Colbert gestured her forward.

'Linda, the whole company wants to express its sympathy–'

'Yes, thank you.'

'You have come to class? It is best. Life must go on.'

'So you said last night,' she replied dully. 'You make it sound so easy.'

'Of course it is not easy. But what, after all, is existence? It is struggle. And for us in ballet, it is struggle for perfection – no, not even that, it is struggle not to lose what we already have.'

The assembled dancers drew in their breath at the words. Who was he, to speak to her of 'loss'? But he went on, self-engrossed as always, unaware of his tactlessness. 'You must not cause us to lose anything, even though you have suffered a great blow. And you must approach life now using all your assets – which include intelligence. Intelligence should tell you we will not please the public if we cancel a performance without warning.'

'There are things more important.'

'Certainly, no one denies that,' Colbert agreed, humouring her. But he intended to get his message across. 'Discipline, however, is also important. And force of character.' He broke off to sweep a glance round his company. 'And incidentally, I forbid any phone calls from now on while the performance is going on. Last night would never have occurred–'

'But it would!' Linda cried, her voice rising and soaring in the empty theatre. 'Alan would have been dead just the same – even if you'd kept the news from me until I'd danced! Dead – do you understand? My husband's dead!'

'Linda–'

'Oh, you'll never understand! Your heart is

made of clockwork!'

'Miss Olliver–' began the stage manager, attempting to take her arm.

She shook him off. 'Don't treat me like an invalid! I know what I'm saying! We work and slave to please the audience, but what are we doing? Creating a world of make-believe, and making it so important we sacrifice real life to it! Alan knew that – he knew all this was illusion – but I wouldn't listen. I thought he was wrong–'

'Miss Olliver, please–'

'For years – half my life – I've thought of nothing else but dancing. And what for? To end up in a company where I'm expected to set aside my husband's death and go on stage as if nothing had happened! And he doesn't even see it's wrong, cold, inhuman!' She pointed a trembling finger at Colbert. 'You're a failure, Pierre. You'll never make a really good ballet because you don't really care about people.'

'Linda, you are hysterical–'

She had burrowed in her holdall and now her hand came out holding the pages of notes for *Messager des Dieux*. She held them out for all to see. Their stricken faces were turned towards her like masks.

'Here's the proof,' she proclaimed. 'The new ballet – the great new ballet! It's about nothing, about humanity's ineptitude, it's full of contempt and patronising amusement!

We're all expected to dance the steps and convey the message, but all it says is, the world is a bore...' She tore the notes into two, into four, and threw them in the air. 'That's all it is – rubbish, rubbish!'

Colbert darted forward to catch the fluttering scraps. 'How dare you!' he shouted. 'After this, let me tell you, you are finished, do you understand? In ballet, you are finished.'

She stared at him, almost as if his words had suddenly struck home. Then she picked up her holdall. 'So much the better,' she said and walked off the stage.

CHAPTER NINE

Betty ran to the door at the sound of Linda's key in the lock. 'Darling, where have you been? We've been so worried!'

'We?'

'Your mother's here–' Betty was appalled at the spasm of distress that cut across her friend's face at the words. Linda turned to retreat, but Betty caught her by the arm. 'Bordi's here too – he's been waiting for almost two hours. Darling, he went to the theatre in search of you, heard what had happened, and came on here. Where have you been?'

'I don't know. The park. Somewhere.' Linda was still trying to extricate herself from Betty's grasp.

'Come on, you can't go wandering off again, Lin. You look whacked.'

Unable to get free, Linda was drawn into the living room. Linda's mother was on her feet already, and rushed to gather her into her arms. 'Oh, my poor baby! How ill you look! Oh, Linda dear, I know how your heart is aching!'

'Don't,' muttered Linda, drawing away, 'don't.'

Betty exchanged a glance with Bordi, who made a fierce grimace of disapproval at the mother's antics. Betty said: 'Have you had lunch, Lin?'

'Lunch? I ... no ... I don't remember.'

'You didn't have any breakfast either. I'll make you a sandwich.'

'No, thanks.'

'But Lin, darling, you must eat–'

'Why must I?' Linda flashed, dragging herself away from her mother's embrace. 'Why can't you just leave me alone?'

'Linda, that's no way to talk–'

'Mrs Thackerley, I believe Linda has a right to privacy. Perhaps we should all go away and let her–'

'I'm her mother! I know what's best for my own daughter! I've come to take you home, Linda dear–'

'No–'

'You need to be looked after. You need to be with people who knew Alan.'

'She perhaps needs a short rest,' Bordi agreed, with a helpless shrug. 'But work is the best cure–'

'I've no work now,' Linda said. 'Colbert fired me.'

'Oh, Colbert! That *insensato!* I heard about all that. I will handle Colbert, Linda. He will take you back.'

She shook her head. 'We could never work together now, not after what I said to him.

And anyway, I don't want to. Alan never wanted me to be a dancer. I see now that I should have heeded him–'

'How do you come to that conclusion?' Betty burst out. 'Alan knew nothing about ballet–'

'He knew what he wanted our life to be. I disregarded him. If I had listened to him, travelled to places where I could be near him, we could have been together more. But no, I went off to follow my own–'

'Linda, why are you blaming yourself? You did better than I did – you disobeyed Gadina for Alan's sake. Alan would have come to understand–'

'No, never. I would have had to give up my dancing. And I should have done it straight away, the moment he wanted me to.'

Linda let her mother guide her to a chair. Mrs Thackerley bent over her protectively. 'You're to come home with me, dear. Back home where you belong, where everybody knows you and knew Alan. Betty, would you put some of her things together?'

'This is a mistake,' Bordi objected. 'She is better here, with her friends of the ballet.'

'Well, I happen to disagree with you, Mr Bordi, and as I'm her mother I think I have a better claim than you.' Like a little ruffled hen, Mrs Thackerley faced the great man.

'All right, Mummy,' Linda said, staring at the floor. 'I'll come home.'

'Linda!' cried Niccolo Bordi.

She didn't look up but she spoke to him. 'It was all a mistake, Nicco,' she said. 'It took a thing like this to show me how wrong I've been.'

Betty raised her eyes to heaven but went to the bedroom to pack a bag. Bordi followed. 'That mother will stifle her!' he hissed.

'What can you do? Leave it a bit. After a week at home Linda will be bored out of her mind, I should think. She'll be back.'

'You are so sure?'

'Listen, Mr Bordi, I saw that kid when she got her first chance a year ago. No one who's had to struggle so hard is going to give up so easily.'

But it appeared she was wrong, for Linda went back to Hedfield and as day followed day, Betty heard nothing.

David Warburton got the news when at last Betty tracked him down by phone in Paisley. 'When was this, Betty?' he asked, horrified.

'Eight days ago. I've written, but had no reply. I telephoned, but the phone seems to be on her dad's business premises and she won't come to it.'

'Oh, God,' groaned David. 'Leave it with me for a bit, Betty. I'll try.'

He rang the number in Hedfield. Mr Thackerley answered. Recognising David's name, and remembering him vaguely from the film premiere, he spoke warmly. 'Thank you for ringing. I'll tell Linda you send your sympathy,' he said.

'But Mr Thackerley, I'd like to speak to her, if you don't mind.'

'We-ell,' said Mr Thackerley, 'her mother thinks it's better if she's not bothered.'

'I wouldn't bother her. I just want to speak to her, see how she is.'

'Well,' said Mr Thackerley in the same dubious tone, 'she's not too great, and that's the truth. My wife says it's just bereavement taking its toll and she'll come out of it, but she's not too great, and that's the fact.'

'Please ask her to come to the phone, Mr Thackerley. Surely she'd want to speak to me?'

'Righto.' There was a long interval, during which David could hear hammering on metal and a hissing sound of compressed air in the garage. Then Mrs Thackerley spoke. 'Mr Warburton? This is Lin's mother. Really, I think it's better if you don't speak to my little girl. She's really not up to it.'

'But Mrs Thackerley! – Linda and I are good friends!'

'She's left all that behind her. It would only upset her. Besides, she really isn't speaking to anybody for the present. It's only natural.'

'You mean she's been shrinking inside herself like this ever since she got the news?

Surely by now she ought to be getting back to normal?'

'You don't know about such things, Mr Warburton,' Nancy Thackerley said stiffly. 'It takes another woman to understand how my little girl is feeling.'

'I see. So I can't speak to her?'

'Better not, I think.'

'Very well. Give her my love.' When he had replaced the receiver David hurried through the dingy little theatre to find Olga Gadina inspecting theatre bills for their next stop in Renfrew. 'Forgive me for interrupting, Madame, but this is very important.'

'Oh yes? Not more trouble with the orchestra, David?'

'No, it's about Linda Olliver.'

'The little film star. And what of her?'

'Her husband was killed. I want to go and see her, Madame.'

'I forbid it!'

He took both her hands, old and thin. 'Olga Gadina,' he said, 'this is outside your command. I'm going. Please don't let's quarrel over it.'

Her eyes filled with tears. 'Ah you are young, you rush to the one you love – Gadina was young once! I understand! But come back soon, *druhgye moy*. I need you.'

'I will, I promise – as soon as I know Linda's going to be all right.'

He reached Hedfield by ten the next

morning. The town boasted few hotels, and most of those were full with directed labour, but he was lucky to get a room at a commercial hotel. He washed, shaved and changed, had a mid-morning snack of *ersatz* coffee and sausage rolls filled with pink paperhanger's paste, then set off in a taxi for Linda's home.

It lay up a cul de sac beyond the garage which gave Mr Thackerley his living. He rang the bell set in the grained-oak door. Nancy Thackerley opened it to him clad in apron and dustcap.

'Oh!' she exclaimed, her hands flying to her unbecoming head gear. 'Oh, Mr Warburton...'

'I hope this isn't too inconvenient, Mrs Thackerley, but after we spoke yesterday I was so worried I felt I just had to come.'

'Oh ... well ... there was no need but of course it's very good of you. Come in, do.' She stood back, waving him beyond a collection of floor-cleaning implements. In the living room, no fire was lit. The hearth contained a carefully arranged fan of red paper. The room was cold and smelt of Mansion Polish. 'Sit down a minute – I'll ... just see if Linda is ... er... Would you like some coffee?'

'No, thanks, I've just had some. How is Linda?'

'Well, she's as well as can be expected,'

said her mother, folding her dustcap and sneaking it into her apron pocket. 'Widowhood, you know... It's a terrible shock.'

'Where is she? Is she in bed?'

'Oh no.' Mrs Thackerley was shocked at the idea of anyone being in bed at eleven o'clock. 'No, she's in our kitchen, where we have the range going, you know. She feels the cold.'

'Then I'll come with you there,' David said, and urged his hostess out of the clammy living room.

Linda was sitting in a wooden armchair close to the old-fashioned kitchen range, within whose polished steel bars a strong red fire glowed. She was holding herself across her middle as if her stomach hurt, and her shoulders were hunched in their childish pale pink cardigan. Her face was turned away from the door. She didn't look round as they came in.

'Well now,' Mrs Thackerley said cheerfully, 'look who's here. David's come to pay you a visit.'

Linda looked up. She frowned. For one dreadful moment he thought she wouldn't recognise him. Then the grey eyes cleared. She smiled. 'Hello, David. What are you doing here?'

'I'm paying you a visit—'

'No, I meant, why on earth have you come to Hedfield?'

Because I was worried, he wanted to say. But already her attention seemed to be waning. 'How are you?' he asked and was ashamed to hear the same false cheerfulness that the mother had used.

'I'm quite well, thanks.'

'I'll just make us all a cup of tea,' said Mrs Thackerley, beginning to bustle about with a fine old iron kettle and the tool for handling the hotplate.

'Oh, no, not more tea!' Then Linda seemed to check herself. 'Unless of course David–'

'No, no, I'm fine. Linda, you look a bit thin. Have you been eating?'

'Not enough to keep a sparrow alive!' her mother put in at once. 'But it's only to be expected, you know.'

'If you don't eat, you won't have energy to dance–'

'Oh, we're not bothering about that – are we, dear?'

'No, Mummy,' Linda agreed.

'But you must bother about it! I remember you once said, there was no one in Hedfield to take class – how will you get back to performance standard if you don't keep up your energy and don't keep in practice?'

'That's all over, David,' Linda said, gazing past him at some scene in her head. 'It's best, really.'

'That's right, dear,' agreed Mrs Thackerley. 'Better to stay here at home with people who knew and loved Alan–'

'But she can't spend the rest of her life like this! Linda, you're a dancer–'

'But Miss Simson will be giving up the dancing school quite soon so Linda can step in there any time she wants–'

'What?' David cried. 'Run a dancing school in Hedfield?'

'It's what Alan would have wanted,' Linda said.

'How on earth do you know it's what Alan would have wanted? Did he ever say so?'

'No, but he always wanted Linda and him settled near his family, you see, David. So really being a teacher would have been the ideal solution.'

'It's the stupidest thing I ever heard–'

Mrs Thackerley bridled. 'Excuse me, David, but you don't understand. Linda wants to do justice to Alan's memory – don't you, dear? And the right way to make good the mistakes she made–'

David leaped out of his chair, took Linda's mother by the arm, and led her out into the passage. 'Are you mad?' he asked in a low, tense voice. 'Why are you implanting the idea that she did some wrong to Alan?'

'Me?' Mrs Thackerley said, genuinely surprised. 'I'm only going along with what my daughter says herself. And I'll thank you to–'

'Can't you see she's in a state of depression? That she's ill?'

'Oh, a bit under the weather and off her food – that's only natural–'

'I mean her mental state, Mrs Thackerley. There's nothing natural about–'

'If you're implying there's anything wrong with my daughter's mind, Mr Warburton, I'll have you know there's nothing like that in our family! Linda is as sane as you or I.'

'Sane. Of course she's sane! What are you talking about? I'm saying she's in a state of mental depression – and you're making it worse. If you're not careful you'll have her devoting the rest of her life to lighting candles in church for Alan–'

'We're C of E, Mr Warburton, we don't light candles–'

He turned from her and marched into the kitchen. Linda was sitting staring at the glow of the fire. 'Linda!'

She looked up at him. 'Yes?'

'How would you like to come with me for a holiday in the country?'

'Mr Warburton!' gasped Linda's mother, coming in behind him. 'My Linda is a respectable girl–'

'Oh, shut up!' he roared, totally forgetting manners. Then, getting a grip on himself, he knelt beside Linda's chair. 'My people live in a nice old stone house with a big garden, and a stream running through. And there's a wood just beyond, where we could go for long walks. And there are horses and dogs, and with Christmas coming on there'll be log fires and carol singers. Would you like to stay there for a while?'

Mrs Thackerley was about to protest again, but some innate honesty kept her silent. The picture David was painting was much better than anything she could offer – except of course that it would lack that important element, 'a mother's love'.

Linda looked at her. 'What do you think, Mummy?'

'It's up to you, Lin, dear. It does sound nice.'

She hesitated. 'Would your parents have room for me?'

'Oh, lord, yes – boffins have taken over half the house but there's still plenty of it, my love. Go on, run upstairs and pack some warm clothes.'

'I'll do it,' said Mrs Thackerley with a suppressed sigh. 'She'll only forget her gloves or something–'

'No, Mrs Thackerley, let Linda do it. Go on, off you go.' He made shooing motions at Linda, who got up stiffly, her arms still about herself, and went out. When he heard her footsteps on the stairs he turned to her mother. 'I'm sorry I got angry with you. I don't think you realise what a change there is in her. A few weeks in the fresh air and quiet surroundings may be all she needs.'

Mrs Thackerley smiled weakly. 'I can't argue with you. You've got so much to offer it would be unfair to stop her going. But I hope you do understand that all that business about a career in ballet is over.'

David shook his head. 'No it isn't,' he said. 'I know it isn't.'

Linda quite enjoyed the journey in a vague way. At the station an aged car was waiting. The driver, an elderly lady with a woollen scarf twisted round her head as a turban, gave Linda a hard stare.

One of her son's odd dancin' friends. Little shrimp of a gel. Looked half-starved, very pale – if one of her poultry had that look about her, Lady Stroud would have had it dosed with hot bran.

'Well, hello there,' she said. 'Feelin' a bit down, are we? Soon put that to rights. I'm David's Ma, you know.'

'How do you do,' Linda said.

'Come on, boy, don't stand there ditherin'. Get her stuff aboard. The boffins need the car by tea-time for a trip to Gloucester.'

The inside smelt of dogs and old leather. Draughts blew fiercely in at the quarter-lights. When Lady Stroud set it in motion it bucked like a bronco. But it met the potholes in the road and the untrimmed hedges with bravura.

They drove between old gate-posts topped

with a coat of arms. The gravel drive was worn into ruts and full of puddles. They lurched up a fairly steep gradient, over a humped bridge that spanned a gurgling stream, and turned into a straight carriage-way which gave a view of the house. It had four gables of Gloucestershire stone, mullioned windows, the remains of Virginia creeper flickering in the last gleam of daylight, and four great dogs lolloping about in greeting.

'Get down, you fools!' shouted Lady Stroud as she tried to open the door against their great pressing paws. David, laughing, got out from the back and dragged them off. They cavorted around him, barking and attempting to lick him.

'Welcome to Cledely,' he said above the clamour, helping Linda out. 'If you can push a way through the canines, the door is under that porch.'

It was being held open by a thickset man with iron-grey hair. She was led into a hall that had once been magnificent, but was now boarded off with plywood partitions. 'This way,' said Lord Stroud, and headed off down an opening between the plywood barricades.

She realised later that the family lived in what had been the north wing. The rest was taken over by a scientific team working on a hush-hush project to do with communications. The roof of the old house was strung with wires and antennae, and from the boffins' quarters came strange hisses and cracklings of atmospherics which had prompted Lady Stroud to christen that area the Goose Fair.

David's family lived very simply but with an ease and enjoyment that was infectious. There seemed to be no set meal times, except in the evenings when Lady Stroud's former nanny produced what she called 'wholesome victuals' for the main course.

A daily, referred to by Lady Stroud as Lallie, came in to do the fires and make the beds. Lady Stroud tended the livestock – poultry, pigs, and the four dogs which needed much grooming and exercising. Her husband had some kind of civil post to do with air raid precautions, which took him three times a week into Gloucester.

At first Linda was scarcely aware of the household. She went out for a walk her first day, guided by David, and thereafter spent almost every moment out in the country-side. It was a mild wet winter that year, the streams full of chuckling water and the winter grass showing emerald green in the fields.

Wearied soon at first, she would come home to nap in the afternoon. In the evening they would listen to the radio until it was made inaudible by the shutting down of

transmitters at the onset of air raids. Sometimes David would play for them, but Linda
noted that his father and mother often
nodded off to sleep towards the end of the
first movement of a sonata.

After a week, David said he must go back
to the Gadina Company. 'Shall you take me
home en route?' Linda asked.

'No, of course not – you're to stay on here
– unless you'd rather not?'

'Oh, I'd love to stay. It's so lovely here!'

It was the first gleam of enthusiasm since
he had found her in Hedfield. He gave her a
hug. 'You're to stay on as long as you like –
it's no trouble, you can see that for yourself.
I'll get home at weekends when I can.'

The first few days after his departure she
felt odd, at a loose end. But she had learned
her way about the lanes and continued her
walks. Once she stopped in the village
church to listen to the organist practise. On
another occasion she had lunch in the pub
of a neighbouring village. The world seemed
to be opening out a little, but she didn't
quite know if she wanted to venture any
further.

David came home for Christmas, which
was a simple affair. Mrs Newby provided a
splendidly roasted chicken and plum pudding made of carefully-saved ingredients.
Carol singers arrived and were offered
mulled wine. At the morning service Lord

Stroud read the lesson and, at the evening service, David did the same. Linda went to bed that night with a strange feeling, as if David's family had adopted her. Her own parents, far off in Hedfield, seemed shadowy to her. Her mother's insistence on the duty of mourning had less force here.

Next day David suggested he should take her into Gloucester 'to see a flick'. She was startled at the idea. It would be her first visit to a town since she came to this country retreat. 'I ... don't know...'

'Oh, come on, Linda. I'd like to go. Haven't been to the pictures in ages. It's Rosalind Russell and Janet Blair in *My Sister Eileen* – should be fun.'

It seemed churlish to refuse. The whole family packed themselves into the ancient Morris, including Lady Stroud's Nanny. The cinema was a surprisingly modern building, well filled with a jovial audience.

Everyone was in a mood to throw themselves into laughter over the escapades of the madcap heroine. Then came the interval, when community singing was imposed on them – 'There'll Always Be an England' and 'Sally!' When the lights went down again Linda was looking around with pleasure at the enjoyment of the audience.

The credits of the next film came up. 'The Ministry of Information Presents...' Then a pair of feet in ballet slippers executing dainty, precise *pas de bourrée*. Over them the words came up: *Count Every Step*.

Linda seized David's arm. 'Let's go!' she said, half-rising.

'Siddown, lady, you're blocking the view!' hissed a voice from behind.

'Sit down, Linda,' David said. 'It's only a film.'

She sat down again. As if in a dream she watched the girl on the screen – hurrying down alleys to the stage doors, running for a train, practising *ballotés* with Alexander Prebble, learning the fish dive and the supported *arabesque penché,* working her way through the problems of interpretation, learning, striving.

Then the comedy dance, 'Music Hall'. The wide flounced skirt swept out, the feet in their little gaiters kicked and stamped, the audience began to sing: 'My old man said, follow the van...'

But then a silence fell as the ballet company were shown dressing for *Swan Lake*. Linda saw the girl in the feathered headdress leaning forward to check her eye make-up. She saw the wings where the dancers were bending and flexing, thrusting shoes into the rosin box, clenching and unclenching fists in tension-release.

The famous music welled up on the sound track. Alexander Prebble ran on stage as the prince seeking his enchanted princess. The swans ran and huddled. The swan princess came forward.

And then the famous *pas de deux*. Linda closed her eyes. She heard the music, and in her mind she went through the steps. She felt her partner's hands on her waist. She felt the perfect beating of her foot against her leg, like the throbbing heart of a captured bird. She felt the turn, the pressure of her foot as the turn was stopped, the stretch of her limbs, the safety of her partner's shoulder where her head rested.

She only looked again when the dance was over, when the camera followed the dancer as she pulled on her outdoor clothes and ran to catch a bus, her ballet shoes tied to the handle of her holdall. A hard life, the dancer's...

The incidental music swelled to a close as the bus took the dancer away. The film ended. There was a pause.

And then to Linda's undying astonishment, the audience in this quiet little country town began to applaud. For perhaps a minute, unbidden, they clapped in appreciation of a life they had never imagined before. Then the clapping died away, the brash soundtrack for the Movietone News throbbed through the auditorium.

As they came out of the cinema, there was a momentary obstacle in the foyer as those at the doors opened umbrellas against yet another shower. An old lady in hornrimmed glasses gave Linda a friendly smile. 'Nice film, wasn't it, m'dear? I like that – a nice bit of dancing.'

'You enjoyed it?' Linda asked.

'Oh yes, made me feel young again. I bet you wish you could do it, eh, young as you are?' She laughed, gave the girl a prod in the ribs. 'Feed you up a bit and you'd be quite like that Linda Olliver.'

The crowd eased, she nodded and made her way out. David said: 'You see? They love you and want you – but not as you are now. As you were then.'

'Don't talk like that,' she said, hurrying away from him.

But all the way home in the Morris she was very quiet. And next morning when David got down to breakfast he heard the strains of the old radiogram in the drawing room. He put his head round the door.

In a sweater and slacks held close with a pair of old socks, Linda Olliver was practising *pliés* as she held on to the back of a chair.

CHAPTER TEN

The neglect of two months cannot be remedied in two days. After a week of exercising alone, Linda borrowed a bicycle from the household and made a daily trip to the little station where she caught the slow train to Cheltenham a few miles off. Here she took class at the Gadina Ballet School with Gadina's principal assistant.

When Gadina, off on tour in Scotland, heard of it, she was pleased. 'A good child,' she said to David. 'I thought her once lacking in character but no – though she bends, there is steel in her.'

David spread the word of Linda's re-entry into the real world. Bordi came to see her at class in Cheltenham. 'So at last you are visible to your friends,' he remarked. 'Why did you not answer any of my letters, or come to the telephone when I called?'

'I'm sorry, Nicco. I can't explain it. But it's over now.'

'What do you intend to do next, *bambina mia?*'

'Work to get back to a decent standard. Then spend some time in London working with Guancini. He is best for strength and stamina and I've a lot of leeway to make up.'

Bordi frowned and then laughed. 'When I ask what you intend to do, you always tell me of studies. I meant, what do you intend to do about performing?'

'I intend not to.'

'*Como?* Why all the work if not to perform?'

'Later, Nicco, when I'm good enough.'

He looked as if he would argue, then with an obvious effort he closed his lips and forced a smile. 'You have become too thin. I will send some steak, promised to me by a second cousin in the United States Air Force Base in Teddington.'

The absurdity of it made her almost chuckle. 'My father keeps saying I'm too thin, too.'

'Your father?' She heard him draw in a breath.

Months spent so much by herself had made her slow to pick up clues about others. But she saw she had hurt him by the implication that he was being fatherly. There was twenty years difference in their ages... All at once her eyes filled with tears at having wounded him.

'I'm sorry,' she said, holding out her hand. 'I was tactless.'

He took the hand she offered. 'Don't cry. It's not that bad.'

'I'm sorry, I get weepy over things these

days. That's another reason why I'm not ready to perform.'

'That will pass, Linda.'

'Yes, but you understand now – I'm not sure enough of myself, so no one else can be sure of me either.'

Bordi shrugged and held his peace. But in the meantime he began a long negotiation with Pierre Colbert.

Colbert was still angry with Linda. Her personal problems didn't concern him, it was her professional slander that had hurt him. True, since her departure there had been a slight falling-off in the attendance at his performances, but not enough to make it vital to re-engage this insolent girl.

However, Colbert now had a project dear to his heart. Having lost the notes for Mercury and the dancer who would have been the ideal performer, he had turned to another idea among his sketch books. He wanted to do a big-scale ballet about the Aztecs. But it would cost a fortune to mount. The décor and costumes would be extravagant. And someone would have to write the score.

Bordi had heard Colbert talk about this longed-for work. He was quite willing to look out for backers for it, but had always felt that during a war the chances were slight. Now, the tide was turning in favour of the Allies. It might be possible to get his rich friends to finance a ballet that symbolised the end of tyranny in Europe.

Naturally, Bordi wanted something out of it. He wanted to make money – his productions usually did. And this time he wanted a reconciliation between Linda and Colbert as well.

Colbert was offended at first. 'It is a restriction on my artistic freedom–'

'It's an even greater restriction not to get the money. Listen, my friend, your ballet may turn out to be a masterpiece. On the other hand, it may turn out to be a great … what is the phrase the English use? … white elephant. I will find backers who will enable you to start on the groundwork – you can hire an artist and a musician and pay for a research team. After that, we shall see whether the thing is good theatre. But I want you to take Linda back. I don't ask you to put her into her former roles – she herself would not expect it, I believe. But she needs to dance, and to dance before the public.'

Colbert shook a stubborn dark head.

'Come, *mi' amico* – she has suffered, she needs help.'

'Oh,' Colbert said, with a very Gallic shrug, 'as to that, it is not my concern. She told me I had a clockwork heart. So why should it be wound up for her?'

'Because you want to produce a parable about the Aztecs and the collapse of society.'

Colbert made him wait two days. Then he rang to say he would see Linda dance, and if she had anything that he felt his company needed, he would hire her. The result of the meeting was a foregone conclusion to everyone except Linda, who sincerely believed she was being given a second chance to prove herself.

Once again Colbert saw her at Guancini's class. This time he didn't take her out for a comradely coffee. He was formal, polite. 'I see you are a little weak with the *petits battements,*' he remarked. 'But if you continue to work with Guancini and come also to my class, I think you will improve.'

'Thank you, Pierre. I hope to.'

'So we shall say that perhaps from the beginning of April you will be of my company again. I may not be able to use you on stage at once, but we shall see.'

'Thank you.' She stood before him, hands clasped loosely in front of the plain black practice tunic, head slightly bent. 'I believe I owe you an apology,' she said in a low voice. 'I don't exactly remember, but I think I said some silly things to you.'

'We will not speak of that,' Colbert said. 'You were distressed, so was I. It is in the past.'

Niccolo Bordi heard the result with satisfaction. To celebrate he took Linda out to dinner. She looked about in pleasure at the shabby elegance of the Cadogan in its wartime guise. 'It's funny,' she said. 'Since I was ill, I keep seeing everything differently. Like having new eyes.'

'I still have the same old eyes,' he replied. 'And it pleases me to see you looking so well. You gave us all a great fright.'

'Did I? I'm sorry. I suppose I got in a muddle because I felt so guilty.' She sighed. 'I know now that I never really loved Alan in the way I thought I did. Does that sound awful?'

'Not at all. I'm glad you can say it without remorse.'

'Oh, you're wrong! I do feel remorse. But I don't blame myself any more. I see now that if Alan had lived, we could never have made a success of the marriage. I never would have settled down to being a dance teacher in Hedfield. I always tried to believe I'd be good and do as he wanted, but I don't think I could have gone through with it.'

'No. It would have been the most tragic waste.'

'It's funny, isn't it? We seemed made for each other when we were children... We were like two trees growing together. Alan grew up straight and upstanding like a pine. I began to bend and turn, like a hawthorn, and...'

'Hawthorn? That is what I call *biancospino*, I think? White thorn...' He smiled and leaned forward to plant a little kiss on her forehead. 'But you are not at all like a thorn flower, my little one. You are a gentler flower, part of the garland of everything beautiful.'

She coloured at his praise. She felt his kiss as a burning spot on her brow. She looked at him with perplexity.

He said no more for the present. She was still a little unsure of herself. But one day soon he intended to tell her how much he loved her, and he had hopes that she wouldn't be indifferent.

To Linda, Bordi seemed so much older. He was perhaps forty-four or forty-five. His black hair was just beginning to show grey threads. He was apt to talk about money rather than art, but there was no doubt he was a man of the theatre, imbued with the desire to surprise and please the public. It was flattering to find that he singled her out, courted her, wanted her.

She began work with the Colbert Company in April. Everyone was kind except Colbert, who was not exactly unkind but kept his distance. She was taken into the *corps de ballet* and noticed at once by the ballet critics. 'Linda Olliver's return after some months absence must be a matter for rejoicing,' wrote the *Telegraph's* reviewer. 'M. Colbert's idea of letting her dance herself back into her former brilliance by putting her into the *corps* is commendable but we must hope such a fine artist does not remain there too long.'

'Let them mind their own business!' Colbert snarled. 'I will promote my ballerinas as I think fit.'

'Listen, Pierre,' Bordi rebuked him, 'this is London, not Paris. Here they don't like factions. Show some sense, give Linda her solos.'

'Ah, you are besotted with her! But I put my company first, and so I make the judgements whether she is ready.'

After so much proclamation about the importance of his company, it came as a tremendous shock when, in late June, Colbert announced his intention of going home.

'Home?' cried Bordi when he was told. 'Where to?'

'France, of course. One of the *aides* of General de Gaulle has told me he can arrange transport.'

The D-Day landing was two weeks behind them. Allied forces were fighting in Normandy. Hopes were high, although the breakthrough towards Paris had not come as yet.

'*Dio mio*, Pierre, what would you do in the middle of a battle?'

'You can laugh. But after all … it is my country. Suddenly I find I want to be with my own people. And the officials of our provisional government say they would welcome my presence. I could put on shows for the Free French–'

'Ballet? In the middle of the Second Front? Come, come, this is nonsense.'

'I want to go, Nicco. It may be nonsense but I suddenly find I am a patriot. I don't know exactly what I could do but I want to go.'

'And the company? The season?'

'My assistant will manage all that.'

'And the Aztec ballet?'

For a moment Colbert faltered. 'Ah... Perhaps that was too big an undertaking in any case.'

'You didn't think so when I was finding backers and hiring researchers! What do you intend to do about it?'

Colbert had clearly not thought that far. 'Perhaps we could defer it? For a year?'

Bordi frowned fiercely at him. 'My friend, you are under contract–'

'And what will you do? Serve a *procés*? That would do you little good when my mind is on the fact that my government has asked me to put myself at their disposal–'

'So that's it, is it? You see yourself as Minister of Culture, or something of that kind. And what about all the people in the company who depend on you – they are to be sacrificed to this ambition?'

'Nicco, it's no use shouting at me. I have made up my mind. I am going to France as soon as it can be arranged.'

The interview was broken off with both men angry. By the time Bordi went to the theatre that evening to collect Linda, he was in a mood of deep dejection. One glance at Linda's face as he came into her shared dressing room was enough to tell him she had heard. She said goodbye to the two other girls and went out with him, taking his arm as if for comfort.

'Nicco, it's so awful! He told us this afternoon and we've all been in a state of misery.'

'Cretino!' growled Bordi, bringing his white teeth together as if he were grinding Colbert's bones. 'Doesn't he realise it's all a public relations move? De Gaulle wants to have big names to bring with him when he makes his entrance into Paris–'

'But that isn't likely for a long time yet, by the looks of it.'

She was right. From the moment the Allied forces had landed in Normandy they had been fighting in a box. Even worse, in a way, was the sudden backlash from the Nazis – a new weapon called a flying bomb had been raining down on the south-east of England and London. It began to look as if after a hard struggle in France the troops might return to find their capital city destroyed.

These new devices had been greeted with some ironic amusement by the population and nicknamed 'doodle-bugs', from the way they cut off their engines and then hesitated overhead before landing to explode. The chug-chug-chug of their engines had become a familiar sound to Londoners; they had learned to calculate that if they heard the engine stop, a count of one-two-three-four-five would tell them where it was going to land – the point being that if you reached five, it wasn't landing on top of *you*. But for all the cartoons and jokes, the machine made people nervous. This was noticeable in a falling off of audiences in theatres and cinemas. It was better to be out of doors; there, you might see the little aeroplane-like bomb, either as a silhouette in daytime or as a glow of exhaust fumes in the night sky. And if you could see its direction, you could run the opposite way.

Linda and Niccolo Bordi walked home through the quiet blacked-out streets of London to her flat. They listened now and again for any sounds in the sky, or for the whistles of wardens or roof-watchers, for there had been an alert, still continuing, at about nine o'clock. But their main attention was on Colbert's plans. Bordi insisted that Colbert wouldn't be leaving immediately, or even soon. De Gaulle's advisers were simply contacting men and women who would look good when numbered among their entourage, Bordi said. Colbert, with his known pro-communist outlook, implied a liberal view of the political future when the de Gaulle government took over.

When they reached her home, Linda invited Nicco indoors for the ever-popular cup of tea. War scarcities had taught him to drink this typically British beverage, and in any case they still had a lot to discuss about Colbert's proposed desertion.

'It'll be so awful without him,' mourned Linda as she set the pot of tea on her kitchen table.

'You will miss him?'

'Of course! He's unique – I can't envisage it without him.'

'Why do you talk so of this selfish, cold-hearted man?' Nicco almost shouted. 'How can you have feeling for him when he is so self-centred?'

Linda paused with her hand outstretched to offer him the sugar. 'You said something like that once about Alexander Prebble,' she said with a faint frown.

'Yes, and for the same reason! I am jealous!'

She thought about that. 'But you never react like this about David?'

'Ah, no.' Nicco allowed himself a curt laugh. 'Of David I have no fears. He is just your brother.'

'I suppose so,' she agreed.

'But with these others it is different. There is an intensity in your regard for them–'

'But it's only because they are important to the ballet,' she explained. 'They're not important to me as men.'

'Thank God for that.' He put a little of her precious sugar ration into his tea, which he drank without milk and, when occasionally he could get it, with lemon. As he stirred his cup he said, 'It didn't surprise you when I said I was jealous?'

She said nothing, gave a little movement of her shoulders that meant embarrassed agreement.

'I am ashamed of being jealous,' he went on, sighing. 'To me it is beneath my dignity, you know? But I can't help it. While you were a married woman I tried very hard not to let it show, but...' He stretched out his hand to her. 'I love you, Linda.'

She put her hand in his. 'I know, Nicco.'

'And you? What do you feel?'

'I ... feel that you're very important to me.'

'Like the Prebbles and Colberts of the ballet?'

'No, different. I've been aware, at the back of my mind, of all you've done for me–'

'But I didn't do it to buy gratitude,' he put in at once. 'I backed Colbert's Aztec ballet, myself, because I wanted to influence him to take you back. But I got others to back it because I thought it would be good. And I would have done all that if you had not been part of it – this is true, Linda.'

She nodded. He got up from his place across the table and still holding her hand, came to her side. He drew her close and put her hand against his cheek. 'They will say that I am old enough to be your father,' he murmured. 'They will say it's because of my feelings that I have helped your career. Does this matter to you, *carissima*?'

She leaned her head against his shoulder. He began to kiss the inside of her hand, little gentle kisses.

Then overhead in the distance they heard the throb of an engine, unmistakable, menacing. He gave a start of alarm and gathered her against him in a protective impulse which he at once recognised as useless.

They stood listening, tense with expectation. The throb-throb-throb grew louder. It passed directly above them. In a second the sound began to diminish, but as they were feeling the first surge of relief there came the awful moment of cut-off.

The silence that followed was worse than the engine noise. The fact that it had gone by meant nothing. The steering had been pre-set so that the machine could swerve in falling or gliding. They stood wrapped in each other's arms, heads tilted up, fearful, prepared for the worst.

There was a swishing, tearing sound as the plane passed close by and near the roofs.

That faded, was lost. The explosion followed – tremendous, shaking the earth, filling the sky.

The room in which they were standing vibrated with the shock. There was the roar of collapsing debris. They could hear shattered glass falling with a waterfall tinkle. Almost at once whistles were blowing, and close upon that came the frenzied ringing of rescue-squad alarm bells. The vibrations from the explosion died away in little tremors of light pendants and blackout curtains.

Niccolo Bordi blew out a breath and released his hold of Linda reluctantly. 'That was close,' he muttered.

'The next street, I think.'

'Let's look at the damage.'

They went through the flat with arms about each other. A window in Betty's room had been shattered, the glass lay across the shabby carpet and Betty's bed.

'Lucky Betty's in Torquay,' Linda said. 'She'd have found it draughty in here tonight.'

Linda's room was unharmed except that the blast had brought a picture from the wall. Nicco replaced it, then stood looking at it absently. 'We have been lucky,' he remarked. 'We might be lying under a heap of rubble now, not putting things to rights.'

Linda felt tears start into her eyes. 'Is that what we are like these days?' she murmured.

'We feel lucky when someone else is killed?'

'Ah, *carina mia.*' He put an arm about her. 'That is the war. We are what we have to be. It would be unnatural not to be grateful that we are still alive.'

'Yes, of course, you're right – I'm glad we're still here, I'm glad not to have lost *you* too.'

'I mean so much to you, Linda? You can think of losing me in the same breath as Alan?'

She threw her arms about him in a convulsive embrace. Her arms were slender but strong – dancer's arms. He felt them straining close, and he gathered her up. 'Linda, say you love me.'

'I love you.' In the aftermath of the brush with death she loved him, treasured and valued him. She kissed him with a passionate gratitude for being alive, there with her, surviving with her in the midst of the dangers of the war.

Nicco returned the kiss. But it was not in his nature to let the woman take the lead. He established his own mastery, and in doing so desire, always held in check when he was with her, rose in an uncontrollable wave.

He picked her up and carried her to the narrow bed. As he laid her on it, her arms clung around his neck, holding him near. He bent over her, kissing her with an unrestrained longing.

Then with trembling fingers he began to undo the fastenings of her dress.

After they had made love he felt guilty. He had been rough and thoughtless, driven by his own needs. When he tried to apologise, she put her fingers on his lips. 'It's all right, I understand. And next time, it will be perfect.'

He laughed. 'You are always surprising me! I thought you would scold me for being cruel.'

'I'd never scold you. You're too important to me.'

'Am I important? Truly? Tell me how you feel.' They lay whispering confidences to one another until his desire rose anew. He began to stroke her lithe, strong limbs so that she turned to him like a flower to the sun.

This time, as she foretold, it was perfect.

Next morning they woke late. Linda began to run about saying she would be late for class – an unheard-of thing. As she bathed and dressed he sat up in bed, arms behind his head, watching her.

'My Linda, I want you to leave this flat and come to me,' he said.

'Leave? But why?'

'Well ... when Betty comes back from her summer show, it would not be very convenient, would it?'

She paused, hairbrush in hand. He was moving too quickly for her. 'No, I suppose not.'

He got out of bed, unregarding of his nakedness, and came to take the brush from her to run through her fair hair. 'How lovely you are,' he said, bending down to kiss her neck. 'Don't go yet, Linda. Stay with me a little longer.'

'But my class–!'

'Oh, *che diavolo!* For once be late! And if Colbert complains, tell him at least you come, you do not desert the company!'

'You're getting me into bad habits,' she said. But she didn't resist when he began to untie the sash of her dressing gown.

Nicco foresaw that she might shy away from actually coming to live with him. He had met the parents; he understood the drag of convention in a provincial town. He had a mother of his own who had ruled his sisters with a rod of iron until they married.

He solved the problem with typical panache. 'This evening I want you to come to a party,' he said.

'Oh? What kind of party?'

'A friend of mine is giving a house-warming. You should wear your prettiest dress. The pale blue one with the white flower at the shoulder.'

'All right,' she said, laughing. 'Any instructions about shoes and bag?' But she took the dress with her to the theatre to change into afterwards, for she liked to please him in every way she could.

He had a taxi waiting. They were driven to a pretty cul-de-sac in Mayfair, where he ushered her into the entrance of a spacious early Victorian building. A lift like a Chinese cricket cage took them to the second floor. Nicco rang the bell. The door was opened by a smiling middle-aged woman in a dark blue dress and apron.

'Good evening, sir, good evening, madam.'

'Good evening, Doris.' He gave her his hat. Linda gave her coat. She disappeared through a door at the end of the narrow hall. 'This way,' said Nicco, and led Linda into a large room lit by a small chandelier of exquisite crystal. Its sparkle shone on a table set for two, with champagne on ice at its side.

'Nicco! Where's the party?'

'We are the party, and it is our house-warming.' He laughed and took her in his arms. 'Say you like it?'

'Nicco, I–'

'First, a champagne toast! To our new home.' He opened the wine, poured it expertly, and handed her a glass. She understood that if she drank, she accepted the new situation. She hesitated only a moment. She couldn't, *couldn't*, hurt him by rejection.

'I have had everything brought here, Linda. All your belongings. This is where we shall live now. It's too late to say no because if you go home to Betty's flat you will find she has someone else sharing with her.'

Helplessly she began to laugh. Champagne spilled over her wrist. 'Drink, drink!' he urged. 'Don't waste it! But first say you are not angry with your Nicco.'

She was not angry with him. She was charmed, touched, enchanted.

Later, as she lay in bed at his side, she thought: I've been swept off my feet. That's the phrase for it. There's something ... luxurious ... about letting someone else take charge. I wonder if I'll go on liking it?

And I wonder what Mummy will say?

But after all, there's no need to tell her, really. And besides ... it doesn't really matter what she says. Because if the war has taught me anything, it's that happiness is too precious to give up just because someone else might disapprove.

As the weeks went by, everyone in the Colbert Company became aware that she and Niccolo Bordi were living together. In the free atmosphere of the group, no one thought it worth more than a passing recognition. More pressing was the problem of Colbert himself. As his journey to his homeland was delayed again and yet again, he grew short tempered, he danced less

305

well, he gave the morning class over to his assistant while he visited officials at the Free French HQ in Belgrave Square.

'I shall be *positivement heureuse* when he goes,' Susanne Lascelles remarked to Linda one afternoon after a shambles of a rehearsal. 'If he cannot pay attention, he should give the direction to someone who can.'

'But to whom, Zou-zou?'

'I don't know. To you, perhaps?'

'Me?' Linda was genuinely taken aback.

'Yes, I notice you are good at stepping in to keep t'ings going when Pierre is called away. And you stay calm, which matters. And also, you have the ear of Bordi, and this pleases us.'

'I've never thought of myself as director of a ballet company, Zou-zou.'

'*Naturellement.* You are young – but it is not a matter of years but of ability. I think you can keep us together. I see no one else who might.'

'It's out of the question,' Linda said, shrinking from the mere idea.

It might actually have come to pass. But in September, when the Allied forces had reached Paris and Colbert packed his bags, she discovered she was two months pregnant.

CHAPTER ELEVEN

Bordi was in a seventh heaven about the baby. 'We will have a son, I know it will be a son,' he cried, 'and we'll call him after my father. Andrea – how is that in English? – Andrew?'

'What if I want to call him after my father? And what, after all, if it's a girl?'

'I'll see Bassett tomorrow,' Bordi proclaimed, 'and have him draw up a marriage settlement. You are not a Catholic, of course, but that doesn't matter–'

'Wait, wait, love,' Linda protested. 'You're going much too fast! Let's just get used to the idea of having the baby, first–'

'Not at all! It's to prevent this that we must act. We must be married when the baby arrives–'

'No, Nicco. I don't want to rush into that.'

'You don't want to?' His face fell. He looked like a small boy who had been slapped. 'You don't want to be my wife?'

Linda couldn't tell him her thoughts. She realised now that she had rushed into marriage with Alan because it was what Alan wanted, but it had been a mistake. She didn't want to make that same mistake again. She knew that to explain all this to Nicco would hurt and offend him so instead she said: 'There's plenty of time. First we must take care of the most important thing, which is what to do about the Colbert Company–'

'Oh, the Colbert Company! The hell with it!'

'No, there are forty dancers and twenty other staff, not to mention the orchestra. You can't just say, The hell with them. We've got to think what to do now Pierre has gone.'

'Very well, let's think about that. What can we do? Pierre's understudy can surely take over–'

She was shaking her head. 'Without Pierre his ballets are nothing. When Renaud dances them they become mere acrobatics. Pierre made them live by sheer force of personality.'

Nicco had been made to concentrate his mind on the problem by her words. 'Perhaps it will prove to be like the Pavlova Company. After she died, it disintegrated.'

'Well, I refuse to let our company disintegrate!' she said stoutly. 'We've got dancers, good dancers, but what we need is a driving force. Say what you like about Colbert, but he made us work.'

'Oh, if all we need is a ballet coach–'

'Be serious, Nicco.' She was scolding him.

Naturally he was not as concerned about the survival of the ballet company as she, for he had opera and musicals to think of too. But he gave her his attention when he saw how earnest she was.

'Well, out with it. What is it you are waiting to say?'

'I was wondering ... Nicco, don't read anything wrong into it – but how about Alexander Prebble?'

To her relief, he didn't at once look jealous. He said, 'He is in the Army, no?'

'No. He's been home about a month – invalided out.'

'Invalided? *Che peccato!*' He was quick to feel for the man. 'Is it serious?'

Linda was uncertain. 'All I hear is he's had a plaster all round his right shoulder. I think it's pretty clear he's not going to dance again. But he always expected that, Nicco. He knew the call-up was the end of his dancing career. I was thinking–'

'For *maître de ballet?* You think he could do it?'

'He taught me so much, darling, when we made the film.'

'Surely it was Leryeva who–'

'She taught me the role, Nicco. Preb taught me how to dance – I mean, how to be with my partner, how to ... to ... use myself so as to *be* the dance.'

'Would he want to teach? It is somewhat

309

less than he should have had from life.'

'*Sicuro,*' said Linda, who found herself picking up little phrases of Italian from him these days. 'But perhaps he'd like to be close to the theatre. And he has a lot to pass on to other dancers.'

'Perhaps the Vic-Wells have something to offer him.'

'That's no reason why we shouldn't ask. It'd be nice, wouldn't it, to give him a choice.'

'Very well. I leave that in your hands, *piccina.*'

'Good.' It amused him to see she'd quite expected this decision. 'Now the next thing to consider is the repertoire. We do the classics well, and there are one or two divertissements we can make up into a programme. But chiefly what we need is items to fill the gaps left by Pierre's ballets. I was thinking, Nicco…'

'What, my love?'

'I wondered if we could approach Gadina for permission to use some of her work?'

Gadina had come home from a long winter tour in April. She was now resting in Cheltenham, while her dancers dispersed to other work or took special classes – or merely rested, if they could afford it.

David Warburton had come south with her, but had let her know he wouldn't be touring again the following winter. The company without Linda was less appealing to him, and in any case he felt that two winters with a small struggling ensemble were enough. He had work of his own he wanted to do.

A film company, having heard his music for the Ministry of Information film, had offered him the chance to write a score for a film about the life of Robert Clive. He had taken the offer, partly because it would let him stay in London, where he could see Linda.

The news that she was living with Bordi came to him swiftly, through Betty Balcombe. He went down to Torquay to see her in the summer show where she was a main attraction, and she mentioned the affair to him as if it were common knowledge.

When Betty saw his stricken face, she was sorry. 'You didn't know?'

'I'd no idea. I saw her in London but... It was just a flying visit.' He paused a moment. 'Perhaps that's what's been wrong – I never gave the impression of being serious about her in that way.'

'I'm awfully sorry, David, I really am. But this is a serious thing between her and Nicco.'

'Thanks for putting me in the picture. Next time I see her I won't put my foot in it by expecting her to act like a free woman.'

He hadn't exactly avoided meeting Linda,

but he hadn't gone out of his way to see her. Linda, busy with the problems of the company, had only occasionally wondered why David didn't drop in to see her.

He was more elusive than Preb, who came as soon as she contacted him and after a moment of astonishment accepted her offer to be *maître de ballet*.

'Don't you want to consult the Vic first?' she suggested.

'No. They've got a lot of men coming back from the war – I'd only be one more problem for them. With the Colbert Ballet I have the feeling that you've actually sought me out. I can't deny I'm flattered.'

She smiled at him. 'You are a love, Preb!'

'That's what my wife tells me.'

'You're married?'

'Last week. It's a bit of a secret – her parents don't approve of ballet dancers, especially out-of-work ballet dancers.' He grinned. 'Wait till I tell Father-in-law! He's about to make a packet in the building industry and probably end up with a peerage, but I hope he'll like having someone in the family to spread a little culture.'

'What about the shoulder?'

Preb gave a smiling glance. 'You asked that *after* you offered the job. Thank you, Lin. Well, it'll be okay. But I'll never be able to hoist ballerinas around six nights a week.'

'Just teach the others how to do it, Preb.'

'Sure thing,' he said.

So that was settled. And Nicco would like it that Preb was married. In some ways Nicco was quite old-fashioned: he considered marriage a binding arrangement, like a good Catholic.

Now she would have to approach David about Gadina's ballets. The musical score belonged to him and though of course he would be pleased to have it performed, it would have to be re-scored for a full orchestra. He was certainly the best person to do the re-scoring.

Gadina was flattered that Linda should want to perform her work and gave permission without demur. She even sent her own choreographical notes. Without telling her, Linda improved the choreography of *The Willing Prisoner* when she put it into rehearsal: she took out some of the pointless variations intended merely for show, and replaced them with dancing passages that conveyed some of the emotions of the plot.

David said he was delighted to be asked to re-set the music. If he seemed less enthusiastic with the orchestra than she expected she put it down to the nerves that were troubling everyone in London during that summer of the buzz-bombs.

Certainly when she told him about the expected baby, he greeted the news with a smile of congratulations. 'I can see you're happy about it,' he said. 'I'm glad for you.'

'It's Nicco, really – it seems to mean a terrific amount to him. I'm happy because he's so happy.'

'He's a lucky man,' David said wryly, and went back to bar sixty-one which the brass section were mincing up.

To lighten the repertoire, Linda introduced the comedy dance called 'Music Hall' which she had put together for the film. She asked David if he would work with her on five more dances from old music hall tunes because she wanted to do a high-spirited ballet for programme balance. She thought he was less willing than she might have expected.

'I'll be busy on this Clive of India thing, Lin.'

'But surely the main work on that comes after they've done the filming?'

'Well, yes–'

'And they've only just started shooting?'

'Yes.'

'So are you fully booked up in the meantime?'

'Well, no–'

'Then what's the problem? Don't you like the subject?'

'Of course I like it. I liked it when we did it for the Gadina Company and I still like it.'

'Then is it money? Nicco is financing it, David–'

'No, no!' He was on the verge of anger. He could see he had backed himself into a corner. And in any case, what was he trying to do? Avoid Linda? It was scarcely possible, if he wanted to be a composer for British ballet. Linda's life was bound up with ballet, she was going to marry an impresario, and thus if he wanted to go on with his plans he had to come to terms with the facts of life.

'All right,' he said, forcing a smile. 'I was just playing hard to get. Tell me what you have in mind.'

Once again it all went well. Within a month David had made arrangements that ran the whole gamut from German band to swooning waltz strings. Costumes were quickly provided almost from stock by the costumiers. The backcloth though freshly done could have come from almost any British pantomime. Linda was still slim enough to dance in the ballet when it went on to form a part of the winter repertoire, but soon after that she had to 'retire' temporarily.

She now had to tell her parents the news. She had kept the relationship with Nicco from them, knowing how shocked they would be. In a way she regretted that now, for the double shock of her loose living and now her pregnancy reduced her mother to a sobbing heap.

And not to want to marry the baby's father!

'We never should have let her keep on that dancing and mixing with those degenerates!' Nancy Thackerley cried to her husband when Linda had gone up to her old room to let them talk in private.

'It's a facer, certainly,' Harry sighed.

'You must talk to that girl and make her marry Mr Bordi,' Nancy wept. 'Otherwise, what are people going to say?'

'I don't see that they'll say much,' her husband remarked. 'I mean, she's got marriage lines to show if anybody wants to get funny about it, she is a Mrs and she's got a wedding ring, Nancy.'

'But Alan's been dead almost a year, Harry! Nobody's going to think it's Alan's baby! No, she's got to marry Mr Bordi.'

'I dunno so much... Look here, Nancy, if it's all so right and inevitable, why's our Lin against it? She's got sense in some ways, our girl. And to tell the truth, I'm not all that keen on having a daughter married to a foreigner.'

'Harry!'

'No, dear, I think we should let her alone. It's a different world, that one she's in. She knows best.'

So rather to her own surprise, Linda found herself supported by her father and protected from the pressure to rush into marriage.

The baby was born in March – a girl,

Carlotta, who became the object of Nicco's adoration from the moment he saw her. 'We will have a son next time,' he said cheerfully when she teased him about it. 'I would truly like a son to leave all my money to, but I am having papers drawn up by Bassett so that our little girl is safeguarded–'

'Darling, I do wish you wouldn't rush to lawyers every time there's a change in our life. Nothing's going to happen to you! It was different when rockets and flying bombs were landing all around, but anyone can see the war's folding up and we're safe at last.'

It was true. Two armies were advancing into Germany, catching the nation between pincers. After one frightening setback in the Ardennes, the invasion forces had pushed on remorselessly across the Rhineland. It was rumoured that, to avoid having to accept defeat by the Russians, Himmler had offered to surrender to the Western Allies – but nothing came of that. However, anyone could see that the fearsome ogre in field-grey who had terrorised the whole of Europe was tottering now – the Wehrmacht was bleeding to death.

There was a feeling of hope in the air of London. Preparations were already being made for victory celebrations, although there were some pessimists who said the Nazis would retreat north as long as they could and wreak vengeance by loosing off rockets from Jutland. Linda had moments when she believed these tales, but she knew it was due to what her mother called 'post-natal blues'. And the remedy for them was to be happy with her baby and get back to work on her career.

She began gentle exercises almost at once, and went back to elementary class after six weeks. At first she seemed to have lost all her lightness. Depression followed. Nicco, mystified, tried to comfort her. To his eyes her dancing looked as wonderful as ever. But Linda knew, Linda could feel in her body an earthbound drag that had never been there before.

'Give it time,' Betty Balcombe counselled when Linda sighed out her fears. 'After all, giving birth is a very earthy business, if you want to look at it that way. I mean, you don't hear much about fairies and sprites having babies – they float about and I suppose any junior sprites are found under rose-bushes.'

Linda laughed. 'You're right! I'm just a human after all, and I'll just have to hope I can get back to my old technique if I work at it. The funny thing is, Betty – I don't really know what to work at. I never did know how I did it.'

'It'll come. You're anxious, you're trying too hard. Relax!'

It was good advice and Linda followed it. She worked as hard as ever at the business of getting back into form, but she stopped mourning her lack of lightness.

She went to see David Warburton one day in late May. She had had a sort of an idea for a ballet, and wanted to talk to him about it. During the heavy, lumbering stages of her pregnancy she had immersed herself in listening to music so that she had discovered many new things. Among these was a work by Brahms called *Die Schöne Magelone*, a series of songs telling a tale of medieval chivalry.

'What I thought was, it would be lovely to make a ballet from the last part of the story, David,' she explained. 'Magelone, the heroine, is living in disguise in a little village, like a farmer's daughter. Her hero Peter has been captured by the Moors. But he escapes with the help of the Sultan's daughter and gets back to Europe, where he searches for his beloved and comes across this simple maiden who of course is Magelone. You see, there are three good roles – Magelone, Peter, and Sulima the Moorish princess.'

'Huh,' David said without much enthusiasm. 'You're not suggesting we should use the song cycle by Brahms as the music?'

'Well ... yes, I thought so.'

'Good God, you'd have musical purists

319

attacking you with swords and cutlasses! Besides, do you think it's particularly danceable?'

'You don't like the idea?'

'It's a bit distant, isn't it? Medieval?'

'But you see, David – I was thinking of all the men coming back from the war soon. They'll be looking for the girls they left behind them, their wives and sweethearts – and of course they won't be the same people they used to know. It was that, really – the story of Magelone is just a romanticised version of it.'

'Mmm...' David doodled in the dust on the top of his piano with one finger. 'If it comes to that, I've been working on a piece of music ... I don't really know what it is so far. But I've always thought of it as being about young loves being re-united.'

'Really? Play it for me, David.'

He searched about among the mass of sheet music paper on the piano top, to emerge at last with a single sheet. 'This is all there is so far,' he said. He played a few experimental chords, mused a moment, then said, 'I'm almost sure it's going to be in the key of F minor. Here goes.'

The melody that lilted from beneath his fingers was hesitant, uncertain, full of little retreats and advances. It was a haunting tune, easy to remember.

'Why, that's beautiful, David!'

'No it isn't. It's pretty, and attractive – but I don't know what to do with it.'

'Give it to me,' Linda said. 'Finish it, orchestrate it, and give it to me. I'd like to do a ballet with it.'

'Is it strong enough for that, Lin? It's quite a slight little piece.'

'I just want to ... I think I can see two people, a boy and a girl – it ought really to be a boy and girl of today but ... that makes costume so difficult, doesn't it? A soldier – perhaps in an idealised version of nineteenth century uniform. And a girl in a pale blue dress – she's telling herself not to be silly, and pushing herself towards this boy she hasn't seen in ... well, years, but we don't know how long exactly. Let me see, David. The boy is being polite but uncertain. He'd bow ... yes ... and let go her hand as soon as he could and turn away. Perhaps a slow turn *à terre,* ending in a broken arabesque, as his anxiety gets the better of him. What do you think?'

'Let's have a look.'

He played, watching her as she tried out movements and steps in his cluttered workroom. Before she left he copied out the music for her on a clean sheet of music paper. 'That's just the melody and what I've thought about it so far. I think it needs a contrast theme, of course, and then it will return to this one for the coda. I take it this is going to have a happy ending?'

She smiled, touching him lightly on the shoulder. 'Of course. Ninety per cent of the men coming back from the fighting are going to settle down with their families. That's what the ballet is going to say that separation needn't mean break-up.'

'You're a romantic.'

'Not at all. I come from a very ordinary family, David. Ordinary people go through a war dreaming of the day when they can get back to being ordinary again. And I think most of them actually do.'

'Then you're an unromantic! This thing of mine is about heartache–'

'I didn't say their hearts don't ache, love. I just said they make it work out in the end.'

'Some of them will have big problems, though, Linda. Wives have been unfaithful, men have done terrible things–'

'Of course. I don't deny that. But our ballet is about the majority, who find a quiet life waiting for them.'

She had no idea as she said it that she herself was about to be numbered among the minority.

As the conquering armies rolled across Germany, concentration camps and slave labour settlements were set free. The horror of the revelations caused more anger than almost anything the war had yet brought. Skeletal figures were seen on the newsreels.

Reports in the newspapers made horrifying reading. At first the reaction was: It can't be true, nobody could really do this to another human being.

But it was true, and little by little those desperate, lost beings were interviewed, identified, given medical attention, and put in touch with relations.

Linda received a telegram from the War Office. Alan Olliver had been found alive though desperately ill near a slave labour camp in Poland.

CHAPTER TWELVE

Soon after Alan's supposed death his commanding officer had come to Hedfield on a visit of condolence. He told Linda that Alan was with his unit on a mission to the coast of Denmark. Their instructions were to destroy an enemy installation of some importance.

The group didn't make their rendezvous with a destroyer standing off-shore in the darkness. After the mandatory wait, the destroyer's captain weighed anchor and left. Later, intelligence reports brought the news that the entire unit had been wiped out: they had clearly been expected, had been ambushed and decoyed into a booby-trapped building. No one had survived.

Part of this story he told to Linda. She was in no condition to ask questions even if any had occurred to her. Now, in full command of herself, though in a state of delight, relief and bewilderment, she went by invitation to an office in the vastness of Whitehall, where a grey-haired major explained what had been learned.

There were in fact two survivors of the Jehnerdal raid, but they had been spirited away by local resistance fighters. These men had decided not to report the true facts to HQ, for clearly either HQ itself or their communications system had been penetrated by the Nazis. Their intention was to move Alan and Len Kitts by farm cart from village to village until they reached a northern port. From there they could be taken across the Kattegat to neutral Sweden.

Delays ensued because Kitts was seriously wounded and needed medical attention. Despite all the Danes could do, he died. Their plan for Alan in fact succeeded in that they got him unnoticed to Grena but there, alas, he fell victim to one of the periodical round-ups for the labour camps.

'But why didn't he own up and say he was a British soldier?' Linda protested. 'Surely that would have been better than slave labour!'

'He couldn't do that. He was in civvies, you see, so that automatically made him a spy. Besides, chaps who go out on raids like that are well briefed. He knew what German questioning would be like. He didn't want to betray the Danes who'd helped him.'

'I see.' Linda sat back, shaking her head.

'You're thinking it's a depressing story, aren't you?' sighed Major Grant. 'War isn't pretty, that's certain. Well, Corporal Olliver kept quiet and had no trouble concealing his true identity. Once you were on one of those cattle-trains, it seems, they didn't make any checks – they counted you on at the beginning and counted you off at the end, and that was that. Your husband just answered 'Ja' when his Danish alias was called and had no problems. It seems he was in a camp in East Germany first, and then was transferred to a factory near Poznan in Poland. In Poland, there was a very active underground movement, as you've no doubt heard.'

'I've read about it.'

'It took Corporal Olliver some time to contact them. You understand, he had to be very careful – there were all kinds of people among the slave labour and some of them not above selling information to their masters for extra food. But in the end he got in touch with a group working from a farm in the woods to the south. Then the Russians began to get close. Unfortunately...' The Major pursed his lips and blew out a breath. 'This particular resistance group didn't trust the Russians an inch, so when the camp discipline began to go to pieces, they took Olliver off to hide in the forests.'

'But the Poles and the Russians are allies!' Linda cried.

'Don't you believe it. There's no love lost between those two nations, I'm afraid. But that accounts for the fact that Olliver wasn't liberated with the rest of the factory's men.

And of course the Russians were too eager to drive on to Berlin to hang about looking for anti-communist resistance groups. It wasn't until June that the unit deposited Olliver on the steps of a military hospital, dangerously ill with pneumonia.'

'How is he now? Where is he?'

'Well, Mrs Olliver, he's much better, and we're moving him west and south by degrees. My info is that in about a week he'll board a hospital ship, probably at Hamburg, and will cross to Harwich where they'll pop him into hospital to feed him up and get him thoroughly fit to muster out.'

'Can I write to him? Is there an address?'

'Well, no. He'll be on the move. My advice is to wait a bit. I'll give you a name and a telephone number to ring. The various welfare branches of the three services are handling these dicey repat. cases, so you'll contact a member of SAAFA who's keeping track of the men coming on that particular ship. I should think you could put through a personal call to your husband once he gets to Harwich. How's that?'

'Thank you, major,' she said, taking the card he handed her. 'You've been very kind.'

'Not at all, not at all. It's a pleasure to be giving good news. I've done so much of the opposite.' He shook hands as he showed her to the door. 'You must be a very happy woman, Mrs Olliver.'

'Oh, yes, I am!' And it was true. No matter how it was going to complicate her life, she was full of thanksgiving for Alan's survival.

Alan had been a childhood sweetheart, her greatest friend for at least three-quarters of her life. He had been her husband, her first lover, awakening her to the joys of physical love. She had a deep, abiding affection for him. It broke her heart to think she must tell him news that would hurt him.

'We will go together to the hospital and tell him,' Nicco said when she got home to the Mayfair flat. 'You cannot do it alone.'

'No, Nicco, it would be too great a shock. He's still a sick man, he'll still be under medical treatment. I must speak to his doctors and see what they think.'

'I refuse to let you go alone!'

'Nicco, darling, you can't prevent me.' She touched his angry mouth with two fingers. 'Don't frown. I would rather do it by myself.'

'You don't understand,' he burst out, seizing her by the arms. 'I'm afraid! When you see him... Who knows?'

'You think I'll discover I'm in love with him?'

'You thought so once, *mia cara.*'

'But that was different. It had been taken for granted so long. And even then ... I don't know whether I would really have married him at the end of the war, as we first planned. It was only when he was going off to take up active service…'

'Yes, you gave in then – he persuaded you. How do I know the same thing won't happen again?'

'But how could it, Nicco? Everything is so different. I've a baby now – your baby. Carlotta and I belong with you.'

'But don't you see – I've no legal claim on Carlotta!' Nicco cried. 'You are legally married to Alan, and in law Carlotta is his daughter!'

'No, Nicco – that can't be so–'

'It is so! I have talked to Bassett–'

'Oh, Bassett… Why must you always rush to lawyers, my darling? Alan isn't going to behave like that. You don't know him. The last thing he'd want is to hurt me–'

'But will he give you up? And when he appeals to you, with his sufferings still plain to see – will you be able to say no, my Linda?'

'Yes,' she said, holding Nicco close. 'Yes, I swear to you, when the time comes I'll tell Alan I'm no longer his wife. But not straight away – not when he's still so ill and likely to be harmed by bad news.'

By a supreme irony, she was to make her return debut as a star of the Colbert Ballet with the new ballet she and David had devised. It was called *Lovers' Meeting* and had been beautifully but simply dressed by

Oliver Messel.

As she dressed her hair for the part, she looked at the girl in the mirror. She was working on make-up to look older, for the girl in the ballet was supposed to be in her mid-twenties. She herself had her twentieth birthday still to come, yet she felt she was in truth the girl in the ballet – so much had happened to her in such a short time.

Although she had done a full class and a long warm-up that day she felt cold and stiff. The ballet frightened her. The steps were simple but the mood of apprehension, regret, and doubt, that must be changed to joy and ardour during the dance, seemed to weigh on her limbs so that she wondered if she could perform.

In the wings she gave her wrap to her dresser. She and her partner, Laurence Mendel, exchanged kisses and the ritual words that meant good luck. The front-of-house lights went down. Mendel walked on stage and took up his opening position. The curtain silently rose.

Then the strains of David's music stole through the theatre. Mendel stretched out his arms, delighting in his freedom, in his wholeness of body after the battles. There was a short passage portraying his impatience as he waited for his sweetheart.

Then came the short, angry bars that Linda thought of as the girl's family scolding. A moment later she had run on stage, almost scurrying in obedience to family commands.

Her nerves vanished. Everything came to her easily. Somewhere among her mental pictures she saw Alan, her young husband, as he had been when they parted. 'Think of me when you dance!' he had called. That couldn't be, for her attention must be on what she was doing – yet he was there with her as she twisted and turned, leapt and soared.

The ballet ended with the two lovers parting from an embrace of renewed passion and then, almost timidly, taking hands to begin their new life. When the music died, there was a moment of breathless silence.

Then a voice from the back of the stalls shouted, 'Bravo!' The word was taken up. A roar of applause broke out. People were on their feet, shouting approval.

Afterwards Linda realised that it wasn't really the dance they were applauding. It was the mood of the work, the anxieties of the post-war world, the human problems thus stated with so much simplicity and sincerity.

The ballet became almost a cult. Young couples came to see it and kept the programme as a souvenir of their honeymoon. The music, too, became famous. David recorded it at the invitation of HMV, expecting little to come from it. But the record sold and sold. What pleased him was that on the other side of the disc David had recorded another of his own works, a suite for chamber orchestra – and that too became so popular that orchestras began to take it into their repertoires.

Yet in a way the thing that was most marvellous to Linda about *Lovers' Meeting* was a totally personal joy. She had got her lightness back. In the midst of the dance, when she was retreating from the young man in a series of frightened little leaps, she felt her foot touch down like a feather. She was too intent on the acting to take any further notice. But when the curtain came down she realised that she had rediscovered the secret that lifted her from the stage in soft airiness whenever she wanted.

She was ashamed to be glorying in something so selfish. Yet she couldn't help the glow of delight that suffused her every time she thought of it. She was herself again – she was the dancer whose speed and lightness had been enough to win over the critics.

At last she was given the telephone number at a military hospital near Harwich where she could reach Alan. She rang him at once, to make arrangements to visit him.

'No, don't come here,' he said at once after the first stumbling introductions. 'I've got an overnight pass due to me – I'll come to London.'

'Oh, but Alan, are you well enough–'

'I've got to get back into the real world some time,' he said, his voice edgy and sharp. 'I've spent a year being ordered about like a slave – I want to do what *I* want to do.'

'Yes, of course, I understand. I was only wondering if it wouldn't be too tiring–'

'I'll manage. Give me the address – I can get a taxi from the station.'

He was too unfamiliar with London to remark on the splendour of the neighbourhood in which she was living. But when he arrived on her doorstep three days later at the appointed hour, he was staring about in surprise.

Linda had persuaded Nicco to go away for the two days of Alan's visit. They had had arguments lasting for hours, but in the end she had won her point. 'He's never met you, doesn't even know of your existence, Nicco. How can I show him in, and then say, "Oh, by the way, this is Nicco, my lover, who pays the rent here"?'

'But at some point you must tell him this – though not in those words.'

'I'll do it. I'll choose the moment. I won't tell him all at once, but I'll explain enough to show him ... to show him our marriage won't work.'

'And then when he breaks down and begs you to give him his life back again – you will

333

say no.' Nicco shook his head. 'Well, I go along with your wishes. But I tell you this, my darling – no matter how reluctant you are to hurt him, in the end he must be hurt, and if you cannot nerve yourself to do it, I am not so tender-hearted. In the end I will tell him if I have to – so don't shrink from it too long.'

'I promise, Nicco.'

Despite the promise, she was full of dread. She felt she would be meeting a stranger – for the Alan who had come back from the brutalities and deprivations of the slave labour camp could not be the same confident young man she had married. She felt, too, that she would be inflicting a cruel wound on a man who had suffered enough. She would be acting selfishly, although the happiness of her baby and Nicco were bound up with her own.

Most of all there was just the simple reluctance to hurt. She had always loved Alan, she simply didn't want to hurt him.

Her first sight of him shocked her. He was very thin. The bones of his hands showed through the skin, his collar seemed too big for his neck. His eyes seemed bigger, in their hollow sockets. His hair had been inexpertly barbered while he was ill and now sat in an awkward tuft on his brow – it made him look almost like an urchin.

'Well,' he said, as she ushered him in. 'You

live well, it seems. Being a ballerina brings in more money than I thought!'

'How are you, Alan? Let me take your overcoat.'

They hadn't kissed. They hadn't even clasped hands. She wondered at that. Had he heard something? But there was a wariness about him altogether – as if he were expecting some alarm, some emergency, and had to be ready.

'I've got sandwiches and tea ready, if you need something after the journey. Then I thought we would have dinner at about seven – is that all right?'

'Oh ... I brought you...' He fished in his overcoat pocket and brought out first a packet of glucose sweets and then a packet of tea. 'I remembered how you always used to need those sweets for energy,' he said. 'They had them in the hospital shop for those with a special card.'

Suddenly she threw her arms around him and began to cry. 'Alan! Oh, Alan! Do you remember how you used to buy fruit drops for me on the way home from school?'

He hugged her. 'There, there! It's only a packet of sweeties! Don't get in a state!'

'No... No, I'm sorry.' She let him go and mopped at her streaming eyes. 'I meant to be very sensible and restrained. But when you held out that packet...'

'Least I could do. You're going to feed me

and give me a bed – I realise that's not easy, with rations the way they are.' He sat down and looked about while she went to fetch the tea trolley with the food. 'My word, this is nice,' he called after her as she moved about the kitchen. 'Big, isn't it?'

'Seven rooms,' she called back. She didn't say that in one of them, fast asleep, was her baby daughter. Her maid Doris was to take care of the little girl for this evening but some time tomorrow Linda was steeling herself to introduce Alan to her.

Alan ate well, although with pauses in between. He explained that he wasn't accustomed yet to large meals. He talked guardedly of his experiences. She was sure he censored out much that he felt unsuitable for her ears. So instead she asked him about his health.

'Oh, I'm okay. They're a bit worried about possible tuberculosis. I have to go for a check-up at a special unit in Brompton Road tomorrow – that all right with you? I mean, you weren't planning to go anywhere with me, or that sort of thing?'

'No, I … I didn't really know what you'd want to do. I'd no idea you had a hospital appointment.'

'They sort of sprang it on me at the last minute. Doesn't matter, it'll only be the morning. We can have the afternoon together.'

'Yes. Alan, I–'

'Let's have a look at your cuttings book, eh? I read what the critics said about this new ballet of yours last week. Quite a hit, isn't it?'

'Oh, you don't want to–'

'I do, Lin. I want to be reminded of your life. I've spent so long concentrating on my own, just staying alive. I want to see what you've been doing, I want to feel you've had a good career...'

'Oh, of course, then ... I'll fetch it.' She knelt to get the cuttings album out of the cupboard next to the fireplace. Alongside it lay the album of photographs that showed her at occasions with Nicco – business dinners, semi-official functions. She pushed that back and went to sit on the sofa with Alan.

The cuttings and her stories about Gadina and Pierre Colbert took them through until dinner. She had the meal ready to be heated up: she and Doris, her live-in help, had concocted it from a Ministry of Food leaflet. It was called 'Vegetable Pie with Cheese and Oatmeal Crust', and when she eyed it doubtfully on its first emergence from the oven, Doris had said with blithe confidence: 'I shouldn't worry too much about it, madam. Your guest's been in military hospital, hasn't he? – I bet they get far better food than we do, so he won't be very hungry.'

Linda forbore to remark that her guest had spent many months in a Nazi slave labour camp and was entitled to all the good food he could get. She had put all the family's cheese ration into the dish, and still it looked insipid. She dressed it up with little sprigs of parsley before bringing it to the table.

Once again Alan made a good meal though it took him some time. Then he began to droop. His eyes began to look drowsy. 'I'm sorry,' he said. 'I get tired easily.'

'I understand.' Now she waited, on tenter-hooks. Would he want to make love? And if he did, would she refuse? The idea of rejecting him was hateful – yet she couldn't bring herself to believe in their relationship as husband and wife.

'Where's the spare room?' Alan inquired. Then added: 'You did realise I … well, I'm used to sleeping alone, if you see what I mean.'

'I understand,' she said, flooded with relief. 'Don't be embarrassed. To tell the truth…'

'I've got a toothbrush and pyjamas in my pocket. I'm used to travelling light.'

'You'll find everything you'll need in the bathroom alongside your room. Look, I'll show you.' She led him to the spare room, switched on the bedside light, turned back the covers. She showed him the connecting door to the bathroom.

'I say,' he said, impressed. 'It's like a five star hotel!'

'Not quite. Would you like anything else – a nightcap?'

'No, thanks, love. I'm out on my feet. Goodnight, Lin. See you in the morning.' He gave her a light kiss on the lips, drew back, smiled and closed his door.

Later, when he was asleep, she went into his room to fetch his clothes. She had noticed how creased his uniform looked – perhaps from being folded in a hospital locker. She decided to give it to Doris for pressing, and have his shoes cleaned for the morning.

She took his belongings out of his pockets. They were few – a new, cheap watch, a wallet that felt thin, and a photograph with a few words in a foreign language written on the back.

The photograph was about snapshot size. It was of a pretty girl in a floral cotton dress and an apron. She looked about twenty or twenty-one years old, dark, with an oval chin and a dimple. She was smiling into the camera hesitantly, head tilted as if she were shy.

Linda sat for a long time looking at it. Then she put it with his other belongings on the kitchen table. She went to the nursery to look at Carlotta. It was just after nine o'clock. The baby was sleeping sweetly.

Doris came to the open door of her room as Linda passed. 'Everything all right, madam?'

'Yes, thanks, Doris. I just wanted to see if Carlotta was all right. Listen, Doris, I've put my guest's uniform over a chair in the kitchen. Perhaps you'd give it a press for the morning.'

'Of course, madam.'

Linda went to the drawing-room. She listened to the radio programme for a time, turned down low so as not to disturb Alan though she knew that in this great rambling flat he was unlikely to hear it.

But the photograph nagged at her consciousness. At last, soon after ten, she went into the kitchen. Doris was busy with iron and damp cloth. Linda picked up the items on the table. She looked at the snapshot.

'I'm just going out for a few minutes,' she said. 'Be back in about half an hour.'

She fetched her coat and hurried downstairs. The theatre was only a short walk away. After the curtain calls, she caught Laurence Mendel coming along the corridor wiping sweat from his face and neck with a grubby towel.

'Hello, what are you doink here?' he asked in surprise. 'Is there some problem?'

'No, Laurence, I just came to ask for your help.'

'Anythink, dear lady.' He gave a gallant bow.

She handed him the photograph. 'Are the words on the back in Polish, Laurie?'

He turned it over. 'Yes, in Polish. It says,' Laurie replied slowly, '"To my own Alan, who must come back to me."'

'Oh.' Linda put her hands up to her cheeks.

'Who is he, this Alan – who lets you see pictures of other women?'

'Never mind, Laurie! It's just … so wonderful! You don't know what a good turn you've done me.'

Next morning Alan slept late. He ate little of the breakfast Linda had ready and asked her to ring for a taxi. He was whisked away to his hospital appointment before they had time to talk.

When he came back about lunchtime she could see he was depressed. 'Keep you hanging about for hours then send you all over the hospital for X-rays,' he complained. '*Then* they tell you nothing.'

'I expect they'll send a report to your hospital,' she soothed. 'Come along, lunch is ready. I hope you like vegetable broth because that's largely what lunch consists of.'

'Everything's good after turnip gravy,' he assured her.

She thought he looked pale and tired. She bustled about getting the meal on the table then took her place across from him. 'What would you like to do this afternoon?'

'Nothing much, Lin. I haven't the energy for it.'

'All right, perhaps we could go for a walk in Green Park later.'

'Yes, if you like.' His thoughts seemed to be elsewhere. After a moment he said, 'They say it'll be weeks before I can be demobbed. Even then, they say I ought to take it easy – not travel about too much.'

'Travel,' she said. 'Were you thinking of travelling?'

He coloured up, the blood very red under his pale skin. 'I … well … as a matter of fact there's something I have to tell you, Linda.'

'About the girl you want to travel back to?' she asked gently.

His hand picking up the spoon jerked so convulsively that he threw it into the soup bowl. Soup splashed over the table cloth. For a moment there was apology and confusion until Linda soothed everything back to order. Then she said, 'Who is she, dear?'

'How did you find out?'

'I saw her photo in your uniform pocket when I was getting it ready for pressing. Forgive me for prying, Alan, but I needed to know.'

'Yes of course, and I was going to tell you! Don't think I was trying to keep it a secret! It's just … I was waiting for the right moment – and to have the control to say it. I get upset easily, you see… But I was going to tell you.'

'It's all right,' she said, getting up and coming to kneel at his side. 'I understand. She's someone you met in Poland.'

'Her name's Natalia. Her brother was with the resistance group who took me in. I want you to know, Linda, it's not a fly-by-night thing. We got to know each other very, very well, in circumstances where our lives depended on each other. She… Her father's got a farm, not much, but it's a decent living. She's twenty-two, she was engaged but the boy was killed by the Germans. I promised her…'

'That you'd go back. Of course. She couldn't come with you because of travel restrictions–'

'She could have done if we'd been married but–' He broke off. 'I want to marry her, Lin.'

'Yes. It's all right. Don't look so desperately unhappy, Alan.' She took his hand, pressed it and let it go. She got up and stretched in relief. 'I have to confess something too, you see. There's someone in my life, someone who came along after I thought you'd been killed.'

'What? Who? You never said!'

'This is his flat. I live here with him. I had a terrible time persuading him to go away

343

for two days so I could see you here and explain everything. Like you, I've been waiting for the right moment.'

He sprang up to catch her in his arms. 'Oh, Linda, thank you! Thank you for telling me! You don't know what a weight it is off my mind! I've got to write and tell Natalia I may not be back for weeks, because of this spot they think they've found on my lungs – and I was dreading having to say you were hurt and unhappy about getting a divorce.'

'A divorce! Yes, that's what we must do – but Alan, isn't Natalia a Catholic?'

'Well, yes, but ... after what we've been through we aren't going to let that stop us. Her father feels the same. He says he's seen too much misery – what he wants now is for Natalia to be happy.'

'He's right! Oh, Alan, dear he's right!'

'And you'll marry your man, will you? What's his name? Shall I meet him?'

'His name's Niccolo Bordi, he's in theatrical management. That's why I live in this marvellous flat – *I* couldn't afford it on a ballerina's salary. And there's more, Alan – I've got a six months old baby daughter!'

Alan stared. 'A baby?'

'She's out now with Doris, my maid. I was trying to think how to ... to introduce you to her.'

'A baby! So you're married to this Bordi?'

She shook her head. 'Well ... no ... I...

No, I'm not married.'

'Not married? Linda!' He was truly shocked. 'Why not? You thought I was dead.'

'It's too difficult to explain. I just felt that … if you want the truth, Alan, I thought I'd rushed into marrying you without enough thought, and I didn't want to make the same mistake twice.'

He sighed. 'I knew I was wrong to drive you into it. To tell the truth, I thought I'd lose you to one of your ballet friends if I didn't tie you down.'

'And now you don't even want me,' she teased.

'It's not your fault, Linda,' Alan said, seriously. 'And it's not mine either. We're different people now, that's all.'

CHAPTER THIRTEEN

The invaluable Bassett warned Nicco that it would not do for him to become too well acquainted with Alan. In fact, it would be well if Nicco could absent himself from felicity a while, until at least the divorce had gone through.

'You see, Linda is the injured party. Her husband has committed adultery–'

'But haven't I?' Linda broke in, surprised into a laugh of bewilderment.

'By no means. *You* have committed immorality, your husband has committed adultery. He knew you were alive when he consorted with this Polish girl. You, on the contrary, believed your husband to be dead, and so in law are innocent.'

'Innocent! With a baby by another man?'

'*Carissima*, you must take Bassett's word for it,' Nicco soothed. 'When he calls Alan "guilty" it is only a *modo di parlare*. No one is really guilty of anything, only the law seems to wish to make a criminal out of someone in order to hear this divorce case.'

'I won't have it!' cried Linda. 'Alan's been through enough!'

Yet Alan was quite indifferent. 'I don't

care about it, Lin, nor does Natalia. Way off there in the Polish countryside, they'll never hear of the case. Who cares what's being said in London?'

'But it just seems so unfair–'

'I don't care about fairness. To tell the truth, Lin dear, what I want is for it to go through as fast as possible.' His wan face seemed even more taut and anxious. 'The Russians are tightening their grip all the while. I want to get back and marry Natalia and make her a British citizen so I can get her out of there before life gets very difficult. Don't forget, she was a partisan – with an anti-Communist group.'

Viewed in this way, all Linda's moral scruples about the rights and wrongs of the case became immaterial. She gave the go ahead to Bassett, urging him to get the case into court as soon as possible.

But not even Bordi's money and influence could get a priority for Olliver versus Olliver. There was a huge backlog of cases in the divorce courts, caused by the delays of the war and a sudden rush of actions now that serving men were coming home to broken marriages.

'I'm sorry, it will be at least six months before the case comes on,' Bassett told them.

'But what about Natalia? Alan is frantic about her. He wants her declared a British citizen so he can get her out of Poland.'

'That is not possible, if he is imagining it can be done quickly through his marrying her. However,' said the lawyer, looking owlishly at Linda through large spectacles, 'I can set in motion various wheels to enable her to travel as Natalia Jerozolimska.'

'Alan says that's impossible. He says the Russians are clamping down–'

'My dear Miss Olliver, the Russians may clamp down on poor peasants in the countryside south of Poznan. I think, perhaps, they would be less strict about a friend of the Assistant to the British Advocate's Department–'

'You know someone out there?' Nicco asked, grinning.

'I don't exactly know him. But he is working on behalf of the case workers for the war crimes trials, and one of his colleagues dined with me in the Inns while we were studying. So I think with a little string-pulling we can get Miss Jerozolimska out of Poland – perhaps not to Britain but at least to the British zone of Berlin. This may not be immediate, you understand – Belmont really is hard at work on important legal matters concerning the trials, but he will do what he can and once it's known someone in the British hierarchy is taking an interest in this young lady, I think she may find she is not harassed by the Soviet's bully boys.'

Alan's gratitude was so great that Linda almost felt she had somewhat evened the debt she owed. She hadn't hurt him by her affair with Nicco, and though she had perhaps been wrong to marry in the first place, she was doing all she could to set him free and help the girl he loved. Her conscience began to feel more at ease in this muddle of emotions.

Nicco was making plans to marry as soon as the divorce was made absolute. 'Then I legally adopt Carlotta, no? – and change her name to Bordi. Bassett says this is very easy. And then she is my daughter in every way.'

'She's your daughter in every way already, darling. She's growing more like you every day.'

But Nicco wanted more – he wanted the legal certainty that the child was his. The marriage – the first step – he was taking for granted. He had ceased to ask Linda if she wanted to take that step; his own panic when Alan appeared had made him imagine that Linda too would want to stabilise their relationship.

'Do you think I should marry him?' she asked David.

David was deep into a search of his brief-case, wherein lay some notes for themes for a new ballet. He had come to the Mayfair flat to play them over to Linda.

After what seemed a long pause he said: 'I'm the last person you should ask.' He snapped the case shut.

'Why?' she countered. 'You know both of us awfully well – you're one of our best friends, certainly the closest friend *I* have.'

He smoothed out the creased sheet of music paper and put it on the music-holder on the piano. He played one or two single notes with one finger, as if tapping out a message to her. When he merged them into a single chord she should have recognised the symbolism; they were in a minor key, and should have told her David was unhappy.

'You see, we never discussed getting married until the baby began to influence him,' she went on, oblivious of David's reluctance. 'What bothers me is that it's for Carlotta that he wants to see me as Mrs Bordi.'

'But he loves you,' David said in a low voice. 'You don't doubt that, surely?'

'Oh no, of course not.' She hesitated. 'It's whether I love him...'

He drew in a hard breath, then turned to give her his most dazzling smile. 'But you do. One's only got to see you together. There's a complete rapport–'

'Of course! We're great companions! We share almost every interest, we're involved in what each other is doing. I'm very, very *fond* of Nicco, David. Is that love? I don't know.'

'Most people wouldn't even be questioning it.'

'Do you think I'm being silly?'

'I think you're being scrupulous.'

She waited. When he said no more she urged, 'Is that good or bad?'

'Oh, how should I know!' He jumped up from the piano stool, strode towards the window, his control finally snapping. 'It's your life, make your own decisions!'

'I'm trying, David, I'm trying!' Suddenly she felt wounded by his reaction. 'It's so important, you see. I was dead wrong about Alan. I don't want to be wrong again.'

David punched at the window frame and said, with his back towards her, 'If you didn't marry Bordi, what would you do – go on living with him?'

'Certainly.'

'And what about Carlotta? Is she to grow up with a father who's different from other children's fathers? Is her name to be your name, or Bordi's?' He sighed. 'I think it would make your life awfully complicated, Lin.'

She nodded. When she didn't speak, he turned to look at her. She was sitting with her head bent, staring at the Persian rug.

'Of course,' David said, 'in our sort of world, it doesn't matter too much about who's the father of who, does it? Theatre people aren't as moralistic as others.'

'That's true.' She shrugged. 'But please don't give me "on the one hand, but on the other" – I've been all through that myself. Just say outright – what do you think?'

He seemed to brace himself. 'Well,' he said, colouring a little, because he couldn't hide what he felt, 'I think where you have so many doubts, you ought not to.'

'In other words, remember the advice in Punch.'

They laughed a little, troubled but suddenly at ease with each other.

'Come on,' cried David, 'listen to my melodies and tell me you see yourself as Tess of the D'Urbervilles, dancing to them.'

'Oh, David, don't! Please don't get your hopes up about a new ballet! Nicco's almost decided to revive the Aztec.'

He frowned at her. 'But I thought that was dead as a dodo?'

'Not a bit. We had all that work done on designs, and the music was partly written. We–'

'But it's Colbert's ballet.'

'Nicco says not. Apparently there's a contract – you know how Nicco loves to have everything signed, sealed and delivered. The rights in the ballet rest with Nicco and if Colbert doesn't want to do the choreography, Nicco can hire someone else.'

'But the cost, Lin–!'

'I know, I know. But Nicco says that we'll soon be relaunching the company on the international level, and he wants something splendiferous to take abroad. There's talk of an American tour in the spring of 'forty-eight. So Nicco thinks it's worth the investment.'

'Who's going to do the choreography, then?'

'No idea, as yet. But as to the music…'

'Yes?'

'We thought you might like to do it.'

'But you've got about a third of a score already.'

'Yes, doors creaking and cats wailing – that was Colbert's choice. You know he loves *musique concrète*. I always thought it was a mistake, David. It was to be a long ballet, and you know, two hours of that kind of thing is just asking for a flop.' She looked questioningly at him. 'What do you think? Would you like to do the music?'

'But Lin–! I've been immersing myself in the Victorian countryside for Tess. I don't know anything about Mexico in the sixteenth century.'

'Oh, come on,' she teased, 'use the same music and throw in a little cactus and tequila!'

The foolish idea set them off laughing. All hopes of serious discussion were gone and they spent the rest of the afternoon fooling about with comedy themes which, a year later, turned up as a short ballet called *Afternoon Tea*.

But, more important to David, he wasn't pressed for his views on the rights and wrongs of Linda's marriage. He was very unwilling to play any part in her decision. He desperately wanted her for himself.

Natalia Jerozolimska was safely conveyed out of Poland to West Berlin. Alan was discharged as fit from his hospital and demobbed, but no amount of string-pulling could get him a permit to travel to Berlin. 'Don't be impatient,' Linda soothed. 'When the divorce is through and you can say you're going to fetch your fiancée, it'll be easier.'

The case was to come on in the Trinity term at the Law Courts. So far no newspapers had wakened up to the fact that the case on a Tuesday in June in Court Two concerned one of the country's leading ballerinas. Most attention was centred on the economic crisis and the fact that the Derby had just been won by a rank outsider called Pearl Diver at forty to one.

Despite Rupert Bassett's protests, Niccolo Bordi had been determined to accompany Linda to the court. 'My dear man,' moaned Bassett, 'don't you understand that if the proctors discover you and Linda are living

354

together and she is not an "innocent" party, the divorce will not be granted?'

'*Che sciocchezza!* If *both* partners love someone else, all the more reason to dissolve the marriage.'

'No doubt,' agreed Bassett with some dryness, 'but English law does not as yet see matters in that light.'

When the morning came, however, Nicco said he thought he would stay away.

'Having second thoughts about the wisdom of it?' Linda asked as she looked out bag and gloves to match her dark dress.

Nicco nodded. 'Our lawyer has advised against it. Foolish to pay him and not take his advice, eh?'

He was still in dressing-gown and pyjamas, very unusual for him. He went to bed late and rose early, saying that the way to run a business was to be busy when other people were asleep. He still had his tray of early morning coffee by his beside, she noticed, untouched.

'Aren't you feeling well, Nicco?' she asked in sudden alarm. He had been much less talkative than usual.

'I'm well, perfectly well,' he said. 'A little too much lobster last night, perhaps. It was unwise to have our celebration dinner before the divorce, I think.'

'Shall I run your bath for you before I go?' she asked.

'No, no. Off you go. Bassett will be waiting for you with the *avocato* and all the papers. Now, *carissima mia,* you will not be frightened in court if they ask you questions? And remember, answer only as much as they ask. Bassett said you are much too likely to let slip all the facts of our life here together. So say little, and only if asked. *Claro?*'

'Perfectly *claro,* darling.' She stooped to kiss him where he was sitting in the bedroom armchair with his head tilted back against the cushions. 'I'll ring you as soon as it's over. Shall we meet for lunch?'

'Of course. I've booked at the Savoy. You'll find me there with the champagne on ice for the celebration.'

But she did not. When she rang home from the Law Courts, there was no answer. After some thought she decided that Doris must be out with Carlotta in the park, and Nicco, beset with impatience as he often was, had gone out to walk to the Savoy.

So she hurried there. The head waiter, always quick to recognise a patron, came smiling to greet her. 'Good morning, Miss Olliver. I have your table ready, as Mr Bordi ordered – this way.'

But when she reached it – one they often had, looking out towards the river – there was no one there. There was a spray of orchids on one of the plates, and a magnum of champagne conspicuous in its silver ice bucket, but no Nicco.

'Hasn't Mr Bordi arrived yet?'

'Not so far, madame. Shall I take your coat?'

She hesitated. Perhaps Nicco was in the lounge – although that was unlikely, since he had specifically said he would be waiting at the table. 'I'll just go and see if–'

'Oh, I'll send a page, madame, if you're thinking Mr Bordi might be in the bar?'

'Would you?'

She sat down at the table and picked up the spray of orchids. They were a small variety, not the hideous mauve Cattleya which American ballet-lovers sometimes sent her. The head waiter supplied a pin. She pinned the orchids to her dress, feeling absurd but knowing it would please Nicco when he arrived.

He didn't arrive. She waited ten minutes, twenty, half an hour. After that, thoroughly alarmed, she gave up the pretence that Nicco was going to arrive any moment. Something was seriously wrong.

She rang the flat. Doris was back by now, giving Carlotta minced vegetables and gravy for lunch. 'No, madame, Mr Bordi was still here when I went out, but he's not here now,' she replied to Linda's questions.

'How did he seem?'

'Seem? All right, really. I didn't notice anything.'

'I'm coming home. Meanwhile, ring his office at the theatre, Doris. Just find out if he's been there.'

She reached the entrance hall of the flat at the same moment as a police constable was examining the names on the bell plates. She knew at once that he was looking for her. 'Is it something about Mr Bordi?' she asked, feeling all the colour fly from her face.

'Miss Olliver?' said the policeman. 'Yes, I'm afraid it's ... not good news.'

'An accident?'

'He's in Charing Cross Hospital. We don't quite understand what happened. He was crossing the road on the Victoria Embankment and got hit by a taxi—'

'Oh, dear God... Is it serious?'

'The hospital said to tell you it was concussion – that's why there's been this problem knowing who to contact—'

'When did it happen? Can you take me there?'

'Surely. As to when – I think it was about half-eleven.'

Just at the moment when she'd been trying to ring him at home. He must have got restless and decided to walk to the Savoy to kill time.

Nicco was in a side-ward. A blue-clad sister came to meet Linda. 'He's not conscious as yet,' she told her. And as Linda was about to brush past her: 'I'm afraid I must ask you not to visit–'

'I know he can't hear me. I just want to whisper some news to him–'

'No, please, if you don't mind, Miss Olliver. He has a strangely high temperature. We don't understand it. We think there might be some infection–'

'Infection?'

'Well, as far as we can gather, he collapsed in the middle of the road before the taxi hit him–'

'Oh, the driver would say that–'

'No, no, there were witnesses. I'm afraid he may have been ill, Miss Olliver, and was hit because he lost consciousness or at least was unable to stay upright for a moment–'

'But what could it be? What kind of infection?'

'Has he been quite well recently?' the sister inquired, watching Linda with shrewd blue eyes.

'Yes, of course – well – no, in fact...'

'What?'

'Well, he's had a headache off and on, and this morning he was shivery...'

'Anything else?'

'Nothing important. Indigestion... Although that's unusual. Nicco can eat anything and never have any tummy upsets.'

'When you say indigestion – you mean what? A pain in the gut region?'

'Yes... A few days ago... But it went away.'

'Thank you, Miss Olliver. I think I must ask you not to approach the patient for the moment. We need to do some tests, and we'll be moving him to a private room in any case. When Doctor has had a chance to assess the case, we'll see whether you can visit.'

'But this is absurd!' Linda cried, trying to push past the nurse. 'Nicco would want—'

'Mr Bordi would not want you to put yourself in danger—'

'Danger? What danger?'

Linda was afraid to ask what the sister was afraid of. Although it was warm in the hospital, she shivered and pulled her thin wool coat about her more closely.

'Please ring me as soon as you can,' she said. 'I'll stay by the telephone.'

'Of course. Don't worry. It's probably nothing. But we're just being careful.'

'I understand. Thank you.'

Doris was already hurrying from the kitchen as Linda closed the front door of the flat. 'Madame, I thought you said you were coming straight home—?'

'I'm sorry, Doris, I met a policeman in the hall and went with him. Mr Bordi is in hospital.'

'Oh, good gracious, how dreadful – I had no idea – but Miss Olliver, what happened?'

'I'll explain in a minute,' Linda said, waving aside the questions as she hurried towards Carlotta's room. 'First of all, tell me – is Carlotta all right?'

'How funny you should ask! As a matter of fact, she's had a little tummy upset–'

'When? What do you mean?'

Doris looked vaguely affronted. 'She sicked up all her lunch–'

'Has she a temperature?' By now Linda was opening the nursery door. Carlotta was asleep, but breathing with a heavy, nasal whine.

'I don't think so, madame–'

Linda tiptoed to the cot and laid her hand on the baby's forehead. It was damp, and felt burning hot.

'Stay with her. I'm going to ring Dr Rostoff.'

'But Miss Olliver, it's only a sick attack–'

Paying no heed, Linda sped to the phone. She didn't know what she was afraid of, but she was deathly afraid. When she had explained in a muddled rush to Dr Rostoff, he sprang to attention at once. 'Keep the child in bed and if she seems restless try to keep her quiet,' he said. 'I'll be there in ten minutes.'

'Keep her quiet – of course I'll–'

'I mean don't let her toss about if you can help it. She ought to lie as still as possible. Don't worry, Miss Olliver, it may be nothing.'

He put the phone down with something a

little less than politeness. Something told her that it wasn't 'nothing'. She hurried back to the nursery, where Doris was sitting with a face puckering up for tears. 'I hope you don't think it's anything I've done, madam—'

'No, no, it's some infection, I think – they seem to believe Mr Bordi has it.' She explained about Nicco's accident to Doris, who listened with wide eyes and a growing look of alarm.

'It sounds serious, madam...'

'No, no, it's just precautions.' But she didn't believe it herself.

Rostoff arrived almost at once. The moment she heard the lift ascending Linda rushed to the door to have it open. He hurried in, went to the nursery, took the baby's temperature, and looked perturbed. 'It's high, there's no use saying otherwise. She was sick, you say?'

'Yes, doctor, brought up her lunch almost as soon as she took it off the spoon. But babies do, you know—'

The doctor gave her a look as if to say, I'm in the business of knowing. He said, 'She must be kept in bed. I'll give you a mixture that may bring the temperature down, but she may not be able to take it.' He paused. 'Just as a precaution, I want you to stay indoors. Both of you, I mean. And don't let people visit you for a few days, until we see

362

how it goes – especially anyone with children.'

Linda stared at him. 'What is it? What do you suspect?'

'Oh, it's just precautions. We don't want to worry unduly–'

'Dr Rostoff!' shouted Linda, startling herself by the anger and rudeness of it. 'Please stop treating me like an idiot! You're looking scared, and the hospital are running tests on Nicco. What do you think it is? What are we taking precautions for?'

The doctor nursed his narrow Hungarian chin in his hand a moment. Then he said with reluctance, 'There's just a chance it might be polio-myelitis.'

'Polio-my... What's that?'

'It's generally called infantile paralysis–'

'But that's absurd! Nicco couldn't get a disease of children–'

'It doesn't attack only children,' Rostoff said, with a brief sigh. 'And just at the moment there are signs of a gathering incidence of the disease that are rather worrying. So if there's the slightest chance it might be that, we want to be careful, very, very careful. The baby may only be in the very preliminary stages – in which case if she's kept very quiet and not allowed to strain her muscles she may not have any damage and it may only be a few weeks in bed for her.'

'And Nicco?'

'I haven't seen Mr Bordi, Miss Olliver–'

'Please, doctor? If an adult has contracted it. What then?'

'It could be very serious,' he admitted. 'But there's no real evidence as yet. Let's just play safe, that's all.' He stopped suddenly on his way to the door and turned to examine Linda with a frown. 'Of course, you're a ballerina,' he muttered. 'Oh, good God... My dear Miss Olliver, you must get some rest now. And if you feel the slightest signs of pain – particularly in the back, or if you have a severe headache...'

Linda heard his words, but they seemed to be growing fainter. Doris's hand came under her elbow. 'It's all right, madam, it's just the shock. And on a day like today, of all days!'

Linda sat down. She felt chilled and dizzy, but she knew it wasn't illness. The events of the last few hours had suddenly caught up with her.

She sat down in the drawing-room within reach of the telephone. Doris brought her some soup and toast, then a cup of strong tea with sugar. She consumed it because she knew she needed it, but she tasted nothing.

Meanwhile in the pathological laboratory of the hospital a count was being made of lymphocytes in the sample of cerebro-spinal fluid taken from Niccolo Bordi. It came out at over a hundred and thirty.

At six o'clock the specialist sat down at his desk and wearily reached for the telephone. He didn't look forward to giving the news to the girl whose name he had on the pad in front of him. He was a ballet-goer when he had the time; he had been distantly in love with Linda Olliver for over a year.

'It's true, then?' Linda sighed when he told her.

'Someone's spoken to you about it already?'

'Our own doctor. I called him to my little girl.'

'How is the child?' he asked quickly. 'You do understand–'

'Oh, of course. She's in bed. If she shows any more of the signs–'

'You must watch for signs in yourself, Miss Olliver. And any other member of your household. It's extremely infectious.' And could put an end to your career, he added voicelessly.

'Yes, I understand that. I'm on the look-out. Can I come and see Nicco now?'

'I'm afraid not.'

'But I–'

'He's very ill, Miss Olliver, and in the infectious stage. We're moving him to an isolation unit as soon as he's able to go – tomorrow morning, perhaps. You won't be allowed to visit because you might contract the disease or spread it–'

'But surely I've contracted it by now if I'm going to? And as to spreading it – I'll stay in the isolation unit–'

'That isn't possible. This looks like being an epidemic. We haven't room for anyone except acute cases. You must wait, Miss Olliver – I'm sorry, but the problem of providing enough sterile clothing and preventative screens for visiting is beyond us at the present time. Our hospitals have had a hard war – we just can't strain our scanty resources for visitors when our patients need the care.'

'I understand,' Linda said. 'I'm sorry, I hadn't thought of any of that. Is Nicco conscious now?'

'Yes, he recovered consciousness about four o'clock.'

'Would you tell him…'

'What shall I tell him, Miss Olliver?'

She wanted to say, The divorce case went through without trouble, in a few weeks I'll be free and we'll be married, Nicco. But it was too long and too complicated. 'Tell him I love him,' she said, her hand going to the orchid on her dress.

CHAPTER FOURTEEN

Next day the baby was no better, although it could not be said that she was any worse. She had had a bad night, snuffling and crying, inclined to be restless despite all that Linda and the maid could do to keep her quiet.

Dr Rostoff arrived almost at break of day. He had been in telephone communication with the hospital and, knowing details of Nicco's condition, was disinclined to take any risks. 'She must go to hospital,' he said. 'I don't know if she has contracted the disease but she has been in contact with a sufferer and–' He broke off to look inquiringly at Doris. 'You feel unwell?' he asked.

The plump little maid shook her head. 'It's just a headache,' she said.

'Indeed? When did it come on?'

'I dunno. I've had it off and on – it's worry about baby.'

'We shall see,' said Rostoff, and asked her to sit down while he took her temperature.

Linda was too shocked to make any expression of concern. All day yesterday and through the night, she and Doris had been with one another, worrying first about Nicco and then the baby. Never once had it occurred to her that Doris's usually friendly face had been creased with pain.

When he had looked at the level in the thermometer, the doctor pursed his lips. 'Would you leave us, Miss Olliver?' he suggested. 'I should like to examine Doris.'

'Of course.' Linda backed out of the nursery, to stand outside in the passage almost with bated breath. By and by Rostoff emerged. 'I think she should go to hospital for tests,' he said in a quiet voice. 'Don't be too alarmed. It's only a precaution.'

'Of course,' Linda agreed, knowing in her heart that it was more. 'I'll go with her and Carlotta—'

'No, you must stay indoors,' Rostoff said. 'You feel quite well? Separate out your tensions and anxieties about Bordi and Carlotta – do you feel pains in the limbs? Headache?'

She shook her head.

'Promise me that if you feel muscle pain, you will not attempt to "exercise it out",' he said in a very serious tone. 'So much damage can be done ... I will telephone about a bed for the child, and then alert the hospital for tests on Doris. Will you put together a few of the baby's things?' The way in which he made the request made her feel they were not going to be needed – she sensed he expected Carlotta to be too sick to want to play with her toys.

When the ambulance came Doris clung to her with sudden, unexpected panic. 'Oh, madam,' she quavered, 'do you think I've really got it?'

'I don't know, Doris dear, I really don't. But if you have, Doctor's caught it very early on, so you'll be all right, I'm sure. I'll come and see you–'

Rostoff shook his head. 'No, not for a time. I'm afraid you must understand that one of the precautions is isolation. But that only lasts a few days.'

Doris burst into tears and was escorted out to the lift. An ambulance attendant took the baby from Linda's arms. 'It's all right, mum,' he told her kindly, 'she looks fit enough to me!' She was wrapped in a bright red blanket and borne away.

Rostoff patted Linda's hand. 'I'll arrange for a nurse to come and keep you company,' he said.

'You mean, stand guard over me–!'

'No, no–'

'I don't want her here,' she cried. 'Don't send her!'

'You ought to have someone. You have a relative who could come?'

Linda thought for a fleeting moment of her mother. But the mixture of overwhelming concern and love of drama that would accompany her mother's visit made her shake her head. 'I'll be all right. Besides, I have work to do–'

'Work? I forbid it!'

'No, not dancing – the theatre. Nicco would want me to make sure things are running smoothly. I'll ring his office. And then I must ring the theatre about the ballet company – I ought to have been dancing tonight but the understudy will have to–'

'Don't overtire yourself–'

'I need to do *something!*' she burst out.

Wisely, the doctor nodded agreement and left, promising to look in on her in the evening.

At first, after he had gone, she wandered about the flat, picking things up and putting them down, half-heartedly doing the chores Doris would have done. She stripped the beds and put the linen aside – she felt the laundering ought to be undertaken by some special firm, since she had no idea if it carried infection. She wondered if a crew would come to fumigate the flat – she had half-memories of such events in her childhood when diphtheria had raged through Hedfield.

When office hours began, she rang Nicco's assistant. He was so shocked he could hardly understand what she was telling him. The last he had heard, Niccolo Bordi had told him he would not be in on Tuesday because he was awaiting the successful outcome of the divorce case and intended to take his future wife out for a celebration. To hear that his employer and friend was in an isolation unit rendered him almost speechless.

'Of course, I'll attend to everything here. 'Oh, Good God, how terrible ... Miss Olliver, anything I can do–'

'Just keep the office going and attend to any problems with *Die Fledermaus* – I'll look after the ballet.'

'Oh, but do you feel up to–'

'I'll manage all that, Paul. Can I leave the rest to you?'

'Of course, of course.'

She was struck by a sudden thought. After all, Nicco had spent his daytime hours with Paul. 'Paul, if you feel unwell – headache or pains in the limbs – see a doctor at once, won't you?'

'What? You think–? Oh, good God, how dreadful! Yes, of course, of course, don't worry about me, Miss Olliver.'

The ballet company was assembled for the morning class when she rang. She told the doorkeeper to fetch Preb to the phone. 'Preb, I shan't be attending class, Nicco's ill–'

'Good God!'

'Will you tell Ludmilla she's got to take over my roles until further notice? I don't

371

know how long I'll be away.'

'Leave it with me. Don't worry about a thing.'

'Just keep it going with the understudy, and if any problems, ring me at home. And by the way, Preb – if anyone in class mentions unusual aches and pains, make them stop exercising at once.'

'What's up?' asked Preb, who was no fool.

She struggled for her voice. 'From the way the doctors have been going on, it seems there's some sort of epidemic going round – so be very careful.'

'I'll come later and give you a report on how–'

'No, don't! I gather I may be infectious – incubating polio, I suppose.' She paused, for control. 'I think you'd better tell everyone not to come here for a week or so. I'm my own isolation unit.'

'Lin, that sounds awful!'

'Never mind about that. Keep an eye on the company.'

'Sure thing. And Linda – take great care.'

Next Linda rang to inquire how Nicco was feeling. The nursing sister in charge of the unit was terse with her. 'Are you a relative?' she inquired.

'Well ... no.'

'Mr Bordi is doing as well as can be expected.'

Only after prolonged conversations with

various authorities did she learn anything more detailed. 'Mr Bordi is rather poorly,' said the specialist when she at last received a return phone call from him. 'I can't tell you more because the fever is changing in its effects all the time. But don't let it worry you – there is a definite time-span in which it makes inroads, and then we can set to work to relieve the symptoms.'

'When can I see him?'

'Not for a few days yet, I'm afraid, Miss Olliver.'

The news about the baby was more cheering. Carlotta had a slight infection, was being kept very quiet, and Linda ought not to be too concerned. If she sensed the words 'As yet' at the end of that sentence, her imagination was perhaps too active. And when she rang to inquire about Doris, she was told it was too early to tell. Tests were still being done. She could ring again tomorrow and they might be able to tell her something.

By that time, surprisingly enough, it was mid-afternoon. She sat in the big empty flat with the telephone beside her and suddenly realised she was faint with hunger. She'd eaten nothing since yesterday. She got to her feet and was directing herself unwillingly towards the kitchen when the doorbell rang.

When she opened the door, David was standing in the hallway. He took one look at her, stepped inside, and put his arms around her.

'Don't,' she said, trying to pull herself away. 'You oughtn't to be here. I may be infectious—'

'Don't be absurd,' he said, almost crossly, and led her into the living room.

He explained he had heard the news from Nicco's office when he called with some query about the music for *Aztec*. He had hurried straight here. 'You look all in,' he said. 'Did you have any lunch?'

'No, I was just going to—'

'I'll make you something. Do you feel like eating? No? That's just as well, really, because I'm a rotten cook, but I make good tea and I can scramble eggs.'

'I'll come with you—'

'No, sit down and rest—'

'Oh, don't!' she burst out in anger. 'I've got to do *something* or I'll go mad!'

'All right, all right, I'll let you start on the spring cleaning if you like. Come on, show me where you keep the eggs.'

He stayed with her the rest of the afternoon and evening. When night came, she expected him to leave, but he inspected the spare room and announced his intention of staying. 'I brought my toothbrush,' he explained, nodding at the briefcase in which he carried music manuscript.

'Oh, David!' she exclaimed, remembering

at sight of that battered old container that he had work of his own to think about. 'Shouldn't you be writing?'

'I can work here, if it's all right by you. All I need is a piano and a pencil, after all.' He hesitated. 'I don't think you should be alone. If I bother you, just say and I'll stop playing. But I think you need someone here, Lin.'

'Yes,' she said, in deep thankfulness. 'Yes, I do, David – and perhaps you're the only one I could bear.'

'That's a compliment, I think.'

'Yes, I think it is.'

He dropped a kiss on the top of her head. 'Night night,' he said. 'There'll be better news in the morning.'

But for days the news remained indefinite. Nicco was not doing well, though the baby was holding her own. Doris was quite ill but the disease had been caught in its early stages. Linda's telephone almost never stopped ringing with friends inquiring after her. David fended off the unimportant calls. Dr Rostoff came each day to check Linda's state of health and, finding David installed, David's. Both remained unaffected by the polio virus.

At length Linda was told she could go out, and visit both Nicco and Carlotta. David accompanied her to the children's hospital but waited for her in the sister's office while she went alone to the glassed-in corridor alongside the ward.

From there she could see a little bundle in a cot, one of a row of six. All that was visible was a little dark head and one hand curled on the pillow. The child was fast asleep.

'She's doing well,' said the nurse kindly. 'You've no need to worry, Mother. We got her while the disease was in its very first stages, which was lucky. How did the doctor catch on so quickly?'

'Because ... her father had just been admitted to hospital with polio.'

'Oh, I'm so sorry. I hope he's doing as well as his little girl.'

'Yes, thank you,' Linda said, hoping it was true.

The drive to the isolation unit in Surrey was not long but seemed to her to last for ever. David, after hearing the news about Carlotta, asked no more questions but concentrated on his driving. He decided to stay in the car while she went alone into the reception block of the hospital, which was in fact a recently vacated army training camp.

A dismal place, he thought as he sat in the car park waiting for Linda to return. I ought to have gone with her. But he had no idea whether she would be allowed to visit Nicco and if so, he himself would have been decidedly *de trop*. He sat patiently in the car park, trying to fill his mind with the theme he was working on for the main third act solo of *Aztec*.

When she came out, he could tell at once that she had had a shock. He scrambled out to greet her. 'What's wrong?'

'David, he's – he's in an iron lung!'

He could think of not a thing to say. He put an arm round her, helped her into the car, got in beside her, and simply sat with her head on his shoulder until at last she muttered, 'Let's go home.'

The figures for the epidemic of poliomyelitis only became available later, after the cases had reached a frightening peak in September. Although it was no new disease, it was the first time it had struck with such ferocity. Children on the whole made a good recovery but a strange factor this time was the number of adults who contracted it, making its common name of infantile paralysis totally inappropriate. The most serious effects were found among the one-third of patients who were adults. The new machine, made by the German firm Drager and called an iron lung, saved many lives by enabling the patient to breathe although muscles of the chest were paralysed.

Although she knew she should be grateful to it, Linda found it frightening. The chamber was a steel cylinder in which Nicco lay on a bed of foam rubber, with his head protruding and resting on an adjustable headrest. The bellows which worked the diaphragm doing Nicco's breathing for him made a strange, sighing sound. Once when she was visiting him something went wrong with the electricity supply and a warning bell rang, bringing a crew of nurses running to work the bellows by hand. She was ushered out without ceremony, to wait scared and tense until the ward sister assured her all was well. 'But you'd better not go back in – after a shock like that we have to do a bit of tidying up, you know, and Mr Bordi doesn't feel like seeing anyone for the moment.'

She went home that day in a state of the greatest depression she had ever known. It was inconceivable to her that Nicco, always so much in control of his life, should now be at the mercy of a fallible machine.

When she questioned the specialists, they were cagey. 'We're making advances all the time,' they told her. 'Mr Bordi is being kept alive and functioning in the respirator so, who knows, before too long there may be some procedure that will enable us to be more help to him.'

'But will he be able to do without it by and by? Will he be able to walk?'

'It's early days yet. We just have to wait and see.'

She went each day to see him. He talked with some difficulty, because he had to match the rhythm of the machine. His first question was always for Carlotta. 'How is she? Are they looking after her properly?'

'She's well, darling – sitting up in bed, playing with toys.'

'No paralysis?'

'No, she seems fine. A little weakness in the left arm and chest but the physiotherapist says that can be remedied by normal exercise.' She didn't tell him – because it didn't occur to him to ask – that Doris would not make such a good recovery, that it seemed as if she might have to walk with a calliper on her right leg. She had kept from Nicco all that might distress him, and was only glad that the news of his little daughter was truly encouraging so that she need not tell lies about her.

She would watch his face in the mirror set above his head on the rim of the steel chamber. He was much thinner now, and the paralysis had affected facial muscles so that he looked very different from the hard, strong man she had first known. His dark eyes would follow her movements; he caught every nuance of her voice. It was as if he were putting all his powers into the senses that were left to him, since the sense of touch and the ability to move were denied him. He, who had always talked with his hands in motion, seemed a different person when he talked now in his halting fashion to the rhythm of the bellows and without gestures.

'When I'm better,' he would say... And then he would watch Linda, to see how she took it. She always smiled and looked encouraging. But she had a feeling he was not confident of getting better.

She understood much of what he was feeling. He had looked forward to marrying her and giving her everything he felt she deserved from life. Now he saw himself as a cripple, with nothing to offer except the money he had amassed.

So she took the initiative. 'I spoke to Bassett,' she told him, 'and he says he'll get a special licence dated for the day after my divorce becomes absolute. We'll be married at once, Nicco.'

There was a long pause, while the machine breathed twice, noisily. Then he said, very low: 'Thank you.'

She knew what he was saying. Thank you for still wanting to marry me, though I'm less than half a man now. Thank you for not shirking it, thank you for still loving me though I'm trapped in this steel cage.

'I made inquiries,' she went on, her tone calm and full of good sense. 'It's possible to buy one of these contraptions privately, Nicco. So by and by, if you like, you could be moved out and we could perhaps buy a house in the country, something big and roomy enough. It would be good for Carlotta, too. A Mayfair flat isn't really right for a toddler to grow up in.'

'No… She would like … a garden…'

'Yes, and to have a pet – a kitten, perhaps.'

'Yes.' A long pause. 'Linda, *mi' amata*… Will you bring Carlotta … to see me?'

She was startled. Her first thought was that the machine would frighten the baby. Then she supposed that they would not allow a child to visit. And then, last of all, it came to her that Nicco perhaps felt very ill, wanted to see his daughter in case … in case…

'I'll bring her tomorrow,' she promised.

Carlotta was still in the children's hospital but regarded as completely out of danger. There had been talk of allowing her home by the end of the week. She had been in hospital a little over three weeks.

When Linda put the suggestion to the paediatrician, he frowned and shook his head. But when she explained the circumstances, he drew in a long breath, thought for a moment, then nodded. 'Children take so much for granted,' he remarked. 'If you tell her the iron lung is a big toy, it perhaps won't frighten her. And she's fit enough to make the journey, I think, so long as she's well wrapped up and not allowed to walk about or tire herself.'

Linda made arrangements. David would

drive her to pick up Carlotta and then take them out to Surrey. It would be best to do it in the afternoon, after Carlotta had finished her after-lunch nap. They would get to the isolation hospital by about four. She would spend only a few minutes in the room with the iron lung and the man who was her father – although Linda doubted if she would recognise him now. They would get her back to Great Ormond Street by her bedtime at six.

None of it happened. At about six that morning Linda's bedside phone woke her. 'Miss Olliver?'

'Yes,' she said, struggling into wakefulness from the fog of a heavy sleep.

'I'm afraid we have bad news for you. Mr Bordi died about half an hour ago.'

'No!' It was a cry of utter rejection.

'I'm sorry. It was a minor infection – the strain on his heart was too great. He told us to say you were not to grieve, Miss Olliver.'

The receiver slid from her fingers. She hunched over in her bed. She didn't know what to do – whether to wail aloud or beat with her fists against the counterpane.

Her bedroom door opened. David said, 'I heard your phone–' He broke off. 'Oh, God,' he said, and ran to her side.

She leaned her head against his chest. Great sobs shook her. 'He's dead,' she told him in a voice he scarcely recognised.

He twitched off the silk counterpane to wrap round her bare shoulders like a shawl. Then in the bright glowing light of the June morning, he held her close and let her cry, conscious, as he felt her taut dancer's body against his own, that it had taken another's death to deliver her into his arms.

CHAPTER FIFTEEN

Linda's friends flew to her side. It astonished her to find how many friends she had. Gadina arrived first, ready to throw open her arms and take a broken child to her breast. Betty threw up a role in a musical to come to her. Preb took up a post outside the door of her flat to keep off reporters. And David was always there whenever she reached out a hand.

She insisted of taking on all the arrangements herself. She went to register the death, she ordered the funeral, she telephoned his mother in Rome and in her pidgin Italian broke the news to her.

'I'll do all that,' David offered.

'No,' she said fiercely. 'I have to do it! I have to keep busy.'

She had no black coat for the funeral and no clothing coupons to buy one. 'I will lend,' said Gadina. 'I have many black clothes. I have been in mourning for my country, every since the revolution.'

And even in the midst of her grief, Linda exchanged a smiling glance with David over this dramatic announcement.

The funeral was a long cortège. Theatre

people, businessmen, politicians, academicians, artists... Even Alan came, shocked and silent in his demob suit.

The newspapermen flocked round her. 'You were more than just a friend to Signor Bordi, I believe?' asked one snidely.

She threw up her head. 'I'm proud to say you're right,' was her reply.

There were seemingly endless conferences with Bassett about the will and then with the managers of Bordi's theatres. There were six, including the London show-place. There were also two touring companies and a musical in rehearsal.

'It will take me some time to wind them all up, but–'

'Wind them up?' Linda interrupted. 'What do you mean?'

'Well, my dear girl, what else can you do? It's too big for one firm to take on but we ought to be able to separate–'

'I am going to run them.'

'You?'

'Why not?'

'But you ... you...'

'Who knows better what Nicco intended? I talked about it so often with him. He told me all his plans–'

'But that's different, Linda. Artistic plans are different from contracts, percentages...'

'That will be your side. You understand negotiation and contract. I understand what

385

Nicco intended and what the public wants.'

'But – it's not that I think it totally impossible, my dear, but what about your own career?'

'Let me worry about that. The main problem at the moment is the livelihood of about five hundred people, five hundred jobs that won't survive if we sell off Nicco's empire piecemeal.'

'She seems quite determined,' Bassett confided to David, the only person who had influence with her. 'I wonder how difficult it will be to talk her out of it?'

'Why should we talk her out of it? Surely it's better to keep Nicco's life's work intact?'

'Well, of course. But she's just a slip of a girl.'

'She has instinct,' David said. 'And she learned a lot from Nicco. They talked theatre almost all the time except–' He broke off. He'd been about to say, 'Except when they were making love.' It still pained him to think that she had belonged to someone else. Alan he had never been jealous of: Alan had somehow never seemed part of Linda's real life. But Nicco had been real. Even in death, Nicco still had power.

'I still think she ought to be prevented...'

'How? As I understood the will, she has a controlling interest.'

'But if you were to point out what a task

she's undertaking, she might change her mind.'

'Don't you see, she needs the task. It's her way of fighting her grief.'

'Did she love him so much?' Bassett said, bewildered. 'I always thought it was ... well ... you know, I thought it was a mixture of respect and affection. I didn't think it went so deep.'

David said nothing. In his opinion it was because Linda herself knew her feelings had not equalled Nicco's that she now felt impelled to protect what he had loved only a little less than herself. It was her peace offering to his ghost, and her lifeline against the tide of guilt.

When she thought Alan was dead, guilt had overwhelmed her. This time she intended to fight back. And the weapon was work – the work to save Nicco's theatrical empire.

'And what about her dancing?' Bassett asked. 'She ought to be performing.'

David shook his head. He knew, as Linda did, that if she walked on stage she'd be greeted with a wave of admiration and love that would destroy her defences. The newspapers would call her 'the brave little ballerina' or something equally trite. Now was not the time to return to the stage. In a while, when the audiences had had time to forget the tragedy... And meanwhile she would always take class, because while she worked her body to exhaustion she could escape from her thoughts.

Bassett gave in. Linda moved into Nicco's great office with its mahogany desk and leather swivel chair. She looked diminutive in it. But her presence was felt.

Alan came to see her, awkward and shy. 'I don't want you to think I'm turning my back on you when you're in trouble,' he explained, 'but I have to get to West Berlin. Natalia needs me. She's got no money left.'

'It's all right, I understand.'

'We're going to wait out the decree nisi and then get married at once in the British zone.'

'Shall you bring her back to England?'

He hesitated. 'I'm not sure, Lin. She's pretty homesick, and I don't know that I could settle down to a building society office now.'

'You're not thinking of settling in *Poland?*'

Embarrassed, he said: 'Why not? There's a nice little farm there, and her father's got no one else to leave it to.'

'Alan!'

'I don't know. It depends. If the Russkies are being bloody-minded, she may not want to go. She could never live under the Russkies.'

She came round the great desk and took his hand. 'Good luck, dear, whatever you do. Write to me sometime.'

He kissed her – a tepid, brotherly kiss. Where had it gone, the young passion of the Cambridge honeymoon? Lost in the wreckage of the war.

Linda's mother was pleased that her daughter had taken over as head of the Bordi business. 'It's got a lot more future in it than dancing,' she said to Linda in a tone of encouragement. 'And after all, office work isn't hard to get the hang of.'

'No, Mummy,' said Linda, and privately shook her head at the lack of perception. No use confiding any of her plans to her mother. An unbridgeable gulf seemed to exist. David Warburton was far closer to her than any member of her family now.

The baby, Carlotta, was home from hospital with only slight muscle wastage after her illness. Doris had had less luck – but was still able to run Linda's household for her with the help of a younger girl to do the more strenuous chores. Linda was home each evening to bath the child and play with her but it was Doris who, with callipers on one leg, saw her through the day.

Britain, now painfully re-emerging into the world after years of austerity, needed all the entertainment it could get. After Nicco died, some of the artists in his companies received lucrative offers from abroad – America in particular was keen to recruit ambitious young dancers for its tentative attempt to form classical companies.

Some of Linda's ballet company left her in search of more money. She didn't blame them. She knew how insecure life was for a dancer. But to her amazement, many of the company simply waited for her to say what she intended to do now that Nicco, the financial brains and guiding force, was gone.

One of the things he would have understood was that to impress the public, now that the company had changed name, there had to be something of a relaunch. It was the Bordi Ballet now.

And now it seemed only fitting that the Aztec ballet should be staged. It had been two years incubating – it was time the chrysalis broke and the creature itself emerged in all its pagan splendour.

When Pierre Colbert, off in Paris, heard the news on the ballet grapevine, he took the first cross-channel steamer to confront Linda in her office.

CHAPTER SIXTEEN

'I forbid it! You cannot do such a thing! The ballet is mine and cannot be staged without my choreography.'

'Do sit down, Pierre. And stop declaiming. I can hear you quite well if you speak in a normal voice.'

'Ah, you use the sardonic tone with me!' he cried. 'You have changed much, Linda!'

'That's quite likely. A lot has happened since I saw you last.'

'And when I say you have changed,' Colbert went on, his voice still loud and dramatic, 'I do not mean for the better.' He thumped Linda's desk with a muscular fist. 'You have become – managerial.'

'That's what comes of having to manage things, I'm afraid. One becomes managerial.'

'Well, you shall not manage me!' roared Colbert. 'My ballet shall not be degraded by–'

'It isn't your ballet,' Linda said, shaking her head and leaning back in the swivel chair which had once been Nicco's.

'But it *is* my ballet!' he insisted at the top of his voice. 'Who else thought of using the setting of the Aztec empire! Who wrote the libretto?'

'And who signed a contract with Niccolo Bordi agreeing that if he withdrew from the staging of the ballet, the rights in it should remain with Bordi Enterprises?'

'Oh, contracts!' Colbert said with a Gallic shrug. 'Pieces of paper! You cannot say that because I once signed a piece of paper, the ballet belongs to someone else! It is *my* ballet!'

'I assure you it is not,' Linda replied. 'The story has been changed, the music has been newly written–'

'Oh yes, by this cretin David Warburton! Oh, I understand all that! Everyone knows how you and he feel about each other, and so of course it's natural you give him work to do – but why should you give him the score of *my* ballet, when already I had a fine score!'

Linda sighed. 'Pierre, you are an idiot,' she sighed.

Colbert studied her. He had thought his remarks about David would make her lose her temper, but no – she simply sat there looking cool and calm in her dark grey dress with its little bright scarf at the neck, matching the small turquoise earrings. She was ... impressive. He had always thought highly of her as a dancer, no matter how he might have raged at her, but now it struck him that she was desirable as a woman. Lucky David Warburton, if the gossip were true.

'You do not deny that I had done much work on the ballet, and had a score ready–'

'No, of course I don't. But then you upped and took off for Paris when fame and fortune beckoned.' She gave him a faint smile. 'What happened? You never got your government appointment after all, did you?'

'Ha!' Colbert cried. 'I do not wish to serve in a government with such people! Neofascists, every one! Always recalling that I am a communist, saying it made me unsuitable – as if a communist Minister of Culture could convert the whole nation by forcing them to read Das Kapital! *Imbecils, tous!*'

'Yes, it's all very sad, and unjust in your view, but that's what brings you back, isn't it?' Linda pointed out. 'You aren't getting the money you thought you'd get in Paris to run an *avant garde* ballet company, you didn't get a government appointment, and so you come rushing back to London crying "Thief!" because I want to do an Aztec ballet–'

'You want to do *my* Aztec ballet.'

'No I don't. I wouldn't have bothered to begin again with yours,' Linda said with greater bluntness than she might have used with anyone else. 'I didn't much care for your plot, and as for the music–'

'Leo Lenard is regarded as a master of *musique concrete*–'

'No doubt. But I'm running a ballet company that has to make money, and one sure way of keeping the public out of the theatre is to inflict three acts of dustbin lids and one-string-fiddles on them.'

'One-string-fiddles?' Colbert repeated, startled. 'What are they?'

'Never mind. The point is, Nicco and I agreed long ago that though the idea of an Aztec ballet was good, we didn't want a propaganda plot, and we certainly didn't want a score that would give the audience a headache. So we've had the story-line re-written and David has done most of the music – and despite the fact that you believe I've given him the work because I sleep with him, the music is damned good.'

'*Ma foi,*' breathed Colbert. 'How you have changed!'

She was silent, wondering if what he said was true. Six months of struggling with account books, lawyers, wages bills, legal documents, difficult critics, design artists, costumiers, and theatre staff had taught her how hard it is to be an impresario.

'Well, I suppose it was inevitable,' Colbert went on cruelly, eager to find a crack in the armour that surprised him so. 'You inherit all the money of the poor dead lover, and you find you have a taste for power–'

Linda got up. 'Excuse me, Pierre, but I have an appointment in a few moments.'

'An appointment? Nothing is so important as to settle this matter–'

'You raged in here without an appointment and I now have someone waiting to see me...'

'Take refuge behind your office routine if you like! But we both know that what I say is true – you only have control of the company because the besotted Nicco–'

She leapt up. Her cheeks flamed red. Ah, he thought, this is where her weakness lies – she is ashamed of what Nicco has done–

To his amazement she came round her desk in one long stride and hit him hard on the cheek with her open palm. She had the dancer's strength, enough to make him rock on his heels momentarily. He staggered against the desk edge, bruising his thigh. He was too astonished to do anything, even to throw up an arm to catch her hand if she slapped him again. But she did not. When her hand came up, it was to point to the door.

'Get out,' she said, 'or I'll have you thrown out.'

Colbert blinked. He had been hit before, but only in a love-struggle that had ended with the woman falling into his arms. He snatched at his dignity. He wanted to put up a hand to nurse his cheek, which he knew would be showing a red mark where she had struck – but that would be too childish. He summoned a grin. 'Ah, so you lose your temper when you hear truth! You don't like to be told your Nicco was–'

She took a step closer to him and gazed up into his eyes with her grey glance that was now like Polar ice. 'Hold your tongue,' she said in a low voice. 'You silly, shallow man! You know nothing. And as for your stupid ballet–'

'I will sue!' he declared, stepping back, because he found he couldn't bear the chill of her anger. 'I will drag you through the court, and everyone will hear how you bewitched that poor man just so as to further your career–'

'Do what you like,' Linda said, turning away from him. Suddenly the fury had gone from her. She couldn't bear to be close to him. It wasn't worth the emotional expense to react to his rubbishy accusations. She took a grip on herself. 'I should get a good lawyer if I were you, someone who'll read the small print on the contract you signed, because you'll find out you haven't a leg to stand on–'

'*Légalité! Légalité!* I am speaking of artistic truth–'

'Oh, stop it! Stop posturing, you fool!' And all at once she offered him the final humiliation. She began to laugh. 'You sound so ... so *daft!* Go away, I have real people waiting to see me about real things, like the cost of paint for the Princess Theatre in Nottingham.'

He went out, head held high and handsome profile displayed for the benefit of the secretary – though the profile was somewhat marred by the red mark where Linda had hit him. The man waiting to see Linda watched the door close on him. 'I hope Miss Olliver isn't going to row with *me*,' he said mournfully as he crossed the outer office to keep the belated appointment with the director of Bordi Enterprises.

Colbert headed straight for the place where he thought he'd get comfort and support. He went to what was now called the Bordi Ballet – but it had been his creation, he told himself. Most of those still dancing with the company owed their roles to him, not to Linda Olliver. He found them breaking up after morning class, mopping sweat from their faces after a long session with Preb.

Zou-zou Lascelles greeted him warmly enough and most of the dancers clustered round to say a welcome. When the purpose of his visit became known, though, he noticed a decided cooling of the atmosphere. He found that their loyalty was now to Linda.

'But she knows nothing,' he insisted. 'She is only able to work on my ballet because she has inherited all this money–'

David Warburton pushed his way into the group. 'What was that you just said?' he inquired.

'Oh, you will argue against it, because you have always been in love with her,' Colbert said, 'but the truth is, she is only able to make claims on my ballet because she has been turned into a millionairess–'

'Wrong. Linda isn't–!'

'Well, a demi-millionairess–'

'Not even that. She didn't inherit a thing. It was all left to Carlotta, Nicco's daughter.'

'What?' cried Colbert, suddenly insecure in his indignation.

'In trust, of course. Nicco's faithful lawyer is the trustee. He's hired Linda as manager and artistic director of Bordi Ballet and Bordi Enterprises–'

'*Ah, merde!*' muttered Colbert. 'How old is this daughter?'

'About two. So if you sue, you'll be suing a baby. How will that improve your image?'

Colbert hunched his shoulders and glared at the floor. 'But the ballet is mine,' he growled.

'If you really believe that, logically you should go to court. And you were always great on logic, Pierre – the triumph of mind over emotions.'

Colbert shook his head as if he didn't want to hear. 'All right, I won't sue the baby,' he said, 'and I was wrong in the things I said to Linda—'

'What have you been saying to Linda?' At once David was confronting him, staring at the other man's face for clues. It didn't improve Colbert's temper that he had to look up to meet David's eyes.

'Oh, I was under a wrong impression,' he confessed. 'I was rude to her, and she ordered me out.' He didn't admit he had been slapped. To his dying day he would never admit that, and if Linda spread it around as gossip, he would never forgive her.

David relaxed. Clearly Linda had handled the matter. 'You always were a clot,' he said.

'Clot? *Qu'est-ce que ça?*' Colbert looked confused. 'I think I have made a mistake,' he said.

'I think you have,' Laurence Mendel said, with earnestness. 'And you are a fool, moreover, because there is still a role in the ballet which Linda has not worked out yet, and it would suit you down to the ground, as the English say.'

'Me?' Colbert was affronted. 'I would not dance in someone else's version of my own ballet!'

'Why not? You are out of a job, no?'

'Certainly not! I have come to London—'

'Because you had a row with the management over the cost of *Léger-Loup* and walked out,' David supplied. 'Come on, Colbert, you know what a small world ballet is. We heard about it a few hours after it happened. The point is, Laurie's right. Linda's having trouble with the role of Cortes.'

'Stay,' suggested Zou-zou. 'We work on it this afternoon, after lunch. Stay to look at it. Who knows – if you apologise nicely, Linda may offer you the part of Cortes.'

Linda found Pierre Colbert lounging on the worn sofa in the green room drinking from a beer bottle. 'What happened?' she inquired. 'Did you come here to show them the wound I inflicted? Or hoping for support in making your claims in court?'

'I've decided against that,' Colbert said. 'I hear now that you don't own the company, after all.'

'I see.'

Suddenly to his own surprise, he set down the beer bottle, leapt to his feet, and embraced her French fashion, a kiss on either cheek.

She freed herself angrily and hastily. 'What are you doing?' she protested.

'I am apologising. I know now I said some silly things to you this morning. I am sorry, Linda. And I know I can help you with *Aztec*. Forgive me?'

She looked at him. He was turning on all

the Gallic charm. She thought, Why does he always have to calculate, play a part? Why can't he just be genuine? And then her sense of humour came to her rescue. He was such a poseur...! It was impossible to hold a grudge against him.

'Very well, let's call a truce, Pierre. But please understand that you have no claims on the Aztec ballet.'

David, sitting at the piano in the rehearsal room, raised his eyebrows at her as she entered with Colbert's arm around her. She let him know, with a hidden smile, that it was another of Colbert's dramatic effects. He smiled back, but took the trouble to rise from his place and lead Linda off for a conference about the music.

Zou-zou Lascelles watched the man-oeuvre with interested eyes. 'This will be fascinating,' she whispered to Laurence Mendel. 'David does not intend the conquering hero to take his lady from under his nose.'

Linda set the two principals in motion at the point where they had had to stop the previous day. The movements she had chosen were stylised, taken from such illustrations of Aztec sculpture as she had been able to see. What she was trying to convey now was the bewilderment of a fierce Aztec princess, brought up in a civilisation indifferent to cruelty, reacting to the first moments of tenderness after falling in love. It was a difficult scene. David's music was helping her. As the strident discords that spoke the Princess's fierce disdain melted into the cadences of the *pas de deux,* she saw it in her mind's eye. She stepped forward, took Zou-zou's hands, and guided them through a swooping movement that might have been attack, but drifted into a caress of Laurence's cheek.

'There. And Laurie – catch her hand. Pull her up on point. Hold her there – no, two beats. She comes down when David plays the dark G minor chord. Now up and down, Zou-zou – twice. You're hesitating, you see. You're ashamed of feeling so soft and yielding. Big leap backwards–'

Zou-zou leapt backwards on her points and staggered over to one side.

'Well, all right, it can't be a big leap, it'll have to be a small one–'

'If Laurie were holding her hands, she could make a big leap,' Colbert broke in. 'Yes, yes – if he holds her hands–'

'No,' said Linda.

The dancers worked on. By the time an hour had gone by, the first three bars of the *pas de deux* were almost right. David rose, stretching. The dancers collapsed on chairs, remembering they had to get a meal and rest before the evening performance. Colbert walked away to a corner where he lit a cigarette and sat looking at the floor. David sauntered up to him. 'Not bad, eh?'

'She is making a lot of mistakes.'

'Well, they're her own mistakes. It's not perfect yet but she's feeling her way.' David touched Colbert on the shoulder so that he looked up. 'Don't undermine her, Colbert.'

'Undermine? What is that?'

'Don't tell her she's wrong. I warn you, if you start making her unsure of her work on this ballet, I'll wring your neck.'

'Oh, really? And what right have you to elect yourself her protector?'

'She doesn't need a protector,' David objected. 'That's what's wrong with your view of her – you can't seem to see...' He sighed. 'You're a pain in the neck, Pierre. You always were and you probably always will be. Just don't hurt Linda, that's all.'

From across the room Linda watched the two men. They were clearly disagreeing. But that was inevitable, perhaps. One was now the closest person in the world to her. The other was an admirer, a would-be lover. As little as a year ago, she would have not have thought that the least amusing. Now she was able to smile a little, and think that very likely Colbert wanted the role of Cortes, and very likely she would give it to him. But only if he promised to behave.

Alexander Prebble had said to her earlier in the year, 'We ought to add another classic to the repertoire.'

'We have *Swan Lake* and the short version of *Sleeping Beauty*, Preb. And if you're going to suggest we do the full-out version, we can't afford it yet.'

'I was thinking of ... *Giselle.*'

'*Giselle?*'

'It doesn't cost too much to mount *Giselle*. Two acts – two backcloths. Peasant costumes for Act One, tarlatans for Act Two.'

'But, Preb–! Zou-zou couldn't uphold a dancing schedule like that – *Swan Lake* and *Giselle*. And even though Nan alternates well as a Swan Princess, I don't think she has the acting ability for *Giselle*.'

Preb flexed his shoulders and spread out his arms to relieve the pain that still troubled him. 'I wasn't thinking of Zou-zou for *Giselle*. I was thinking of you.'

Sometimes the longing, the physical need to dance, engulfed her like a tidal wave. When that happened she would make plans to train Paul up to take full charge of the business side and return herself to the stage. She had been away too long already.

There was a long silence. Linda didn't reply because the idea had taken her breath away. At last she said, 'We can't afford to mount another ballet until we get some financial return from *Aztec*, Preb. The question is academic.'

But the thought stayed in her mind, as her

ballet master had intended. Preb didn't make idle remarks. If he suggested Linda could dance *Giselle*, he meant it. He who had taught her how to dance with the inner meaning of every action, he above all knew if she was ready for this, the greatest role in ballet.

That fact alone meant that the idea had to be taken seriously. Although Linda herself might feel unfitted for the part, Alexander Prebble thought otherwise. But in any case, any serious dancer must feel unworthy of the role of Giselle until after she has danced it for the first time, and perhaps even after that.

If she now examined her deepest feelings, it began to seem to Linda that she had lived enough, experienced enough, to do justice to the role. She knew what suffering was. She had endured loss and grief. If she had not yet learned the complete acceptance implied by the end of the ballet, that might come in time.

Perhaps next year… Perhaps next year she might think about *Giselle*. But first she must return as a dancer. Soon – after *Aztec* was given its first performance.

The Bordi Ballet was to open its American season with the ballet which had taken London by storm. 'I think it will interest them,' Linda had said. 'Being about American Indians, after all…'

They were to give *Aztec* for the first three nights. Then Linda was to make her first appearance on the American stage in the role which had placed her at the top of her profession – her *Giselle*. If the rest of the company were nervous, Linda was doubly so, on their behalf. It had been her decision to take British ballet abroad to show the rest of the world. Whether the rest of the world were the least bit interested remained to be seen. The eight weeks tour would show.

A small group of half-interested newspapermen and photographers were waiting for them on the tarmac when the plane touched down. The entrance of the Bordi Ballet in the New World was quite dramatic: Susanne Lascelles fell down the slippery landing steps and injured her leg.

'Dear God!' cried Linda when the first panic was over and it proved the leg was only badly bruised, not broken. 'What are we going to do now? We'll have to cancel *Aztec* and put in *Giselle*.'

'No, you can't do that,' said the entrepreneur who had booked them into the Shubert Theatre. 'We've had all the balleyhoo–' he paused, wondering if he should make a joke about the word, then decided this was not the moment. 'Everybody's all keyed up for *Aztec*. There's been articles in the Smithsonian about the costumes, the research that was done, speculation about whether the music bears any resemblance to the real thing. Yma Sumac's songs–'

'We can do *Aztec* with the understudy,' Linda said. 'But Nan isn't a patch on Zou-zou.'

David, fidgeting about the room an unnatural twenty floors up into the sky, turned with a sudden impulse of determination. 'We can do *Aztec*,' he said. 'You can dance Ichtecua.'

Linda drew back and shivered. Everyone else turned and stared at her. 'No!' she said.

'Why on earth not? No one knows it better than you–'

'But I've never danced it!'

'Not on stage. But you've danced every step of it a hundred times in the rehearsal room–'

'But I've never danced it on the Shubert stage–'

'Neither has Zou-zou,' said Colbert with a shrug. 'And moreover, we rehearse tomorrow – you can get the feel of the stage.'

'But I'm the wrong colouring–'

They all looked at her. Everyone knew that for this ballet they all had to wear suntan make-up, even that child of the Midi, Colbert. As for her fair hair, it would be hidden in the first act under the great feathered headdress with its broad jewelled chinstrap, and in the rest by the wild black wig Zou-zou would have worn. And if she couldn't change her eyes and lashes to look like a flashing Indian princess, what was she doing in ballet?

Stefan Wohlheim put his hands together in a beseeching gesture. 'Do it, girlie,' he begged. 'Apart from Lascelles, yours is the only name our audience knows.'

'My name is known,' Colbert said indignantly.

'I meant among the girls,' Wohlheim said pacifically, but not changing his opinion unduly. 'They don't want an understudy, especially an understudy who doesn't sound good enough. But if you dance it, we can make a special news item of it– "After the unfortunate mishap to Mme Lascelles at the airport this morning, it is announced that the ballet's leading role will be danced by its creator, head of the company, Linda Olliver. This will be not only the debut of *Aztec* in America, but the debut of Mme Olliver in the role. New York is doubly honoured!"' He beamed about him, pleased with his public relations effort.

He was right. It made sense. Linda ceased to argue.

But she felt a thrill of fear as she stood in the wings before the first performance, her body tightly sheathed in a calf-length tunic of gold cloth split at the thigh, her head weighed down by the wide, fan-like head-dress of feathers and gold.

The rest of the company were about in the backstage area warming up, parting reluctantly with shawls and cardigans, testing out *pointes*, or simply clutching each other in fright. New York! They might die out there tonight in front of the most sophisticated audience in the world, and be slain anew by the Butchers of Broadway in the morning papers.

Pierre Colbert, in his dirty finery as Cortes, came up to give her a kiss on both cheeks. '*À la lanterne!*' he remarked. She laughed and returned his kiss. He drew back, surprised. In general, she tried to avoid his approaches. But of course, she was in a *crise de nerfs* this evening.

David said crisply, 'Well, you can't start until I get down there. Break a leg, Linda.'

'You too – for the music.'

'See you first interval.'

'If we survive that long.'

The call came for opening dancers on stage. The orchestra finished its tuning up. The stage manager at his board looked them all over on stage and pressed the cue for the light to come on in the orchestra pit, to tell the conductor to begin the overture. David raised his baton.

The first wailing crash rang out. The entire audience sat up as if it had been shot. The brass blared its Aztec fanfare. The first melody filtered in, the tune already famous in London as the Aztec Princess Dance. The audience got its breath back and relaxed: after all, it wasn't going to be one of those awful screech-and-bang scores.

The overture was short, because David always believed that folk at the ballet wanted to see dancing, not wait for it. The curtain went up on a phalanx of Aztec soldiers, shields to front, drawn up in lines on the steps before the temple. Cortes leapt on, sword drawn, supporters at his heels. Colbert, thoroughly enjoying himself, sneered and swaggered his way round the temple precinct until...

A sonorous sudden note from the trombone. The soldiers parted. And there, seated in all her power and beauty, was the Princess Ichtecua.

The whole theatre gasped in awe. An utter silence reigned. Even the orchestra was still. And then, at the faint flutter of violin bow against strings, Ichtecua arose and took four slow, particular steps down from her dais. She pointed at Cortes, arm outstretched. At the same moment she came up on to full point on one foot and spread out her other in a perfect, effortless arabesque. The orchestra gave out a cry of glory.

'My God,' breathed Alexander Prebble in the wings, 'oh, my God, she's incredible.'

So the audience thought. At the end, they stood up and applauded and shouted.

410

Flowers rained on the stage, the little black page-boy came staggering in with bouquet after bouquet. Laurence Mendel, playing her peasant lover, handed her out to take a bow again and again. He felt her trembling with fatigue and reaction but he would not let her withdraw. She had deserved every plaudit and he would make her accept them so that she could treasure them in years to come, in those inevitable years when the dance was done.

There was a party backstage afterwards to wait for the morning papers. But it was scarcely necessary. Only a madman could have written anything unkind about the debut that had just taken place. And on every other count the reviews were favourable: costumes beautiful beyond belief, music a triumph of dramatic invention, the entire company a standard by which future ballet visitors would be measured.

'Well, now we can go home,' Colbert said, pulling himself off a spindly chair with relief. 'I think we are what the Americans call "a wow".'

Linda was walking about embracing her dancers, mingling tears of relief and gratitude with theirs. Zou-zou Lascelles was limping here and there, weeping different tears, for the chance she had lost. It would have been asking too much of human nature that she didn't feel some envy at Linda's

411

success. Yet even so, she bore it well. 'It had to come some day,' she said to Laurence. 'There is greatness in her. I only hope it isn't spent too much in her choreography.'

'I will see you home,' Colbert said to Linda. 'I will order a cab.'

'Thank you, Pierre.'

'You should have a light meal and a long bath. You will not sleep, of course.'

Linda said nothing to this masterful advice.

'I will stay and talk to you until you are tired. That will be best.'

'I don't think so, Pierre. It might disturb Carlotta.'

Colbert shrugged. Really, the foolishness of it, bringing the infant on tour. But she had refused to be parted with the baby for eight weeks. *Quel empêchement!* How could one get a love affair going when there was a three year old *bebée* always in the way? Huffily, and a little drunk from too much champagne, he stalked away.

David watched him leave. 'Want to walk home?' he offered. 'Manhattan by moonlight.'

'That would be good, David. Pierre's right, I'm not ready to sleep yet. You feel like a walk?'

'Love it. Theatres are great, but they don't have fresh air, they have dusty draughts.'

They went out into Shubert Alley, the

little lane the Shubert Brothers had had to construct when first they put up the Shubert and the Booth Theatres. Nearby, Sardi's was still doing a roaring trade.

They walked down the now deserted sidewalk. A trash truck was on its rounds. 'After the Lord Mayor's Show, the dustcart,' Linda quoted.

'But that doesn't apply to us. What are you going to do next, Lin?'

'Have a heart! I've still got to do *Giselle!*'

'I've been thinking – our programmes are a bit short on light stuff now we're doing *Swan Lake, Giselle* and *Aztec*. How about a nice little frothy ballet for when we re-open in London next autumn?'

'What kind of thing? Divertissements?'

'I thought – something linked by a typical British event.'

'Bank Holiday?'

'Not bad. Flowery hats and coster-mongers.'

'A period piece? I thought ... present-day.'

'Well then – jitter-bug? No, that'll date. Brass band in the park?'

'Kids dancing to a hurdy-gurdy.'

'And an elderly gentleman who breaks out into a waltz to the horror of his wife–'

'And a handsome young officer with his girl–' he grabbed her hand.

She gave him a wide smile of perfect understanding.

413

Immersed in discussion, tonight's triumph already behind them, they walked on arm in arm. In a few hours the audience would file into the theatre to see work already completed and made ready for their entertainment.

But now Linda Olliver was reaching out towards the next creative work, towards the future that waited for her. She was weaving one more strand into the garland of her life.

The publishers hope that this book has given you enjoyable reading. Large Print Books are especially designed to be as easy to see and hold as possible. If you wish a complete list of our books please ask at your local library or write directly to:

Magna Large Print Books
Magna House, Long Preston,
Skipton, North Yorkshire.
BD23 4ND

This Large Print Book, for people
who cannot read normal print,
is published under the auspices of

THE ULVERSCROFT FOUNDATION